On the run
from the past,
Tasya Flynn enters a
world of revenge, passion,
magic, and mystery,
where she encounters
a man more
charismatic than she's
ever known . . . and a
love more powerful
than she's ever
dreamed.

"Just tell me the truth, Tasya. That's all I ask," Ian said.

"If you're here to steal the tourmaline, fine. I'm a thief. You're a thief. No hard feelings. Tell me who you're working for, and you're free to go."

"I didn't come here to steal the jewel. I'm not Interpol, and I'm not working for anyone."

"Damn it, Tasya. I can forgive anything but a lie."

"I know how crazy this is going to sound, but the truth is, I'm from the future. Your future. I traveled back in time to save you."

Silence reigned for a heartbeat, then Ian said scornfully, "You wouldn't know the truth if you heard it directly from God Himself."

"I don't blame you for not believing me. I wouldn't believe me either. But I slept with you because I loved you. I loved you old and I love you young. Even if you go through with this, even if you end up crippled and imprisoned again for thirty years, I will still love you. I will always love you."

CATHERINE MULVANY

Run No More

Pocket Star Books
New York   London   Toronto   Sydney

This book is a work of fiction. Names, characters, places, and incidents are products of the author's imagination or are used fictitiously. Any resemblance to actual events or locales or persons, living or dead, is entirely coincidental.

An *Original* Publication of POCKET BOOKS

A Pocket Star Book, published by
POCKET BOOKS, a division of Simon & Schuster, Inc.
1230 Avenue of the Americas, New York, NY 10020

Copyright © 2004 by Catherine Mulvany

ISBN:0-7434-9383-4
First Pocket Books printing October 2004

10 9 8 7 6 5 4 3 2 1

POCKET STAR BOOKS and colophon are registered trademarks of Simon & Schuster, Inc.

Front cover design by Lisa Litwack. Front cover illustration by Tom Hallman. Stepback art by Craig White.
Manufactured in the United States of America

For information regarding special discounts for bulk purchases, please contact Simon & Schuster Special Sales at 1-800-456-6798 or business@simonandschuster.com

What is the use of running when you are on the wrong road?

——Proverb

Run No More

Prologue

IAN MACPHERSON LOWERED himself through the sky-light of the Sodré mansion like a spider on a dragline. He tried to ignore the twinge in his gut, a warning that something was off-kilter. Or perhaps nothing more than his ulcer flaring up. Damned if he knew which.

That's what happened when one approached thirty. The instincts faded. The reflexes slowed. The mind played tricks. Wasn't that why he'd retired to Tahiti six months ago? Wasn't that why, if not for Alex Farrell, he'd be there now, practicing his French on one of Papeete's exotic beauties?

Ian paused for a moment, and the silence enveloped him. Most old buildings expressed themselves in creaks and groans and sighs. This one was mute, its still air heavy with the sickly scent of dying flowers. His gut gave another twinge.

Ignoring it, he resumed his descent.

Halfway down his headlamp died, and inky darkness swallowed him whole. His heart lurched. Damn it, he'd checked the equipment. Double-checked it.

"Cat? You all right?"

Ian glanced up to see his former apprentice's head and shoulders silhouetted against an oval of star-smeared sky. "I'm fine, but this wretched headlamp's giving me fits." No sooner had he uttered the words than the light blinked on.

"Seems to be working now," Alex said. "Maybe a short?"

"Most likely." Ian's mind embraced the logic of Alex's explanation, but his gut wasn't convinced.

Again he resumed his descent and moments later spotted the target, a stone known as Milagre—the Miracle. His twinge blossomed into a full-blown ache. They'd been had, by God. No one in his right mind would pay them a million for this rock.

In a glass case positioned under the skylight lay a tourmaline. Granted, it was an enormous tourmaline, half again the size of a man's fist and a rich ruby red, but a tourmaline all the same. Cut, polished, and mounted, it might have fetched six figures. Perhaps. Uncut and hung like an amulet from a heavy gold chain, it was worth a quarter that at most.

So why had the owner refused to sell? And, more to the point, why had the L.A. producer who'd tried to buy it financed its theft?

Ian swiveled in a semicircle. Roughly fifty feet square and almost as high, the vaulted space seemed even larger. Aside from the tourmaline, the room held only seven statues—crude, garishly painted plaster figures representing the *orixás,* the deities of Macumba, the local version of voodoo. Spaced at five-foot intervals, they formed a protective circle around the stone.

Was the tourmaline a religious icon? That would explain why the owner had refused to sell, if not why a Hollywood producer would be so determined to possess it. Perhaps Afro-Brazilian fetish cults were the latest L.A. craze. After all, these were the people who built multimillion-dollar mansions on major fault lines. Fools, yes. But rich fools. Ergo, if Alex's client was willing to pay an astronomical sum for the stone, his rationale was irrelevant. And no reason for alarm.

With a diamond-edged blade, Ian scored a circle in the glass case's domed lid, then attached a suction cup before tapping the incised curve with a small rubber mallet. A half-dozen faint *tinks* echoed in the silence. The glass circle broke free.

"Hurry," Alex said. "The guard's due back in five minutes."

"Relax. We've plenty of time." Ian slipped the glass circle into his pocket, secured his tools, then reached for the stone. Even through his glove, it felt warm. He jerked his hand from the case with a muffled exclamation.

"What's wrong?" Alex said.

"Nothing." He'd slashed his wrist on the sharp glass edge. Blood welled from the cut, but it wasn't deep, an annoyance rather than a handicap. His own fault for being so damned suggestible. The warmth of the stone had been an illusion. Just as it was an illusion that the seven plaster deities were crowding closer in the darkness.

Danger. He could smell it in the musty air, taste it as a metallic sourness at the back of his throat. The silence pressed on him, a tangible weight that made it hard to breathe, harder yet to think.

He caught a flicker of movement from the corner of his eye and whipped around.

Nothing. No one. Except those damned plaster idols. Bedecked with beads and flower petals, they should have looked ridiculous. Instead, they looked menacing.

He took a deep breath.

"Four minutes," Alex whispered.

Which meant the guard might check in sometime between now and dawn. He'd yet to meet the South American who stuck to a rigid schedule.

Focus. Ignore the guard and Alex, too. All you have to do is grab the stone. He stared at the tourmaline. God help him, his skin crawled at the thought of touching it again.

He caught another flutter of movement in his peripheral vision and spun around to face a sword-wielding figure, its face frozen in a permanent snarl. The statue's fierce eyes glittered like bits of polished onyx. Had the warrior always been a few inches closer to Milagre than the other *orixás*? As Ian watched, a single white petal detached itself from the cluster bunched at the god's shoulder and drifted to the floor.

Get out!

Ian wasn't sure if the voice reverberating through his head originated from an outside source or was the product of his own fear. Not that it mattered. Good advice was good advice.

This time he was careful not to touch Milagre itself. Instead, he threaded the heavy gold chain between his fingers and lifted the tourmaline from the case. A faint vibration thrummed in his ears like the hum of an electrical power line. Hair rose along the back of his neck. His fingers tingled.

Just your imagination, he told himself. He yanked on the rigging to signal Alex.

"Christ, what took you so long?" Alex pulled him toward the roof in jerky increments. "Did you get the rock?"

"I—" The chain suddenly writhed like a snake in his hand, slithering through his grip. He made a wild grab for it and snagged the end of the chain with two fingers. The tourmaline swung in an arc, then smacked against bare skin at the pulse point in his wrist.

Dear God, not just warm. Hot.

Deep inside the gem, a tiny point of red light throbbed in concert with the frantic beat of his heart. He stared, mesmerized, unable to move or speak or think.

"Cat? Cat? What's wrong?"

Alex's urgent whisper broke the spell. Stretching as far as he could, Ian thrust the stone toward his apprentice. "Take it," he said, mortified to hear the panic in his voice.

Alex reached down to pluck the gemstone from Ian's grasp, seemingly oblivious to both Ian's agitation and the heat radiating from the tourmaline. He studied it for a moment, then with a grunt of satisfaction tucked it into his knapsack.

Ian's wrist still tingled. He glanced down and drew a sharp breath. Where seconds ago blood had welled from a narrow cut, the skin now stretched unblemished. "Bloody hell," he said.

"Is there a problem?"

Ian stared at his apprentice. "Either I'm going mad, or there's something damned peculiar about that tourmaline. Look at my wrist."

"What about it?"

"I cut it trying to get Milagre out of the case."

"Looks fine to me," Alex said.

"My point exactly. The tourmaline touched my wrist, and the cut healed as if by magic."

Alex raised his eyebrows. "Magic?"

It did sound absurd, but it had happened. Hadn't it?

"Magic?" Alex repeated.

"Never mind. Pull me up before the guard comes back."

The light from Ian's headlamp turned Alex's features into the face of a stranger. "You pull capers like this for the thrill, don't you?"

Ian welcomed the sudden rejuvenating spurt of irritation. "This is hardly the time or place to discuss motivation."

"But it's the rush you crave, right?"

Ian frowned. "I . . . yes. Don't we all?"

"I get off on the danger, but for me, the excitement's secondary." Alex paused. "The money doesn't mean a thing to you, Cat, but it does to me. Damn it, it does to me."

Some odd quality in the tone of Alex's voice set Ian's nerves on edge. "You're wasting time. Pull me up."

Alex's eyes glittered. "I don't think so. Not this time."

"No!" His lips formed the word even as Alex released the tension on the rigging with one quick jerk.

Untethered, he plunged toward the floor in a petrifying slow-motion free fall, all flailing limbs and wide-eyed, gut-curdling terror.

Then pain, as fierce and red as the eye of the tourmaline, struck a sledgehammer blow to his spine. The marble pedestal had broken his fall and, *oh God,* from the feel of it, his back as well.

PART ONE

Revenge

No more tears now,
I will think upon revenge.

—MARY, QUEEN OF SCOTS

1

IAN MACPHERSON sat hunched in his wheelchair with a Colt Python .357 shoved in his mouth. Blowing his brains out would take care of his problems, but leaving Paulinho to deal with the resulting mess hardly seemed sporting. His ex-cellmate barely spoke English.

On the other hand, what did he have to live for besides revenge? A revenge that shimmered like a distant mirage forever beyond his grasp.

The kitchen lay deep in shadow, the only illumination a pale swath of moonlight admitted by the window over the sink and the eerie green glow of the digital clock on the microwave. Two-thirty-seven.

How very appropriate, he thought in sour amusement, dying in the dead of the night. His finger tightened on the trigger.

The creak of the dog door distracted him. Not a particularly alarming noise . . . unless, of course, one didn't own a dog.

He leveled the pistol at the plastic flap.

Thin and agile, a young woman squeezed through the narrow aperture, a penlight clenched between her teeth. He waited until she was all the way in, then said, "Burglary's against the law."

She gasped and dropped the light. It spun across the kitchen tiles, throwing weird, flickering shadows into every corner of the room, briefly illuminating in turn the cupboards, the appliances, the butcher block, and finally Ian with his revolver.

"Don't shoot." She got to her feet, extending her hands in surrender.

"Why not? It's what one does to intruders." He flipped on the overhead light, and she blinked in the sudden glare. With her odd monochrome coloring—skin and hair almost the same shade of pale honey beige—she reminded him of an old sepia print. Portrait of a waif. He wondered if the effect was calculated.

"All I was looking for was something to eat." She met his gaze, and her eyes captured his attention. Unusual eyes, a pale silvery gray ringed in black. Even more unusual, the expression in their depths—neither fright nor defiance, just a sad resignation, a sterile lifelessness.

Abused, he thought. She looked like someone who'd endured so much in the past that she was prepared now to suffer quite stoically whatever new horror presented itself. Even a crazy, gun-toting, gray-bearded cripple.

"Hunger seems an unlikely motive for breaking and entering."

"Are you going to call the police?"

He studied her a moment in silence. "When did you last eat?"

"A truck driver bought me dinner yesterday. I didn't stick around for breakfast." She shifted her gaze to the toes of her ragged sneakers. "I don't have any money, but I can pay you for the food the same way I paid the trucker."

"You'd barter your body for a crust of bread?"

Her soulless eyes locked on his. "And count it a fair trade."

Bitterness welled up, all but choking him. "Your sacrifice won't be necessary." He glanced down at his ruined body. "My injuries preclude it. I have minimal sensation below the waist."

He was used to pitying looks and polite murmurs of, "I'm sorry." But the dead-eyed girl drew a deep breath, then released it in a ragged sigh. "Some people have all the luck."

Tasya huddled naked in the dark. Richard would be coming soon. He saved his nastiest games for the hours between dusk and dawn. Though she had no clock, she knew it was late. Like a threat, darkness pressed against the barred window high up on the cellar wall. The color of midnight.

Every instinct urged her to run, but there was nowhere to go. Nowhere to run and nowhere to hide. If only I could die, she thought. Just curl up and die, leave her body behind, go to a place where Richard couldn't follow. But he would never permit it. He enjoyed torturing her, but he was careful not to inflict life-threatening injuries. He liked her to fight, to scream, to beg, and dead women did none of those things.

Suddenly the fluorescents buzzed on overhead, flooding her prison with a harsh glare. He was coming. Oh, God, he was coming.

The lock clicked, and the door at the top of the stairs swung open. She didn't want to look, tried not to, but she couldn't help herself. His gaze met hers. He stared at her for an endless minute, then smiled, his eyes bright with anticipation.

And she knew it was going to be bad.

Tasya awoke with a start, shuddering at the memory of the joyous malevolence in Richard's blue eyes. *He can't hurt me,* she told herself over and over in what had become her own personal mantra. *He can't hurt me anymore.*

Slowly the nightmare faded and her surroundings registered. She lay tangled in the sheets of an antique four-poster, the sort of bed normally found in the pages of glossy magazines.

Oh, God. Another of Richard's games? She shoved herself upright, panicking, her heart beating frantically.

But no. Richard couldn't hurt her anymore. She was alone now. Alone and safe for the moment. Only . . . alone where?

Disjointed memories of the night before teased her mind. She frowned, forcing her brain to sort through her impressions.

She'd thought at first the old man intended to shoot her. Instead, he'd fed her hunks of crusty bread and something he called *feijoada*, a filling dish of garlic-flavored black beans and meat, ladled over rice. She'd eaten one big plateful and half of a second, the only sounds in the room the click of her fork against the blue-and-white stoneware and the soft creaking of the wheelchair as the old man moved about the kitchen.

She'd gobbled her food, afraid he would realize his

mistake any minute and call the police. But he hadn't, and when she'd eaten all she could hold, he'd shown her to this sumptuous room, a room she'd been too tired to explore last night. She slipped out of bed to rectify that oversight.

An enormous mural of Venus rising from the sea foam, so cleverly painted that it might have been the work of Botticelli himself, covered the wall beside the bed from polished wooden floor to beamed cathedral ceiling. Centered on the opposite wall, long, shuttered casement windows leaked buttery sunlight, striping the brown leather club chair that sat in front of them. Flanking the chair were a brass floor lamp and a flat-topped trunk piled high with books and magazines—*Time, National Geographic, The New Yorker.*

A postcard marked someone's place in one of the books. *L.A. Requiem* by Robert Crais. A second Crais book, a Harlan Coben, and a Tony Hillerman constituted the rest of the collection. All hardbacks. All mysteries. The old man's choice of reading matter? Or someone else's? Whose room was this? Whose bed?

She frowned at the rumpled covers of the four-poster. The old man had claimed sex was out of the question, but he could have been lying. In her experience, that was what men did best.

But she had to admit, she'd done her share of lying. Last night she'd claimed she'd broken in to look for food. In truth she'd planned to rob the old man. Still planned to rob him. She needed cash, and from the looks of this place, he wouldn't miss it.

A smudge on the sheet caught her eye. She'd slept in

her clothes, too exhausted the night before to undress. Now she realized with embarrassment that her filthy clothing had soiled the bedding. Surely one of the room's three doors led to a bathroom.

At random she tried the door to the left of the armoire, but it opened into a walk-in closet larger than the living room of the Idaho farmhouse where she'd spent the first fifteen years of her life. The closet was full of clothes, men's clothes. And the lightweight collapsible wheelchair parked against the back wall confirmed her earlier suspicions. This was the old man's room.

A headache throbbed at her temples. Nausea churned her stomach. Had she escaped one exploitative male only to have been captured by another?

Luck was with her on her second try. The door opened into a spacious bathroom equipped with both a whirlpool tub and a tiled shower enclosure. Tasya opted for the shower.

She dropped her soiled clothing in a pile, adjusted the water temperature, and stepped under the pounding spray. She scrubbed herself, then stood there, eyes shut, body relaxed, as the grime sluiced away. She reveled in the luxury of herbal soap, the balm of warm water cascading over her battered body, even though she knew cleanliness was an illusion. Once you'd wallowed in filth the way she had, the dirt worked its way down to the bones, where soap and water couldn't touch it.

Only after the water grew tepid did she turn off the faucets and step out of the shower. She dried herself on one of the thick blue towels that hung from the heated towel rack, wishing she had a change of clothing. Instead she'd have to dress again in the same dirty clothes she'd filched from the Salvation Army four days ago in Carson City, Nevada.

If she could find her dirty clothes, that was. She wrapped herself in the towel, frowning at the spot where she'd dropped her things. Either they'd evaporated or someone had taken them.

Payback time already? Cynically, she speculated about the old man's intentions. Normal sex was out of the question if what he'd told her was true, but she knew firsthand about the other ways a man could use a woman to pleasure himself.

Angry now, she shoved the bedroom door open, then stopped dead just inside the room. She'd expected to find him waiting for her in bed, but the room was empty. Someone—presumably the same someone who'd taken her clothes—had been here, though. The bed had been made, the room tidied.

In the doorway behind her, someone cleared his throat.

Startled, she spun around, tightening her grip on the towel. "Who are you?"

An ebony giant examined her, his impassive gaze flicking up and down her body. He grunted, sounding so much like the Charolais bulls her dad had raised that she almost smiled, would have smiled if she hadn't felt so vulnerable and he hadn't looked so intimidating.

"Who are you?" she repeated, but instead of answering, he turned and bellowed something incomprehensible down the hall. Tasya didn't recognize the language. Neither French nor Spanish, though with elements of both.

"Quiet," the old man said from somewhere beyond Tasya's line of sight. "The girl needs her rest."

Another torrent of impassioned speech erupted from the giant.

"No wonder," the old man said, "with you carrying on like a demented idiot." He wheeled his chair into the doorway and nodded at Tasya. "You're up early. Did you sleep well?"

"Well enough, thank you, though I seem to have misplaced my clothes."

"Ah, yes." The old man held a low-voiced consultation with the giant, then turned to her. "Paulinho put your things in the washer. They'll be ready in an hour or so. In the meantime, feel free to borrow something." He gestured toward the closet door, then spoke again to Paulinho. The giant shot a glare in her direction, grunted, then moved off down the hall, grumbling under his breath.

A sardonic smile tilted the corners of the old man's mouth. Though his face was lined, his hair graying, he had the saturnine good looks of a fallen angel. With his piercing dark eyes and devilish black eyebrows, he'd have broken a few hearts in his day. "Join me for breakfast on the deck when you're dressed." He delivered the invitation in a rich baritone, deep and resonant, another reminder of the man he'd once been.

"I'd like that," she said, meaning breakfast. She wasn't so sure about the company.

"Did you see the bruises on her arms and shoulders?" Paulinho said in Portuguese.

"Yes, and the ligature marks on her wrists and ankles," Ian answered in the same language.

"And her neck. Did you notice? Someone tried to throttle her. The girl is trouble." Paulinho tied an apron over his khakis.

"The girl is *in* trouble," Ian said. "I think we both can relate to that."

A muscle twitched in Paulinho's cheek as he stood at the sink, scrubbing his hands. "You know nothing about her, Senhor Ian. She might be a thief, a murderer even."

"A thief like me? A murderer like you?" Ian laughed. "Besides, the bruises were on *her* neck."

"Humph." Paulinho dried his hands on a blue-checked towel and began preparing breakfast.

"She's been abused. I knew that. I saw it in her eyes."

"And did it not occur to you that there are women—whores—who let men do these things to them in exchange for money?" Paulinho slapped a side of bacon on the meat board. Wielding a knife with the élan of a surgeon, he cut paper-thin slices.

"Does she look like anyone's paid her lately?"

"No," Paulinho admitted. He broke eggs into a bowl, poured in some cream, and whisked the mixture to a froth. "But what if she is a runaway? What if the police are after her? If they come looking for her, they may get suspicious, and our papers—"

"Don't worry about our papers. They're the best money can buy. Don't worry about the police, either. I have enough to buy them as well, should it become necessary." He ran his chair over to the window. Redwoods and eucalyptus screened the rooftops of his neighbors down the hill but allowed glimpses of the ocean.

"I, too, noticed her eyes, Senhor Ian, and I am telling you, this one has been touched by Exú."

"Exú?" Ian shot a skeptical glance at his friend.

Paulinho rubbed the gold crucifix that hung around his neck, then crossed himself quickly, oblivious to the irony of using Christian symbols and Catholic rituals to protect himself from a Macumba devil.

Ian turned back to his view of the distant ocean. "I'm sixty-one years old. I have no family, no life beyond the constraints of this damned mechanical contraption." He smacked the arm of his chair. "Last night I came close to blowing my head off. This morning instead of grilling bacon and chopping chives, you could have been scrubbing my brains off the wall and trying to explain to the police in your damned poor excuse for English how you had nothing to do with the senhor's death."

"You thought of killing yourself?" Paulinho sounded shocked. "But suicide's a mortal sin!"

"The strange part is, just as I was about to pull the trigger, the girl squeezed through the dog door I've been threatening to have sealed off for the last six months."

"I will fix the latch after breakfast," Paulinho said.

"You're missing the point. If the flap had fastened properly, she couldn't have shoved her way in. And if she hadn't shoved her way in, I'd have pulled the trigger. The girl saved my life. In fact, I haven't felt quite so alive in years."

Paulinho's spatula clattered on the counter. "So now you want to keep her? This skinny girl someone tried to throttle?"

"Keep her?"

"For your woman." Paulinho grated cheese with a vengeance. Fine shreds of cheddar flew from his grater like confetti.

Ian shook his head. "Are you mad? What good is a woman to me at my age? In my condition?"

"There are many roads to pleasure."

"Not for that child. You saw her poor dead eyes, Paulinho. She needs help. For once in my life, my motives are entirely altruistic. I assure you, I have no designs on her virtue."

"Humph." Paulinho scowled at the pile of shredded cheese.

"Don't stand there grunting like a Neanderthal. Speak up."

"Very well." Paulinho's troubled gaze met his. "You're fooling yourself, Senhor Ian. She attracts you, with her long limbs and smooth skin, her eyes like silvery mirrors."

"She's interesting looking, yes, even beautiful, but—"

"Only a fool trusts a beautiful woman. Who is she? Where did she come from? What does she want? Do you know the answers? No. I pray to God she will not end up destroying you."

"Impossible. Alex Farrell already did that." Hatred stirred in the depths of his soul like an oily black sludge. "I'm not a religious man like you, my friend, but I believe that girl was sent as an act of divine intervention. It was not destined that I die last night. Why? The only answer I can come up with is, I have something yet to accomplish. I think the girl was sent to help."

Paulinho snorted and dumped the bowl of eggs into an omelet pan. "Help you to an early grave, perhaps."

Sunlight gleamed off the big black man's shaved head. Paulinho didn't like her much, Tasya thought, judging by the sullen look he sent her way as she took her place across from the old man at the table on the deck. She couldn't fault his cooking, though.

She stuffed herself with bacon and omelet, fresh fruit, and hot buttered rolls, a meal consumed in silence broken only by the rustle of turning pages as the old man read his way through a stack of newspapers.

Finally, he set the papers aside and turned to her with an inquiring glance. "More fruit? Some coffee perhaps?"

"No, thank you. I couldn't eat another bite." Her smile included Paulinho, standing guard behind the old man's chair. He glowered back at her as if he suspected she'd try any moment now to slit his employer's throat with her butter knife.

The old man said something to him she didn't understand, and Paulinho took his scowl into the house.

A sparrow balanced on the deck railing as if waiting for crumbs. She broke off a bit of roll and tossed it to him. "What language is it that you and Paulinho speak?"

"Portuguese," he said. "I lived in Brazil for many years." He shot her a quick smile, and she caught another glimpse of the charmer he'd been in his youth. "But how rude of me. I never introduced myself last night. I'm Ian MacPherson, also known as Cat." He held out his hand, and they shook across the remains of their breakfast.

"Cat?"

"A nickname." He leaned back, a wry half smile twisting the corner of his mouth. "My turn to ask a question."

"Of course." Wary, but not wanting him to see it, she lowered her gaze to the tablecloth.

"What's *your* name?"

She didn't know how much the police had figured out or what they'd released to the press, and Ian MacPherson was obviously a man who stayed abreast of the news. She couldn't chance the truth. "I-Ivana. Smith."

"How original." Again that cynical twist of the lips.

"My mother was a Russian immigrant, my father American." That part, at least, was true.

"And where are they, your parents?"

"Dead." Her mother and the man she'd called Dad for the first fifteen years of her life had died in a two-car pileup on Highway 55 south of Horseshoe Bend, Idaho. Only after the funeral had she learned that Joe Flynn wasn't her biological father. She knew nothing about the man who'd provided half of her DNA.

"Do you have other family? Friends perhaps?"

"No." The sparrow finished the crumb and took flight. Just as she would . . . once she located her crumb.

"You're on the run, aren't you?"

Speechless, she stared at him.

"From whom? The police?"

"They might be looking for me. I don't know for sure."

"Is that why you lied about your name? Because you think the police are after you?"

"I'm sorry. I can't tell you any more. Thank you again for the food and the bed, but it's time I was on my way." She stood.

His fingers closed around her wrist, his grip surprisingly strong. "Don't go. Not yet." She must have made some involuntary sound of protest, because he released her instantly, his voice softening as he added, "Please."

Please. She couldn't remember the last time she'd heard that word. She sat down.

"I didn't mean to frighten you."

Tasya stared at the remains of her breakfast. "You didn't. I don't like being touched, that's all." She took a deep breath. "You've been very kind, but I can't involve you in my problems."

"Too late. I *am* involved." His gaze captured hers. His eyes were so dark a brown, she couldn't distinguish his pupils from his irises, their expression so intense, she couldn't look away.

"You don't understand. Getting involved in my troubles would be a mistake. A dangerous mistake."

"I've been in and out of trouble all my life." He smiled. "And I rather enjoy danger."

She gazed at him helplessly. How to explain without telling him everything?

He cocked his head to one side. "If you don't let me help you, what will you do? Where will you go?"

"I'm not sure. Maybe L.A."

"Stardom. The American dream." A trace of condescension colored his expression.

Her cheeks grew warm. "I'm not some pathetic starstruck runaway, deluding herself that she's the next Julia Roberts. I plan to try my luck as a stunt double."

His mouth twitched as if he were suppressing a smile. "A profession requiring its own talents."

"Talents I have. I trained in gymnastics for eleven years. I have excellent reflexes. I'm fast, flexible, and well coordinated."

"Ideal attributes for a stunt double." He was humoring her.

Tasya's temper flared. "Watch." She jumped onto the railing and, using it as a balance beam, moved through the elements of an old routine, only slightly hampered by the baggy borrowed sweat pants. She finished with a round-off triple-twist dismount.

"Brava!" The condescension had vanished, replaced by genuine enthusiasm and a hint of something that might have been speculation. "You are, indeed, talented."

She sat down across the table from him. "Why didn't you call the police last night?"

"Let's just say I have a soft spot for thieves."

She studied his face. "That's not the only reason."

"Do you believe in fate, Ms. Smith?"

She frowned. Was he trying to change the subject?

"I do," he said. "I believe you were destined to enter my life at a critical moment, as I, perhaps, was destined to enter yours." He paused. "Who hurt you?"

The blood drummed in her ears. "I can't tell you that."

He inclined his head. "Fair enough. I dare say there are things I'd not wish to share with a stranger, either."

She studied the harsh lines of his face. "You seem a decent man. You've treated me kindly, but—"

"You're curious about my motivation. Wondering what I expect in return for my 'kindness'?"

She nodded, then looked away, unable to face his dark scrutiny.

"Nothing you're unwilling to give. I promise."

Men always promised. And they always lied. "Then why did you put me in your room last night? In your bed?"

He raised his eyebrows at the accusation underlying her tone. "The guest room beds weren't made up, and you were asleep on your feet."

A simple explanation. Possibly even true. She flicked a glance at him. He seemed to find her amusing.

"Even were I not . . . incapacitated, you'd still be safe with me. I'm not a child molester."

"And I'm not a child." She stared steadily at him. A shadow passed across his face, a flicker of emotion there and gone so fast she couldn't name it.

"Quite so," he said and shifted his gaze to the distant ocean.

Quite so? How many Americans talked like that? She crumbled the remnants of her roll as she puzzled it out.

A querulous chirp drew her attention to the deck railing. The sparrow was back. She tossed him another crumb, and he pecked at it, studying her all the while with black ball-bearing eyes.

"You don't sound American," she said abruptly.

He laughed. "I'm a Scot by birth, originally from a village northwest of Inverness. I emigrated in my teens."

"A Highlander?"

"Aye, lass." His exaggerated accent mocked her. "The MacPhersons belong to Clan Chattan. 'Touch not the cat, but a glove.' Our motto."

"'But a glove'?"

"Archaic language for 'without a glove.' In other words, watch out. We have claws."

"That explains your nickname."

He made no comment but smiled again, a charming smile this time that crinkled the corners of his dark eyes and revealed strong white teeth.

Tasya broke off eye contact. Condescension, she could handle. Mocking irony, she could handle. But charm set off her internal alarms. "So . . . how long were you in Brazil?"

"Thirty years, more or less."

"Thirty years! Doing what?"

He laughed again. "Avoiding gang rape, for the most part. Not that I could have felt anything, you understand, but one doesn't care to be used."

His careless words stirred the murky depths of her memory. Tasya bit the inside of her lip until she tasted blood.

He hadn't noticed her distress. She swallowed hard. "Are men often raped in Brazil?"

He tugged at the corner of his mustache, smoothed his neatly trimmed beard. "Only in prison."

She shuddered. "How did you end up behind bars?"

"I trusted the wrong person." A bitter smile twisted his mouth. "I'd been a thief all my life, so I suppose I deserved incarceration. But I didn't deserve to lose the use of my legs. I didn't deserve this damned wheelchair. Dreams of retribution were all that kept me alive in that pesthole, but I've been free for over six months, and I'm no closer to achieving revenge now than I was the day I got out." He paused. "Then last night fate sent you."

"Me?"

He'd been staring at some point over her head, but now he focused on her. She wanted to look away but found she couldn't. "If I'm not mistaken, you, too, have been betrayed. So you'll understand how I feel."

"Yes," she said, even though it hadn't been a question. He knew. Somehow he knew. "What do you want from me?"

He examined her face, a smile hovering around the corners of his mouth. "I'm a cat burglar confined to a wheelchair. I need an assistant, someone young and agile. All those admirable skills of yours—speed, flexibility, co-ordination—make you ideally suited for the job."

"I don't mean to insult you, but"—she felt herself flushing again—"I'm not sure I want to make a career of thievery."

He frowned. "You had no such qualms last night."

Oh, God, he knew about that, too. "That was different. I was desperate."

"So was I. I'd decided to kill myself. When you interrupted, I believed it was a sign." He smiled. "And when you demonstrated your gymnastics skills just now, I knew it for another. Fate has smiled on me at last."

"But—"

"Don't worry. I'm not proposing a crime spree. One caper. That's all you'd be involved in. One payback caper."

"Revenge," she said.

"Yes. I'd get satisfaction, and you'd get money. A million dollars. No strings attached."

A million dollars? "But—"

"Don't say no. Try the training first," he said. "You can

back out at any time. No hard feelings. But if you stay the course, you can build a new life with the money you earn."

She considered his proposal. Outrageous, yes. Dangerous, without a doubt. But with a million dollars at her disposal, she could do as she pleased and never have to answer to any man again. "A new life," she said, the words sweet on her tongue. A life without Richard. Without fear. She nodded. "All right, I'll try it."

"Very well, Ivana Smith, shall we—"

"Don't call me that. You were right. I lied about my name. It's Tasya."

"Tasya what?"

She hesitated. "Flynn."

"A good Irish name." Smiling, he reached across the table to seal their bargain with a handshake.

His grip was warm and firm, his expression kind, but Tasya had learned the hard way not to accept anyone at face value. Only time would tell if Ian MacPherson would deliver the salvation he promised . . . or if she'd just made a pact with the devil.

2

"D ONE." Tasya said.

"*Oito.*" Paulinho, who'd been timing her lock-picking speed, held up eight fingers.

"Eight seconds." Ian nodded approval. "Not bad." In truth, very good, almost as good as he. Young Tasya was a natural.

Ian had turned the family room of his Half Moon Bay home into a schoolroom of sorts. The crème de la crème of lock-pick tools, collected bit by bit since his release from prison, lay scattered across the big mahogany table. The box housing his eclectic lock collection sat on the floor next to him. He reached inside to choose another lock, this one more challenging than the last. "Try it again," he said. "This time with your eyes closed."

The clock on the mantel chimed six times, and he glanced up, startled. Tasya'd been at it for hours, ten to be exact, not counting a twenty-minute break for lunch. She must be exhausted. But if he'd expected a protest or a re-proach, he should have known better. The girl was like a well-trained soldier. She never complained, no matter what he asked of her, not even when she was frustrated, in pain, or worn to a frazzle as she was now.

Sometimes he wished she would whine a little. Her unquestioning compliance worried him. He suspected her obedience was less a matter of self-discipline than self-preservation, a survival skill learned at the hands of a brutal master. Over the past weeks, her bruises had faded. The damage to her spirit would take longer to mend.

She closed her eyes, and he handed her the lock he'd chosen.

"Go." Paulinho punched the stopwatch as she fitted a pick to the keyhole.

Seconds later, the lock sprang open. She opened her eyes.

Paulinho nodded approval. *"Seis."* Six seconds flat.

"Good." Excellent, in fact.

Tasya set the lock on the table. "I think it's easier with my eyes shut. I can concentrate on what I feel without interference from what I see. Shall I try it again?"

"No, you've mastered the lock pick. Let's call it a day. Tomorrow I'll start you on combination locks."

"Safecracking 101." She grinned. "I can hardly wait."

Tasya was surprised—and curious—when Ian called her into his study after dinner. As a rule he was careful not to encroach upon her free time.

"This came in the mail." He passed her an article cut from the entertainment section of the *Los Angeles Times.*

She shot him a puzzled look. "A story about a health spa?"

"Read it."

She scanned the text. "'La Magia's hydrotherapy is truly miraculous,'" she quoted. "'My arthritis disappeared overnight.' You don't buy any of this, do you? The owner's claims? The testimonials from satisfied guests?" He didn't really think immersing himself in some magic pool was going to mend a severed spinal cord, did he?

He tapped a photograph at the bottom of the page. "Look."

Tasya didn't see what Ian was so excited about. And he was excited. She could hear it in his voice and see it in the barely contained energy of his movements.

The man in the photo was generic Southern Californian, slim and tanned with a big toothy smile and lots of dark brown hair, a baby boomer battling middle age. And winning. She read the caption aloud. "As lean and fit as a man half his age, owner Alexander Peyton Farrell attributes his youthful appearance to a regimen of vigorous exercise, a healthy diet, and daily sessions in one of the spa's six hydrotherapy pools." She frowned at Ian. "I must be missing the punch line."

He bared his teeth in a predatory smile. "Alexander Peyton Farrell is Alex Farrell, the double-crossing bastard who destroyed my life."

Tasya's abdominal muscles clenched. No wonder . . . She examined the picture more closely. Tall, dark, and handsome, the spa owner was a living, breathing cliché. "He looks more like a leading man than a villain," she said. "You haven't seen Alex Farrell for thirty years. Are you positive this is the same person?"

"You don't forget the face of the man who ruined your life."

She shut her eyes for a second. "No. No, you don't."

Ian took the clipping from her. "Besides, my investigators already verified the facts. They sent me the article, part of a more detailed report."

"You hired detectives?" A chill ran down her spine. Had he researched her background as well?

"How else could I find Alex? I have neither the mobility nor the technical know-how to do the job myself."

"But—" She paused, choosing her words with care. "If something . . . happens, won't the investigators go to the police?"

"They might, but as they think they're working for a retired stockbroker named Arthur Ramsdale, I foresee no repercussions."

"You've thought out every detail."

"I had over three decades to plan."

"How exactly did Alex Farrell betray you?"

"I never told you the whole story, did I?" He moved to the window and scowled out at the lengthening shadows. "By the time I hit my late twenties, I'd acquired a fortune. Before retiring, though, I decided to pass on my expertise as a cat burglar. I took an apprentice."

"Alex Farrell."

"Yes, for my sins. He quickly mastered the requisite skills, but I think a part of me knew from the beginning he wasn't going to work out. Alex had the talent, but he lacked the temperament. He was too impatient. Too egocentric."

She studied Ian's stiff shoulders. "But he was like the younger brother you'd never had, so you made excuses for him and hoped for the best."

He turned to face her, bitterness in his expression. "All he ever cared about was the money."

She curled up on one end of the sofa. Careful to keep her voice neutral, she asked the question that had been bothering her for weeks. "How did you end up in a Brazilian prison?" In a wheelchair.

"Once I'd taught Alex the tricks of the trade, I retired to Tahiti. Bought a house near the beach. Spent my days fishing and my nights learning French." He grinned suddenly. "Useful phrases like *Tu es tellement belle* and *Veux-tu coucher avec moi?*"

"I don't speak French."

"Just as well," he said.

Tasya frowned. "But how did you get from a beach in Tahiti to a prison in Brazil?"

"Alex coaxed me out of retirement, promised me half his million-dollar fee to help with one last score. A Hollywood producer had hired him to steal a tourmaline known as Milagre."

"A tourmaline?" she said. "Jewelry?"

"No, an uncut stone. Large and flawless, a deep blood red, but worth only a fraction of the fee the producer promised Alex."

She glanced at him, startled. "Then why—"

"Precisely. Only I was so anxious to get back in the game, I didn't question the producer's motivation. It wasn't until after the fact that I learned he'd coveted Milagre for its reputed healing powers. His daughter, his only child, was dying of an inoperable brain tumor."

"And he thought a stone could help?"

"The man was desperate. Apparently he tried to buy Milagre first, but the wealthy Carioca who owned it refused to sell. That's when he hired Alex."

"Who couldn't pull off the heist on his own."

"He tried, but he hadn't done his homework. He tripped over the owner's Siamese, and its yowling woke the entire household. Alex barely escaped."

"So he coaxed you out of retirement."

"Didn't take much coaxing. The fishing had begun to pall."

"How about the French lessons?"

A smile flicked at the corners of his mouth. "It's an overrated language."

"So you flew to Brazil?"

His smile faded, and his features set in a grim expression as he recounted the details of the double-cross.

Tasya listened in rapt silence. At one point she must have made some involuntary sound, though, because he met her gaze. "I know how peculiar it sounds."

Did he? A stone that felt hot to the touch? A stone that healed a cut like magic? "Perhaps you imag—"

"It happened." He held out his wrist to display the unblemished skin.

"Okay, but if it healed your wrist, why didn't it heal—"

"My back? Because Alex took possession of the stone before he sent me plummeting to the floor."

Neither of them spoke for a moment. Then Ian continued, his voice emotionless. "From that point on, my memories are confused. I remember pain. And noise—the alarm, the shouts, the screams, the weeping."

"Weeping?"

"While making his getaway, Alex shot and killed the night watchman. Paulinho's father, Januário Vieira."

She'd wondered about Paulinho's involvement. "So

Alex escaped, and you went to prison for thirty-plus years." She frowned. "Why such a harsh sentence? You didn't murder anyone."

"A fire in the late seventies destroyed prison records. Twelve hundred inmates—including me—got lost in the bureaucratic shuffle."

Dear God. Betrayed, crippled, imprisoned, and forgotten. "No wonder you're bitter."

"Alex destroyed my life." He crumpled the La Magia article into a ball and tossed it in the fireplace. "Now I'm going to destroy his."

Paulinho sat cross-legged on the floor in the middle of his bedroom, frowning over the *opele*. This particular *opele*, or necklace of the Ifa cult, had been in his family for generations. In the hands of a trained *babalaô*, the chain of pods from the African opele tree was a powerful divination tool.

But Paulinho was no *babalaô*. His clumsy Brazilian tongue stumbled as badly with Yoruba as it did with English. Try as he might, he could not understand the *opele*'s message. The girl was the question mark. Good or evil? Saint or demon? Savior or nemesis? "Father," he prayed, "You-Who-Touched-the-Miracle, show me what I must do to return the magic to its rightful home. Guide me by the secrets of the *babalaô*."

He repeated each step of the ritual, but again it resulted in an ambiguous pattern.

He heaved a sigh, then bowed his head in acceptance. The spirits had spoken. If he could not understand the message, the fault was his. "I have failed you, Father. I am sorry."

Have faith. In time, all will be put right.

He didn't so much hear the words as feel them, a resonant vibration in his heart. Tears of relief blurred his vision.

Ian awoke with a start, not sure for a moment what had awakened him. Then he heard it again, a scream.

As he flipped on the bedside light, Paulinho, resplendent in red silk pajamas, materialized in the doorway like a jinn from a bottle. "I heard a noise. Are you all right, Senhor Ian?"

"I'm fine. It's Tasya. Another nightmare." The girl was prone to bad dreams. Several times a week, she would wake them with her sobbing. He'd never heard her scream before, though.

"Shall I check on her, Senhor Ian?"

"We'll both go." Ian threw back the covers and maneuvered himself into his chair. He and Paulinho made their way to the wing off the kitchen where Tasya slept. Even muffled by the closed door, her sobs tugged at Ian's heartstrings.

Paulinho eased the door open and light spilled into the hall. Terrified of the dark, Tasya slept with a lamp on.

Ian entered first, with Paulinho right behind him.

Tasya cringed against the headboard. Her eyes were open, but she gave no sign she'd seen them. "No," she pleaded, a long, drawn-out note of anguish. "Please, no."

Paulinho moved closer to the bed. He shot Ian a troubled glance. "Shall I . . . ?" He reached out as if to touch her shoulder.

"No," Ian whispered. "You might frighten her."

"Senhor, she is frightened already."

Paulinho had a point.

"No," she screamed, thrashing her legs as if kicking at an invisible adversary. "No, Richard. Please."

Richard. Though she often spoke in her sleep, Ian had never before heard her use a name.

"No. No, not again." She caught her breath on a sob. "Why can't you leave me alone?"

"Tasya?" Ian pitched his voice low, but she flinched as if he'd struck her.

"No!" She stared wide-eyed at a spot on the wall. "You can't be here." Her breathing quickened. "You're dead."

Ian moved closer. "Tasya?" he said, trying to soothe her with his voice. "It's all right. You're safe now. Richard can't hurt you anymore. Paulinho and I are here to protect you."

Her body twitched. Her face convulsed, then went very still. Expressionless. She blinked several times in rapid succession, then slowly focused. Her breath came in quick, shallow gasps, and tears glistened on her cheeks, but her fingers no longer gripped the edge of the sheet as if it were her only link to sanity. "What's going on?" She looked from Ian to Paulinho, then back to Ian. "Did I have another nightmare?"

"Yes," Ian said. "A bad one."

"We hear the screaming," Paulinho told her in his fractured English. "Like a soul in torment," he continued in his own language. "A shriek ripped from the bowels of hell itself."

She frowned. Paulinho had been giving her Portuguese lessons, but Ian suspected she'd only understood a word or two of the big Brazilian's rapid speech. "I'm sorry," she said.

"No need to be." Ian smiled. "You frightened us, but we can see now that you're all right." A lie. She wasn't all right. All wrong was closer to the truth. Whatever this Richard had done to her had taken its toll.

She eyed them, her expression wary, her fingers clenched again on the edge of the sheet.

He backed away. "Go to sleep. And sweet dreams this time. That's an order. Paulinho and I need our beauty rest, even if you don't." He shot her a reassuring smile, then moved into the hall, motioning for Paulinho to follow. "Good night."

"Good night," she echoed.

Paulinho closed the door and accompanied Ian back to his room. "It is not tired muscles bothering the girl. Her mind is troubled," he said. "Exú haunts her dreams."

Ian levered himself into bed. "She's haunted all right, but I think the devil goes by a different name."

"Yes?"

"Richard." He tucked the sheet around his useless legs.

Paulinho gave him a solemn look. "Do you think he is the one who hurt her? The one who made her so wary of human contact?"

"I do."

Paulinho fell silent a moment, then said slowly, "She spoke to him as if he were dead. Do you think she . . . ?"

"Killed him? I don't know. It would explain a few things."

"If she did . . ."

"We'll cross that bridge when we come to it."

*   *   *

Tasya lay in bed, haunted by her nightmare. Richard. She'd dreamed she was back in his control. But that was impossible. He was dead. All that blood where his face had been. No one could survive that. Not even Richard.

She should tell Ian the truth. But if he knew what she was, what she'd done, he wouldn't want her around.

She didn't want to leave Ian's house, but how much longer could she hide the truth? Sooner or later the authorities would catch up with her. Richard had taken so many pictures. Evidence of her motive. Clues to her identity. If she'd had her wits about her, she'd have destroyed them before she left. But she hadn't been thinking straight, just reacting, running on adrenaline and fear.

Finally, exhaustion claimed her, and the dreams came. Not of Richard this time, but the sweet dreams Ian had ordered.

She found herself in a walled garden, surrounded by luxuriant ferns and exotic flowers. A breeze whispered through palm fronds overhead, wafting the delicate scent of frangipani. An elegant dark-haired woman sat in the shade of a vine-covered trellis. She smiled at Tasya, her brown eyes warm and kind. "*Bem-vinda ao Brasil. Bem-vinda, viajante.*"

Portuguese. The woman was speaking Portuguese. Paulinho had been teaching her the language in his spare time, but she was far from fluent. Welcome to Brazil. That was how the first part translated. But the last part had her stymied. *Viajante*? She didn't know that word. "What's a *viajante*?" she asked, but the woman seemed not to hear her.

Tasya woke, heart pounding, but she was more excited than frightened this time. Four-forty-three, according to her alarm clock. Still dark outside, though the lamp on her bedside table kept the shadows at bay here in the sanctuary of her room.

Strange dream. Not a nightmare. Not frightening. Yet somehow unsettling. Maybe because it had seemed so real, every detail vivid.

She grabbed paper and pencil and scribbled down the woman's words before she forgot them. In the morning she would ask Paulinho to translate for her. *Bem-vinda ao Brasil. Bem-vinda, viajante.*

Tasya gave an involuntary shiver as she stared at the words she'd just written.

How could she have dreamed in a language she didn't speak?

3

June 2004
Orange County, California

CHRISTINA FARRELL CROSSED La Magia's wide tiled lobby. Kelly Bradshaw, the efficient young blonde manning the main desk, glanced up. Her smile wavered for an instant, then gained conviction.

"Mrs. Farrell. What can I do for you?"

Like all the employees at the spa, Kelly had been chosen for her upbeat personality, glowing good health, and physical attractiveness. Christina's husband, Alex, did the hiring, and he placed a high premium on beauty.

Kelly shot her a concerned look. "Is something wrong?"

"Have you seen my husband?"

The young woman hesitated for a second. "He's been in and out all morning. Would you like me to buzz his office?"

"Don't bother. He's not there. I already checked."

Christina, who hated confrontations, thought of all the things she'd rather be doing with her morning: riding, working on her herb garden, consulting with the architect on the planned changes to the house. If only things were different . . . If only Alex were different . . . *Till death do us part.* If only she didn't take her vows so seriously . . . "It's important, Kelly, or I wouldn't be here."

The girl shrugged. "Maybe he went out."

"His car's in the parking lot."

"Hmm." A slight frown wrinkled the desk clerk's brow. "I suppose I could page him for you. He doesn't like us to do that, not when he's with one of the Level III guests, and if he's not in his office, I expect that's where he is." Level III was in-house code for their high-profile clients, mostly international jet-setters and assorted celebrities wealthy enough to pay for privacy as well as first-rate care.

"It's important," Christina repeated. Damn Alex and her father, too, for putting her in this position.

Kelly held her gaze for a five count, then nodded. "Diana Lindsay checked in yesterday."

"Diana Lindsay?"

"British pop star. Does some elaborate dance sequences as part of her act. She fell from some scaffolding during a concert in L.A. a week ago. Hurt her back."

"I see," Christina said.

"Mr. Farrell likes to personally oversee the treatments of our celebrity guests."

The attractive young females anyway. Bitterness churned Christina's stomach even as she told herself she didn't care, that Alex's flirtations didn't matter. The infatuations never amounted to anything. He valued their marriage more than that.

Kelly keyed in some information, studying the computer screen in front of her. "According to the schedule, Ms. Lindsay's down for hydrotherapy this morning."

"Where?"

"Mrs. Farrell, I—"

"Where?"

"If Mr. Farrell finds out I've released Level III scheduling information, I'll lose my job."

Christina took a deep breath. "You work for me, too, Kelly. La Magia is half mine."

"Yes, but Mr. Farrell's my direct supervisor, and if he thinks I've talked out of turn, he'll fire me."

"You're right," Christina said. "Tell me what I want to know, and he *might* fire you . . . if he finds out. Don't tell me, and I *will* fire you. Guaranteed."

Kelly's mouth opened and closed, but no words came out.

"For the last time, where's my husband?"

"In one of the private rooms."

"Which one? St. Blaise? St. Florian? No?" Christina studied the young woman's panicky expression. "St. Fiacre then."

"Mrs. Farrell, maybe this isn't such a good idea. . . ."

Christina started back across the lobby, then spun to face the young receptionist. "Warn him I'm coming, and you'll be looking for a new job tomorrow. Are we clear on that?"

Kelly shot her a startled look, then dropped the house phone handset back in its cradle. "Clear," she said.

Christina made her way toward the vaulted corridor that led to the private treatment rooms. She didn't want to be here. She didn't want to do this. But her father had insisted.

"If Alex sold off our stock, I'm sure he had a good reason," she'd told him.

To which her father had responded with a few pithy expletives.

"It was his stock, Dad."

"*Your* stock," he'd said. "Your stock and my production company. I need to speak with that slippery bastard one-on-one, but he won't return my calls. All you have to do is arrange a meeting."

All she had to do . . . Easy for her father to say. He was used to giving orders, making arrangements. Whereas she had trouble planning dinner menus and choosing clothes. Or rather planning dinner menus and choosing clothes that suited Alex. Nothing she did ever quite met his standards.

Awash in a golden glow from the skylights overhead, the broad corridor, furnished with a veritable jungle of tropical greenery, stretched for sixty feet before opening onto the solarium. Along its length six recessed doors led to private treatment rooms named for the various patron saints of healing. A discreet red light signified that St. Fiacre was in use. Squaring her shoulders, Christina used her keycard to open the door.

Music blared from the sound system, loud enough to cover the noise of her entrance. One of Diana Lindsay's top ten hits? Christina couldn't say. She'd always preferred classical music, had even entertained the notion of becoming a concert pianist at one time. Before cancer. Before Alex.

She saw him then, and her heart shriveled. Dear God. She should have followed Kelly's suggestion. She should have waited in Alex's office.

Because it was one thing to know your husband was a flirt, quite another to catch him cheating on you. Not even the turbulent churning of the hydrotherapy pool could disguise the fact that both Alex and his client were naked and engaged in an activity not listed on La Magia's treatment schedule.

Christina turned away almost immediately, but the image of Alex's suntanned hand fondling the young singer's breast had already burned itself onto her retinas. She reached blindly for the door.

June 2004
Half Moon Bay, California

On a Monday ten weeks into Tasya's training, Ian rented a local gym for the entire afternoon. He wanted Tasya to experience the climbing wall and spend some time developing her upper-body strength. Because he planned to work her unmercifully later in the day, he gave her the morning off, figuring she'd either spend the time sunbathing in the garden or reading in the study, her two favorite leisure-time pursuits. Despite his warnings about UV rays, she had a passion for sunlight, a passion equaled only by her passion for books. She'd read every novel in the house, some of them twice.

As for himself, he'd intended to use the morning to work on his plan to exact revenge from Alex Farrell. Unfortunately, he made little progress.

Investigator Jim Harper had sent him half a dozen lengthy reports covering the last three decades of Alex Farrell's life. Ian had all but memorized them, but he still hadn't decided what form retribution should take. Thirty years ago, Alex's besetting sin had been greed. Now he was a wealthy man with an even wealthier wife. Was greed still a factor? Ian didn't know.

Hunger finally drove him to the kitchen a little before noon. Tasya sat on a bar stool with her back to him. "So according to you, Paulinho, women are less intelligent than men," she said in her increasingly fluent, if grammatically challenged Portuguese.

Paulinho stood at the butcher block, chopping vegetables. If the sarcasm lacing her words bothered him, it didn't register on his face. "Yes. The man has the bigger head, the bigger brain, and thus, the bigger intellect."

"Not to mention the bigger ego," Tasya muttered in English.

"Que?"

"Nothing. If, as you say, intelligence is a function of gender, how do you explain Madame Curie? Margaret Mead? Sandra Day O'Connor?"

Paulinho shrugged. "Genetic anomalies. Freaks of nature."

"I beg your pardon? Freaks? Freaks!"

Paulinho raised his eyebrows. "No need to turn this into a shouting match. You females are so emotional."

"You insult my entire gender, then blame me for reacting emotionally? That's irrational."

"No, silly girl," Paulinho said. "Irrational is screaming at a man with a knife in his hands."

She scowled. "Silly *woman*."

"How dare you!" Paulinho drew himself up to his full six feet, eight inches.

Tasya leapt to her feet, tilting her head to look him in the eye. "Not you, me. I resent being called a girl."

Paulinho's frowned. "And I resent being called a woman. My vow of celibacy does not make me any less a man."

"Look, you thick-skulled Brazilian, I wasn't casting aspersions on your manhood."

"I accept your apology," Paulinho said.

"What apology?"

"Stop while you're ahead, girl," Ian said.

Tasya whirled around to glare at him. *"Woman,"* she said before stomping from the room.

Paulinho threw his hands up in disgust. "And now she insults you, Senhor Ian."

Ian spent a few minutes soothing Paulinho's injured sensibilities, then went in search of Tasya. He found her in the study, her fingers flying across the computer keyboard. "Are you angry with me, too?"

"No," she said, though she sounded it.

"What are you doing?"

"Accessing that translation website to find out how to say 'asshole' in Portuguese."

Ian laughed.

She frowned. "What's so funny?"

"You."

She glared at him, then turned back to the computer screen.

"What are you doing now? Searching for a site to translate 'asshole' into Gaelic?"

"How'd you guess?"

He touched her shoulder and felt her tense up. "A waste of time. I don't speak Gaelic. Why not tell me what's really wrong?"

She shifted in her chair, dislodging his hand and angling her face away from him. "Why do you have to be so kind?"

"Kind?" He'd never thought of himself in quite that way.

"Yes, you've given me a home—food, shelter, clothing, even an education of sorts. And why? You don't really need my help. If I hadn't sneaked in the dog door, you'd have found another way to get even with Alex."

"If you hadn't appeared when you did, I'd be dead."

She shuddered. "You never would have pulled the trigger. You're not a quitter, not a victim."

Was that how she saw herself? As a victim? Someone undeserving of kindness or respect? "Like you?"

She jerked around to meet his gaze. Something sparked in the depths of her silvery eyes, but before he could identify it, she lowered her gaze, screening her eyes from view with a sweep of dark lashes. "I'm not worth the time and effort you're investing. You don't know me, Ian."

"Don't I? Tasya Ivanova Flynn," he recited, "illegitimate daughter of former Olympic gymnast Natassia Nikolaevna Krestyanova. Born August 28, 1983, in Boise, Idaho. Adopted as an infant by Natassia's American husband, Joseph Orrin Flynn. Reared on a dairy farm near Caldwell, Idaho. Trained in gymnastics under Natassia's tutelage. Winner of numerous national competitions."

Tasya stared at him, wide-eyed. "How do you know this?"

He ignored her question. "Following the deaths of Joseph and Natassia Flynn in December 1998, Michael and Brenda Dietz of Portland, Oregon, assumed guardianship. Brenda was Joseph's older sister. Shall I go on?"

"How can you possibly know this?" Her voice shook.

"I'm a wealthy man. Money equals power."

She frowned. "Those private investigators you have searching for information on Alex Farrell. You had them do a background check on me, too."

"Yes. Want to rescind what you said about my being kind?"

She smiled sadly. "You have the statistics, but not the details. You don't know me. You only think you do."

June 2004
Orange County, California

Alex Farrell's father-in-law crouched like a toad in the corner of one of La Magia's steam rooms. The old man's mouth tightened in acknowledgment as Alex took a seat on the bench opposite. "It's about damn time."

Alex flashed an easy smile. "Sorry I'm late. Something came up."

His father-in-law grunted. Grenville Gentry had never been attractive. At seventy-four, he was repulsive. With scrawny limbs, no chin to speak of, and pale bulbous eyes, the man looked like an experiment in cross-species hybridization gone awry.

"You wanted to talk to me?" Alex said.

"What can you tell me about those shares of Gentry Consolidated that went on the market yesterday?"

Blunt as ever. Grenville could christen himself with an upper-crust name, but he was still the same crude little man who'd started his career in the entertainment industry working as a bouncer in a strip club.

Alex arranged his features in a regretful expression. "La Magia's had some losses lately. I didn't say anything to Christy because I didn't want to worry her, but the new herbal center cost more than we anticipated, and the—"

"Bullshit. You've been gambling again. What I want to know is, who with, and how much are you in for?"

Alex took a deep breath. "Okay, you're right. I lost a bundle to a guy in Vegas with serious underworld connections. Stupid of me, I know. And I'm sorry. God, I'm sorry. I never would have touched those stocks, I swear, but I was desperate. He said if I didn't pay up, he'd hurt Christy."

The old toad glared. "The truth, you lying sack of shit."

"That *is* the truth." All except the part about Casale threatening Christy. It was *his* well-being at stake, specifically the well-being of his knee caps.

"Eddie Casale is scum, but he doesn't victimize innocents. He didn't threaten Christina. He threatened you. And in order to pay what you owed, you sold off my daughter's stock, putting the stability of my company in jeopardy."

So the old toad knew about Casale. He'd just sat there asking questions he already had the answers to and let Alex make a fool of himself.

Though fury and humiliation roiled his gut, Alex pasted an ingratiating smile on his face. "Okay, I admit I stretched the truth a little. I probably should have talked it over with Christy first, but it's not like I broke any laws by selling that stock. In case you've forgotten, California is a community property state."

"Only you signed a prenup," Gentry snapped. "That stock wasn't yours to sell. How'd you do it anyway? Have your secretary call the broker and pretend to be Christina?"

"I was up against a wall. I had no choice."

"There's always a choice," the old man said. "In fact, I'll give you one now. We can prosecute, destroy your reputation, and send you to jail for fraud. Or you can agree to a quiet divorce and walk away a free man. A poor man, of course, but a free man."

"Divorce? Isn't that a little drastic?"

"I've already spoken to Christina. It's what she wants."

"I don't believe that. Christy knows I love her."

"Does she?" Malice edged Grenville's smile. "I sent her out here earlier to ask you about the stocks. Apparently you were too busy sticking it to some little slut to notice Christina. She saw you, though, and this time, Alex, my boy, you're not going to be able to sweet-talk your way out of the mess."

"I don't know what Christy thought she saw, but—"

"Save your breath. It's over. My daughter has finally realized what a worthless bastard you are. She wants a divorce."

"But—"

"Shut up and listen. This is the way it's going to be. You're going to sign everything over to Christina, everything except your clothing and personal effects."

"This is ridiculous. I want to talk to Christy."

"Haven't you hurt her enough?"

"Hurt her? I'm the one who saved her life."

"Yes, you did." Gentry eyed him steadily. "But you canceled that debt when you broke her heart." The old man's mouth stretched in a travesty of a smile. "Face it, you're fucked."

June 2004
Half Moon Bay, California

"How did your detective trace me?" Tasya asked halfway through dinner. She and Ian were eating on the deck. Grilled chicken, snow peas, and rice pilaf. Up to now their conversation had been a desultory discussion of the food (good), the weather (good), and state politics (not so good). He hadn't said another word about her past. She had to find out how much he knew.

"More ice water?"

She shook her head. "How did he trace me?"

Ian refilled his own glass, then set the pitcher down. "It wasn't difficult."

She didn't look up, but she knew he was watching her, trying to see inside her head. "I know part of what happened after you moved to Portland," he said.

"A small part, if all you've uncovered are official records." She stared at the deck railing, trying not to think, not to feel.

"I'm no fool, Tasya. I can read between the lines."

Her throat tightened. Her eyes prickled.

"Dietz abused you, didn't he?"

She didn't answer, didn't look at him.

"According to court records, you became pregnant.

You claimed Dietz was responsible, but he denied it. His wife backed him up."

"Yes." She poked at the snow peas on her plate, impaling one on the tines of her fork. "Even when DNA tests proved the twins I'd carried were his, even when it became obvious he'd lied, she stood by him." He'd changed his story, of course, twisting the facts to his advantage. "He told Aunt Brenda I seduced him one night when he'd had too much to drink." She jabbed at another pea pod.

"And she believed him?"

Tasya nodded. Mike Dietz was a good liar.

She scraped the peas off her fork and buried them under a pile of rice. They hadn't buried her twins. She knew, because she'd tried to find their graves. Her caseworker had explained later that miscarriages didn't count as births or deaths. Fetuses didn't merit a cemetery burial.

"You lost the babies."

His words stripped away the protective scar tissue. "They said it was a blessing in disguise. Statistically, sixteen-year-olds don't make the best mothers." She swallowed hard. "Even if I'd carried them to term, they probably would have been taken from me." The social worker, Mrs. Penzler, had said as much.

"You didn't go back to the Dietzes."

"No. Aunt Brenda believed Mike's lies, but the judge didn't."

"You lived in a series of foster homes."

"Some good, some indifferent. None as bad as living under the same roof as Mike Dietz."

A faint frown wrinkled Ian's brow. "Yet you ran away."

"Aunt Brenda showed up at my school one day. She

said she and Mike were ready to forgive and forget, ready to resume custody. They'd somehow managed to get the first judge's order overturned." She took a sip of water, hoping to ease the tightness in her throat. "I ditched class next period, hitchhiked from Portland to Seattle." She shoved her food aside uneaten.

"There's a gap in the official record," Ian said. "Over three years from the day you ran away until the night you crawled through my dog door."

She forced herself to look him in the eye. "You said you'd never ask for more than I was willing to give. You promised."

"You need to talk about this, to exorcize your demons."

"Talking about it is like living it all over again. I can't. I won't."

"All right. Fair enough. But if you change your mind—"

"I won't."

He covered her hand with his. "You're safe here."

She met his gaze. "No one's safe. Anywhere."

4

Tasya overslept Saturday, waking stiff and sore after a strenuous workout Friday afternoon. She showered, pulled her hair into a ponytail, and dressed in black leggings and a leotard.

Paulinho was stuffing the last of the breakfast dishes in the dishwasher when she walked into the kitchen at a quarter to eight. "*Bom dia,*" he said. "You are late."

"Slept through my alarm." Ignoring his disapproving grunt—Paulinho didn't like people messing up his kitchen once he'd put things to rights—she poured herself a glass of juice, snagged a leftover blueberry muffin, and perched on a stool at the counter.

"I think when you don't get up that maybe you are sick." Paulinho scrubbed the already spotless countertop.

"I'm fine. Just a few aches and pains from my workout yesterday." She stuffed a chunk of muffin in her mouth.

"You do not have more bad dreams?"

"No nightmares." She sipped her juice. "But I did dream of that woman again. The woman from my other dream. Remember? I told you about her. The one who said, 'Bem-vinda ao Brasil. Bem-vinda, viajante.'" The morning after the first dream she'd asked him to translate. He'd looked at her strangely for a moment, then said, "Welcome to Brazil. Welcome, traveler."

Paulinho was staring at her now with that same odd expression on his face—half wary, half excited. "Did she speak this time?"

"No. She was preoccupied." The dark-haired woman had been standing alone at the center of an enormous room. Light poured through a skylight in the ceiling, illuminating a domed glass case atop a marble pedestal.

"What did she do?" Paulinho paused, one big paw clenching the dishcloth.

"Nothing." Just stood there, silent, immobile, the expression on her face ineffably sad. Tasya had found the dream as disturbing in its own way as the Richard nightmares. Afterward, she'd tossed and turned for a long time before finally falling asleep again.

Paulinho gave a grunt and went back to scouring the counter. "You'd better hurry. Senhor Ian is waiting for you in the *sala de estar*."

Just as Ian had transformed his family room into a schoolroom, he'd made his living room into a workout area equipped with weights, a treadmill, exercise mats, and a climbing rope.

The first thing she noticed was Ian's empty wheelchair. The second was Ian himself, sliding down the rope like a trapeze artist. She squinted at the rafters. "How did you get up there?"

He swung himself into his chair with a cocky grin.

"Climbed. Nothing wrong with my upper body strength."

Had she imagined the slight emphasis on the word *my*? She met his gaze and saw the challenge in his. She hadn't imagined anything. "You're suggesting there is something wrong with mine?"

"How many pull-ups did you manage yesterday?"

"Ten."

He laughed. "I'm three times your age and I can do forty."

"Men have more upper body strength than women."

"So this is a weakness we need to address. Climb the rope." He handed her a pair of leather gloves to protect her hands.

She tugged them on. Her muscles ached from yesterday's workout, but she refused to complain. Gritting her teeth, she shinnied up the twenty-foot rope. When she reached the top, she grinned down at him. "How fast?"

He shrugged. "I didn't time you, but it wasn't bad. Try it again. I'll use my stopwatch this go round."

She let herself down the rope. Her muscles were loosening up. With any luck, she'd be even faster this time.

"Go." Ian's command caught her off guard.

She went, leveraging with her feet and knees, pulling with her arms and shoulders. Again she made the top in what must have been record time. "How'd I do?"

"Fair," Ian said. "Try it again."

So she tried it again. And again. Until her shoulders were on fire and her arms felt as limp as month-old celery stalks. When Ian said, "Let's try something different," at the end of the first hour, she was so relieved, she nearly wept.

Feigning indifference, she peeled off her gloves. "What weakness are we addressing next?"

"Overconfidence."

Tasya frowned.

Ian raised his eyebrows. "You're going to need the gloves."

"I thought you said I was done climbing."

"No, I said we were going to try something different. Spread the tumbling mats under the rope."

"Why?"

"To cushion your fall."

"I'm going to practice falling?"

"That's one way of looking at it."

"What's the other way of looking at it?"

"You're going to climb the rope without using your lower body. No feet. No legs."

No way.

"You can do it, Tasya. I have confidence in you."

"Right. That's why you told me to spread the mats."

"MacPherson's Rule Number Three: Whenever possible, work with a safety net."

Ian and his rules. *Prepare for every eventuality. Think before you act. Never approach a potentially dangerous situation without backup. Control your emotions and control the job.* She needed a three-inch binder just to keep track of them all.

She positioned the mats under the rope. "Ready." Despite what Ian said, she knew he thought she'd lose her grip. But he thought wrong. She squared her shoulders, determined that she'd rip both arms from their sockets before she gave him the satisfaction of seeing her fall. She shot him a narrow-eyed look.

He was smiling. No, he was smirking. "Go," he said.

The spirit was willing, but the flesh was weak. Halfway up, her body stalled. Her arms trembled. Her hands cramped.

"Problem?" Ian called.

What did he think? That she'd stopped to admire the view? "No." She fought the groan clawing its way up her throat.

"Good." He sounded encouraging, but his expression said he thought she was only seconds from defeat.

What did he know? She glanced up. It wasn't that far to the top, not more than seven or eight feet.

Okay, what if the mats weren't there? Would she give up if she knew she'd land on the hardwood floor? Or worse yet, what if someone replaced the mats with hungry alligators? Or razor-sharp spikes? *Bet you could haul yourself up the rope then, wimp.*

"Hungry alligators. Razor-sharp spikes," she muttered under her breath and pulled herself six inches closer to the top. "Hungry alligators. Razor-sharp spikes. Hungry alligators. Razor-sharp spikes," she repeated. And before she knew it, she'd run out of rope. She hooked an arm over the rafter and clung there, panting, but victorious.

"Now that wasn't so hard, was it?" Ian grinned at her.

Scowling, Tasya made a very rude suggestion in Russian, one she'd once heard her mother make in an argument with a Ukrainian judge who'd scored Tasya's floor exercise five-tenths of a point below the other judges.

"That would be Russian for 'asshole,' I presume."

"Worse than that."

His smile grew broader. "Good. I'm glad to hear you're recovering your spirit."

Her irritation evaporated. He was right. Eleven weeks ago, when they'd first started the training regimen, she never would have permitted herself to complain, let alone abuse her instructor. Free of Richard's domination, her true personality was reasserting itself.

She let herself back down the rope, lighthearted despite the nagging pain of her overworked muscles. "Okay, what's next? What new torture have you devised in the name of training?"

"I want you to practice maneuvering in the hanging harness later on, but right now you need a break."

Yes. A break. She heaved a sigh.

Then Ian's mouth curved in that sardonic smile she was growing to hate. "Hit the treadmill. Warm up for a minute. Do five miles at a jog, followed by a minute of cool-down."

Five miles. At a jog. Some break.

Ian reread the *Los Angeles Times* article reporting Grenville Gentry's hit-and-run. The producer's death seemed too convenient to be coincidence. Harper Investigations reported that Alex had been gambling again and was seriously in debt to Eddie Casale, a well-known Vegas underworld figure. According to a La Magia employee, Alex and his father-in-law had had an angry confrontation after Alex dumped some Gentry Consolidated stock, presumably to raise cash to cover his debt to Casale. The next day Alex's wife—perhaps egged on by her father—had filed for divorce, a divorce that would leave Alex in a precarious financial situation.

Desperate and angry, Alex might have engineered his father-in-law's accident, but if the police suspected him, they were keeping it quiet. The article didn't even hint at foul play.

Someone knocked at the study door, and Ian laid the newspaper aside. "Come," he said.

Tasya poked her head in the room.

"Did you need something?"

"No, never mind. It's not important."

"Don't go," he said. "I've been sequestered in here for the past two hours. I'd welcome some company." He waved toward the sofa. "Have a seat. Talk to me."

"How's your plan coming?" She sat on the edge of the sofa.

"Slowly but surely. Alex has been gambling and owes more than he can pay. I think I've figured a way to use that against him. How about you? What have you been doing?"

"Reading. And thinking. Mostly thinking."

"Troubling thoughts?"

She nodded. "I've been feeling guilty since this morning."

"No need." He laughed. "I've been cursed before."

"Not guilty about swearing at you. You deserved it." A spark of animation lit her face for an instant, then faded, leaving her cheeks ashen. "But you also deserve the truth."

"What truth?"

"About me." She moved to the window and stared toward the shaggy eucalyptus tree across the street. "I'm . . ." She turned to face him. "I'm not the person you think I am."

He watched the rise and fall of her breasts as she tried to control her agitated breathing. "Who are you then?"

She closed her eyes for a split second, then focused on his face through a glaze of tears. "A murderer," she said. "I killed a man, Ian. Not accidentally. A premeditated murder." Tasya watched for signs of the distaste he must be feeling. But the only emotion visible was sadness.

"You're referring to Richard."

He knew. "How could you—"

"You talk in your sleep." Ian paused. "He's the one, isn't he? The one who hurt you."

She stared at her fisted hands. Dietz had hurt her, too, but Richard had taken the abuse to a higher level. "Yes," she said, still not looking at him.

"Then it wasn't murder. It was self-defense."

"No, he was asleep when I hit him. I smashed him in the face with a billy club." One of Richard's favorite toys.

"He didn't wake up?"

"I don't know. I just kept hitting and hitting. The blood . . ." She shuddered, unable to look at Ian, afraid of what she might see in his face. Revulsion. Repugnance. Loathing.

"Tasya?"

She didn't answer. What more was there to say? She'd killed a man, the ultimate in unforgivable sins.

"Tasya, look at me."

Look at me. Richard's three favorite words. He'd liked to see her eyes so he could savor her fear, revel in her despair.

"Tasya?" Ian's voice was gentle, nothing like Richard's. Ian was nothing like Richard. Or Dietz.

She looked at him then, and all she saw was sympathy.

"Come here." He extended an arm.

She closed the space between them and placed her hand in his.

He held it tightly. "Paulinho and I saw the evidence of long-term abuse on your body. No jury in the country would convict you of murder."

"But—"

"No buts," he said. "You did what you had to do."

Her hand still in his, she knelt on the floor beside his chair, leaning into him, resting her head on his knees. She shut her eyes, feeling safe, truly safe.

Ian didn't say a word, just smoothed the hair back off her face, but his tenderness proved her undoing. Tears welled up and spilled over. She burrowed into him, sobbing quietly. And through it all he held her hand, comforting her with his presence.

She clung long after the worst of the emotional storm had subsided, reluctant to relinquish contact. Ian was bedrock in a quicksand world. And she loved him for that.

Frowning, Paulinho studied the *opele*. This could not be right. He must have done something wrong. Not concentrated hard enough, misinterpreted the *odum*. He started over, proceeding through each step with meticulous care, but the end result was the same. Death.

But who was going to die? The *opele* refused to tell him. Possibly because the murderer had not yet chosen his victim. More probably because he, Paulinho, had misinterpreted the signs or asked the wrong questions.

He pounded his head in frustration. If only he knew, he could . . . what? Thwart the murderer? Protect the victim? Change destiny?

What arrogance! As if any of this was his concern. Vengeance and the retrieval of Milagre. That was where he needed to focus his attention.

Only what if the victim-to-be was Tasya? Yes, the girl complicated the situation and might at some point interfere with his agenda. Despite that, he did not wish to see her hurt.

He studied the pattern again. He liked Tasya. His heart told him she was a good person—which made the *opele*'s warning even harder to understand. Because according to all the signs, Tasya posed a danger.

Tasya's tears had relieved some of the pressure, but she still felt as if she were lost in an emotional fog, a confusing mixture of fear and rage, guilt and dread.

"Feeling better?" Concern softened Ian's features.

"A little."

"It might help to talk about it."

"I'm not sure I can." She shuddered, staring at the jar of cinnamon red hots on the desk but not really seeing them, seeing instead the ugliness of her past. "What Richard did was sick, but he couldn't have preyed on me if I hadn't made a bad choice."

Ian raised an eyebrow. "Are you suggesting Richard was your punishment for poor judgment?"

She frowned. "In a way."

"That's bloody nonsense."

"You don't understand."

"Then fucking well explain it to me."

She stared. Ian used profanity so seldom that the harsh words surprised her.

"Enumerate your so-called sins." He rapped the words out. "Make me understand."

She gazed into his eyes. Ian cared for her. Could she bear to see that caring shift to loathing? She should have left the first day, before their lives became so intertwined.

But she had stayed. She had, once again, chosen the easy road, and it had led her to this moment. She had to tell him the truth—all of it—but she couldn't find the words. She stood, separating herself from him.

"Tell me what happened after you went to Seattle," Ian said.

She moved restlessly, pacing back and forth, back and forth, then stopped abruptly by the window. "I can't."

"You have to. You need to get past it."

She didn't want to get past it. She wanted to forget it. She wanted to bury it deep, deep down in the depths of her mind.

Deep, deep down where it would fester, erupting from time to time in hideous nightmares. She leaned against the windowsill and drew a shuddery breath. Ian was right, but that didn't make the ordeal any easier.

"I had no money," she said finally, "no friends. The first night I slept in an alley behind a Dumpster, terrified some junkie was going to slit my throat and steal my jacket. The next day I discovered University Avenue. Lots of street kids hang out on the Ave.

"I tried to get a job, but nobody would hire me without a social security number. I was afraid to use mine for fear the authorities would trace me and drag me back to Portland." Back to Dietz. She frowned. "I could have sold my body, of course, but I'd decided no one was ever going to use me again the way Mike Dietz had. So instead I got by living out of garbage cans, panhandling until I had saved enough to purchase a fake ID. After that I worked a series of minimum-wage jobs."

"Is that how you met Richard?"

She turned to face Ian. "It rains a lot in Seattle."

He raised an eyebrow at this apparent non sequitur.

"Whenever it rained, I would hole up at the public library. Did you know libraries offer free Internet access?"

"A chat room. You met him in a chat room."

She frowned. "He seemed so sweet, so shy. He said he'd never had a girlfriend, that computer nerds like him didn't attract women. I . . . believed him."

"Men like Richard can be very manipulative."

"And women like me can be very gullible." A wave of self loathing engulfed her. "My life was a disaster. I wanted to trust him. I wanted to believe he was a knight in shining armor come to rescue me."

"Only he wasn't," Ian said, his voice harsh.

"He asked me to marry him." She heard Ian's quick intake of breath. "So I told him about Dietz, thinking he'd change his mind. Instead, he offered to pay my way to Reno, said we'd be married at an all-night wedding chapel."

"But it didn't turn out the way you expected."

"No." She took a deep breath. "He met me at the airport. He looked exactly the way he'd described himself: medium height, pale skin, freckles, and rusty brown hair with a cowlick. When he smiled, he looked like a teenager. I found out later he was thirty-two."

She took another deep breath. "He proposed next to the baggage carousel. The people nearby applauded. It was very romantic. Then after the ceremony he took me to a hotel room, ripped my clothes off, and took me so hard and fast I bled."

Ian made a sound. Tasya glanced up. His mouth was a tight line, his eyes narrowed. "You mean he raped you."

She shut her eyes to avoid the accusation in his expression, but she couldn't shut out the shame. "I . . . he . . . I was crying. He said he was sorry. He said he hadn't meant to be so rough. He said he'd been carried away. He said he'd go easier next time."

"But he lied." Ian spat out the words.

Yes. By the time she'd figured that out, though, it was too late. "He took me to his cabin in the Sierras. Our love nest, he called it." Prison was more like it. She paced again, back and forth, back and forth, halting finally near the bookcase, careful to keep her face turned away from Ian.

"And he just kept hurting you, didn't he?" Ian's voice sounded raspy, as if he'd been yelling.

"Yes." She could still see the smile on Richard's face, hear the soft caress of his voice as he tied her to the bedposts. *Open your eyes, Tasya. Don't you want to see my new toy?* "I tried to run away, but he caught me. And after that he kept me locked in a basement room with bars across the window. Twice a day he brought me food." Twice a day he . . .

"Someone must have noticed—a family member, a neighbor."

Tasya stared at her clenched hands. "His cabin was isolated. No neighbors. No visitors. Once or twice a month he'd drive down the mountain for supplies, but he never stayed away long."

"Where did he get his income?"

"Writing software programs for a Reno-based company. He did all his work at home. Sometimes he'd get so engrossed in a project, I wouldn't see him for a couple days. I looked forward to those times, even though it meant going hungry." Better an empty stomach than the degradation of one of Richard's games.

"He enjoyed hurting you, didn't he?"

"And humiliating me." A lump grew in her throat as she remembered. She swallowed hard. "At first, when things got unbearable, I disconnected, escaped inside myself." She paused. "But Richard wanted to control my mind as well as my body. When he couldn't, he lost his temper. That's how I got this." She touched her crooked right collarbone. "He broke it to get my attention."

"My God." Ian looked ill.

"When the bone healed crooked, Richard blamed me. He hated imperfections."

Ian muttered something under his breath.

"After that he was careful not to cause any permanent damage."

"How long were you his prisoner?"

"Two years, three months, thirteen days."

"Christ!"

She faced Ian squarely. "All that's beside the point. I make no excuses. I killed Richard in cold blood. And I'd do it again."

"Good."

Good? She stared at him, thinking he'd misunderstood. "Ian, I'm a murderer."

His nostrils flared. "Some people don't deserve to live. Killing them's not murder; it's justice."

5

T HERE WAS NO JUSTICE in this world. Richard Zane
had learned that lesson early on. But he also knew if you
were smart enough and lucky enough, you could get
even.

As he washed toner powder off his hands, he caught a
glimpse of his face in the mirror above the sink. Three
surgeries had repaired the damage, but he didn't look like
himself anymore. Ironically, he looked like his father. He
shared a conspiratorial grin with the man in the mirror.
Wouldn't old Reverend Otis shit a brick to see his face on
Richard?

As a boy, Richard hadn't understood why his father
hated him. Most fathers in their rural Kentucky community took a belt to their offspring on occasion, but the Reverend Otis's belt spent more time flaying his son's
backside than it did holding up the reverend's trousers.
Sleep past six? Ten lashes. Stumble over a Bible verse?
Twenty. Dip into the collection plate money? Fifty. And
the time he'd got caught smoking behind the revival tent?

Sweet Jesus, he'd lost count after a hundred. Lost consciousness, too.

His mother had finally explained things after the old man died. Seemed the Reverend Otis thought Richard was a bastard. He didn't believe brown-eyed parents could spawn a blue-eyed child.

Richard dried his hands, then winked at his reflection. *Joke's on you, Otis. I was pure-dee yours all along.*

He made his way down the hall to his office, then sat in front of the computer. Pure-dee. Now there was a folksy expression he hadn't heard since he left Cumberland County, since Otis Leroy Bodine Jr., reinvented himself as Richard Martin Zane.

Muttering, "Pure-dee, pure-dee," he typed in the URL of the website he'd just put up and hit Enter. Tasya's face stared at him, mouth tense, eyes wide and frightened. HAVE YOU SEEN THIS WOMAN? it said in bold black caps below her picture. Underneath he'd added a few details. *Delusional. Mentally unstable. May pose a danger to herself and others. Answers to the name Tasya. Wandered away from her caretaker in the vicinity of Lake Tahoe. Concerned family offers reward for information regarding her whereabouts. Contact_Dr_Zach_Arien@yahoo.com.*

He thought the e-mail address was a particularly clever touch. Dr. Zach Arien. An anagram of Richard Zane.

August 2004
Los Angeles, California

Christina Farrell sat in the sunny morning room overlooking the rose garden, nibbling croissants and melon because Mrs. Wolfe, her father's housekeeper, had insisted that she eat some breakfast. Six weeks had passed since her father's funeral. And for six weeks she'd been staying in his big house off Mulholland, going through his personal effects, trying to come to terms with his death. Though the house swarmed with people—servants and other employees—Christina had never felt more alone.

"More coffee, Mrs. Farrell?" Preoccupied, she hadn't noticed the maid slip into the room.

"No, thank you." Christina had drunk too much coffee lately, which was probably at least half the reason she wasn't sleeping well.

"Mr. Culbertson called half an hour before you came downstairs." Harold Culbertson, longtime friend of her father, had agreed to handle the divorce. "He said he had a few things to take care of at the office, but that he'd be here at eleven."

"Thank you, Blanca."

She hadn't spared a thought for her cheating husband since the moment she'd heard about her father. Alex had attended the funeral, of course, but she hadn't seen him since. He'd phoned numerous times. She hadn't taken the calls. She hadn't felt like arguing with him, not with her grief so fresh and raw.

"Will there be anything else, Mrs. Farrell?" the maid asked.

"No, Blanca. Thank you. I'm finished here, I think." She rose, abandoning her half-eaten breakfast. "If anyone wants me, I'll be in the rose garden."

Originally, her father had planted the roses to please her mother, an expatriate Irishwoman who'd longed for the sights and scents of home. After Christina's mother, Meg, died of cancer at thirty-one, the roses had become her father's solace. Now Christina sought a measure of that solace for herself.

She wandered the paths at random, stopping now and then to enjoy the scents and textures of her favorites: Summer's Kiss, a yellow blend with a spiced honey fragrance; La Ville de Bruxelles, an old damask rose; Frederic Mistral, a pink both sweet and potent; and Angel Face, a mauve cluster-flowered floribunda with delicate ruffled edges and a sweet lemony scent.

She skirted an elaborate redwood arbor showcasing a pink climbing rose called Fourth of July. Paying more attention to the abundant blooms than to where she was putting her feet, she nearly tripped over the head gardener, who was squatting at the edge of the path, tinkering with one of the drip pipes. "Oh," she said. "Sorry."

He straightened to his full height, though straightened wasn't entirely accurate. Nothing about Michael Ryan— not his knotted arthritic hands, his bowed legs, or his curved spine—was straight. At five-feet-five she topped him by a good two inches.

"Miss Christina, how are you then? I was that sorry to hear about your dad. He was a good man, Mr. Gentry was. Tough, but fair."

"Thank you." She didn't know what else to say. Thinking about her father made her sad. Talking about him made her cry.

The old man squinted down the length of the garden. "Loved the flowers, he did."

"Yes." Christina stared hard at the showy pink blooms.

"Reminded him of your mother."

She nodded. "I miss them both."

"Then I'm thinking you're in the right place, miss. They each left a part of themselves here amongst the roses."

But not the parts she needed so desperately. No gentle arms to hold her close. No soothing voices to ease the ache in her heart. She sighed.

"Do you remember your first day of school? Your mother brought you out here and let you choose some roses for your teacher."

She smiled at the memory. "An armful of pinks and whites."

"Pristine and Gruss an Aachen." He cocked a bushy eyebrow and rubbed his chin. "And do you remember playing hide-and-seek with your dad?"

Again she nodded.

He patted her hand. "So your parents aren't truly gone, are they, miss? Nor will they be as long as you hold fast to your memories."

Tears stung her eyes, tears of gratitude at his kindness and understanding. "Thank you, Michael."

"Ah, miss. None of that now, or I'll be after disgracing meself." He cleared his throat. "'Tis a dirty shame what happened to your dad, but you'll do all right, miss. You look like your mother, saints be praised, but there's more than a bit of your dad in you. Don't you be letting them shove you about now. Not the lawyers. Not the studio executives. Not *anyone*."

She studied the old man's wizened face, puzzled by his vehemence. Then from behind her, she heard a familiar voice call out, "Christy!" and suddenly Michael's warning made perfect sense. What he meant was, she didn't need her father's help to stand up to Alex. She could do it on her own.

God, she hoped he was right. Panic fluttered in her stomach, but she squared her shoulders.

"Left me spade in the shed," Michael murmured, tactfully removing himself.

With a sigh she turned to face her husband, wondering how he'd gotten past security.

"I've been calling and calling, but the officious Mrs. Wolfe always insists you're not to be disturbed."

"Mrs. Wolfe was only following orders. My orders. I didn't want to speak to you when I first issued them, and I don't want to speak to you now."

"Don't speak then, sweetheart. Just listen." He smiled at her.

That smile. Even knowing what she knew, she responded, her heartbeat accelerating and her hands trembling.

Pretend he's a stranger.

But he wasn't a stranger. He was her husband.

"I've missed you. I've missed you so much." His voice caressed her aching heart. "Let's walk," he said, taking her arm.

For a second, her legs went rubbery in reaction. She stumbled, and Alex steadied her. Her heart skipped a beat, then raced to make up for lost time. Dear God.

A glimpse of Michael Ryan disappearing around the corner of the potting shed stiffened her resolve. What sort of fool was she? How could she respond to this man?

•

Alex stepped closer. "Please, Christy?"

"All right. But I can't be away from the house for long. I'm expecting someone."

Alex smiled again, dropping her elbow and weaving his fingers through hers. "Do you have any idea how beautiful you are, Christy? Beautiful inside as well as out. How could I help but love you?"

She pulled her hand free of his. "It's Christina," she said.

"What?" He gave her a baffled look.

"My name. It's Christina. Not Christy."

"But I've always called you Christy." He flashed the smile again.

She frowned. "And I've always preferred Christina."

His smile slipped a notch or two. "All right, Christina then." He shot her a look, half puzzlement, half hurt feelings. "I can't talk to you like this." He pulled her down beside him on a wrought-iron bench and gathered her hands in his. "Sweetheart, I'm so very sorry about your father. If they ever catch the drunk driver responsible, I hope they throw the book at him."

Christina studied his face. She'd been married to Alex Farrell for almost thirty years, but sometimes she wondered if she knew him at all. Was he as sincere as he seemed? Or was it all an act?

She felt so tired.

Alex leaned closer. "I know how close you and your father were. He was a good man. Grenville and I had our differences, but I always respected him."

She jerked her hands free and sat up very straight. "And you showed that respect how? By jeopardizing his company's stability? By making his daughter miserable?"

"Christy, I never meant to hurt you."

"It's Christina, damn it, and the truth is, you never meant to hurt yourself. Me, you couldn't care less about."

He gave her his wounded expression, the one designed to garner sympathy. "Sweetheart, you know that's not true. I love you. I've always loved you."

She studied his face. Had he *ever* loved her? Even in the beginning? Or had it always been about the money?

"It's over, Alex. I'm divorcing you." Simple and direct. A chip off the old block. Michael Ryan would be proud of her. So would her father.

For a split second she saw anger flash like lightning across Alex's face. The next instant, the smile was back in full force. "You're upset. You've been through a terrible ordeal."

"You're right. A twenty-seven-year ordeal." She stood up, and his expression sobered.

"I'm sorry for what I've done. I didn't mean to hurt you. I made a mistake."

"More than one."

"The stock—"

"And the women. And the gambling. You're addicted, Alex."

"Yes, but it's not the women or the gambling I'm hung up on. The excitement's what I crave. It's like the adrenaline rush I used to get from pulling off a perfect caper. Would you prefer I resume my career as a jewel thief?"

"I don't care what you do as long as you're no longer doing it married to me."

"You don't mean that, Christy . . . na. You can't. Yes, I

have my faults, but I love you. I don't believe you'd give up on our marriage without a fight."

"You don't get it, Alex. This is a fight. And you just lost."

August 2004
Half Moon Bay, California

Just as Ian and Tasya broke for lunch, Paulinho appeared in the doorway. "Telephone, Senhor Ian. It is Senhor Harper."

"An update on your former apprentice?" Tasya said.

"No doubt." He smiled. "Go ahead and eat without me. Harper likes to dot all the i's and cross all the t's. This is apt to take a while."

Tasya shot him an odd look. Could she tell he was lying? She held his gaze for a moment or two, then nodded and left the room.

"Transfer the call to the study," he told Paulinho.

Immediately following Tasya's confession, Ian had searched the archives of Reno area newspapers for mention of Zane's murder and come up empty. A discomforting result. Either the body had yet to be discovered or the monster was still alive. Either way, Ian needed to know. He couldn't protect Tasya unless he understood the full extent of the danger.

He'd contacted Harper Investigations and asked them to run surveillance on Zane's cabin and report any activity. He'd been in limbo ever since, waiting for a call.

Ian thought he was prepared, but the news was even worse than he'd expected. He scowled at the phone, trying to think. "Very well," he said when Harper finished. "Have your man keep an eye on Zane. I want to know every move he makes."

He heard a sharp intake of breath behind him and spun his chair around. Tasya slumped against the door frame, her face chalky. "Richard?" Her mouth formed the word, but she made no sound.

"May I call you back?" he said so peremptorily it didn't sound like a question.

"Ah . . ." Harper hesitated. "Actually, I'm headed out of town. Fishing trip. But if you can hang on for a couple more minutes, there's something else you need to know. Not about Zane. About the Flynn girl."

"Just a second, Jim." Ian covered the mouthpiece with his hand. "Tasya, Harper's people have located Richard in Nevada. They're keeping him under surveillance. I'll tell you all about it in a moment, but right now, I need to hear what else Jim has to say, and you need to go sit down before you collapse." He raised his voice. "Paulinho!"

Tasya had already begun to collect herself by the time Paulinho stuck his head in the study. "What is wrong?"

"Help her to the kitchen."

Paulinho put a hand under Tasya's elbow, but she shook him off. "I don't need help," she said, leaving the room under her own steam.

Paulinho raised his eyebrows in an unspoken question, but Ian had no time to explain. "Keep an eye on her," he said. "She's had a shock."

Ian removed his hand from the mouthpiece. "Are you still there, Jim? I apologize for the interruption. You were saying?"

"Right. About the girl. I've been doing routine Internet searches on her name since we opened the investigation and finally hit pay dirt. You might want to take a look." He gave Ian the web address for the site.

Ian hung up but didn't head immediately for the kitchen. Instead, he tried the URL Harper had given him. Tasya's picture appeared on his monitor. HAVE YOU SEEN THIS WOMAN? said the banner underneath it.

Ian swore, then swore again when he read the lies Richard Zane had posted. He scowled, staring at the monitor, but no longer seeing it. The twisted bastard was still alive. Perhaps he'd have to do something about that.

Tasya glanced up as Ian entered the kitchen, his face grim. She drew a shaky breath. "The investigator's positive it's Richard?"

He rolled his chair up to the table, poured himself a glass of water, and nodded. "He's living in Richard's cabin, driving Richard's 1X1, writing software for Richard's company."

"Oh, my God." A second wave of nausea washed over her.

Ian took her hand. His touch felt warm and comforting. She met his gaze and saw the compassion in his eyes. "He's in Nevada, Tasya. He can't hurt you as long as he's in Nevada."

She shook her head. "I don't understand. I thought I'd killed him. All that blood . . ."

"Head wounds bleed heavily."

"Head wounds. How about faces beaten beyond recognition?"

"You hurt him that badly?"

"I thought I'd killed him."

"So he's probably had reconstructive surgery." Ian frowned. "I'll ask Harper to have someone take photos of Richard's new face. We don't need any surprises."

"No." She drew a long, shuddery breath. "Tell me everything. Every single thing Harper told you."

"You already know most of it. Richard's alive, and Harper's promised to have his best operatives keep him under surveillance. If Richard makes a move, we'll know about it."

Tasya clenched her hands together.

"Don't be frightened," Ian said.

She jerked her gaze up to his. "I'd be an idiot not to be frightened. Don't underestimate Richard. He's smart, and he's relentless. Given enough time, he'll track me down."

Ian met her gaze. "You're not alone anymore. You have Paulinho and me to watch your back. Let Richard come. We'll be ready for him."

"How do you get ready for someone who lives his life out of bounds?" She sighed. "You have no idea what he's like."

"I think I do," he said quietly. "I've seen the look that comes into your eyes whenever his name is mentioned. To be on the safe side, I'm going to have a new security system installed."

To be on the safe side. That was a joke. There was no safe side. "Richard's a tech genius," she said. "There's not a system made that he can't breach."

"How good is he at dodging bullets?"

"What do you mean?"

"Paulinho and I can teach you how to handle a gun. I'll even invest in a couple of silver bullets."

Tasya squared her chin. "Don't joke, and don't underestimate him. Richard's a dangerous man."

Ian smiled. "So am I."

Ian was more worried about Tasya than about Richard Zane. She'd refused to eat lunch and had spent the entire afternoon alone in her room. Now Paulinho reported she didn't want any dinner, either. She was giving in to the fear, letting it control her, and that was far more dangerous than any external threat.

Ian wheeled his chair down the hall to her room and rapped on the door.

"Go away. I told you I'm not hungry."

"It's Ian. Open up. We need to talk." He knew he sounded brusque, but gentleness was not what she needed at this juncture.

Tasya didn't respond, but after a few seconds the door swung open. She looked like a ghost, pale and insubstantial, staring at him from haunted eyes.

"Put on your shoes and come to the table. Dinner's ready."

She shifted her gaze to her bare feet. A faint frown wrinkled her forehead, as if she were surprised to see she wasn't already wearing shoes. "I'm not hungry," she said.

"You're going to eat anyway. You need your strength."

She turned that dazed frown on him. "Why?"

"Because tomorrow night is your final exam."

"I don't understand." A spark of animation lit her eyes. He'd piqued her interest.

"I've taught you everything you need to know. It's time you started earning your keep."

She narrowed her eyes. "I agreed to help you get even with Alex Farrell. You didn't say anything about extra capers."

"This one's just practice. Acquisition's not the goal."

"Okay," she said slowly, then pinned him with a sharp look. "What I think you're saying is, I'm going to steal something but not keep it." His strategy seemed to be working. Tasya was looking more normal by the second.

"Exactly. Now get your shoes on and meet me in the dining room. We'll discuss the plan in detail over dinner."

"Ever heard of the Orion Museum?" Ian said as Paulinho set out fruit and cheese at the end of the meal.

"No, should I have?"

He shrugged. "It's a small private art museum in San Francisco. Tomorrow night they're hosting a special exhibition, a collection of gemstones."

Tasya frowned at him. "This has something to do with Alex Farrell and Milagre, doesn't it?"

"In a roundabout way, yes. Kenji Takimoto, owner of the gemstones, is—as collectors tend to be—extremely acquisitive. While you're testing your skills as a jewel thief, I plan to drop a few hints about Milagre."

She took a sip from her water glass. "Why?"

"Alex is in debt to a nasty piece of work named Eddie Casale. In the past, whenever he got in over his head, he'd dip into his wife's considerable personal fortune. Unfortunately, she recently filed for divorce. With her money out of reach, he's going to have to liquidate assets in order to pay Casale.

"My guess is, considering the higher-than-normal cure rate at La Magia, Alex still has Milagre. That means Alex has something Takimoto covets. If Takimoto's as grasping as I think he is, he'll make Alex an offer for the stone."

Tasya didn't get it. "So Alex sells Milagre and uses the proceeds to pay off Casale. How does this help you? Unless . . . We're going to steal the money before he can pay off Casale, aren't we?" She grinned. "Not bad."

"Oh, it gets better," he assured her. "We're going to steal Milagre, too, and set it up so Takimoto thinks he's been double-crossed. Did I mention his yakuza connection?"

"Yakuza?"

"Japanese organized crime. Rumor has it Takimoto's the number-one man on the West Coast."

Obviously not a person to mess with. Tasya studied Ian's face. Did he know what he was getting into? "If we steal the stone, won't Takimoto come after us?"

"Not if he thinks Alex was the one who cheated him. We're going to switch Milagre for a lookalike."

Tasya didn't say anything.

"I know what you're thinking," Ian said. "You're wondering how Takimoto is going to figure out he doesn't have the real Milagre, because if he doesn't know the difference, he's not going to go after Alex."

She nodded.

Ian shot her a mischievous grin. "Takimoto knows what Milagre can do. He's been asking questions, trying to locate a ruby tourmaline reputed to have healing powers.

When the stone he buys from Alex doesn't perform, he'll realize he's been cheated."

Tasya frowned. "But how could he know about Milagre? It's not famous, is it, like the Hope diamond?"

"No, but the stone's been around a while, and I doubt I'm the first person to notice its peculiar properties. Takimoto likely ran across an obscure reference."

Tasya heard a noise behind her and froze. *Richard,* she thought, then, realizing how illogical that was, turned to see Paulinho in the doorway.

"Did I startle you? I am sorry."

"It's okay." It wasn't Paulinho's fault her nerves were on edge. Relax, she told herself. Richard doesn't know where you are.

Maybe if she repeated that often enough, she'd start to believe it.

"Tasya?"

She turned to meet Ian's concerned gaze.

"Trust me," he said. "You're safe."

"Safe," she repeated. At least for now.

6

August 2004
San Francisco, California

T ASYA PROWLED THE ROOMS of the Orion Museum, noting the placement of guards and security cameras. Steal a diamond. Any diamond. That was her task. Her final exam.

She, Ian, and Paulinho had driven up to San Francisco earlier in the day. They planned to stay the night in the city, then, if all went well tonight, head down the coast to La Magia tomorrow.

As she passed the mirrored case displaying the showpieces of Kenji Takimoto's gemstone collection, she caught a glimpse of her own reflection. Since her assigned role in this pseudo caper was dumb blonde, Ian had brought a colorist to the house to add highlights to her hair, pale streaks ranging from wheat to platinum. With makeup and a glitzy black evening dress added to the mix, she didn't recognize herself.

"May I offer you a glass of wine, Mrs. Durrant?"

It took her a split second to remember that *she* was Traci Durrant, trophy wife of retired investment banker and amateur gemologist Charles Durrant, aka Ian.

She turned to a slender young man too well dressed to be straight. They'd been introduced earlier. She knew he was on the staff of the Orion, but his name eluded her. He held out a glass.

"Thanks," she said. "I'm sorry. I don't remember your name."

"Jason Wright. My friends call me J. W."

"And mine call me Traci."

"What do you think of Mr. Takimoto's collection, Traci?"

Tasya took a sip of Chablis and gave him a vacuous smile. "It's really big, isn't it?"

"He owns the world's largest collection of uncut gemstones."

"Wow! Really?" She frowned. "You work here, so you're an expert, right? Maybe you can answer a question that's been bugging me. So many of the stones are red—rubies, spinels, garnets, tourmalines. How do you tell them apart?"

"If you look closely, you'll notice subtle differences."

She pursed her lips in a pout. "I'm no good at subtlety."

He gave her a look that said, *No shit*, though he was too well trained to put his observation into words. "Which is your favorite?" he asked instead.

"I really like that green one." She caught a flicker of movement from across the room. Ian, signaling that he'd disabled the security cameras.

"The emerald?"

"Are you sure it's an emerald? It doesn't look anything like mine." She tilted her hand so her ring caught the light.

A pained expression crossed J. W.'s face. "That's the difference between cut and uncut stones." His gaze slid away from hers to focus on someone behind her. A smile lit his handsome face. "Mr. Takimoto, have you met Mrs. Durrant?"

Tasya turned and found herself face to face with a short, slight middle-aged man, unremarkable except for his eyes—small, black, and reptilian.

They shook hands. "A pleasure, Mrs. Durrant. You're interested in my collection of crystals?"

"She prefers faceted stones." J. W. smirked. "If you'll excuse me . . ." He melted into the crowd.

Takimoto caught her hand and examined the ring Ian had given her to wear, part of the stage dressing. "Very nice."

"Charles gave it to me on our three-month anniversary." She turned, caught Ian's eye across the room, and blew him a kiss.

Takimoto, who had followed her gaze, raised his eyebrows. "You are married to the man in the wheelchair?"

"Almost six months now. Some people think he's too old for me, but I adore older men." She giggled. "They're so generous."

"I'd say so." Takimoto gave a tight little smile. "At a guess that ring is worth a quarter of a million."

"Three hundred thousand. I had it appraised."

He nodded. "I take it from what the assistant curator said that you're not impressed with my gemstones."

"Oh, no, you have a *very* nice rock collection."

"Darling." Ian pressed a proprietary hand to the small of her back.

Tasya hadn't heard him coming. She stiffened at his touch, falling out of character for a moment. Then, recovering herself, she leaned over to kiss his cheek. "You surprised me," she said.

"I try." His smile was so overtly lecherous, she had to fight off an attack of the giggles.

She leaned over again, this time to wipe an imaginary smudge of lipstick from his cheek.

His gaze met hers. He winked as if to say, *Nice save.* "I'd like to chat with Mr. Takimoto for a moment. Could you run and fetch me a glass of wine?"

"Whatever you want, sweetie." She stroked his cheek, then kissed him full on the lips. She saw by the widening of his eyes that she'd startled him. So they were even. "I think I saw some hors d'oeuvres on the other side of the room. Are you hungry?"

His gaze locked on hers, and the heat in his eyes sizzled along her nerves. "Not for hors d'oeuvres." One up for Ian.

"Be right back," she said.

He shot her a wicked smile, patted her rear end, then turned to Takimoto. "Your collection is truly magnificent," she heard him say before she moved out of earshot.

Okay, two up for Ian. She took a deep breath. If the man could arouse her this much with a touch here and a glance there, what havoc could he wreak if he really put his heart into it?

Tasya glanced back over her shoulder at the two men, deep in conversation. Had Ian seen her swipe the diamond ring off Takimoto's pinkie when they shook hands?

*   *   *

The hired limousine eased away from the curb in front of the Orion. Ian closed the privacy divider, then turned to Tasya. "How did you plant Takimoto's ring in the assistant curator's stuffed mushroom? For that matter, *why* did you plant Takimoto's ring in the assistant curator's stuffed mushroom?"

"I had to put it somewhere. It kept slipping off my finger."

"You were wearing the damned thing?"

"I didn't think anyone would notice one more diamond ring in a jewel-bedecked crowd like that. Besides, where else was I supposed to put it? This overpriced Versace doesn't have pockets. I could have stuffed it in my bra, I suppose, but the fabric of the gown is so clingy, I was afraid the lump would show."

The way her nipples showed? Ian felt an unusual stirring and froze in horror when he realized what he was doing. Lusting over Tasya, a woman forty years his junior. *You're a lecherous old bastard, Ian Thomas MacPherson.*

But he was still staring at her breasts.

He snapped his gaze back up to her face. Tasya gave him a sphinxlike smile. Had she intentionally drawn his attention to her nipples?

Ian cleared his throat—and his mind. "You purposely targeted the assistant curator, didn't you? Why? What did he ever do to you?"

She shrugged, and he did his best not to dwell on the enticing movements beneath the beaded dress. Maybe he should lend her his jacket. "I didn't like his attitude," she said.

It took him a moment to remember what they'd been

talking about. Not full, round breasts. Not tight, hard nipples. Not narrow waists or rounded hips.

Tasya chuckled. "Did you see the expression on the curator's face when his assistant spat a mouthful of ring and half-masticated mushroom on that antique Persian rug?"

"Amusing," he admitted with a reluctant smile.

"Priceless," she said. "So, did I pass?"

He nodded, still smiling. "With honors. Even though you knew quite well when I specified a diamond, I meant one of the uncut stones from the collection."

"You said, 'Any diamond.' That's a direct quote. And personally, I think stealing the ring off Takimoto's finger was a stroke of genius and certainly as great a challenge as swiping a stone from a display case." She smoothed his lapels, and he swallowed hard. "Admit it," she said. "You're proud of me."

"I am." He paused. "I wasn't sure how you'd react in a pressure situation. Practice is one thing. An actual job is something else again. Were you frightened?"

She cocked her head, considering his question. "A little. But more excited than anything else."

"That's the adrenaline. The energy can be a real plus, but if you let the chemicals take control, you're in trouble."

"Avoid adrenaline addiction. Check."

"What are you talking about?"

"The rules according to Cat MacPherson. I'll add it to the list. Avoid adrenaline addiction. Rule Number Seventy-two."

"Tasya, I'm serious."

"Indeed you are." Another inscrutable smile. "Paulinho's meeting us at the hotel?"

Ian nodded. "Later." They hadn't needed Paulinho for the evening's caper, so Ian had given him a much-deserved night off.

The limousine driver pulled under the porte cochere, and a scarlet-uniformed bellboy opened the door, unfolded Ian's wheelchair, and escorted them to the two-bedroom suite Ian had reserved as part of their cover.

"Your luggage arrived earlier, sir," the bellboy said. "We put it in the larger of the two bedrooms."

"Very well." Ian handed him a tip.

"Enjoy your stay, sir."

"Yes, we will." Ian closed the door and flipped the security latch. "I'll have Paulinho move my luggage to the other bedroom."

Tasya raised her eyebrows. "Where will Paulinho sleep then? I'm not having him in with me. The man snores."

"I booked him an adjoining room. It has its own separate hall entrance, but there's also a second door that opens into the suite's sitting room."

"I see."

What did she see?

She tossed her purse on an end table. "You can have the master bedroom. I'll take the smaller room. I need a shower."

"And I need to get out of this tux. I feel like a maître d'."

She laughed. "You look more like Bond, James Bond. The Sean Connery version."

"You've been watching too many old movies," Ian said.

"I like old movies. Especially old Sean Connery movies."

She gathered her luggage and disappeared into the

smaller bedroom. Minutes later Ian heard the shower running.

Doing his best not to think about soapy water cascading down Tasya's naked body, Ian shut himself into his own room. He stripped off his evening clothes and tossed them onto a chair.

Bond, James Bond. He smiled, remembering the way she'd delivered the line, lowering her voice in the worst Sean Connery imitation he'd ever heard. Ah, Tasya.

He considered reading for a while but knew he couldn't concentrate. Despite his caution about the dangers of adrenaline addiction, he'd been riding an adrenaline high all evening. He'd been tempted—more than once—to empty those display cases himself. One emerald in particular had offered an almost irresistible challenge. That and an enormous ruby tourmaline that looked so much like Milagre he'd stared at it in slack-jawed astonishment for half a minute before he realized it wasn't the same stone. Quite a temptation.

Almost as great a temptation as Tasya.

He'd pushed a little harder tonight than he should have. The "darling" would have done it. He hadn't needed to pat her rear end. But adrenaline sometimes urged a person to act in ways he would normally not consider. And he'd definitely had a buzz on. He still did.

Maybe Tasya had the right idea. A good long soak in the whirlpool tub might calm him down.

August 2004
Half Moon Bay, California

At a little after ten Richard parked the stolen Camry under a eucalyptus across the street from the house where Tasya was living with a man named Ramsdale.

When his Internet site hadn't yielded anything but a bunch of crackpot sightings, he'd managed to get his hands on a bootleg copy of the software the government used to vet e-mails for terrorist communications. Only instead of searching for keywords like *jihad* or *Great Satan*, he'd entered Tasya's name and hit the jackpot.

Ramsdale and San Francisco–based private investigator James Harper had carried on quite a correspondence over the past few months. Ramsdale knew almost as much about Tasya as Richard did.

Just as Richard knew a thing or two about Arthur Ramsdale. According to Ramsdale's California driver's license, he was sixty-one years old. Six-feet-two, a hundred ninety pounds. Salt-and-pepper hair, brown eyes. Not bad looking even in his DMV picture, though the Reverend Otis wouldn't have trusted him. Not with those devilish black eyebrows.

Richard rolled down the windows. A breeze rustled the eucalyptus tree's long, narrow leaves, filling the air with a strong medicinal scent. Crickets chirped. Quail clicked somewhere out of sight in the empty lot. A dog yapped off to the east.

No lights on inside the house, and Richard wasn't sure what that meant. No one up? Or no one home? Only time would tell. He adjusted his seat and settled back to wait.

August 2004
San Francisco, California

Ian had been soaking in the whirlpool tub for half an hour, long enough to shrivel the skin of his fingertips but not his erection. After thirty years of impotence, that should have been good news. Instead, guilt sickened him even as the image of Tasya in the curve-hugging black Versace teased his memory. He ached to touch her smooth skin, to kiss her laughing lips, to . . . A fresh wave of guilt shuddered through him. God forgive him. The last thing Tasya needed was another man to take advantage of her.

"Want some help?"

Tasya. The swirling water had masked the sound of her entrance and, he hoped, his embarrassing state of readiness. Ian met her gaze with a look that brought a smile to her lips.

"Sorry if I startled you."

"What are you doing?"

"I thought you might appreciate a little assistance. Would you like me to scrub your back?" She wore a thin white tank top that left little to the imagination and a pair of low-slung blue silk pajama bottoms. Two inches of bare midriff filled the gap.

Keep your eyes on her face, he told himself. And with a superhuman effort, he dragged his gaze back up to hers. She stared at him, eyebrows raised, waiting for his response.

"I beg your pardon?" Stupid remark, but the best he could come up with, since he hadn't a clue what they'd been discussing.

She knelt next to the tub. The flowery scents of body wash, lotion, and shampoo added to his sensory overload. "I asked if you'd like me to scrub your back." Leaning across him, she plucked a washcloth from the basket of bath accessories.

Her breasts moved beneath the snug knit fabric—bounced, by God, the taut tips of her nipples clearly outlined—and he quickly averted his eyes. *You're going to hell, MacPherson.*

Or maybe he was already there.

"Lean forward," she said.

He should tell her to go. He should tell her he wanted his privacy. He should tell her he didn't need her help. Instead, he leaned forward without saying anything at all.

The warm water bubbled around him, but all he could feel was the slick touch of soapy fingertips sliding up and down his back, followed by the slightly rough texture of the terry cloth as she rinsed off the soap. Seconds seemed to stretch to hours.

Agony or ecstasy? He wasn't sure. All he knew for certain was if she didn't stop soon, he was going to come right there in the tub. "That should do it," he said in a strangled voice.

A smile teased the corners of her mouth. "Are you sure?" She squeezed a little liquid soap into one palm. "I could do your chest, if you'd like."

She reached toward him, but he caught her wrist. "What game are you playing, Tasya?"

Her smile faded. Something moved in the shadows of her smoky silver eyes. "No game. I only wanted . . ." The corner of her mouth twitched. "Pulling off that caper was the biggest thrill of my life. I feel so excited. So happy. So alive. I just wanted to thank you for helping me experience emotions I thought I'd never feel again."

"Thank me how? I don't expect sexual favors. I don't want sexual favors."

"Liar," she said, pulling free of his grip. She wiped the soap on the washcloth and stood. "I'm not blind. You were as aroused as I was. *Are* as aroused as I am."

He closed his eyes, shielding himself from the hurt in hers. "More," he said at last. "More aroused. The problem is, considering the disparity in our ages, my urges are completely inappropriate. Were I to take advantage of your gratitude . . ." He shuddered. "I have little left to me but my self-respect. Don't ask me to give that up, too."

"But, Ian—"

"No." He opened his eyes and saw the pain he felt reflected on her face. "I care for you too much to take advantage of you."

"But—"

"It's the adrenaline, Tasya."

"No."

"Yes," he said quietly.

"Okay, maybe that's part of it."

"And gratitude. That's the other part of it. I took you in when you had nowhere else to go."

"I am grateful, but that's not why I'm doing this. I'm grateful to Paulinho, too, but I have no desire to make love with him. The way I feel about you is different. With other men I shy away, but I want you to touch me." Tears trembled on the tips of her lashes.

"You're confused. I know you don't believe this, but

one day you'll thank me for my restraint. In time you'll meet a man nearer your own age—"

The tears spilled over, running down her cheeks. "Shut up." Kneeling, she captured his face between her hands and kissed him with all the pent-up passion in her young body.

He fought the impulse to kiss her back, though the effort cost him.

Abruptly, Tasya released him, perhaps frustrated by his lack of response. She sat back on her heels and frowned at him through her tears. "I love you," she said in the same tone of voice another woman might have used to say, "I hate you." Then she jumped to her feet and ran from the room, slamming the door behind her.

"God help me, I love you, too," he whispered, too softly to be heard above the rush of the water.

August 2004
Half Moon Bay, California

Richard paused in the tiled foyer of the house on Oceanview Drive, congratulating himself. Ramsdale's electronic security system was top-of-the-line, but he'd disarmed it in less than five minutes.

He stood there, motionless, listening hard, thinking, Sweet Jesus, but this place was darker than six inches up a cat's ass. Gradually, his eyes adjusted to the gloom.

A cavernous, two-story living room with a wall of uncurtained windows overlooking the back of the property lay directly ahead of him. An archway to his left opened into the kitchen. He could see the glowing green numbers on the microwave. To the right a carpeted hall led to what he assumed was the bedroom wing.

He padded cautiously down the hall. Even less light here, but too risky to chance a flashlight. Leather whispered a sibilant threat as he drew his knife from its sheath. He pictured the shock in Ramsdale's eyes in the instant before Richard slit his throat. Tasya would be even more entertaining. He'd take his time with her.

The first door led into a study, the second to a half bath. Nobody home in either. The third room was the master suite, also unoccupied.

He checked the bathroom, just in case, but found it empty, too. A second door led into an enormous walk-in closet, and there, of necessity, he risked the flashlight. Not Tasya's room, he realized. The closet housed men's clothing.

Light glinted off metal at the far end. Curious, Richard moved closer. A collapsible wheelchair. Interesting. Was Ramsdale a cripple? He hadn't noticed mention of a disability on the man's driver's license. The irony of the situation tickled him. Tasya's protector was an old man in a wheelchair. The odds were more in his favor than he'd thought.

The phone rang, the noise shocking in the silence of the sleeping house. Richard jumped, then froze, flicking off the light as a precaution. Just because Ramsdale wasn't in his bed didn't mean the place was deserted.

Two rings. Three. He slipped back down the hall, listening hard, but heard no telltale sounds of life. No creaking bedsprings. No muffled curses. No footsteps.

The answering machine picked up in the kitchen. He

moved closer to listen as the digital version of Ramsdale's voice announced, "You have reached 555-7485. Please leave a message at the tone."

"Ramsdale, this is Harper. The Nevada state police just found the body of one of the operatives I assigned to Zane. He was stuffed in the trunk of his own car, his throat slashed so deeply he was nearly decapitated. If you're still alive"—he paused—"get the hell out of Dodge."

So they'd found the body. And what was worse, the state cops were onto him. Probably taking his place apart right this minute, uncovering a few other secrets in the process.

Luckily he'd prepared for such an eventuality. He had two sets of fake ID in his money belt. At a moment's notice he could become Mark Jackson of Fort Wayne, Indiana, or Miguel Garcia of Chico, California. After all, it wasn't the first time the leopard had changed his spots.

Richard erased the message, then continued his search. The first bedroom he checked was unoccupied, the closet bare, but the second showed signs of habitation. Tasya's room, he thought at first, until he realized the closet was full of men's clothing. Size extra extra large.

Was there a third player? Someone his research hadn't uncovered? If so, then Tasya had two protectors, the cripple and the giant who owned all that oversized clothing.

Or did she? He'd been through all the bedrooms and found no trace of female occupancy. Had he been wrong to think Tasya was staying here under Ramsdale's protection?

Unless . . . What about the maid's quarters? Houses this size often had an extra bedroom near the service entrance.

Sure enough, off the kitchen he found a self-contained suite. The walk-in closet was nearly empty. No dresses. Nothing overtly feminine, but he'd swear on a stack of Bibles the few shirts hanging there belonged to Tasya. He recognized her scent.

Damn it, where were they? Where was she?

Richard grabbed the ceramic lamp on the bedside table, ripping the cord from the socket with an impatient snap of his wrist. He swung the lamp by the cord and heaved it across the room, where it smashed into the mirror over the chest of drawers, shattering both lamp and mirror.

Thwart me, will you?

He ripped the curtains from the rod, tore the bedding off the mattress, dumped drawers, emptied toiletries. By the time he finished, he was breathing hard, sweat rolling down his face.

He surveyed the damage with satisfaction. A good beginning.

But just the beginning.

7

August 2004
San Francisco, California

WHEN PAULINHO LET HIMSELF into the suite via the connecting door, he expected to find Ian and Tasya celebrating. Instead he found Ian alone, poring over blueprints of the La Magia complex. He glanced up with a smile. "I was beginning to wonder where you'd got to." But his casual manner did not fool Paulinho. Something had upset him. Negative energy charged the air.

"Where is Tasya?"

"In bed." Ian buried his nose in the blueprints.

Though he would have preferred a more thorough description of the evening's events, Paulinho recognized a dismissal when he saw one. "Good night," he said, and retired to his own room.

Forty-five minutes later he stood by the window, staring out at the lights of the city. He should be relaxed. The soothing warmth of the shower and the tactile pleasure of silk pajamas against his skin should have guaranteed it. But his muscles felt tense and his mind uneasy. Something was wrong. Something more than a minor disagreement between Ian and Tasya. But what?

His gaze fell on his open suitcase. One corner of a carved ivory box poked out from beneath a pile of underwear. Perhaps the *opele* could enlighten him.

He set the box on the bed and carefully removed the necklace.

Macumba priestesses foretold the future with cowrie shells. The Ifa cult used the *opele*. According to the priestess of the *terreiro* he had attended as a child, the difference was, the *babalaô*s of the Ifa cult did not have to rely on the trickster Exú as their spirit intermediary. Hence, their predictions were more accurate.

So Paulinho had the optimal tool at his fingertips, but his natural gifts could not entirely compensate for his lack of education. The five years he had wasted in prison would have been better spent in Africa. Learning the *odum*s, their histories and prayers, required intensive study under the guidance of a trained *babalaô*.

Paulinho took the carved box into the bathroom and set it on the smooth tiled floor. He knelt and removed the necklace, then closed his eyes, breathing slowly and steadily, clearing his mind.

The *opele* felt warm and heavy in his hands. A living entity. His lifeline to another dimension of existence. Voices seemed to whisper secrets just beyond the threshold of his hearing. His heartbeat thrummed with heightened awareness like the beat of a distant drum.

Eyes shut, he murmured the ancient words, a Yoruba chant he had learned as a child. He did not know what the words meant, but he liked the music of the syllables, just as he liked the rhythm of the Ave Maria he repeated next. In Latin, of course. The old languages conjured more power.

He fished a fine copper chain from the ivory box and arranged it in a U, the open end facing him. The stones came next, a handful of pebbles he kept in a small white cotton bag. He arranged them around the chain to sanctify the area set aside to welcome the spirits and to connect it to the earth from which the stones had come.

He held the *opele* at arm's length for a moment, then touched it to his forehead. Concentrating on the vague sense of unease plaguing him, he tossed the necklace into the enchanted circle. It landed in a twisted *odum*, confirming his suspicions. Danger.

From what source? he asked silently, dreading the answer. Not Tasya. Not the girl. Holding his breath, he tossed the necklace a second time.

Again it landed in an intricate pattern, an *odum* fraught with contradiction. He frowned, sensing something beyond the pattern, something malevolent. *Richard.* The name flashed through his mind, accompanied by a series of disturbing images, like scenes from a movie shown in fast-forward.

Ian heard a muffled sound. Tasya having another nightmare, he thought at first, then realized the noise was coming from the opposite direction.

Paulinho burst into the sitting room, babbling an incoherent jumble of English and Portuguese. He tripped over an ill-placed ottoman and flipped end over end. Pure slapstick. It would have been funny, if not for the terror in his eyes.

Ian frowned. "What's wrong?"

Paulinho shoved himself upright. "I saw the man who tortured Tasya. By Xangô, I swear it."

Ian suppressed a shiver at the thready note of panic in the big Brazilian's voice.

"He was in the house, Senhor Ian. Our house. He had a knife." Paulinho held his hands a foot apart. "Very sharp. He used it twice. Not in the house. Before. On a man first and later on a woman. He meant to use it on us. He—how you say?—hurt to use it? No, *ached* to use it."

"Are you certain? Perhaps it was a nightmare."

"I am not sleeping. I am seeing. Seeing through his eyes." Paulinho lowered his brows in a scowl.

"Through his eyes? Meaning what? You didn't actually see the man?"

"No." Paulinho pressed a fist to his chest. "But for a few moments, I was this Richard, this monster, seeing what he saw, feeling what he felt."

Another shiver ran down Ian's spine. Superstitious nonsense, he tried to tell himself, uncomfortably aware that he had once felt a presence in an empty room and watched a wound heal as if by magic.

As if by magic? Or *by* magic? That was the real question.

"Operatives from Harper Investigations have Richard Zane under twenty-four-hour surveillance. They would have contacted me if he'd left the Sierras."

"How? Do they know you are staying at this hotel?"

"No, but they could've left a message on the machine at the house. And they didn't. I checked my messages half an hour ago."

"Call, Senhor Ian. Have them double-check."

Ian glanced at his wristwatch. "There won't be anyone in the office this late. And tomorrow's Sunday. I've got Harper's home number, but he's out of town."

Tasya poked her head out of her room. "Is there a problem?"

"*Sim*," Paulinho said.

"No." Ian shot him a warning glare. No point in worrying Tasya. Not until they had something more solid to go on.

"*Não*," Paulinho said.

Tasya glanced from him to Paulinho. "Which is it?"

Paulinho struggled to his feet. "*Não*. No. Is no problem. I am walking in my sleep, is all. I am having the bad dream."

"About what?" She wandered farther into the room, barefoot, a two-inch strip of smooth golden skin visible between the lower edge of her tank top and the low-riding waist of her pajama bottoms. Not that the few clothes she *was* wearing did much more than call attention to the warm curves underneath. With her hair tousled and her skin flushed, she posed an even greater temptation now than she had earlier.

Bloody hell. Ian stared at the knuckles of his left hand, clenched on the arm of his chair.

"About knives," Paulinho said. "About bodies with their necks slit from ear to ear. Pfft." Ian glanced up in time to see him draw a finger across his throat in illustration.

Tasya wrinkled her nose. "Disgusting. No wonder you made so much racket. I, on the other hand, was having a wonderful dream." She glanced at Ian, the hint of a smile hovering around her mouth. "You should have been there."

"Go to bed," he snapped. "Paulinho's fine. The excitement's over."

She sauntered toward her room, then paused, glancing back over her shoulder. He did a slow burn at the look in her eyes. "Is it?" she said.

"Brat," he muttered under his breath.

Paulinho shot him a curious look. *"Que?"*

"Não é importante," he said. "It's not important."

Ian was gone by the time Tasya got up. Business meeting, he'd told Paulinho, but she suspected he was avoiding her. Afraid if he hung around, she might try to change his mind about taking their relationship to the next level. Which, of course, was exactly what she intended to do.

Her plans temporarily on hold, she ordered breakfast from room service, then settled down in front of the television to watch the news as she ate.

Halfway through her French toast, she called to Paulinho, who was in Ian's room, packing. "Did you hear that?"

He poked his head out the door. "Hear what, *moça?*"

"What they said on the news. It's just like your dream. Yesterday Nevada state police found a man's body locked in the trunk of his car, and this morning a second body, female, was discovered locked in the trunk of a car at San Francisco International. Both victims had their throats slit, and investigators suspect the two murders may be related."

Paulinho's face went gray. He sank onto the nearest chair. *"Meu Deus."* He knuckled his forehead with clenched fists, then jumped to his feet, looking agitated. "Where is Senhor Ian?"

"You told me he had a breakfast meeting with someone."

"*Sim*. I remember now. The Japanese."

"So he did have a meeting? That wasn't just an excuse to avoid me?"

Paulinho frowned. "Why would he avoid you?"

She shrugged, feeling her cheeks grow warm. "No reason."

She feared he might pursue the matter, but apparently he had other things on his mind. "I must talk with Senhor Ian."

"About your dream? About the murders?"

He paused at the door, one hand on the knob. "Yes, there is no time now to explain." He turned then to face her. "When I come back, I will knock so." He hammered out a series of three raps, followed by a pause, then two more raps. "That will be our signal. You need to promise me, *promise me, moça*, that you will not open the door for anyone until I come back. Not for room service. *Ninguém*. Nobody."

Upon returning to the hotel after his meeting with Kenji Takimoto, Ian found Paulinho in the lobby.

"*Senhor Ian, graças a Deus*. Thank God you are back. I have been searching for you everywhere, in all the restaurants, all the nearby hotels."

Fear sent Ian's pulse rate skyrocketing. "What's wrong? Has something happened to Tasya?"

"No, but I am very worried. According to the news, police found a dead man stuffed in the trunk of his car near Lake Tahoe yesterday. This morning they found a woman in similar condition in a car at the San Francisco airport. Both victims had had their throats slit. The police believe the two cases are related. So do I. It is just as I saw."

"Richard." The name tasted bitter as alum.

"He was in the house, Senhor Ian. I saw it."

But where was he now? Ian's gut clenched. "Where's Tasya? You left her alone?"

Paulinho looked bewildered at the accusation implicit in Ian's question. "Richard has no way of knowing we are here."

"He had no way of knowing we were in Half Moon Bay, either."

Paulinho's eyes grew round. "*Meu Deus*, I am a fool! I will go to her now."

"No," Ian said. "I'll guard Tasya. You check the house."

"*Sim.*"

"But don't go in unless you're sure Richard's gone."

"I threw the *opele* again this morning. He is gone." Paulinho scowled. "Besides, I am not afraid of him."

"You should be," Ian said. "I bloody well am."

Paulinho's certainty that Richard Zane was responsible for the two murders headlining the morning news unnerved Ian. If Paulinho was right, Richard had graduated from torture to murder, and that meant Tasya was in terrible danger. The elevator to the twenty-second floor seemed even slower than usual. Each moment's delay raised his anxiety level.

By the time he keyed himself into the suite, he was half convinced he'd find Tasya's lifeless body sprawled across the floor. Instead she sat on the sofa, reading. Or pretending to. Posture erect, expression wary, she seemed poised for flight.

"I thought . . . For a minute I thought . . ." She pressed her lips together in a tight line. "Paulinho and I worked out a code. When you inserted the keycard without knocking first . . ." She pulled a poker from behind the sofa cushions and set it aside.

"Glad to see you were prepared. Sorry if I frightened you."

Her gaze met his with the force of a physical impact. "Richard is involved, isn't he?"

"Paulinho thinks so."

"And you? Do you think so?"

He nodded. "I wish I could dismiss Paulinho's concerns as superstitious nonsense, but I can't."

She frowned. "You're talking about his so-called dream?"

"It wasn't a dream. How much has Paulinho told you about Macumba?"

"Not much, but it's like voodoo, isn't it?"

Ian paused, choosing his words carefully. "Macumba is like voodoo and Santería and Candomblé in the same way the Catholic religion is like the Lutheran, the Baptist, and the Seventh Day Adventist. They share basic commonalities, but there are differences. At the heart of Macumba is the old African religion, but it's a syncretic belief system. Added to the mix are new ingredients—mysticism, Roman Catholicism, and French spiritism."

"Okay, but what does Paulinho's religion have to do with his vision of the murders?"

"Paulinho felt uneasy last night. He's very sensitive to

undercurrents. Maybe he sensed something of Richard's intent. Or perhaps our unresolved issues"—she gave him a speculative look—"left traces of tension in the air. I don't know. He probably doesn't, either. But in such circumstances, he tosses the *opele*. Apparently if you do everything correctly, the spirits answer your questions in *odums*."

"*Odums*?"

"They're like words or symbols. You toss the *opele* and it lands in a pattern. The pattern's the *odum*. I gather the tricky part's in interpreting it." He frowned. "One of Paulinho's ancestors was a *babalaô*, a famous seer. Perhaps Paulinho inherited some psychic ability from him. I don't know, but in addition to whatever answers he might get from the *opele*, he sometimes sees what he calls 'lightning pictures,' brief, vivid vignettes of things that have happened or are happening."

"So last night, when you two led me to think he'd had a nightmare, what he'd really had was a vision. He saw the two murder victims, didn't he?"

"Yes. Through Richard's eyes."

Her face went blank. "Richard killed those people. That's why Paulinho was so upset."

"Part of the reason," Ian said. "What really frightened him was realizing that Richard was inside the house in Half Moon Bay."

She paled, and Ian thought for a second she was going to faint. "In the house? Oh, God." She buried her face in her hands.

His own emotions—fear, confusion, anger, and a fierce protectiveness—twisted in his chest like a knot of vipers.

He maneuvered his chair next to the sofa, then levered himself onto it. "Tasya?" He touched her shoulder.

"I'm okay," she said, but she didn't sound it.

He pulled her into his arms. She didn't cry. Perhaps her terror was too acute for tears. He could feel her tension, the stiffness of her back, the quivering of her muscles. "It's going to be all right," he said. "Trust me."

"I do," she said. "But you're only one man. It would take an army to shield me from Richard."

"Then I'll hire an army."

Tasya stilled. After a long, tense moment, she leaned back, angling her head to look him in the eye. The shadow of a smile touched her lips. "You would, wouldn't you?"

She smelled of soap and gardenias. She was warm and soft, her palms splayed against his chest. Could she feel the thunder of his heart?

The shadow smile faded. Her eyes widened and her breathing quickened. "Ian?"

He kissed her. He didn't plan it. It just happened. One minute he was gazing at her lovely face and the next he had his mouth pressed against hers. Softly at first, but when she slid her arms around his neck and leaned into him, he increased the pressure, deepening the kiss. He knew it was a mistake, but he couldn't stop, didn't want to stop. She tasted so good, like the one perfect dessert he'd been craving all his life. Sweet and warm and delectable.

Ian felt a quiver in his stomach, as if the world had suddenly tilted on its axis, skewing his perspective, altering his reality. By any normal standard, he and Tasya were wrong for each other. He was old. She was young. He was crippled. She was whole. And yet . . .

He needed her. For over thirty years he'd lived for revenge, but he saw now it wasn't enough. Revenge couldn't save him, but Tasya might. She lightened the darkness of his hate-scarred soul and made him forget the limitations of his ruined body.

Moaning softly, she returned his kiss, tasting him delicately, tentatively, and the world swung free, whirling out of control, a cosmic carnival ride. She slid her tongue along the inside of his lower lip in tactile confirmation of the truth he'd already realized: she needed him, too.

She sought safety in a dangerous world, but safety wasn't what she needed. Tasya was an old soul in a young body, a woman who'd never had the chance to be a child. What she truly needed was time to play, to laugh, to grow young again. And he could give her that once Richard was out of the way.

Richard. The carnival ride shuddered to a stop.

As if she sensed his mood swing, Tasya pulled away. "Ian?" She stared at him, bewilderment clouding her eyes.

He smiled. "Enter reality."

"What?" She bit her lip, a lip moist and swollen from his kisses.

"I have to contact Jim Harper. His men have been keeping tabs on Richard. We need to know what they've learned."

She frowned. "I forgot. Oh, God, what's wrong with me?" She sat up, putting some distance between them.

"Nothing," he said, reaching for the phone. "You needed a respite, that's all."

He dialed the agency, intending to leave a message, but someone picked up on the second ring. "Harper Investigations. Jim Harper speaking."

"Ramsdale here. I thought you were fishing."

"I came back early. Where are you?"

"San Francisco, why?"

"You got my message then."

"What message?"

"I left a message on the machine in your house, telling you to get out of Half Moon Bay."

"Because of Richard Zane," Ian said. It wasn't a question. "How did he get away? I thought you had someone watching him."

Harper didn't say anything for a second. "Did you catch the news this morning?"

"You're talking about the bodies that were stuffed in car trunks? Those were your people?"

"The man was one of my best operatives." He sighed. "Hard to believe, but he must have gotten careless, tipped Zane to the fact he was under surveillance."

"And the woman?"

"The woman they found in the white Camry? The car was registered to her. Apparently she offered Zane a ride after his rental car broke down. California and Nevada have launched a joint investigation. When the Nevada state police contacted me about my investigator, I filled them in on the case he was working. They consider Zane their prime suspect. They'll be searching his house—if they haven't already. No doubt they'll have questions for you, too, Arthur. Do you have a number where you can be reached?"

Ian thought about that. The hotel number was no good, since he was registered as Charles Durrant, not Arthur Ramsdale. And he made it a practice not to give out his cell phone number. "I'm going to be moving around, but I'll check in from time to time."

"Moving around sounds like a good idea," Harper said. "Zane may have traced you to Half Moon Bay. I don't think it's a coincidence that he left the second corpse at the San Francisco airport. Be careful, Arthur."

"I will." Ian hung up, then filled Tasya in.

"How did Richard know I was in Half Moon Bay? That's what I don't understand."

"We can't be a hundred percent certain he did. Just because Paulinho 'saw' it doesn't make it true. At any rate, that's where Paulinho is now, checking the house for signs of forced entry."

"What if Richard's still there? He's killed two people. He wouldn't hesitate to kill Paulinho, too. How could you send a friend into a potentially dangerous situation?"

"Paulinho's certain Richard left the house last night, and I'm inclined to agree. He dumped the car with the second body at the San Francisco airport this morning. Logic argues he wouldn't drive all the way to the airport to abandon one car only to steal or rent another, then drive back to Half Moon Bay."

"Much of what Richard does wouldn't strike a normal person as logical. He's crazy, Ian."

"Yes, but he's on the run, the prime suspect in two suspicious deaths. The police launched a manhunt after finding the first body. When the second corpse turned up this morning, I'm sure they intensified their efforts. With any luck he'll soon be behind bars."

Tasya frowned. "I'm going to pack. You *are* still planning to drive down to La Magia today?"

He nodded wearily, and she left.

Ian pulled out the La Magia blueprints and the file folder of information Harper had dug up on Alex Farrell, but it was hard to concentrate. He was staring off into space, sunk in gloomy reflection, when the phone rang a little before noon. Tasya came running out of her room. They both stared at the telephone for a second. Then Ian lifted the receiver. "Durrant here."

"Senhor Ian, *graças a Deus.*"

"It's Paulinho," he told Tasya. "What's wrong?" he said into the mouthpiece.

"He was here." Paulinho spoke in Portuguese, either because he was concerned about being overheard or because he was too rattled to communicate in English. "The security system was disabled. Tasya's room is ruined." He drew a shaky breath. "Senhor Ian, I—"

"What?" Ian snapped.

"Her room. How can I explain? This Richard is sick, a demon. He did not just destroy the room. He savaged it, defiled it."

Ian's anger flared, hot and fierce.

"Senhor Ian, did you hear me?"

"Yes, I heard you." He fought to control his temper. "Did you check around the neighborhood to see if anyone noticed anything out of the ordinary?" Ian knew how unlikely that was. He'd chosen the Half Moon Bay property because of its isolation.

"Yes, I rang doorbells all down our road. A woman walking her dog a little after midnight noticed a white Toyota Camry parked across from the house and assumed we had company."

"She was positive about the make and model?"

"Yes, she said her granddaughter drives a red one. "

Dread lodged like a stone in Ian's chest. "According to Harper, the car that was left at the airport, the one with the body in the trunk, was a white Camry."

Richard had been inside the house. That meant he'd had access to the study. Fortunately, Ian never went anywhere without his laptop, so all his e-mails from Harper were safe. And since he'd been working on the La Magia plan, he'd brought those papers along. But if Richard had checked the file cabinet, the desk, and the wastebasket, as Ian assumed he had, then he might have pieced together enough information to figure out where they were now.

"Get back here as quickly as you can," he told Paulinho. "We're checking out."

Tasya stared at him, panic in her eyes.

"Finish packing," he told her. "We'll leave for La Magia as soon as Paulinho returns. It's not safe here anymore."

8

August 2004
Orange County, California

"AND IF I GET ONE MORE complaint, you're out on your ass. We clear on that, Peck?" Alex glared at the masseur, who slouched in one of the purple director's chairs like a grade-school bully who'd been sent to the principal's office for tripping kids in the lunch line. "We clear on that?" Alex repeated.

Peck grunted what might have been an acknowledgment. The man was a gifted massotherapist. If only he could learn to keep his hands off his female clients' tits.

"Senator Bingham is threatening to sue," Alex added.

"Screw him," Peck said. "Hell, the broad grabbed me first."

"That's not *her* story."

"Then screw her, too."

"I think that's the point, Peck. You already did. Find yourself a dictionary and look up the meaning of discretion."

Peck stood, brow wrinkled in uncertainty. "So I'm not fired?"

"Not yet." Alex escorted him to the door.

Halfway out, Peck stopped. "Holy shit," he said.

Alex shouldered him aside to see what had prompted the remark.

The blonde responsible for his reaction turned toward him, and their gazes met across the crowded lobby. She stared at him for the space of three heartbeats. Then a tiny provocative smile tilted the corners of her mouth. She held his gaze a moment before turning back to her elderly companion.

The white-haired old man huddled in a wheelchair, shoulders rounded, head sagging toward his chest, hands flaccid as dead fish in his lap. The blonde tucked in the blanket swaddling his legs and hips.

The old boy's nurse, Alex thought for a split second, then realized a nurse wouldn't be wearing designer clothes. Probably wouldn't be showing so much skin, either. So that made her what? A relative? Daughter? Granddaughter?

Heavy breathing told him Tommy Peck was still rooted to the tiles, hyperventilating. "Peck?"

"Huh?" The masseur looked even more vacant than usual.

"Get back to work."

"Work?" He blinked a couple times. "Right. Sure, boss." But he didn't move. "Any idea who the blonde is? She's never been here before. I'd have remembered."

Alex would have remembered, too. "Her name's none of your business. Just do your job, Peck. Not the clients."

La Magia sat atop a rocky promontory overlooking the Pacific. For a small fortune, guests could rent suites on the second floor of the main building. Or for a considerably larger fortune, they could stay in one of the private cottages scattered over twenty acres of manicured grounds. Ian had opted for the privacy of a cottage, and Tasya applauded his decision.

She leaned against the rock balustrade that edged the terrace, gazing across the inlet. A bee buzzed among the flowers in a nearby planter, a sound echoed by a little red speedboat cutting troughs in the sun-spangled water. Farther off, waves crashed against the rocks at the base of the headland. She breathed deeply, filling her lungs with the scents of freshly mown grass, sweet williams, and the sea.

Ian rolled his chair up next to her. "Paulinho has finished scanning for audio and video surveillance devices. The cottage is clean."

She smiled at him. "You sound almost disappointed. Did you expect to find the place bugged?"

"Not really, but nowadays, one never knows. It would have been foolish not to check."

She turned back to the view. "What a beautiful spot for a spa."

"La Magia's a gold mine," Ian said. "Alex should be able to manage nicely on the revenue it brings in, but he has a serious gambling addiction. Casalet not the only one he's in debt to, either. When his creditors heard about the divorce, they started pressing for payment. He's desperate." Ian smiled. "And a desperate man doesn't always make wise decisions."

"Great imitation of a feeble old codger back at the registration desk, by the way. Very convincing. That colorist in L.A. did a fantastic job. The silver hair and beard look totally natural. As long as you keep your mouth shut, I don't think there's any chance Alex will recognize you."

"I'm not worried. He hasn't seen me in over thirty years. The Ian MacPherson he knew was clean-shaven."

With two good legs, Tasya thought.

"Old age is a great disguise." A wry smile tilted one corner of Ian's mouth.

Tasya studied him, trying to imagine Ian without the beard. "I wonder if you'd still look devilish if you were clean-shaven."

"Devilish?" He cocked an eyebrow.

She traced its arching contour. "Positively satanic."

He stared at her a moment, his face unreadable. She was the first to look away. She frowned at the tower perched on the headland. "If I were Alex Farrell, I'd cut my losses and run."

"Wouldn't work," Ian said. "Even if Alex could run fast enough and far enough to elude Casale, he'd still be penniless, and poverty wouldn't suit him."

"Surely broke is better than broken."

Ian gave a bitter laugh. "My former apprentice is an egotistical bastard, confident of his ability to charm his way out of any tight spot. But this time, charm's not going to work. Casale's immune. Alex is going to have to pay his debt. The way I see it, he's down to a single option: liquidate assets. And the only thing he owns that isn't mortgaged to the hilt is the tourmaline, Milagre."

"That's where Takimoto comes in." Scary eyes. Scary man. "Not a person to cross."

"No." Ian smiled.

* * *

Alex knew it was downright un-Californian of him, but he hated Oriental cuisine. Octopus, seaweed, raw fish. Disgusting. You could douse the stuff in soy sauce or smother it with rice, but as far as he was concerned, it still tasted like day-old bait.

The thing was, when you had Eddie Casale breathing down your neck and out of the blue a well-heeled investor like Kenji Takimoto proposed a business lunch, you damn well let him choose the restaurant.

Finally, after ninety minutes of small talk, Takimoto said, "I am a collector," and placed a couple of rocks in the center of the table.

Alex picked one up. Not just a rock. A gemstone. Cradled in his palm was an uncut diamond, the largest he'd ever seen. The emerald on the table was even larger. "Nice," he said. "African?"

Takimoto inclined his head.

"If you'd like me to hook you up with a diamond cutter—"

"No, I much prefer the stones in their natural state. Cutting often diminishes the crystals' power."

The crystals' power? What kind of flaky New Age shit was that? Alex had asked around. He knew all about Kenji Takimoto and his extensive financial holdings—even the rumors about possible connections to organized crime and the opium trade—but not one whisper that the man had metaphysical leanings. Easy enough to get sucked into that crap, though. Southern California was lousy with crystal therapy practitioners and other assorted wackos.

Alex laughed. "You'd never convince my wife that cutting a stone diminished it. The more facets, the better, as far as Christy's concerned. You ought to see *her* rock collection."

Takimoto rested his chin on his steepled fingers. "I assume she'll keep it as part of the settlement." It wasn't a question. Takimoto had researched him as thoroughly as he'd researched Takimoto.

Tired of games, Alex set the diamond on the table. "What do you want from me?"

A muscle twitched in the man's left cheek. "Americans are so impatient."

And Japanese are such dickheads. He wanted to say it so bad he could taste it, but hell, he'd already suffered through two hours of kelp and cat food. Be damned if he'd blow the deal now. So he smiled instead. "I'm sorry if my blunt approach offended you, Mr. Takimoto. You hit a nerve with your mention of the divorce. I love my wife, and I refuse to give up hope that Christy and I can eventually work things out."

Takimoto's mouth curved in a Buddha-esque smile. "Are you a gambling man, Mr. Farrell?"

Alex felt the smile slide off his face. Not only did Takimoto know about the divorce, he knew about Casale. "Unfortunately, I am," he said. "The addiction destroyed my marriage."

"And your credit." Takimoto paused. When Alex made no response, he shrugged slightly and continued. "You owe a great deal of money to a very unpleasant person named Eddie Casale."

Still Alex said nothing. What was there to say? Takimoto seemed to have his number—which was, as close as he could figure, somewhere in the negative six figures.

"I may be able to offer you the means to repay your debt."

"Oh, yeah? Who do I have to kill?" he asked, half seriously.

Takimoto stared at him for a moment, unsmiling, his black eyes as empty and emotionless as a corpse's. Then he laughed, the genial sound at odds with those vacant eyes. "Why would I hire an amateur when I have two dozen professionals on my payroll?"

A shudder worked its way down Alex's spine. This guy made Casale look like an altar boy.

"It has come to my attention that you have in your possession a stone, a large red tourmaline."

"I'm afraid my wife's tastes run more to diamonds and—"

Takimoto interrupted him with an impatient wave of his hand. "Don't take me for a fool, Mr. Farrell. I know about Milagre."

How? The only people in southern California who knew about the stone were Christy and her father. Surely Christy wouldn't have had any contact with a man like Takimoto. And Grenville was dead. Unless the old toad had blabbed before the hit-and-run . . .

He frowned. Did Takimoto realize the rock was stolen? Was this the prelude to blackmail? But no, he'd said something about helping Alex repay his debt. "I'm confused," he said.

Takimoto tilted his head to one side. "As I told you already, I'm a collector. You have a gemstone I covet, and I'm prepared to pay handsomely for it."

"How handsomely?"

"A million dollars."

Alex's heart skipped a beat. A million would clear his debt to Casale and then some. But four or five million would buy him a villa in the south of France, far from Casale's sphere of influence. Of course, by upping the ante he risked pissing off Takimoto, but hell, nothing ventured, nothing gained.

"A million's what my late father-in-law paid for the stone thirty years ago. Factoring in inflation on top of three decades of appreciation, I'd say ten million would be a fairer price."

"It's an uncut tourmaline," Takimoto pointed out. "Not the Kohinoor diamond."

"Yes, but an uncut tourmaline with special properties."

Takimoto drew a sharp breath.

So that was it. The man must have heard exaggerated tales of Milagre's reputed healing powers, powers Alex had never believed in. Yes, Christy's cancer had gone into remission shortly after her father forced her to wear the damn rock around her neck day and night. But cancer victims did experience remissions from time to time, even without tourmaline therapy.

Ever since they'd opened La Magia, clients had been raving about the miraculous restorative powers of the spa's hydrotherapy pools, located directly above the safe housing the tourmaline. Proof of the stone's magical healing power, according to Christy. Which was bullshit, of course, but if Takimoto bought it . . .

"Two," Takimoto said.

"Eight."

"Three."

"Six."

"Four."

"Deal."

"Enjoying your breakfast, Mrs. Durrant?"

Tasya glanced up from a plate of whole-wheat waffles smothered in fresh raspberries. Good, though not as good as Paulinho's omelets. "Yes, thank you, Mr. Farrell."

"Call me Alex," he said.

She smiled. "And I'm Traci. Would you like to join me? I hate eating alone, but my husband's such a late riser, I'd starve to death waiting for him."

"How *is* your husband? Are the treatments helping?" She would have bought the concerned expression if she hadn't known better.

She shrugged. "According to the doctors, his prognosis is poor. The treatments here at La Magia are a last-ditch effort." She sighed. "Quite frankly, I see no change."

Alex reached across the table to cover her hand with his. "I'm sorry to hear that. Our therapies work well for some, and yet for others . . ." He shrugged. "Sometimes results take a while."

Tasya bit her lip. "I'm afraid my husband may not have a while. At his age . . ." She shook her head. "I hate to watch him going downhill so fast." She met Alex's gaze. "It's not fair. We've only been married six months. If he dies, I'll be all alone again." *All alone with all those millions. Poor little me.*

"Surely you have other family."

"No, just—"

A waiter approached. "Excuse me, sir, but there's a phone call for you. A Mr. Casale. Shall I bring a phone to the table?"

"No, I'll take it in my office." Alex dismissed the waiter with an impatient wave of his hand, then turned to Tasya. "I'm sorry to end our conversation so abruptly, but I need to take this call." He stood.

"It was nice talking to you." She gave him the big eyes combined with a provocative pout. When Ian had caught her practicing the expression in front of the mirror, he'd sworn it made her look mentally deficient, but she suspected Alex Farrell preferred his females brainless.

He studied her a moment, a half smile on his lips. "Why don't we continue our discussion later . . . over dinner?"

Tasya fluttered her eyelashes. "I'd like that," she lied, "but I'm dining with my husband."

Ian's hydrotherapist, a muscular young Swedish woman named Gerda, handed him a pair of blue swim trunks with the La Magia logo embroidered on one leg and pointed to a changing stall in the corner of St. Blaise, one of six hydrotherapy rooms equipped with whirlpool baths the size of small swimming pools. "Do you need help?" she asked.

Perish the thought. "I can manage, thanks."

"*Ja,* I thought so. According to your records, you're an S-5," she said, meaning the damage to his spinal cord was located low on his back at the site of the fifth sacral vertebra. She clapped her hands. "You change then. I wait."

Growling imprecations under his breath, Ian did as he was told, changing as quickly as possible for fear Gerda would tire of waiting and decide to help.

The only challenge involved in his therapy session was remembering to feign weakness and shortness of breath. After a while, he fell into a rhythm, alternately trembling and gasping.

"You need to build your stamina," Gerda told him. "You are weak as a kitten."

"Or a drowned rat." He arched his neck backward, dipping his head underwater to slick the hair out of his face.

"*Ja,*" she agreed with a deep chuckle. She squeezed his biceps. "You have retained some muscle, but you must build your wind. Push yourself. It's the only way to improve." She hoisted herself up onto the deck, using only her arms. "You saw how I did that, *ja?* You try."

Ian knew he could not only try, but succeed. Compared to climbing a rope, the maneuver was no challenge at all. But since the fictional Charles had neither the coordination nor the strength for such a move, Ian slapped at the water, repeatedly losing his grip on the side of the pool until Gerda finally took pity on him. "Here," she said, regarding him with a mixture of compassion and disdain, "grab hold of my hand."

He did, and she jerked him out of the water. He lay on the tiled deck, gasping for air like a landed fish.

She frowned. "You need to get in shape, Mr. Durrant. Do they have you on a vitamin regimen?"

He nodded.

"And a high-protein diet?"

He nodded again, shoving himself to a sitting position, letting his legs hang over the edge of the pool.

"Good." She glanced at her watch, then scrambled to her feet. "I must report to my next client. Can you dress yourself?"

"I'll manage."

She gave him a doubtful look. "Take your time. No one else is scheduled in here until after lunch. If you run into difficulty, there's a buzzer in the dressing room. Use it to summon assistance." She tugged on a blue and white La Magia T-shirt, shuffled into a pair of rubber thong sandals, and hustled toward the door. She paused with one hand on the knob. "Vitamins," she said sternly. *"Ja?"*

"See you tomorrow," he replied, but she was already gone.

He smiled. Despite Gerda's bossiness, today's hydrotherapy had been several giant steps above yesterday's mud wrap and herbal steam bath. At least the hydrotherapy pool bubbling around his dangling feet felt comfortably warm, neither as unpleasantly chilly as the mud nor as miserably hot as the steam.

And then it hit him. The water felt warm. Felt. Warm.

No bloody way. His legs couldn't feel anything. Not pain. Not pressure. Not temperature. And yet, he could swear the water felt warm.

He poked his thigh. Nothing. He pinched his thigh. Again nothing. The sensation of warmth must be a product of his overactive imagination. Still, it seemed real enough.

All right. Try this then, MacPherson. Wiggle your left foot.

His left foot jerked. And his heart threatened to slam its way past his rib cage.

Calm down, now. It's probably just a coincidence. Most likely one of those involuntary spasms you're prone to when you overwork the muscles in your lower extremities.

So why not try the right foot? He concentrated on his right foot. *Move.*

The foot twitched, but so feebly he was afraid he'd imagined it. Again he ordered the foot to move, and again it twitched, more noticeably this time.

He stared at the mural of St. Blaise that covered the opposite wall, his mind churning as frantically as the frothing water. Dear God, how was this possible?

Paulinho left to go collect Ian after his hydrotherapy session. Bored with her own company, Tasya turned on the television. She was just getting interested in a morning talk show when regular programming was interrupted by a news bulletin. She reached for the remote, then froze.

Minutes ticked past, but she stood immobile, her thumb arrested in the midst of punching the button. When the men returned, part of her brain registered the fact, but she didn't move. She couldn't move.

"Tasya, where are you?" Ian called. His voice chipped away at the icy fear paralyzing her.

"In here," she said, each word an effort.

Ian entered with Paulinho right behind him. "I want to talk to you," he said. And then he saw her face. "What is it?"

"You need to hear this." She punched up the volume.

". . . in an attempt to defuse a potentially dangerous situation," the TV reporter said, her expression serious.

"What's going on?" Ian said.

"It's Richard." Her voice was barely audible. Someone needed to punch up her volume.

"For those of you just joining us, here's an update on this breaking story. Acting on an anonymous tip, Oakland police have traced a man believed to be Richard Martin Zane, prime suspect in two homicides, to this motel." The camera swung around to show a sign in dire need of paint: Nite Owl Motel.

"The motel is surrounded, a SWAT team poised to go in," the reporter continued. "But we understand authorities have sent for a negotiator to try to talk Zane out. The suspect has threatened to blow himself up if police attempt to take him by force."

"He's crazy enough to do it, too," Tasya said.

Paulinho scowled. "Let him."

"Suspect Richard Zane has reportedly severed communications with the police," the television reporter announced, information confirmed by a policeman in the background who could be heard yelling through a bullhorn: "Pick up the phone, Richard!"

Frowning, the reporter pressed a finger to her earphone. "My producer tells me—"

Without warning, a thunderous explosion rocked the scene. The windows of unit 10 blew outward in a deadly hail of splintered glass. People screamed and ran for cover as dust and debris rained down. Pandemonium ruled the airwaves. "Oh, my God! Oh, my God!" the reporter screamed in a voice several octaves higher than her news anchor drone.

"He did it," Tasya whispered. "He blew himself up." She stared at the television, shaking her head in disbelief. "I knew he was crazy, but—"

"Not just crazy," Paulinho said. "Sick. Perverted."

A muscle jumped in Tasya's cheek. She stared at the TV, at the inferno that had once been the Nite Owl Motel.

"You're safe," Ian told her. "Richard's dead."

With an effort she pulled her gaze away from the chaotic scene on television and focused on Ian's face. "He's been dead before," she said.

9

ALEX SAT AT A TABLE in a corner of La Magia's juice bar, nursing a papaya smoothie as he waited for Traci Durrant to emerge from the women's locker room. The young blonde intrigued him. Though she looked like a typical California girl, he suspected there was more to her than met the eye. She'd surprised him on the court. Though it was obvious she'd never played tennis before, she caught on quickly. She was a natural athlete, and, he suspected, more intelligent than she let on.

She breezed through the door. He caught her eye and smiled. Smiling back, she sauntered to his table, turning heads in a curve-hugging black halter top, matching boot-cut hip-huggers, and enough museum-quality turquoise and silver jewelry to stock her own specialty shop on Rodeo Drive.

"I ordered you spring water with a slice of lemon."

She sat down, crossing her long legs. "Perfect. Thank you." As she leaned forward to sip her drink, her breasts swung forward. No bra. He'd lay money on it. "Thanks again for the lesson. That was the most fun I've had all week." She sighed, and her breasts bobbled again. He wondered if they were real.

"I'm sorry you're not enjoying La Magia."

Another sigh. She recrossed her legs.

Alex imagined those long legs wrapped around his waist, those big, bouncy tits filling his hands. "I'm free later. How about a swim?" Traci in a bikini. The mind boggled.

She pushed out her succulent lower lip. "I'd love to, but I can't. Charles is taking me shopping."

"How about tomorrow?"

"You're pathetic, Alex," a woman's voice said from behind him.

Shit. Talk about lousy timing. He turned. "Christy, what a surprise!"

"I'm sure it is."

He maintained the smile in spite of Christy's hostility, in spite of an almost overpowering urge to smack the prissy look off her face. "What brings you to La Magia?"

She glared at him. "I heard a disturbing rumor."

About his daily breakfast meetings with the toothsome Traci Durrant, no doubt. "You're the one who filed for divorce. Who I spend time with now is none of your business."

Her glance flicked toward Traci, then quickly back to him. "Not a rumor about your sex life. A rumor about your plans to dispose of my property."

Alex assumed an expression of baffled innocence. "I'm afraid I don't follow."

"I heard you're planning to sell Milagre."

"To a gemstone connoisseur, yes. The man's determined to add the tourmaline to his collection."

"My tourmaline," she said.

"Our tourmaline."

Her mouth tightened. "My father bought the stone for me. He paid you a million dollars for it."

"Fine. I'm not greedy. I'll give you a million in compensation."

"You don't get it, Alex. Milagre saved my life. I don't want money. I want the stone."

"Okay, two million."

Her expression hardened. "You're not listening. This isn't about money."

The hell it wasn't.

"Cancel the deal, or I'll make enough waves about the illegal sale of my Gentry Consolidated stock to drown you."

Alex stared narrow-eyed at her retreating backside. No way was he reneging on the deal with Takimoto. Milagre was his ticket out of the danger zone.

Traci touched his shoulder. "Are you all right?"

"I will be once the divorce is final. My soon-to-be-ex-wife keeps coming up with new demands. Every time I think we have things settled, she raises a new issue."

"I'm sorry." Traci leaned closer, treating him to a nice view of her cleavage. She stroked his arm, as if unaware of what she was doing.

Damn, she was hot. The perfect distraction from all the stress in his screwed-up life.

She moistened her lower lip with the tip of her tongue. "You know, I don't think I've ever seen a tourmaline."

"Really?"

"What do they look like?"

"This one's a long hexagonal crystal, transparent and flawless."

"What color?"

"Dark red—what's called rubellite." He twined his fingers with hers. "Want to see it for yourself?"

Her eyes lit up. "I'd love to."

Alex helped Tasya to her feet and ushered her out of the juice bar toward the private elevator at one end of the broad corridor that connected the lobby and the solarium. He unlocked the outer door, then keyed open the inner door.

"An elevator?" she said. "Going where?" Easy to understand her confusion, since this section of La Magia was a single-story structure.

"The lower levels," he said. "A basement and subbasement where the mechanical equipment's located—pumps, heaters, and whatnot." He let her precede him into the elevator, then closed the doors behind them and punched in B for basement. "The vault's carved out of bedrock. Very secure." The elevator door slid open with a discreet ping, and he led her into the empty corridor.

"It's so quiet down here." Alex wondered if she realized she was whispering. "Where are all the employees?"

He smiled. "This part of the building's computerized. Aside from the security staff, the only time anyone works down here is when something goes haywire with the system."

She shivered. "It's creepy."

"Don't worry. Just stay close. It's a maze down here

easy to get lost." Industrial-grade carpeting muffled their footsteps as they made their way down the wide corridor. Halfway along, he drew her to a stop. "Here we are."

"Here we are where?" She glanced around, looking so adorably confused that he pressed a quick kiss to her mouth. "Oh," she said, her eyes widening.

"Sure I can't talk you out of that shopping trip?"

She caught her lower lip between her teeth. "It's tempting, but I really can't disappoint Charles."

He slid aside a section of paneling to reveal the vault, then put his hands on her shoulders and spun her around. "No peeking."

She giggled. "Cross my heart."

He worked the combination and opened the heavy steel door. "You can turn around now."

"Wow!" She leaned forward to touch the nearest stack of hundreds. "When you see so many bills all together, it doesn't even look real."

He reached past her for the velvet-lined case.

"Is that it?" She crowded closer, so close he caught a whiff of her perfume. Something flowery.

"Yeah." He raised the lid and lifted out the stone. "Here." He dropped it in her hand.

She sucked in her breath with a hissing sound. "Oh, my God!" She shoved the stone at him. "It burns."

Damn. Freaking her out was not what he'd had in mind. Alex took the tourmaline, fitted it carefully back into its box, and returned it to the vault.

Traci stared at her palm as if searching for scorch marks. He cupped her hand in one of his. "I'm sorry. I never dreamed it would affect you that way. Most people aren't so sensitive."

Her face was pale, her eyes huge. "You mean it doesn't feel hot to everyone?"

"I don't feel a thing when I touch it. Christy's always claimed it feels warm to her, though."

"Warm? That's an understatement. I could have sworn it was burning right through my skin."

"No kidding? I've only known one other person to react so strongly." *Cat MacPherson.*

Strange thinking of Cat after all these years.

After a week of hydrotherapy, Ian could walk the length of the living room. Granted, he wouldn't be running any marathons in the near future, but he could stand upright and use his legs after a fashion, two things he never would have believed possible before coming to La Magia.

He reached the far end of the room, turned, and started back, one foot in front of the other, so focused on what he was doing that he didn't realize Paulinho had entered the room until he heard the big Brazilian gasp. "*Meu Deus,* Senhor Ian! How is this possible?"

Startled, Ian stumbled and nearly fell, catching himself on the back of an armchair. He grinned at Paulinho. "It's magic. La Magia has lived up to its name."

"Not magic," Paulinho said. "A miracle. Milagre did this, didn't it?"

Ian lowered himself into the chair. "I think so, yes. According to the blueprints, the vault is located directly under the hydrotherapy rooms, close enough, apparently, for the stone to have a restorative effect." At least for a chosen few. In compiling statistics on the spa's success rate, he'd noted only a dozen or so cases where patients reported a complete cure.

Paulinho clenched his hands. "Then you understand its power, its importance. We cannot allow it to fall into the wrong hands. Milagre belongs in Brazil."

Ian raised his eyebrows. "I had no idea you felt so strongly about the stone. I thought you were helping me because you had your own score to settle with Alex."

"*Sim*, I do. Alex Farrell is a cowardly dog who shot and killed my father, a man armed only with a flashlight. But Milagre is more important than revenge. The stone can heal, but it can also harm. You have no idea how dangerous it is. People have died trying to unlock its secrets."

"What secrets?" Ian said. "What aren't you telling me?"

Paulinho's face shut down. "I have said too much already."

The small hairs prickled on the back of Tasya's neck. Alex Farrell had insisted upon accompanying her to the cottage, but his presence was an annoyance, not the source of her uneasiness. Was she under surveillance? That's how it felt, as if someone were tracking her every move.

Richard? Dread squeezed her heart even though she knew how absurd it was to suspect Richard of spying on her. Richard was dead. One of Harper's operatives had identified the body at the morgue. She herself had seen Richard's picture on the news, a picture taken by a security camera at San Francisco International. It had been the same face she'd seen in the digital shots Harper had e-mailed Ian. Richard without a doubt. Plastic surgery had altered his appearance in other ways, but his eyes had remained the same—cruel, predatory. Nightmare eyes. She suppressed a shudder.

Glancing over her shoulder, she saw no one aside from the two gardeners weeding ground cover under a clump of ornamental Monterey cypresses. Farrell, preoccupied with the inane story he was telling about one of the spa's more famous clients, didn't notice her discomfiture.

You're imagining things, Tasya.

She risked a second look and this time caught one of the groundskeepers staring. The sun glinted off his mirrored sunglasses. An insolent smile revealed a row of even white teeth beneath his thick black mustache. He tipped his cap in mock obeisance.

She turned away without acknowledging him. Just another lech, she told herself. Like Tommy, the massotherapist. Like Alex with his hands-on approach to tennis lessons.

"The seagull flew off with his toupee," Alex said as they reached the front door of the cottage, "and some joker snapped a picture. Sold it to the *National Enquirer*."

"How embarrassing!" she said.

He smiled at her, a smile full of masculine appreciation and sensual promise. "Sure I can't change your mind about that swim?"

The man was so vain, confident no woman could resist him. Tasya hid her amusement with a flutter of eyelashes. "Not today."

"Tomorrow then?"

"We'll see." She let herself into the cottage and closed the door firmly behind her.

"See what?" Ian said.

She turned and saw him standing at the edge of the tiled entry just inside the archway that led to the living room. She stared, speechless.

He took a halting step toward her. "Tasya? Are you all right? You're not going to faint, are you? I meant to surprise you, not shock you."

"I'm . . . I'm . . ." She made a sound that was half laugh, half sob. "How is this possible? I thought the specialists told you you'd never walk again."

"Obviously they were wrong."

"But how? I don't understand." She closed the gap between them.

"It's the hydrotherapy. I noticed improvement the very first day. I was going to tell you as soon as I got back to the cottage, but that was the day Richard—"

"Blew himself up," she said. "But how could hydrotherapy effect such a change?" Unless . . . "This has something to do with Milagre, doesn't it?"

"I think so, yes. I told you how it healed the cut on my wrist."

"Yes, but Milagre touched your wrist. It didn't touch your spine."

"Not directly, no, though apparently it's close enough."

"Why didn't you tell me?"

"I couldn't quite believe it myself at first. I thought maybe the improvement was only temporary, and I didn't want to get your hopes up."

Or his own.

"But I've been growing stronger all week. My back. My legs. I can feel pressure, variations in temperature, pain.

And best of all, I can control my leg muscles again, though I'm still shaky. My walk's halfway between a lurch and a totter. I wanted to surprise you and Paulinho once I had it down, but he caught me earlier." He smiled again, and her heart skipped a beat.

So tall. She hadn't realized Ian was so tall.

"Since Paulinho knew, it seemed only fair that I let you in on the secret, too."

"Oh, Ian." She moved a step closer, so close she could smell the clean detergent and fabric softener scent of his shirt, the spicy fragrance of his aftershave, and the faintest hint of cinnamon on his breath. She wanted to throw her arms around him, but she didn't, afraid she might knock him off balance.

As if he'd read her thoughts, he backed away. "Let's sit. I've been standing too long. My legs hurt."

True, no doubt, but she didn't believe he'd moved out of reach because his muscles ached. No, Ian was avoiding her. Ian was afraid if he didn't keep his distance, he'd be tempted to kiss her again the way he had in San Francisco.

"You shouldn't push yourself so hard. Give it time. " She perched on an armchair.

Ian lowered himself onto the sofa with a muffled groan. "At my age, how much time is left? I want to do everything I once did, to be everything I once was."

His recovery was a miracle, but surely even miracles had limits. A man in his sixties could never hope to match the physical condition of a man in his thirties. If Ian refused to recognize his body's limitations, he was doomed to disappointment. "You're not thirty anymore."

He said nothing for a moment. Then he laughed, a sound that grated on her ears. "No, I'm not."

She hadn't meant to hurt him. He must know that. "Ian." She moved to the sofa and took his hands in hers. "When I said you weren't thirty anymore, I didn't mean it as an insult. You're the only one who's worried about what you can or can't do. I don't care if you can run as fast as a steaming locomotive or leap tall buildings in a single bound." She sighed. "You don't have to be Superman." *I love you just the way you are.* She released his hands and leaned back against the cushions. Had he heard a word she'd said?

He stared at the floor. Silence stretched between them, an arid wasteland of misunderstanding.

Look at me, you stubborn man. I'll help you if you give me half a chance.

He met her gaze for an instant, his eyes dark and tortured. Then he looked away. Was he afraid if he held her gaze, he'd be forced to acknowledge the bond between them?

"Did he kiss you?"

"What?"

"Alex. Did he kiss you during your tennis lesson?"

Where had that come from? "Yes, but it was nothing."

"Did you make love with him?"

She wrinkled her nose in distaste. "No! Why would you—"

"You were late. . . ." Ian wouldn't look at her. Was he jealous? Surely not. Common sense should tell him she wouldn't risk involvement with a murderous, double-crossing bastard even if she did find him wildly attractive—which in Alex Farrell's case was definitely not an issue. The man made her skin crawl.

She frowned. "There's only one man I want to make love with, and he keeps turning me down."

"Someday you'll—"

"Someday I'll die, and then and only then will I stop wanting you." *Loving you.*

He shook his head. "Tasya, you're so young."

"Damn it, not this again!"

He ignored her outburst. "When I was your age, I fancied myself madly in love with an actress I met in Cannes."

"I don't think I want to hear this."

"You need to hear this." He scowled at her. "Caroline was there for the film festival. I was there for the jewels."

"Is this going to be a long story?"

"On the contrary," he said. "The festival ended, and so did the big romance. She headed back to the States, and I moped around for a good two days." He paused. "Then I met Jennifer."

"Your point is . . . ?"

Ian narrowed his eyes. "If anyone had tried to convince me what I felt for Caroline was anything but true love, I'd have called them insane. And yet—"

"I know what I want."

"You think you do." His gaze locked with hers in a silent battle of wills. She glared at him, determined not to be the first to break eye contact.

His lips parted as if he were on the verge of saying something. Then he pressed them together in a thin line.

But emotion flickered in his eyes in the instant before he looked away. An admission of sorts.

She smiled. *I know what you want, too, Ian MacPherson.*

Ian tried not to think about Tasya's eyes, Tasya's mouth, Tasya's sweet young body. Dear God, where was Paulinho? Ian willed the big Brazilian to walk in the door. Now. He needed someone to run interference. If he had to spend another half hour alone with Tasya, he was going to do something he'd regret.

Regret later, perhaps, but enjoy like mad while it lasted.

Right, and that would be what? All of thirty seconds? His spinal cord wasn't the only thing Milagre had repaired; his libido had been growing stronger all week. At the moment he wasn't sure if that was a blessing or a curse.

"Oh," Tasya said. "I almost forgot. Alex showed me Milagre."

Her words were like a good-natured cuff to the side of the head. *Hey, MacPherson, remember why you're here. Sex is not your top priority at the moment.* At least it shouldn't be.

"You guessed right," she said. "He does keep it in the vault under the hydrotherapy pools."

"Guards?"

"None I saw."

"Security cameras?"

"Two. One at either end of the corridor."

"Is there a time-lock mechanism?"

"No. Combination lock. He made me turn my back while he opened it, but I could hear the tumblers click."

"That's good news."

"Yes," she said, but her expression was troubled. "I held the stone, Ian. It burned my hand yet left no mark. I don't understand how that could happen any more than I understand how your spine could regenerate or Christina Gentry's cancer could disappear. Things like that defy the laws of science."

He shrugged. "*Milagre* means 'miracle.'"

"We have to make sure it doesn't fall into the wrong hands."

"Meaning Takimoto's?"

"Have you looked into his eyes? He's an evil man. A criminal."

Ian laughed softly. "And I'm not?"

"A cat burglar's one thing. A gangster's another. You may have stolen jewelry, but you never profited from the drug trade. You never ordered anyone killed."

"He offered Alex four million dollars for the stone."

Tasya frowned. "He must need it badly, either for himself or to save someone he loves."

"If that's his motivation, then why doesn't he check himself or that hypothetical loved one into the spa and save the four million?"

"Maybe he's come up with some scheme, some way to use Milagre to make such an enormous profit that four million seems a paltry investment by comparison."

"Or," Ian said, "perhaps he believes the stone can grant him virtual immortality by curing his every ill."

"That evil man living forever?" Tasya shuddered.

He touched her hand briefly. "Don't worry. Takimoto will never even see the real Milagre."

"When do I pull the switch?"

"Tonight. The word is, the buy is set for tomorrow."

"Alex is hosting a party tomorrow," Tasya said. "I know because we're invited."

"Throwing a party to celebrate his change of fortune. That sounds like Alex."

"Do you have the substitute?"

"Paulinho collected it from the jeweler yesterday. I had them attach a chain."

"How close a match is it?"

"Judge for yourself." He retrieved a large jeweler's box from his bedroom and set it on the coffee table in front of her.

Tasya opened it and, hooking the chain with two fingers, lifted the tourmaline from its nest of cotton. About five inches long and three inches in diameter, it resembled the original in every aspect. "Whoa. Déjà vu."

"Uncanny, isn't it?"

"Is it safe to touch this one? It won't burn me, will it?"

"No." He smiled. "Oddly enough, not everyone feels a burning sensation even when they touch the real Milagre. Alex doesn't. That night in Rio I watched him hold it in the palm of his hand, then stuff it into his knapsack. He didn't even wince."

Tasya nodded. "He told me it doesn't affect everyone." She shook her head. "So what's wrong with us?"

"Nothing."

"Then why—"

"I suspect a slight variation in our body chemistry is to blame. We're like those people who can't wear wrist-watches."

"What people? I don't follow."

"After an hour or so of direct body contact, some people's watches quit working. I'm not sure why. Maybe it's chemical. Maybe it's something to do with the body's magnetic field. But whatever the cause, I think this works on the same principle."

Tasya stared at the stone. "Can Milagre cure a person who doesn't feel the heat?"

"I suspect not. According to La Magia's records, about fifty percent of the patients experience some amelioration of their symptoms—regardless of the ailment. Nearly ten percent exhibit marked improvement, and a very small percentage report a complete cure. That suggests that at least half the population is sensitive to the stone, but that the sensitivity runs the gamut from mild to extreme."

"And we're extreme."

"That's my guess."

"What about Takimoto? If he can't feel the heat, how will he know he's been cheated?"

"Just in case he's in the wrong half of the population, someone's going to tip him off. Anonymously, of course."

"What makes you think he'll believe an anonymous tip?"

"Because the tipster's going to tell him where Alex bought the replacement stone and who he hired to affix the chain." He smiled. "I had the foresight to place the order in Alex's name. Even paid for it with his credit card."

She gaped at him. "How'd you manage that?"

"I'm a thief, Tasya. Identity theft is a walk in the park compared to second-story work."

She smiled, a smile that quickly faded. "After you even the score with Alex, what do you plan to do with Milagre?"

He shrugged. "Paulinho thinks we should return it to Brazil."

"To the woman you stole it from."

"Elizabete Ribeiro Sodré. Yes."

"And you agree with him?"

"Don't you?"

She looked troubled. "I'm not sure. Think of the potential benefits to humanity. A stone that can repair a damaged spinal cord could conceivably cure any number of fatal or debilitating diseases—cancer, AIDS, diabetes, MS, Alzheimer's. Would the Sodré woman use Milagre to help mankind? Or would she hide it away in some private shrine?"

Ian smiled. "Your heart is in the right place, Tasya, but I don't think we have any say in the matter. Milagre belongs to Elizabete Ribeiro Sodré. Milagre belongs in Brazil."

Paulinho knelt in the center of his bedroom, his heart hammering so hard and fast, he feared it would slam its way past his breastbone. *Meu Deus*, had Kenji Takimoto somehow discovered the true extent of Milagre's power?

Carefully, he opened the ivory box and removed his *opele*, setting it aside. The copper chain and bag of stones followed. When the box was empty, he hooked a fingernail under the velvet-covered cardboard liner and removed that as well.

Though the room was cool, he was sweating as heavily as if he had been digging ditches all morning. He wiped his forehead with the tail of his shirt. Then, hands trembling, he used his thumbs to depress latches camouflaged by the box's carved surface. *Meu Deus, meu Deus,* please let it be there.

The false bottom popped free, and he sobbed with relief. Inside the hidden compartment lay a slim black leather-bound volume. He pressed his fingertips to the cracked leather, reassured that however Takimoto had learned the truth, he, Paulinho, was not to blame. Father Duarte's diary was safe. The secret of Milagre was secret still.

10

PAULINHO SLUMPED IN A CHAIR on the terrace; Tasya perched on the balustrade. But Ian was too fidgety to sit still. "You're sure the police were called in? It's not just a rumor?"

"I myself saw them," Paulinho said. "Two men in uniform."

"Alex told me about the theft over breakfast. He said someone broke into the vault last night and stole Milagre." Tasya frowned. "Could he be telling the truth? Could someone have beat me to it?" She'd slipped past the guards with no trouble, but she hadn't been able to switch the stones as planned. By the time she'd cracked the vault, Milagre had vanished.

Ian raised his eyebrows. "Take the tourmaline but leave the cash behind? Absurd. He moved the stone himself. Nothing else makes sense."

Tasya looked thoughtful. "His wife and her lawyer showed up this morning. She insists Milagre belongs to her. I bet they came to collect it."

"There's his motive then," Ian said. "Alex faked the robbery so he wouldn't have to hand over the stone, and he's hidden it somewhere until he can complete his transaction with Takimoto."

"We cannot allow Milagre to be sold. The tourmaline belongs in Brazil," Paulinho said, his voice husky with emotion.

"I agree," Ian said.

"We can't return what we don't have," Tasya pointed out. "At this point we don't even know where Milagre is."

"In Senhor Farrell's office?" Paulinho suggested.

"Maybe," Tasya said. "Though it wouldn't be my first choice. Too much traffic."

Ian leaned on the balustrade next to her. "For all we know, Alex has moved Milagre off the premises. He owns two houses, one here in Orange County and another in Santa Barbara."

"Yes, but his wife has access to their houses. He wouldn't hide the stone anywhere she might find it. But . . ." She paused. "Ever since his wife filed for divorce, Alex has been living in the tower." She pointed to the three-story structure on the headland, a modern interpretation of the Italian campanile.

Ian raised his eyebrows. "And you know this because . . . ?"

Tasya shot him a mischievous look. "Because Alex offered to give me a tour the second day we breakfasted together."

"Fast worker," Ian said dryly.

"Naturally I declined," she said. "Claimed my poor pathetic old husband was waiting for me to help him dress."

"Brat," Ian said. He gazed thoughtfully across the narrow inlet at the tower. "You really think that's where he's stashed Milagre?"

"I do," she said. "It's private and accessible, the ideal spot to hide the tourmaline, the ideal spot to pull off the exchange with Takimoto."

Ian was inclined to agree.

"Even if you are right—" Paulinho glanced at his watch. "It is half past noon already. If we are to prevent the exchange, we must act soon."

"Daylight heists are tricky," Ian said. Doubly so when one's mobility was compromised. He stared at the tower. Three stories, damn it. Three flights of stairs.

"But necessary in this instance. Let me retrieve the stone," Tasya said.

He turned to her with a frown. "No. I'll do it."

"Climb all those stairs? Ian, be reasonable."

"I can do it."

"And I can do it faster."

"The plans show a lift."

She shook her head. "Which wouldn't do much good if you had to make a run for it. You'd get into the elevator on the third floor, and by the time you got down to the first, there'd be a posse waiting for you. Besides . . ." She placed her hand on his arm and met his gaze. "This is what you trained me for, isn't it?"

Paulinho and Tasya had waited until Alex hit the showers after a session in the weight room. Then Tasya swiped a blank keycard from the front desk and sent Paulinho to exchange it for the master key Alex left in his locker. The two cards looked identical. Even if they didn't have a chance to swap them back, Alex wouldn't get suspicious. He'd just assume the card's magnetic strip had become desensitized, a common problem.

Paulinho stood lookout outside the tower. If he saw anyone approaching, he was to call her on Ian's cell phone, set to vibrating mode and stuffed in her jeans pocket.

Tasya pulled on thin leather gloves to avoid leaving prints and to protect her hands from the stone's heat in the event her search proved successful. Then she took a deep breath and keyed herself in.

The front door opened into a three-story entry where light from windows near the ceiling bounced off the cream-colored walls. Bright with the spicy-scented geraniums banked along the curved outer wall, the entry offered a gracious welcome. Terra-cotta tiles paved the floor, and a graceful wrought iron staircase spiraled up to the other levels.

Tasya decided to start at the bottom and work her way up. The first floor—kitchen, pantry, dining room, and powder room—was a bust, though she did find a couple ounces of a suspicious white powder and a plastic sandwich bag full of pink pills. Probably not vitamins.

The second floor comprised a bedroom, a walk-in closet, and a shiny black-tiled bathroom. The bedroom's focal point was a round bed covered in black satin. Filmy black chiffon draperies hung in swags from a crown canopy, a writhing jungle of black metal, vaguely Rococo in style. French whorehouse meets Hollywood tacky.

Again she came up empty.

As she climbed the stairs to the great room on the top floor, she wondered if they'd been wrong to assume the stone was hidden in the tower. What if someone else—Takimoto, for instance—had broken into the safe and stolen the tourmaline? What if Alex had taken it but hidden it elsewhere?

Her doubts evaporated a few minutes later when she spotted a leather-covered box wedged behind a row of books on the shelves beside the fireplace. Heart pounding, she dug the replacement tourmaline from the fanny pack cinched around her waist.

Milagre didn't burn her this time, but she felt its heat even through gloves. If she hadn't known better, she'd have sworn the stone was alive. A faint throbbing seemed to emanate from deep inside the crystal, a slow, steady oscillation that triggered a tingling response in her fingertips.

She wasted no time making the exchange. In seconds, the fake was in the box behind the books and Milagre lay nestled safely in her fanny pack.

She was halfway down the second flight of steps when she felt the cell phone vibrate. She flipped it open and punched Talk. "What?"

"Senhor Farrell, and he is not alone." Paulinho broke the connection.

Should she retreat up or down? Down was closer to the exit, but there were no good hiding places on the first level. The second floor was probably her best bet.

She ran up the stairs, pausing to peek out the window overlooking the walk. Alex Farrell and Kenji Takimoto approached at a leisurely stroll. Apparently, the exchange was going down now.

Hiding herself definitely topped the agenda. But where? A quick glance in the bathroom told her the shower was out. It had a transparent glass door instead of the usual frosted variety, a detail she hadn't noted earlier. The closet wouldn't work, either. Not enough hanging clothes to use as camouflage. She couldn't even wedge herself under the bed, since it sat on a solid platform.

Which left the third floor.

She raced up the staircase, panicking when she heard the sound of the key in the lock.

I've got the real key, she told herself. His won't work.

And it didn't—at least not on the first try. Alex's second attempt was more successful. Voices floated up from the entry below.

"Sorry about the delay. These keycards can be temperamental."

"It is fortunate you had a spare hidden outside."

"I like to be prepared. May I offer you a drink?"

"No, thank you. I prefer to get right to business. May I see Milagre?"

"Of course. This way."

Her way. Frantic now, Tasya scanned her surroundings, but the room offered no cover. Which left . . . the balcony.

"A most interesting home, Mr. Farrell," Takimoto said, glancing around the great room with obvious approval.

"The tower used to be a convenience, a place to sleep if I had to work late, but since my wife sued for divorce, I've been staying here full-time."

"It has much to commend it. Compact, uncluttered, elegant. A most restful retreat."

"Wait until tonight, when it's full of guests. Won't seem so restful then. You are planning to attend my party?"

"I don't think so, no." Takimoto paused in front of the sliding glass doors. "Ah." He smiled in obvious pleasure. "And your view is splendid."

"On a clear day you can see Catalina," Alex said. A lie, but hard to disprove, since between the natural marine layer and the smog drifting down from L.A., they rarely had a clear day.

"Living here must be like living in a lighthouse."

"Because I'm perched at land's end? Or because of all those stairs?" Alex laughed. "Actually, see the doors behind you? That's the elevator. I use it to move heavy objects— that's how we got all the furniture up here—and for the convenience of my frailer guests, of course."

Takimoto nodded. "Plus, two exits are better than one."

Was that an observation? An Oriental aphorism? Or a veiled threat? Takimoto's stolid expression offered no hint.

"Yes, well." Alex cleared his throat, then walked to the bookcase, where he dug the tourmaline from its hiding place. He passed the box to Takimoto, who cradled it in one hand and raised the lid with the other.

"Oh," he said. "Magnificent. Just as I imagined it."

"We have a deal, then?"

"I shall have my men bring the money immediately. A million-dollar down payment as per our agreement, the additional three million to be wired to your offshore account." He set the box on the coffee table, closed the lid, then pulled a cell phone from his pocket. After punching in some numbers, he spoke a few words of Japanese in short staccato bursts, then frowned, paused, and spat out a few more syllables.

"Problem?" Alex asked. Was this the prelude to a double-cross?

"A slight delay only while one of my men answers the call of nature."

A pit stop. Right. Alex wondered what was really going on. Was a platoon of ninjas about to descend on the place? He wouldn't put such a tactic past Takimoto. The man had a reputation as a devious son of a bitch.

Alex wasn't into martial arts himself, much preferring the solid weight of a .357 in his hand. Luckily, he had his favorite Luger tucked into the waistband of his jeans at the small of his back, hidden by a loose-fitting polo shirt.

"While we're waiting, would you like to see the view from the balcony, Mr. Takimoto?"

Takimoto shot him a searching look, then, apparently satisfied with what he saw in Alex's expression, nodded once. "Very much, yes, thank you."

Tasya dangled from the balcony railing like a human windsock. She worried the wrought-iron posts she clung to would rip free of their moorings, and she'd crash to her death on the rocks below. She worried that even if the posts held, her arms would fail her, and she'd crash to her death on the rocks below. She worried that seagulls, mistaking her for a tasty tidbit, would peck at her exposed flesh, and she'd crash to her death on the rocks below.

Luckily, the birds kept their distance, the railing held,

and her arm muscles were good for at least ten more minutes, perhaps longer if she could get a toehold in the rough stuccoed wall of the tower.

"This is fantastic!" Takimoto's voice came from so close, she nearly lost her grip in surprise.

"I like it." Alex's voice came from farther away. Was he worried Takimoto might flip him over the edge of the balcony if he ventured within jujitsu range?

"Smell that air. So fresh and clean. I envy you this. My Tokyo penthouse has a rooftop terrace with a view of the city. Equally exhilarating. Unfortunately, the air reeks of hydrocarbons."

"That's a shame." Tasya thought Alex sounded uneasy. Or maybe what she interpreted as nervousness was simply boredom.

"The thunder of waves dashing themselves against the rocks. Such a primal sound," Takimoto said. "Humbling, a reminder of how puny we humans are compared to the forces of nature."

MacPherson's Rule Number Forty-seven: When suspended more than six feet off the ground, resist the impulse to look down. Tasya didn't remember this bit of advice until, half mesmerized by Takimoto's words, she risked a quick glance at the jagged rocks and churning water below. Far below. Big mistake.

Terrified, she clamped her mouth shut on the scream clawing its way up her throat. Shut her eyes, too, to keep herself from taking a second look at the maelstrom below. Hungry alligators and razor-sharp spikes were nothing compared to the fury of pounding surf.

Her arm muscles ached, and she could no longer feel

her fingers. She was going to fall. She knew it, was almost resigned to it. If Alex and Takimoto didn't go back inside in the next few seconds, she was doomed.

What? Die before you've had a chance to live? Before you've loved and been loved? She could almost hear Ian's voice, badgering her. Goading her.

All right. Fine. She wouldn't give up. Unfortunately her body wasn't so easy to convince. Her arms quivered. Her shoulders burned.

The next instant something exploded on the other side of the compound.

"What the hell was that?" Alex said.

"A bomb?" Takimoto said. "A terrorist attack?"

"I doubt terrorists would consider La Magia a politically significant target."

"Perhaps your boiler blew up."

"Our system's all electric. It might fry a few wires, but it wouldn't explode."

"Then perhaps—"

"Speculation's a waste of time. I'm going to go check it out. You coming?"

"Of course."

A second explosion ripped through the afternoon calm.

"Holy shit!" she heard Alex say, and then the sliding glass door banged shut.

She'd just shifted her weight, preparing to swing a knee up to help lever herself back onto the balcony, when her numb right hand slipped free with no warning at all.

*   *   *

Ian had been prepared to break into the tower, but that hadn't proved necessary. Alex had left the door unlocked. "Tasya?" he called. "Tasya, where are you?"

No answer.

Please let her be safe. If Alex had . . . Ian refused to finish the thought.

And then he heard it, a muffled thunk from overhead.

"Tasya?"

No answer.

Fear constricted his chest. He took the elevator to the top floor, then paused just inside the great room, listening intently. "Tasya?"

"Out here." An answer so faint, he thought at first he'd imagined it. Then, "On the balcony," she said. Tasya's voice. No doubt this time.

He crossed to the sliding door, pulled it open, and stepped outside. She lay prone and still near the edge of the balcony. His heart skipped a beat. "Tasya?"

She rolled onto her back and gave him a wan smile. "Ian, thank God. Help me up. We've got to get out of here."

By the time Ian and Tasya made it back to the cottage, Paulinho was already there. He brightened when he saw them. "You found her safe, Senhor Ian. *Graças a Deus.*"

"Thanks to you, too, *meu amigo.*" Ian settled Tasya on the sofa in the living room. "Can I bring you anything?"

"New arms?" she suggested. "I think mine are shot." She turned to Paulinho. "I assume you had something to do with those explosions I heard."

"*Sim.*" Paulinho appeared both pleased and surprised. "I meant to start a fire."

"He panicked when Alex escorted Takimoto into the tower," Ian said.

"That makes two of us." Tasya flexed her hands.

"I told him to create a distraction, something to draw them away so I could get you out of there."

Tasya turned to Paulinho. "So you blew something up?"

He nodded. "I poke holes in the gas tank of a car. The *gasolina* makes puddles. I think if I throw matches in the puddles, the *gasolina* makes fire."

"Only the flame must have ignited the fumes," Ian said.

Paulinho mimed an explosion. "*Ka-boom*. Two cars. Two *ka-booms*. But the second was an accident, parked too close to the first."

Tasya sat cross-legged, massaging her biceps. "Accident or not, your distraction worked. If Alex and Takimoto hadn't left when they did, I'd probably be splattered all over the rocks at the base of the cliff right now."

Ian's stomach did an elevator swoop. "I never should have let you go in there alone."

"If you hadn't, I wouldn't have discovered Alex's secret escape hatch."

"What are you talking about?"

She grinned. "He has a coil of rope stored in the space between beams under his balcony."

"*Under* his balcony?" Ian fought to keep his voice even. "What the bloody hell were you doing under the balcony?"

"Hiding, hanging off the edge. Wasn't like I had much choice. When Alex brought Takimoto outside to enjoy the view"—she shrugged—"I had nowhere else to go."

Ian swore under his breath. He never should have involved her in his vendetta. Never.

"When Alex and Takimoto finally left, I tried to haul myself onto the balcony and almost ended up on the rocks. While I was flailing around, trying to get a handhold on something, an eighteen-by-twenty-four-inch section of end trim swung open on hinges."

"A hidden door?" Ian said.

She nodded. "It looks just like the rest of the trim but opens onto an enclosed space between floor beams. Inside, a rope is secured to an eyebolt."

"Why would Alex have rope stowed under his balcony?" Ian wondered aloud.

Tasya frowned. "Plan B in case Casale corners him?"

"He couldn't suspect *we're* after him, could he?"

"I don't think so," she said.

"Fire exit," Paulinho said. "When I was small, my family lived in a fourth-floor apartment. We kept a rope in a trunk near the window for emergencies."

Ian nodded. "Perhaps Alex learned something from me, after all. I always encouraged him to plan ahead."

"Thank God he did," Tasya said. "I got a foothold on the bottom edge of the storage space and levered myself back up onto the balcony. His fire escape saved me, and I saved this." She unzipped her fanny pack, gingerly lifted the tourmaline by the chain, and set it on the coffee table.

"Milagre." Paulinho reached for the stone. Light reflected off the crystal, flickering like fire.

"Be careful," Ian warned.

"Careful? I do not understand." Paulinho gazed at the stone, his expression almost reverent. "*Maravilhoso!*"

"Marvelous indeed," Ian said.

"Doesn't it hurt?" Tasya asked.

Paulinho shot her a puzzled look. "*Não.*"

"It burned me," she said.

Paulinho glanced at Ian, his eyebrows raised. "And you?"

"Yes. It seemed to sear my skin, but left no trace."

Paulinho frowned. "Both of you feel the burning?"

"Yes," Ian said.

"Yes." Tasya echoed him.

Paulinho's frown deepened. "*Meu Deus*, I did not know."

11

A HOT SHOWER HAD EASED Tasya's aching muscles. Or maybe Milagre was responsible for her sudden rejuvenation. Before the men left on an unexplained errand, Ian had insisted she let Paulinho massage her arms and shoulders with the towel-wrapped tourmaline. Her skin had tingled at the contact, even with a double layer of fabric—her shirt and the towel—protecting her from the worst of the heat.

Whatever the reason, though, she felt refreshed and energized as she dressed for Alex's party in a blood-red Armani. She studied her reflection in the full-length mirror in her bedroom, pleased with what she saw. The gown's color warmed her skin and complemented her lightened tresses. Plus—and this was the true source of her pleasure—Ian had chosen the dress. Which meant Ian liked it. Liked *her* in it. And maybe, just maybe, if all went as planned at the party tonight, he might like her out of it, too. As in naked. In his bed.

The front door slammed, announcing Ian and

Paulinho's return. Tasya fastened diamond studs in her ears, gave the blonde in the mirror a thumbs-up, then clicked her way down the hall in her high heels. She paused at the entrance to the living room and struck a pose.

"*Meu Deus!*" Paulinho goggled, his mouth agape.

Ian stared, his expression unreadable.

Not quite the reaction she'd been going for. Had she overdone the makeup? "What's wrong?"

"*Nada.* All is right. Very, very right."

"Ian?"

"You look incredible." Her heart fluttered at the expression on his face. "Alex doesn't stand a chance."

Alex. Right. All this lily gilding was intended to distract Alex, not seduce Ian. "What have you two been doing?"

The men exchanged a look she couldn't interpret.

Ian met her gaze. "Paulinho's been keeping an eye on Alex."

Paulinho nodded. "I see him load a suitcase into the trunk of his car."

"The parking area's so chaotic, he probably figured no one would notice," Ian said.

"He's planning to run away?"

"I think so, yes." Ian smiled. "When Alex left, Paulinho popped the trunk and opened the suitcase."

"I take it the case wasn't full of underwear."

"Money," Ian said. "Presumably the million-dollar down payment from Takimoto."

"I transferred the suitcase to the trunk of our limousine," Paulinho said. "No one noticed. Everyone was watching the fire."

"Meanwhile, I emptied the vault," Ian said.

She stared, appalled at his audacity. "In broad daylight?"

"Everyone's focused on the fire. I didn't see a soul downstairs, and even if I had, I doubt they'd have questioned me, disguised as I was as a maintenance man." He grinned. "I carried the money out in a garbage bag and stashed it in the trunk of the limo. When Casale shows up for his payoff, Alex is going to find himself in a bind. No cash in his trunk. No cash in his safe. No cash, period."

"And when Takimoto figures out the stone he has is not the stone he paid for . . . ?" she said.

"Alex will have two sets of thugs determined to bring him down." Ian smiled. "And I'll be there to watch him fall."

Alex surveyed the crowded great room with satisfaction. He'd done it. Despite the apparent assassination attempt that had destroyed Takimoto's Rolls, the exchange had gone off without a hitch. Alex had his money, and Takimoto had Milagre. By now, the collector and his prize were well on their way back to San Francisco in a rented limousine.

This party was Alex's farewell bash, though he was the only one aware of it. He'd booked a nonstop flight to Paris leaving LAX at 7:35 A.M., which left ample time to seduce the lovely Traci Durrant. Hell, fifteen minutes would probably do it. She'd been hanging on him most of the evening.

Not at the moment, though. Her husband had summoned her to his side a minute ago. Ready to leave, maybe. It was almost eleven, late by old-fart standards.

He watched as Traci bent to whisper something in Durrant's ear, inadvertently giving Alex an excellent view of her tits. She straightened the lap robe across the old man's knees, then wove her way through the crowd to Alex's side.

"I thought you said the treatments weren't helping. Your husband looks ten years younger than he did at check-in."

Traci sighed. Her gown was so low-cut that every time she inhaled, he half expected her nipples to pop free. "An illusion, I'm afraid."

He glanced at her in surprise, forgetting for a moment what they'd been discussing.

"There's been no change in Charles's prognosis." She sighed again. "That's one reason I appreciate your inviting us tonight. Who knows how many more parties are in his future?"

Alex stared at her mouth, red and luscious, and wondered how she'd react if he suggested a quick blow job. Who'd notice if they slipped away for a few minutes?

A hamlike fist closed painfully on his upper arm. "What's with the party, Farrell? I thought we had an appointment."

Casale. Alex twisted free as unobtrusively as possible. "I didn't forget. In fact, I have something for you."

The gambler grinned, an expression scarier than most people's scowls. "That's what I like to hear." He turned his ferocious grin on Traci. "I don't believe we've met."

"Traci Durrant," she said.

His big hand swallowed her smaller one the way a

shark swallows lunch. Alex half expected her to emerge from the handshake with only a bloody stump where her hand had been.

She smiled uncertainly, as if the same possibility had occurred to her. "I'm afraid you have the advantage of me, Mr.—"

"Casale. Eddie Casale."

"Pleased to meet you, Mr. Casale."

"Likewise, I'm sure." Casale stared at Traci's cleavage. "Farrell and I have some business to discuss. If you'll excuse us a moment—"

"I'll go freshen my drink." Traci seemed relieved to retreat to the far side of the big room. Alex didn't blame her. Too bad he didn't have that option.

"Here's the deal," Casale said. "I get my money in the next"—he consulted his watch—"forty-two minutes, or I drop you off the balcony."

"If I'm dead, you'll never get your money."

Casale nodded. "Yeah, but it's good advertising. Next time some jerk tries to stiff me, I say, 'Pay up, sport, or you'll be taking a dive like that lame-ass Alex Farrell.'"

Casale might talk like Punk Number Two from one of Grenville's low-budget *Godfather* rip-offs, but he was dead serious. If Alex didn't pay up, Casale would dump him off the balcony. Make it look like an accident maybe. Or a suicide.

"Here. Take my keys." Alex dug them from his pants pocket. "The money's in a black leather suitcase in the trunk of my car."

"What car? You signed the Lamborghini over to me, remember?"

"I leased this one a couple weeks ago. A red BMW. It's parked in my reserved spot."

Casale took the keys. "If the money's not there—" He mimed a diver. "Splish-splash."

The instant Casale left, Traci migrated back to his side. "Your friend didn't stay long."

"He's no friend of mine." Alex draped an arm around her shoulders. "But you could be."

She smiled at him over the rim of her wineglass. A come-hither look if he ever saw one. Encouraged, he leaned closer, whispering a few friendly suggestions in her ear.

She jerked away, glaring at him.

Okay, so apparently he could forget the blow job. Damned if this farewell bash wasn't going to hell in a handbasket.

Movement at the edge of his peripheral vision drew his attention, and he turned to see Kenji Takimoto and his bodyguards coming up the stairs. Odd. He'd figured Takimoto would be back in the Bay area by now. Apparently something had changed his mind. Maybe some insurance problem with the Rolls.

Alex approached the trio, his hand outstretched in welcome. "Mr. Takimoto, what a surprise. I'm pleased you decided to drop by after all."

Takimoto ignored his hand. "Do you take me for a fool?"

Alex's heart skipped a beat. Though Takimoto hadn't raised his voice, it was obvious he was pissed. "Is there a problem?"

Takimoto leaned closer. "You tried to cheat me."

"No, I didn't. What are you talking about?"

"Milagre."

He stared blankly at the man. "What about it?"

"I want it."

"You have it."

"No, Mr. Farrell. What I have is a fake. You tried to cheat me out of four million dollars."

"Do you think I'm crazy? I know who you are, what you are. Believe me, you're the last person I'd try to cheat."

Takimoto signaled one of his bodyguards with a jerk of his head. He snapped out an order, and the man produced the box containing the tourmaline. Takimoto flipped back the lid and grabbed the stone, pushing it at Alex. "Then explain this."

Alex studied the crystal, wondering what the hell had Takimoto frothing at the mouth. "What's the problem?"

"The problem is, you tried to cheat me."

"Hey, hold on a minute. I'm not the one who set up the deal. You came looking for me, remember? And I'm sorry if the rock didn't cure your lumbago or whatever, but if you'll think back real hard, you'll recall I never made any claims about its supposed healing powers."

"This tourmaline"—Takimoto made it sound like a swear word—"is not Milagre."

That's what this was about? Takimoto thought Alex had pulled a switch? Substituted an inferior stone? He studied the crystal, and the first doubts crept in. Not that he'd spent much time looking at Milagre, but he was familiar enough with its conformation to suspect Takimoto might be right. This stone was about the right size, but it didn't have the same depth of color. Only if this wasn't Milagre . . . His head buzzed with unanswered questions, the most important of which were who and why.

He caught a flash of red from the corner of his eye as Traci and her husband moved out onto the balcony. She paused on the threshold to smirk at him, as if she knew exactly how much trouble he was in right now, as if . . .

Damn. She'd played him. The bitch had played him, conned him into showing her the stone, even staged the little charade about being reluctant to touch it, then turned right around and pulled a switch. Which answered the who, if not the why.

"Trifling with me was a fatal error, Mr. Farrell." Takimoto's soft voice and flat black eyes frightened Alex far more than Casale's wiseguy bluster.

He set his empty glass on a nearby table and shoved his trembling hands into his pockets. "There's been a mistake."

Takimoto's eyes narrowed. "And you made it."

Alex took one cautious step backward.

Across the room, the elevator doors pinged, and Casale stepped out. He scanned the room, his gaze fixing on Alex. "Hey, sport!" Casale's mouth smiled, but his eyes told a different story. Alex's blood froze in his veins.

Casale plowed a swath toward him across the crowded room.

Oh, shit.

Casale's smile vanished. "I don't like wild goose chases."

"What do you mean?" Alex took another step backward. People were starting to notice. Maybe somebody would have the sense to call security before this got out of hand.

Casale seized his arm, squeezing damned near hard enough to snap the bone. "I'm talking about the money you owe me." He cinched down even harder, and Alex thought for a second he was going to piss himself.

"There's been some mistake."

"Two mistakes, apparently," Takimoto said.

Casale released Alex, and he staggered back a step before regaining his balance. The gambler grinned. "Splish-splash."

The balcony. Casale was going to toss him off the balcony . . . if Takimoto didn't beat him to it. Casale, Takimoto, and the two bodyguards barred his path to both the elevator and the stairs. No way out. If he made a break for it, he wouldn't get five feet. But if he did the unexpected . . .

He spun around and dodged out onto the balcony, upending a folding deck chair to jam the door shut. It wouldn't delay them long, but perhaps long enough.

Except for the Durrants, the balcony was empty.

Casale rattled the door handle. "Open this damn thing!"

Christ, he had to think. There must be some way out of this mess. Maybe he could grab Traci, threaten to toss her over the railing if Casale and Takimoto didn't back off.

But no, that wouldn't work. Neither man would balk at a little collateral damage.

"Your friend sounds royally pissed," Traci said. "Maybe I should move the chair."

"Stay where you are, damn it. I don't want to have to hurt you."

"Charles, did you hear? He just threatened me!"

The old man didn't even glance around. He slouched in his wheelchair, staring out at the ocean. Probably so doped up on pain pills that the life-and-death drama playing out behind him didn't register.

Inside, confusion reigned. The bodyguards were taking turns ramming themselves into the slider, but the double-paned glass was stronger than it looked.

"There's no escape, you bastard!" Casale smashed a brass lamp base against the glass, shattering it.

Escape. Of course. Alex raced to the far end of the balcony and slung a leg over the railing.

"What are you doing?" Traci asked.

He didn't answer, just swung his other leg over and balanced precariously on the edge of the balcony.

"Alex, *what* are you doing?"

"Taking a leap of faith," he said.

Casale, Takimoto, and the two bodyguards kicked at the remaining shards of glass. When Traci turned to watch the assault, he seized his chance.

He doubled over, got a firm grip on the bases of a couple of railing supports, and lowered himself over the edge. He'd intended to fake a scream to add realism, but there was nothing phony about the shriek he let out when his right arm—the one Casale had tried to snap in half—unexpectedly gave out on him. He dangled from the base of the upright by the fingertips of his left hand with only a couple hundred feet of cool night air separating him from the churning surf and deadly rocks below.

Scrabbling madly, he finally got a grip with his right

hand, any noise he might have made drowned out by the cacophony of screams and shouts that erupted above.

"Where'd the bastard go?" Casale's voice.

"Oh, my God!" Traci gasped. "He must have jumped!"

Alex's "suicide" had brought the party to an abrupt end. He'd managed to slot himself into the coffinlike, two-foot storage space between the balcony's support beams before anyone spotted him. He'd been there ever since, biding his time and hoping to hell he wasn't sharing his cramped hideout with any stray black widows.

Gradually, the excited babble died away as the tower emptied and the partygoers moved to the base of the cliff. A crack between boards gave Alex a bird's-eye view of the activity below—random searches at first, then more organized efforts once the sheriff's deputies arrived, equipped with searchlights, trained rescue dogs, and a boat. The deputies divided the volunteers into squads, then spent the next few hours scouring the rocks below.

Eventually they concluded that Alex's body must have been washed out to sea. Calling it a night, they strung crime scene tape, abandoning the rocks—and the search—until first light.

Alex gave it a full thirty minutes after the last of the voices had faded to silence before making his move. He shoved the hidden door open, tossed the loose end of the rope down the cliff, and began his descent. He'd lowered himself a half dozen yards when he heard a low laugh from the balcony above.

"You almost got away with it, Alex." A male voice. Familiar, but neither Casale's nor Takimoto's.

"Who are you? And what do you want?"

"You know who I am. Think. Rio, 1972."

Rio? The only time he'd been to . . . Oh, shit. "Cat?"

"So you do remember. That was a nice trick, that dive you took. You fooled them all. I taught you well."

"I don't understand. How can you be here? I thought you'd died in prison."

"God knows I came close a time or two. Thirty years of hell, confined to a wheelchair, locked away with the dregs of society. All that kept me alive were dreams of vengeance."

A muscle twitched in Alex's cheek, and he thanked God for the darkness that masked his fear. Masked Ian as well. All he could make out was an indistinct shape looming over the balcony railing.

"What are you doing here?" Alex was proud of the way his voice sounded, confident with a slight edge of irritation. No hint of the icy dread freezing the blood in his veins.

"That's no way to greet an old friend."

"How did you get past security at the main gate?" As soon as the words were out of his mouth, the truth hit him. "You're staying here, aren't you? You're a guest."

Ian laughed again, and the sound sent a chill down Alex's spine. "Charles Durrant, at your service."

The feeble old geezer in the wheelchair? It didn't seem possible. Alex tried to remember Durrant's face, but the only memory that surfaced was the image of pale hands lying limp as dead fish on a plaid lap robe. "Traci's your wife?"

"Her name's not Traci, and we're not married. Tasya's my new apprentice."

"*She* switched the stones."

"Yes."

"And she took the money, too, the money I owed Casale."

"Actually, someone else handled that part of the caper while I cleaned out the safe. We couldn't let Tasya have all the fun." He paused. "I thought Casale would take you out, but you outsmarted him, didn't you? Outsmarted Takimoto, too."

Alex's apprehension gave way to fury as he realized all Ian had stolen from him. He couldn't go back to his old life, not with Casale and Takimoto after him. And he couldn't start a new life in the south of France or anywhere else without money. "I'm going to get you for this, Cat, if it's the last thing I do."

Ian laughed again. "I don't think so. Not this time." He swung a leg over the railing and bent low. The paltry light of a new moon gleamed off something in his hand. The rope vibrated.

Full-blown panic sent Alex sliding down the rope faster than common sense allowed. Too fast. Out of control. Abrading his hands, rope-burning his knees even through his pant legs. He ignored the pain, his only concern reaching the bottom before Ian sawed through the nylon fibers.

He was almost halfway down when he felt a quiver and heard a snap. The rope went slack.

How could this be? He'd figured all the angles, planned for every eventuality. He should be on his way to Paris. "No!" he howled as he plunged untethered toward the jagged rocks below.

Though the drop took only seconds, it seemed longer, a petrifying slow-motion free fall, all flailing limbs and wide-eyed, gut-curdling terror, culminating in a split second of excruciating pain. And then nothing. Nothing at all.

12

THE VOICES WOKE TASYA a little after four. She got out
of bed and went into the living room.

Paulinho, wet and bedraggled, glanced up, a guilty expression on his face. "Did we wake you, *moça?*"

"What are you doing?"

"Celebrating a successful caper." Ian held up a bottle of
champagne. "Join us?"

"What happened? Did Alex finally make a break for it?"

Ian and Paulinho exchanged a look.

"I went along with the act to help convince the authorities, but I know Alex didn't kill himself. He hid in the
space between the beams, didn't he?"

Neither man answered. They didn't have to.

Ice pick in hand, Ian hollowed space in the wine cooler
for the bottle of A. Charbaut et Fils.

Paulinho refused to look her in the eye. She let her gaze
drift from his shuttered face to the rope at his feet. A rope
like the one she'd seen under Alex's balcony. His
makeshift fire escape.

She glanced quickly at Ian. A muscle twitched in his cheek. "He was scum, Tasya. If I hadn't stopped him, someone else would have. Takimoto. Casale. His wife."

"Stopped him? Murdered him, you mean."

"Murdered, exterminated, executed. What does it matter how the pig died as long as he is dead?" Paulinho's voice shook with the violence of his feelings. "He killed my father in cold blood."

"Harper suspects Alex was responsible for his father-in-law's death as well, that he either ran the man down himself or hired someone to do it," Ian said, his voice expressionless.

"You cut the rope."

Ian's mouth twisted. "Thirty years imprisoned in the worst pesthole in South America. Thirty years confined to that damn wheelchair. Thirty years when all that kept me alive were dreams of revenge. Yes, I cut the rope."

Tears spilled hot on her cheeks. She tried to speak but couldn't find any words.

Paulinho grabbed the rope, then turned to Ian. "Where is the piece he tied to the balcony?"

"On the kitchen table. You'll take care of it?"

Paulinho grunted assent. The door shut behind him, and a terrible silence filled the room.

Ian stabbed the ice. Once, twice. "Damn it, I did Alex a favor, and he repaid me with betrayal. He stole everything from me. My freedom. My mobility. My life. How can you cry for him?"

"I'm not," she said. "I'm crying for you."

"For me?"

She nodded.

A series of emotions played across his face: surprise, relief, confusion. "Oh, bloody hell." He dropped the ice pick and gathered her close, holding her until she'd sobbed herself dry.

It was going to be all right. Suddenly she was sure of it. Without the cancer of bitterness eating at his soul, Ian could live again, love again. She heaved a gusty sigh.

"Better?" He held her at arm's length.

She nodded.

His hands tightened for a moment before he released her.

Why did he do this? Why did he always back away? Was he still obsessed with the age difference? Or did she fall short of expectation in other ways?

Tasya forced a smile. "What's next? Do we pack our tents and steal off into the night?"

"I don't want to arouse suspicion. We'll check out in a day or two."

"And tonight?"

He didn't say anything for a moment, but then, just when she was beginning to wonder what she'd said or done wrong, he smiled. "Tonight we drink champagne to celebrate our new beginnings."

Beginnings. Plural. As in two people going their separate ways. "So this marks the end of our partnership."

He eased the cork from the bottle, filled two flutes, and handed her one. "It's the end of your apprenticeship, Tasya. The beginning of the rest of your life."

Without him. Oh, God, was he going to make her beg?

He glanced at her with the politely expectant look of a grown-up waiting for a child to explain her plans for the future. *And when I grow up, I want to be a doctor and a balle-rina and a mommy and the president of the United States.*

Damn him. Why couldn't he see past her face? Though young chronologically, in soul-searing experience, she was nearly as old as Ian himself. She was grateful to him for giving her a chance at a real life and for protecting her from Richard, but her feelings transcended simple grati-tude. He'd given her back her self-respect. And she loved him for that.

But she also loved him for himself, for the courage she saw in his fight to overcome his infirmities, for his cool head and analytical mind, for the way he furrowed his brow when he was thinking, for the way his eyes danced when he was pushing her buttons, the way they softened when she entered the room.

She loved his broad shoulders and his weathered face, his lean body and strong, capable hands. She loved his devilish winged eyebrows and saturnine good looks and the way he always smelled of soap and spray starch and cinnamon red hots. "I know our agreement was for a lim-ited engagement. What did you say all those months ago? One caper. One payback caper."

"A caper that's over," he said. "It's time to move on."

"What if I don't want to move on?"

He sipped his champagne, then gave her an indulgent smile. But his eyes looked so sad, so dull and lifeless, she knew his indifference was an act. As he opened his mouth to utter some stupid platitude like, "You're so young. You don't know what you want," she set her glass on an end table and invaded the protective space he'd put between them.

His eyes widened. His shoulders went rigid in a defensive posture. And it all clicked into place.

"You don't trust me," she said. "You think I'll betray you the way Alex betrayed you. The way life betrayed you. But I won't. I swear I won't."

He took a deep breath and exhaled slowly. "I know you mean what you say, but life isn't static. People change."

"I won't."

"When I'm in my eighties, you'll be in your forties."

"So?"

"What if I develop Alzheimer's or have a stroke?"

"What if I die in a car accident or get hit by lightning?"

"It's not the same."

"It's exactly the same. No one knows how long he or she has. Which is why it's important not to waste a second of precious time." She bracketed his face with her hands. "Tell me you don't love me, and I'll leave you alone."

"I don't . . . love you," he said from between clenched teeth.

"Yes, you do," she said, and kissed him. And kissed him. And kissed him some more, until finally, finally he kissed her back. Excitement sang along her nerves—Beethoven's Fifth, Handel's Hallelujah Chorus, and Queen's "Bohemian Rhapsody" all rolled into one. He tasted of champagne and hot, sweet urgency.

Ian pulled her roughly to him, one hand at her waist, the other higher, touching the bare skin above the deep U back of her tank top. Her breasts felt tight and swollen, her legs, boneless. She strained closer, aching for more. Aching for Ian.

After a time, he pulled away. "You lied. You promised if I said I didn't love you, you'd leave me alone."

"You lied first, so my lie doesn't count. You do love me, don't you?"

"Damn it, Tasya, it's impossible."

"You didn't answer my question." She paused, suddenly afraid to push the issue. "Do you love me?"

"Oh, bloody hell, woman, you know I do. I want you so much my guts tie themselves in knots every time I see you. But it won't work. I'm all used up. My joints ache in damp weather. My hair's going gray. I can't read without glasses."

She traced the lines scoring his forehead, the crinkled skin at the outer corners of his eyes. "I love your face. The lines describe your character. It's all there—your determination, your kindness, your intelligence, your humor." She laughed softly, smoothing the furrow between his brows. "Even your stubbornness."

"That isn't stubbornness; it's caution. I love you, Tasya. That's why I don't want you to do something you'll regret."

"The only thing I'll regret is not following my heart."

He closed his eyes for a second, then opened them again. His fierce black gaze scalded her. She grabbed his lapels to steady herself. "Yes," he said, his voice low and gravelly.

Yes. He'd said yes. Tasya raised up on tiptoes to press a kiss to his lips, then quickly, before he could change his mind, dragged him into his bedroom and locked the door. "Just in case," she said. "I wouldn't want to shock Paulinho."

Ian raised an eyebrow. "I doubt we could. He predicted this the day after you crawled through the dog door."

"Now I'm shocked."

"And just yesterday, he gave me these." Ian crossed to the nightstand and pulled a box of condoms from the top drawer.

"Shocked and appalled."

"You don't look shocked and appalled. You look"—his smile upped her pulse rate—"like a walking temptation."

She held his gaze as she crossed the room. Her emotions cartwheeled out of control, but it felt as if everything else were happening in slow motion. Ian set the box of condoms on the nightstand, an action that should have taken moments but seemed to last forever. Half a dozen packets bounced out, scattering like dice.

He shot her a wicked grin, then took her in his arms, and the instant he touched her, time caught up with itself. "You have the most beautiful eyes," he said. "Like polished pewter." But it wasn't her eyes he was touching. It was her cheek, her neck. Her shoulders, her lips. She pressed a kiss to his fingertips and watched his eyes darken.

Ian. Ian touching her. She'd dreamed of this, but her dreams paled in the face of reality. Dear God, Ian *touching* her. She focused on the nerve endings tingling to life at the brush of his fingertips. Ian touching her.

"I . . ." she started, then lost her train of thought when he slid his hands beneath her tank top to cover her breasts. She moaned. "I . . ."

Ian eased her onto the bed, his hands gentle, the look in his eyes anything but.

". . . love you," she said.

And he kissed her. Deep, dark, dangerous kisses that tasted of champagne and cinnamon.

She kissed him back with an urgency that verged on desperation. "Please."

He peeled her tank top over her head, baring her breasts. "Beautiful," he said, his breath warm on her nipple. He took it in his mouth, sucking, pulling, and stroking with his tongue.

She knew she was making too much noise—cries of delight, moans of desperation—but she couldn't help it. She'd relinquished control the instant his tongue began its first lazy circle around her nipple.

Desperate to feel his skin under her hands, to torture him the way he was torturing her, she loosened his tie and pulled his jacket off. But the studs on his shirt front defeated her. She fumbled, her clumsiness increasing exponentially with her need. "Can't," she said, the word a sob of frustration.

Ian lifted his head, smiled at her, then grabbed his shirt and ripped it open. The studs popped loose, pattering like hail as they bounced off the wall, the nightstand, the floor.

He shrugged out of the shirt. Light gleamed off the bunched muscles of his arms, the sculpted lines of his torso. He wasn't old. He was . . . "Magnificent," she said, and touched him. Silken steel. A contrast in texture. A soft layer of skin over the denser, harder muscle, bone, and sinew. She dug her fingers into his shoulders, wanting him, wanting him.

He slid his hands beneath the elastic waist of her pink satin boxers and stripped her naked.

"You, too," she said.

"Me, too." He stood up, undressed quickly, then sat on

the edge of the bed, his back to her as he tore open a foil packet.

Tasya wrapped her arms around his chest, rubbing her aching breasts against his back, biting at his shoulder. She. Tasya. Touching Ian. Tasting Ian. Wanting Ian.

He angled his head to smile at her over his shoulder, and she kissed him hard. No finesse, just right to the point. *I want you. I want you now.*

He rolled over, pulling her down on top of him. And then he was there, right there, inside her, hard and warm. Filling her. Fulfilling her. Tasya thought her heart would burst, it was hammering so loudly.

So loudly she didn't realize someone had kicked open the door, not until that same someone grabbed her by the hair and dragged her off Ian. She screamed and lashed out with her fists.

Shouting obscenities, her assailant slapped her hard across the face. She fell back, scrambling for the sheet, and got her first good look at him. It was the groundskeeper she'd caught staring the day Alex walked her back to the cottage. His insolent scrutiny had bothered her then. Now it made her skin crawl.

"Who are you?" Ian demanded. Tasya felt him tense, as if he were preparing to pounce on the man.

"I'm the one with the gun, Grandpa." Laughing, the intruder pulled a pistol from his belt and leveled it at Tasya's head.

She knew that laugh, that voice. The man had a stranger's face, but he wasn't a stranger. The attitude, the threats, the blunt-fingered hands, awakened memories of another time, another place. "Richard?" she whispered.

"Richard's dead," Ian said. "He blew himself up."

"I know, but . . ." This man didn't look like Richard, not even the post-plastic-surgery version in the photos Harper had sent. Richard had been pale, blue-eyed, clean-shaven. This man was swarthy, with brown eyes and a mustache.

Ian gave her arm a warning squeeze. "Careful," he whispered. "He's high on something. Look at his eyes."

Aside from caffeine, Richard didn't do drugs, but this man's eyes did look odd. "Contacts," she said suddenly. "Contacts, a fake mustache, and tanning spray."

"Bright girl." He smirked, and she knew for certain. This was Richard. This was nightmare made flesh.

Ian's grip tightened as he realized the true extent of the danger.

Richard scowled. "Get your paws off the merchandise, Grandpa. She's mine."

He reached for her, but she batted his hand away.

His nostrils flared. "Stupid move, Tasya. I was planning to slit your throat once I'd pulverized your face the way you did mine, but now I'm thinking I might prolong the pleasure. . . ."

Tasya tuned out the gruesome details. Instead she watched the spittle gathering at the corners of Richard's mouth, the angry spots of color riding his cheekbones. He'd been certifiable before. He was completely over the edge now.

Behind her Ian stirred, preparing himself, she suspected, to lunge at Richard if the opportunity presented itself. Time was on their side. The longer Richard's rant continued, the greater the chance he'd relax his vigilance for an instant. All they needed was the narrowest window of opportunity. . . .

Suddenly Richard ran out of venom. A deadly silence gripped the room. His gaze crawled over her body, up and down, back and forth. She shuddered.

Smiling, he took a step nearer.

"How did you find me?" She blurted the words, not because she cared, but because she knew she had to keep him talking. Her survival—hers and Ian's—depended on it.

Richard smirked. "Technology rules. Ever heard of Carnivore? No? It's a sophisticated software program the government uses to trace terrorists' e-mails. I obtained a bootleg copy, used your name as a keyword, and hit pay dirt—all those e-mails between Grandpa here and that firm of private investigators. Did you know he'd hired them to research you as well as Farrell?"

"But you blew yourself up. I saw it."

"Smoke and mirrors," he said. "I figured the best way to become invisible was to become dead. A televised suicide. Clever, huh?"

"They found a body with your face," she said.

"Not my face," he snapped. "You destroyed my face. All that's left is this bland reconstruction. Now I look like everybody else."

"Who really died in the explosion?"

"Another generic-brand average Joe." He laughed. "Found him in a shelter in Oakland. Kept him supplied with Jack Daniel's, and he did whatever I asked. The resemblance was close enough to fool Grandpa's investigator—especially after the explosion did its damage."

"You blew up an innocent man," Tasya said. "That's disgusting."

"The poor bastard had already fried his brain. Think of his death as a mercy killing." His expression hardened. "And now it's your turn."

"You'll never get away with this," Ian said.

Richard dismissed him with a contemptuous curl of his lip. "Shut up, old man."

Paulinho, she remembered. Paulinho should return any minute now. When he did, she and Ian could take advantage of the distraction. . . .

She must have glanced toward the door, because Richard's eyes narrowed. Then he laughed. "If you're waiting for the giant to come save you, forget it. I took care of him already."

Took care of him? A chill ran down her spine. "If you hurt him—"

"If I hurt him, what? I don't think you're in any position to make threats." His mouth twisted in a sneer. "Sweet Jesus, don't tell me you've been doing the giant, too."

"You're a sick bastard," Ian said.

Richard shook his head. "I just know her better than you do. The little slut used to fuck her uncle. Bet she never told you that." He shifted his gaze back to Tasya. "How much does the old man pay you?"

"Go to hell." Ian enunciated each word.

"Someday." Richard bared his teeth. "But first things first. This is how it's going to work. Tasya, you're going to help the cripple into his wheelchair, then duct tape him down so he can watch while I finish what he started."

Dear God, Richard didn't know Ian could walk.

"Cooperate, and I promise to kill you within a week. Fight me, and I'll make sure you last for months."

"You bloody psychopath!" Goaded beyond endurance, Ian lunged for the gun. He was fast, but not fast enough. Richard shot twice at point-blank range.

Ian crumpled in slow motion. Or maybe it was the adrenaline flooding her veins that once again slowed time to a crawl. "No!" she screamed, her voice echoing in her ears. *No, no, no, no.* Over and over in an endless litany of despair.

Richard was still gloating when she dashed past him. She raced into the living room and grabbed the ice pick Ian had left beside the wine cooler.

She ran back to the bedroom, catching Richard off guard. He hadn't expected her to go on the offensive. He brought his gun up, but too late. Before he could aim and fire, she buried the ice pick in his heart.

His eyes widened. His mouth fell open. The gun slipped from his fingers, and then he too crumpled in slow motion.

Ian tried to sit up, but the movement made him cough. Out of habit, he covered his mouth, and his hand came away red.

Both shots had hit him square in the chest; he'd felt the impacts. No pain, though, which was odd. Perhaps shock had temporarily delayed the normal pain reflex.

Tasya? he thought suddenly. Had Zane shot her, too? He rolled to his side and precipitated another coughing spasm. He spat blood, staining the carpet. "Tasya?" He couldn't seem to get enough air to produce any volume. "Tasya, where are you?" Oh, bloody hell, he didn't want to die here. Alone. Not knowing what had happened to her. "Tasya?"

And then she was there, cradling his head in her lap.

"Blood," he said. "You'll get it all over you."

She smoothed his hair, his beard. "It's okay. Don't talk. I called 911. The ambulance will be here soon."

"Richard?"

"Dead," she said in a voice stripped of emotion. "For real, this time. I stabbed him with the ice pick."

"Get it," he said.

"Why?"

"Don't ask questions. Just get it." He shut his eyes, garnering strength. Talking was an effort.

Tasya laid his head down gently and scrambled to her feet, returning in seconds with the wood-handled pick. Its metal point was sticky with gore.

He took it from her, wiped it on his discarded shirt, then deliberately grasped the handle in his own right hand, leaving bloody fingerprints as evidence. "*I* killed Richard," he said. "If anyone asks, I killed him. Self-defense. He broke in, planning to rob us as we slept. When he found us up, he panicked and shot me. I grabbed the ice pick and stabbed him before he could shoot you." He closed his eyes again, panting for breath.

"Don't talk." Tears slipped unheeded down her cheeks. "Save your strength."

"No," he said. "No time. I'm dying."

"You can't die. I need you."

He dropped the ice pick and reached up to wipe the

tears from her face. His gesture only made her cry harder. "Listen, Tasya. The money in my numbered account. It's yours now."

"I don't want the money. I want you."

"You can start a new life, be anything you want to be. Money is freedom."

"I don't care about freedom. I care about you!" Her face contorted. "The paramedics—"

"Couldn't save me even if they were here now." He tried to focus on her face, but his vision blurred. Time was running out.

"Don't die, Ian. Please. I can't live without you."

"You can," he said fiercely, "and you will." He groped for her hand, unable to see her anymore. "Listen carefully. To access the money, you'll need my number." He repeated it for her. "Copy it down so you don't forget."

"I won't forget. Ian? Look at me, Ian."

He wanted to but couldn't. His eyes were open, but all he saw was darkness. He knew her hand lay in his, but he could no longer feel it. "I love you," he said, his voice thick.

"And I love you," she whispered. Or maybe she hadn't whispered at all. Maybe his ears were shutting down on him, too.

He felt cold now, almost detached from his body's struggle to drag air into lungs rapidly filling with fluid. *So this is how it feels to bleed to death. This is how it feels to drown from the inside out.* He tried to speak, but his mouth wouldn't form the words.

"Don't die, Ian. Please." Tasya's tears fell warm on his face. Then suddenly she stiffened. "Oh, my God, Milagre! Ian, tell me where you hid Milagre!"

* * *

Paulinho came to, disoriented for a moment. What was he doing lying in the shrubbery, his head throbbing like the drumbeat of the *ogãs* in a Macumba ceremony? He wasn't hung over, was he?

And then he remembered. He had been on his way back to the cottage after burying Alex's rope in a flower bed when a groundskeeper had attacked him. The man had cracked him over the head, then apparently rolled him into the bushes, though his memory was unclear on that part.

He touched his head, wincing at the pain.

Pondering possible motives for the attack—a case of mistaken identity seemed most likely—he shoved himself upright, then staggered back to the cottage.

Inside he heard weeping. Was Tasya having another nightmare? He hurried toward the sound, but it was not coming from Tasya's room. It was coming from Ian's. Paulinho stopped dead on the threshold, shocked immobile by the carnage inside.

A groundskeeper, the same man who had attacked him earlier, lay near the door, his eyes open, a look of surprise on his face. A small red circle bloomed like a flower in the center of his chest. A pistol rested next to his right hand.

Less than a meter away lay Ian, two gory holes in his chest. Tasya knelt on the blood-soaked carpet, streaks of gore on her face, her hands, her arms, her breasts. She held Milagre by its chain. The stone itself rested on Ian's chest.

"*Meu Deus*, what happened?"

Tasya stared at him as if he were a ghost. Her mouth opened, but no words emerged.

"Tasya, what happened here?"

She swallowed and tried again. "Richard said . . . I thought he'd killed you."

"Richard? But he is dead."

She nodded toward the uniformed corpse. "Now he is." Then she turned to him again, blinking as if she were having trouble focusing. "You're injured. There's blood on your head."

"This man—this man you say is Richard—hit me with a shovel."

"He shot Ian. I couldn't stop the bleeding." Her voice edged toward hysteria. "I pressed my hands to the wounds, but the blood kept welling up. It wouldn't stop." Her voice broke. "And I didn't know where he'd hidden Milagre."

"In the box with my *opele*," he said.

She did not seem to hear him. "By the time I finally found it, Ian had quit breathing." She shut her eyes. "It's my fault. Milagre could have saved him if only I'd acted more quickly. . . ."

PART TWO

Regret

Deep as first love, and wild with all regret.
Oh death in life, the days that are no more!

—ALFRED, LORD TENNYSON,
"THE PRINCESS"

13

A BLACK STONE MARKED Ian's final resting place in Buena Vista Memorial Park, a small San Mateo County cemetery within walking distance of the house. Buena Vista. Good view. Except on days like this one when the fog rolled in off the water.

Tasya placed a bouquet of red carnations on the newly laid sod, just as she had every day for the last three weeks. Carnations for reincarnation. A custom she'd first heard about from the woman who ran the flower shop. A custom Paulinho said the florist had invented.

The mist tangled itself in the cypresses that edged the cemetery. She knelt on the wet grass, staring into the swirling mist, searching for a sign.

She felt so alone, isolated in a vaporous wasteland. *I miss you, Ian. If you can find a way, come back.*

The sheriff's deputies responding to her 911 call had accepted Ian's revised version of the truth. Tasya didn't know if they suspected a connection between the two dead men on the cottage floor and Alex's so-called suicide.

She'd been too numb at the time to pick up on nuances. All she knew was, no one had tried to stop her or Paulinho when they finally left the spa.

"Tasya." Her name echoed eerily across the graveyard. Gooseflesh raised along her arms. *Ian?*

"Tasya? Where are you?"

Not Ian. Of course, not Ian.

A dark figure loomed up out of the fog, and even though she knew who it was, her heart gave a sickening jolt. "You frightened me, Paulinho."

"You frighten me, *moça*. You do not eat. You do not sleep. You spend too much time crying, too much time haunting this place." He scowled. "Senhor Ian would not approve."

"I feel closer to him here."

"It is time to come home, *moça*." Paulinho glanced around uneasily. "It will be dark soon. I brought the car. Senhor Ian would not like you walking home in this weather."

"In a minute," she said.

"Very well." He frowned. "I shall wait in the parking lot."

She watched him disappear into the mist, then turned back to Ian's grave. She'd promised herself she wasn't going to cry, but tears blurred her vision. She dug her fingers into the grass. "I moved into your room. I couldn't stand sleeping anywhere Richard had . . . been." And besides, Ian's room offered comforting reminders—his books, his clothes, his wheelchair, his stash of cinnamon red hots.

She sighed. What was wrong with her? In the unlikely event Ian could hear what she said, did she really want to bore him with household trivia? No, but what else did she have to say?

I love you?

He knew that.

I miss you?

He knew that, too.

I'm sorry?

Yes. Regret colored her every thought. If only . . . The two saddest words in the English language.

She stared at his headstone. "You saved me." Her voice broke. Tears rolled down her cheeks. "If only I could have saved you."

Paulinho had served Tasya her favorite teriyaki chicken and stir-fried vegetables for dinner, but she had scarcely touched the food. She did not eat, she did not sleep, she did not even speak unless spoken to. Ian would not want Tasya to torture herself this way. Paulinho knew this, but he did not know how to ease her grief. He only knew that he must try.

After tidying the kitchen, he went looking for Tasya and found her in the study, staring at a photograph of Ian. He cleared his throat to get her attention, and when she swiveled to face him, he saw again the pain in her eyes. "We must talk," he said.

She shook her head. "Not now."

"It is important, *moça*."

"Can't it wait? I'm tired." She stared straight ahead, not making eye contact.

"I have delayed too long already. I need to go home," he said. "Home to Rio."

"Why, Paulinho? Returning to Brazil can only stir up

bad memories. Ian told me about the miseries you two endured in prison."

Had Ian told her of Paulinho's attempt to kill him? Had Ian described their desperate battle for control of a homemade knife? Had Ian explained how he had held its razorsharp edge to Paulinho's throat for the endless minutes it had taken him to convince Paulinho he was not the man who had killed Paulinho's father?

Probably not. There had been so many other miseries to recount.

The inmates at Castelo Sombrio had been afraid of Ian—partly because he was foreign, partly because he was white, partly because he was crippled, but mostly because of his face. *Diabo*, they had called him. Devil.

Ian had used that fear along with his quick reflexes and considerable upper-body strength to protect himself and those he called friend. A month after Paulinho's abortive attempt to slit his throat as he slept, Ian had helped fight off two prison bullies who were trying to kill Paulinho.

"Castelo Sombrio is not Rio," Paulinho said. "Rio is long white beaches. It is samba and pretty girls in bikinis. It is Carnaval and *futebol*. It is my home . . . and, more importantly, the home of Milagre. I must return the stone."

"But, Paulinho, you're the only friend I have left. I don't think I can bear losing you, too." Her throat moved convulsively.

"You misunderstand, *moça*. I think we both should go to Brazil. We must return Milagre to Dona Elizabete. She can protect the stone better than we can."

She gazed at him in surprise. "You know the owner?"

"*Sim*. From the time I was a child."

Surprise turned to speculation. "Ian knew this?"

"*Naturalmente*."

"Milagre's the reason you agreed to help him."

Paulinho scowled. "Alex Farrell killed my father. Revenge motivated me. Milagre is important. I am not disputing this. But when I agreed to help Senhor Ian, I did not know for certain that Alex Farrell still had the stone."

"When you heard the rumors about miracle cures at the spa, you must have suspected."

"I hoped." He smiled. "And thanks to you, *moça*, we now have the tourmaline in our possession. It is only right that we return it to Dona Elizabete. Do you not agree?"

"Fine. Return it. You don't need my help."

This was true, but she needed his. If he were to leave her alone, he was not sure what she might do. With no one to cook for her, she might quit eating altogether. With no one to wake her, she might stay in bed forever. With no one to anchor her to this world, she might decide to join Ian in the next. None of which he could say out loud, of course.

"The trip will do you good. They call Rio de Janeiro *a cidade maravilhosa*, the marvelous city. She is beautiful, my Rio. She will steal your heart."

Tasya's eyes turned an opaque, smoky charcoal. "I have no heart. It died with him."

Nossa Senhora, how was he to get through to her? "You are young," he said. "Ian would not wish you to waste your life mourning him."

"I don't want to argue, Paulinho. I'm too tired for this."

"*Exatamente*. You need a rest, a change of scenery."

"I need a good night's sleep," she said.

"The doctor gave you pills, *sim*?"

"They don't work." She refused to meet his gaze, and a nasty suspicion slithered through his brain. Was she hoarding the pills, planning to use them all at once?

"Tasya?"

"Yes?" Still she did not make eye contact.

"I do not like what you are thinking."

"You don't know what I'm thinking."

He paused. "Ian would want you to come with me. I know this is so. What would it take to convince you?"

"A sign," she said.

A sign? "*Muito bem.* Very well. I will paint such a sign."

A weary smile lightened her expression for a second. "Not that sort of sign. An omen. A message." Her eyes filled with tears. "But that's not going to happen. Ian's gone. I can't find him anywhere. Not in the cemetery. Not here in the study. Not even in his room. I stare at his pictures, sit at his desk, lie in his bed, praying for some hint of his presence—a whisper, a touch—but there's nothing. Nothing." The tears spilled down her cheeks.

Paulinho pulled her from the chair and into his arms, holding her close as her tears soaked his shirt. "Oh, *moça*. What would Ian say if he knew what you were doing to yourself?"

At length Tasya regained her composure, stepping back out of his arms. "What would Ian say?" She sighed. "Quote one of his rules no doubt. Number Thirty-two, maybe. 'If the goal appears beyond your grasp, examine it from a new perspective.'" A strange expression crossed her face. "Oh, my God," she whispered.

"You asked for a sign, *moça*, and I think Ian just gave you one."

September 2004
Rio de Janeiro, Brazil

A cidade maravilhosa, Paulinho had called Rio. The marvelous city. Perhaps he was right; Tasya couldn't say for sure. She hadn't really been paying attention as the taxi drove them from the airport to their hotel on Copacabana Beach. She retained a vague impression of heavy traffic, white buildings with red tile roofs, and a hazy sun, glimpsed through a gauzy layer of low clouds.

Though these days everything seemed a little vague, a little gray, a little out of focus. And even more so after twenty-four hours of airplanes and airports. They'd left San Francisco at night. It was mid-morning here in Rio. She wasn't sure what day. So many miles. So many time zones.

Still, she felt more at peace now than she had in weeks. Somewhere over the Andes with the cabin lights turned low and Paulinho snoring gently in the seat next to hers, she'd decided. Once they'd returned Milagre to Elizabete Ribeiro Sodré, she'd lock herself in her hotel room and swallow all her carefully hoarded sleeping pills—leaving a note, of course, to exonerate Paulinho from any blame.

"Are you all right, *moça?*" His voice jerked her back to the present. Concern etched his features. Could he somehow know what she was planning?

"I'm just tired."

"Jet lag." He pushed the heavy draperies aside to peer out the window of her hotel room. "You are lucky. Your room faces the ocean. Mine"—he flapped a hand, indicating the room across the hall—"overlooks the city."

"I'll trade you." She didn't care about the scenery.

He looked appalled at the thought. "Never would I take advantage of your exhaustion. Sleep now. Later you will—how you say?—appreciate your view of the beach." He beckoned. "Come look."

She forced herself across the room.

Paulinho drew her close to the window. "See?"

"What? The water?" Gray-green under an overcast sky, the Atlantic slapped irritably against a nearly deserted beach where a group of teenage boys played volleyball and a scattering of middle-aged tourists slathered on sunblock despite there being no sun to block.

"*Não*, the sidewalk. Do you see?"

A wide black-and-white mosaic promenade curved along the ocean as far as the eye could see, dividing the traffic on the Avenida Atlântica from the beach itself.

Paulinho's hands traced curlicues in the air, mimicking the swirling design of the mosaic. Showing his gold tooth in a broad smile, he spoke fervently in his native tongue. "The undulating ocean, the rolling hills, the rise and fall of the samba beat, the generous curves of Rio's many, many beautiful women—all this is captured in the sinuous patterns of the promenade."

"It's nice," she said in English.

"Nice?" His nostrils flared. "Rio de Janeiro is many things: seductive, glamorous, exotic, cosmopolitan, chic—even dangerous. But never, never is she 'nice.'"

"Sorry." She hadn't meant to offend him. "I'm tired. I hardly know what I'm saying."

Affront faded from his expression. Remorse took its place. "*Não*, I am the one who is sorry for badgering you. I will leave you alone now so you can rest."

Paulinho left, but Tasya didn't lie down immediately.

First she dug the sleeping pills from her suitcase. She'd refilled her prescription twice, the maximum allowed. Twenty-four pills. She hoped it would be enough. How terrible to drift off thinking, *This is it,* only to wake with a headache and the sick knowledge that she'd not only failed but wasted her best opportunity.

What she needed was a backup plan. Like a bottle of brandy. Didn't the label on her pills warn not to mix them with alcohol?

Despite the long flight, Paulinho was too excited to feel tired. In Rio, modern skyscrapers bumped elbows with old colonial buildings. Hillside *favela* shacks sprang up within a few miles of elegant five-star hotels. Gloria Church lit the night sky every August 15 to celebrate the glory of God while candles flickered at crossroads, marking furtive Quimbanda ceremonies. Poverty and wealth, scholars and fools, drug dealers and do-gooders—all found a home in the *cidade maravilhosa,* city of contrasts. In Paulinho's opinion, though, Rio's flaws only served to highlight her perfections.

A wave of *saudade* swept over him. *Saudade,* that bittersweet Brazilian emotion that translated so imperfectly to English as homesickness. His *saudade* was more, a yearning, a piercing nostalgia for all he had left behind: his city, his family, his friends, his wife.

Former wife, he reminded himself. Angela had cheated on him, betrayed him, testified against him.

So why did he feel this almost overwhelming compulsion to see her again?

Because she had not been entirely to blame. He was the one who had invoked the curse, a curse meant for his father's killer. "Death to the man who has wronged you," the Quimbanda priestess had promised him. And the very next day, he had discovered his wife in bed with a stranger.

He had lost his temper, yes. He had hit the man, yes. But only black magic could have converted a single punch to a fatal blow. The man had staggered back, tripped over a pile of discarded clothing, and fractured his skull on the windowsill. He had died within minutes, and Paulinho had gone to prison for murder. His friends blamed Angela's lies—she swore he had deliberately slammed the man's head against the windowsill—but Paulinho knew his was the greater guilt. He had called disaster down upon himself by invoking the powers of darkness.

He showered quickly, shaved, and dressed in jeans and a loose sport shirt, all the while telling himself, I am going to visit Dona Elizabete. But the address he gave the taxi driver was for a shabby stucco dwelling in the north zone of the city.

A low stone wall enclosed a small paved courtyard. The planting bed that had once held pink and red hibiscus had been overtaken by an aggressive jungle vine. Its tendrils twined around the pillars supporting the porch roof, threatening to encroach upon the house itself.

"Wait here," he told the driver. "I will not be long."

Dust, dead leaves, and desiccated insects littered the tiled porch. The shutters had not been painted in so long, half the paint had chipped away. What remained was an anemic, sun-bleached blue instead of the rich aquamarine he remembered.

The house looked deserted, but he stood on the sidewalk, clapping his hands sharply to announce his presence. He had not lived in the United States for so long that he had forgotten that Brazilian custom.

No one appeared.

He clapped again, shouting Angela's name.

And again nothing happened.

Why are you so surprised? It had been almost six years, after all. Perhaps she had moved.

He was just about to get back into the taxi when the old man who had been sweeping the steps of the house next door hailed him. "You looking for that Angela?" The man's coffee-black skin, creased by a thousand wrinkles, contrasted sharply with the thin white fuzz on his scalp.

"Yes," Paulinho called back. "Angela Mesquita Vieira." Or had she dropped the Vieira?

"She doesn't live there anymore."

Paulinho frowned. "Where did she go?"

The old man leaned his broom against the porch railing and shuffled over to the stone wall abutting the sidewalk. He pulled a crumpled pack of cigarettes from his trousers pocket, stuck the filter end between his puckered lips, struck a match, and lit up.

Aware of the taxi's meter ticking up reais, Paulinho wished he could hurry the old man's pace but knew any such effort would likely have an opposite effect. He held his tongue and waited.

"She was a wild one, that Angela," the old man said. "Every night a different man. Up until two years ago. During Carnival, it was. Suddenly the stream of men stopped." He gave a cackle of laughter. "And the stink started. After two days it smelled so bad, we called the police."

"She was dead?"

"Oh, yes. With her head smashed in and maggots where her face had been. I did not see this myself," he hastened to add, "but I heard the policemen talking."

"Did they catch the murderer?"

The old man sucked his lungs full of smoke, held it a second, then blew it out his nostrils. He shook his head. "They thought it might have been the ex-husband, but as it turned out, he was in prison."

"Who owns the house now?"

The old man shrugged. "A Paulista." He scowled, as if he did not have much use for anyone from São Paulo. "Or so I heard. People rent the house from time to time, but no one stays long." The old man took another deep drag, exhaling with a sigh. "They say the house is haunted, but me, I do not believe in ghosts."

"I do not believe in ghosts," Tasya whispered to herself, but the face looking back at her from the mirror above the sink in the hotel bathroom told a different story. Those haunted eyes believed. Those trembling lips believed.

He had come to her in a dream. Ian.

They'd made love, hot, fierce, frantic love, and then again, taking it slower the second time, lingering over each kiss, each caress. She had awakened to harsh reality still naked, flushed, and satiated, every detail of the dream as vivid as a memory.

"He's dead," she said aloud, but her body refused to accept the truth.

He touched me. I felt him. His mouth on my mouth, my breasts, my . . .

She touched herself. She was damp, still swollen. Her body gave a residual tingle, a faint reminder of the shuddering climax of her dream. Could it be? Was it possible?

She started guiltily at a knock on the hall door. "Yes?"

"It is I. Paulinho."

"Just a minute." She shrugged into an oversized terry cloth robe, cinching the belt as she made her way to the door. She removed the chain and let him in.

Paulinho registered surprise. "You are not ready."

"For what?"

"Dinner. I told you earlier. We have been invited to Dona Elizabete's house. The driver is picking us up in half an hour."

"What time is it?"

He glanced at his watch. "Four-thirty."

"What's the rush then? Surely we won't eat before seven."

"Dona Elizabete thought you might enjoy a tour of the city first."

A tour. Well, why not? "How considerate."

Paulinho beamed. "I knew you would be pleased." He examined her closely. "You must have rested well, *moça*. You look better."

She felt better. Warmth flooded her cheeks as she remembered the intimate details of her dream. Afraid Paulinho would notice, she grabbed some clothes and ducked into the bathroom. "What have you been doing?" she called. "Did you catch up on your rest?"

"No, I visited my old neighborhood."

She poked her head out of the bathroom, alerted by an odd note in his voice. "Which old neighborhood? The one where you grew up? Or the one where you and your wife lived?"

Paulinho's swarthy skin made it hard to tell when he was blushing, but the beads of sweat on his forehead gave him away.

"You went to see your ex-wife," she said. "Why? Are you crazy? Or just a glutton for punishment?"

"She was not there," he said. "She is dead."

"And if she hadn't been? What then?"

He shrugged. "I do not know, *moça*. I loved her once." He shrugged again. "I loved her once."

They took the elevator down to the lobby, where Paulinho collected Milagre from the hotel safe. He handed her the box. After tucking it into her purse for safekeeping, she followed him to a lounge area near the entrance. Heads turned as they passed.

Tasya knew she and Paulinho made a striking couple, he with his shaved head and liquid brown eyes, she with her gymnast's body and blond-streaked hair. A stranger might assume they were lovers, but Tasya knew Paulinho's feelings for her were those of a brother. A bossy, interfering, but well-meaning older brother.

They took seats facing one another on a pair of red velvet armchairs. "What is she like, this Dona Elizabete?"

"You will like her. Everyone does."

A woman in a navy blue chauffeur's uniform pushed through the front door and approached the reception desk.

Tasya tapped Paulinho's knee to get his attention. "Is that our driver?"

Paulinho turned to look. *"Meu Deus,"* he said in a tone of voice that made it clear he wasn't praying.

"What's wrong?"

"That woman. The chauffeur. I know her."

"Not an old friend, I take it."

"Não." Paulinho swore under his breath, mostly gutter language Tasya didn't understand.

"What is your problem?"

"She—" Words seemed to fail him momentarily. "She is my problem. Vania Marcia Freire da Rocha." He scowled at Senhorita da Rocha's back. "She made my childhood a misery. Teasing me, following me. That one is a devil disguised as a female."

The desk clerk pointed them out. The she-devil chauffeur and Paulinho made eye contact with a nearly audible click.

Tasya found herself quite looking forward to the ride to Laranjeiras.

14

"SENHORITA FLYNN? Senhor Vieira?" Even in a tailored uniform and sensible black oxfords, even with her wavy auburn hair confined in a knot at the nape of her neck, even with her face frozen in a polite mask, Vania Marcia Freire da Rocha was a beautiful woman. Not at all Tasya's image of a she-devil.

Senhorita da Rocha had well-defined cheekbones, wide-set gray-green eyes, a generous, full-lipped mouth, and dimples. Her skin, a warm mocha color halfway between Tasya's pale honey and Paulinho's rich mahogany, was spiced with a sprinkling of cinnamon freckles.

"*Sim.*" Tasya stood. Paulinho did, too, though he didn't say anything. He hadn't looked at Senhorita da Rocha since that first blistering moment of eye contact.

"I am Vania, your driver. If you would follow me, please?" she said in Portuguese, then turned without another word, leading the way toward the double doors of the main entrance.

Say something, Tasya mimed behind Vania's back.

Paulinho pinched his lips together and flared his nostrils. Body language for *Mind your own business*.

A venerable English Bentley, as immaculate as it was ancient, sat parked on the cobbled apron beyond the hotel's porte cochere. Vania held the door for Tasya.

"It was very kind of Dona Elizabete to send you to pick us up," Tasya said in Portuguese. She stepped into the cavernous backseat, and Vania shut the door.

"Dona Elizabete is a kind woman."

"Unlike others I could name," Paulinho said in English. He folded himself into the backseat next to Tasya.

Judging by the tightening of Vania's lips, Tasya suspected she'd understood every word. "I'm Tasya," she said in English, "and I believe you already know Paulinho."

"We knew each other slightly as children, yes."

Paulinho muttered something under his breath. Tasya caught the phrase "short memory." Or maybe "she-devil."

Vania pulled into traffic, then glanced at Paulinho in the rearview mirror, one fine eyebrow raised. "Did you say something, Senhor Vieira?"

His upper lip curled. "Slightly? You say we knew each other slightly? You, Vania Marcia Freire da Rocha, were the bane of my existence."

She shrugged. "I don't know why you say that."

Paulinho snorted.

"All right, I may have played a few childish pranks."

"Pranks?" He turned to Tasya. "She used to let the air out of my bicycle tires."

"Self-preservation," she said. "I couldn't keep up with you unless you were on foot."

"Why was it so important to keep up with me?"

"Because you were my hero."

"Oh," Paulinho said. He looked and sounded like someone who'd been punched in the solar plexus.

"And just for the record, it's not Vania Marcia Freire da Rocha anymore. It's Vania Marcia Freire da Rocha Bousquet."

"Oh," he said again in that same wind-knocked-out-of-him voice. "You're married."

"I'm thirty-five," she said. "What do you expect?"

Little Vania da Rocha married. It did not seem possible. Paulinho studied her reflection in the rearview mirror. A faint frown furrowed her forehead but did nothing to detract from her beauty. The Vania he remembered was a skinny schoolgirl with frizzy hair and an acid tongue. The tongue had not changed, but everything else had. Vania was a lovely woman. A lovely *married* woman, he reminded himself. A lovely married woman who apparently had outgrown her youthful crush.

Since starting the city tour, she had not once made eye contact nor addressed a single comment to him directly. It was "Senhorita, notice to your right Sugar Loaf Mountain, one of the city's most recognizable landmarks," and "On your left, senhorita, is the Municipal Theater, a copy of the Paris Opera House." Never "Paulinho, do you remember how Dona Elizabete used to scold us for hanging out the windows of the trolley up Santa Teresa Hill?"

"We go now, senhorita," Vania said, "to the top of Corcovado to see the famous statue, Christ the Redeemer. Designed by Heitor da Silva Costa . . ."

Paulinho tuned out the rest of Vania's lecture, pleased

that Tasya seemed to be enjoying the long, circuitous drive up the mountain.

Vania parked in the lot near the top, and Tasya jumped out of the car, her face alight. "What a beautiful spot!"

"To get the best view, we need to go on up to the platform. We can take an elevator, the escalator, or the stairs. Your choice."

"How many stairs?" Tasya asked.

"Thousands," Paulinho said.

Vania gave him a disgusted look. "Two hundred twenty."

"It seems like thousands," Paulinho said.

Tasya smiled. "I vote for the stairs. Sounds like a good way to work up an appetite." She headed for the steps. Paulinho and Vania followed.

Tasya's enthusiasm pleased Paulinho. He had not seen such animation in her face since Ian died.

They reached the base of the statue just as the lights came on. "Oh!" Tasya cried. "It's incredible."

"Wait until you see the view," Vania said, leading them to the overlook, where tourists lined the railing, enjoying the spectacle as the sky darkened to indigo and the lights of the city flickered on one by one. When a group of Germans in shorts and backpacks drifted toward the souvenir stands, Tasya, Vania, and Paulinho took their place.

Rio. Emotion grabbed Paulinho by the throat. His heart thumped. Tears sprang to his eyes, blurring his vision. He blinked them away, then caught his breath as the incredible vista swam back into focus.

The lights of the city fanned out toward the sea, sparkling like a million glittering diamonds against the inky backdrop of Sugar Loaf Mountain. The beach highway, a shimmering river of light, trailed blurred reflections onto the glassy obsidian surface of the bay. In the distance, ebony mountains reared up from the sea, rugged silhouettes outlined against the darkening sky.

Paulinho nudged Tasya with his elbow. "Well? What do you think of my city?"

"It's magic."

"*Sim.*" Paulinho shut his eyes. Cool air, redolent of damp earth and tropical vegetation, flowed over him with a lover's touch.

"You must return in daylight," Vania said. "It's even more beautiful then. In fact, many consider the view from the top the most spectacular in all of South America. Of course, as a native Carioca, I may be prejudiced."

"That's what I thought when Paulinho first described Rio to me, but the reality far exceeds his claims." Tasya took a deep breath. "I'll remember this. Thank you. You're a wonderful tour guide."

"My pleasure," Vania said. "I've had a lot of experience."

"As a tour guide?" Paulinho said. "I thought you were a chauffeur."

She gave him a long, level look. "I am filling in tonight as a favor to Dona Elizabete. Her driver sprained his ankle playing *futebol* yesterday."

"So you're not her regular chauffeur."

"I'm not a chauffeur at all. I work for Carioca Tours."

"Lucky for us." Tasya twirled, her arms outstretched as if to embrace her surroundings.

Paulinho also found the view entrancing—especially

the view of Vania's lovely profile. Perhaps he had been hasty in describing her as a she-devil. . . .

She caught him staring, and her eyebrows met in a scowl.

Definitely a she-devil expression. He shifted his gaze back to the lights of the city below. The years had improved Vania's appearance but not her temperament.

"We should go," he said. "Dona Elizabete is probably wondering where we are." He turned to Tasya. "Are you ready?"

"I suppose."

Taking Tasya's arm, he escorted her down the steps, fighting the impulse to look back to see if Vania was following. Once they reached the Bentley, he helped Tasya in, then climbed in beside her.

Without a word, Vania slid behind the wheel, started the engine, and headed back down the mountain.

They drove in near silence. Occasionally Vania indicated a point of interest or vouchsafed a bit of local history, but Tasya answered only in monosyllables. Her brief flare of excitement on Corcovado had faded. She leaned against the door, eyes closed, expression pensive. Still grieving, Paulinho thought. Still missing Ian

As night fell on Rio, Tasya's depression deepened. Eyes closed, she rested her head against the cushioned backseat of Dona Elizabete's Bentley and prayed for the tour to end. Vania was an excellent guide. Like Paulinho, she was passionate about her city. But frankly, Tasya didn't care how many species of palm flourished in the Jardim Botânico, which teams were scheduled to play next at Maracanã soccer stadium, or whether São Francisco da Penitência's interior was covered in gold foil or tinfoil. All she wanted to do was hand over Milagre, return to the hotel, and down a lethal cocktail of pills and brandy.

Vania cleared her throat. "I hate to alarm you, but—"

Tasya forced her eyes open. "What is it?"

"We're being followed." The strain in Vania's voice jerked Tasya out of her stupor.

"By whom?"

"A man in a Lexus."

Tasya peered out the back window. "I don't see him."

"I do," Paulinho said. "Two cars back. Behind the SUV."

"He's been tracking us ever since we left the hotel," Vania said. "I didn't mention it earlier because I wasn't sure. I detoured up Corcovado to see if he would follow. When he didn't, I thought I was mistaken, but he was waiting at the bottom. He's been behind us ever since."

Tasya's head throbbed. Who would follow them? "I've heard reports of kidnappers holding tourists for ransom," she said slowly.

"Perhaps it is the police," Paulinho suggested. "Did you break any traffic laws, Vania?"

"No. And I seriously doubt either kidnappers or police would be driving a Lexus. More likely it's someone who's after Milagre."

Neither Tasya nor Paulinho spoke for a moment. Then, "What do you know of Milagre?" Paulinho said, leaning forward.

Vania flicked a sideways glance at him. "Just the stories Dona Elizabete told us as children."

"Why would you assume Paulinho and I have the stone?"

"Because Paulinho wouldn't return to Brazil without it." She met Tasya's gaze in the rearview mirror. "It's in your bag, *não?*"

Tasya pressed a protective hand to her purse. Even through the heavy leather, she could feel the warmth. She glanced at Paulinho, looking to him for a cue, unsure how much to admit. For all they knew, Vania was after the stone herself. Maybe no one was following them. Maybe this was a trick.

"My father died protecting Milagre. I would gladly do the same." Paulinho spoke quietly but with conviction. "The stone belongs to Dona Elizabete."

"Would the man you took it from agree?" Vania asked.

"Perhaps not, but he is dead."

"Then who is following us?"

"Takimoto," Tasya said.

"Who's Takimoto?" Vania stumbled over the unfamiliar syllables.

Tasya frowned. "A ruthless gemstone collector with underworld connections."

"You are leaping to conclusions, *moça.*"

"Who else could it be? How well did you see the man in the Lexus?" she asked Vania. "Was he Asian?"

"I couldn't tell. But I think you should call Dona Elizabete for help. She has many friends, many connections." Vania passed her cell phone to Paulinho.

Which put Tasya's fears to rest. Vania wouldn't have offered the use of her phone unless she was on their side. "Call," she told Paulinho. "Tell Dona Elizabete what's happening."

"And hurry," Vania said, "before whoever's back there gets suspicious."

Paulinho placed the call. He spoke so quietly Tasya could make out only a few words, a reference to Milagre and *perseguir,* Portuguese for "to chase." He flipped the phone shut and handed it back to Vania. "False alarm," he said. "The man in the Lexus is Dona Elizabete's nephew José Antonio, assistant secretary of public security."

"And what exactly is an assistant secretary of public security?" Tasya asked.

"A very high-level law enforcement officer," Vania said. "We have a police escort."

Vania dropped them off in front of the Sodré mansion, a towering gray stone fortress enclosed by a walled courtyard. Bleak as a prison, Tasya thought, even with its harsh lines softened by tropical foliage.

Paulinho pressed the buzzer next to the gate.

Tasya glanced up and down the quiet street. "Not much like Copacabana, is it? Hard to believe this is the same city."

Paulinho shrugged. "An old, established neighborhood with many elderly residents. Naturally it is less hectic here."

The gate creaked open then, and a gray-haired, liveried manservant ushered them into a tiled courtyard heavy with the scent of gardenias.

The mansion's elegant interior provided a sharp contrast to its stern exterior. Tasya admired the lofty molded plaster ceilings and polished parquet floors, the costly Persian rugs and gilded picture frames, as the elderly majordomo led them to the second-floor sitting room, where Dona Elizabete awaited them.

"Paulinho Vieira and Tasya Flynn." The servant made the announcement without butchering Tasya's name too badly.

"Come in, come in!" Dona Elizabeth greeted them in Portuguese.

"It is good to see you again," Paulinho said.

Dona Elizabete, a tiny silver-haired, dark-eyed woman, approached, her arms outstretched. "Welcome, my dear." She enfolded Tasya in a quick hug, kissed the air next to her cheeks, then held her at arm's length. "Welcome to Brazil."

"Have we met?" Tasya frowned. "You seem familiar."

"No, I haven't had that pleasure." Dona Elizabete smiled, patted her hands, then turned to Paulinho. "You brought it?"

He nodded. "Tasya?"

She dug the box from her purse and handed it to Paulinho, who opened the box and lifted Milagre by the chain. The tourmaline swung back and forth, a blood-red pendulum that captured the light from the chandelier and magnified it tenfold, shooting dazzling rays in all directions.

"At last." Dona Elizabete cupped trembling hands, and Paulinho dropped the stone into them. Tasya winced, but if Dona Elizabete felt the searing heat, she gave no sign. "Thank you." She beamed at Paulinho, then turned to

Tasya. "And you, my dear. Paulinho told me how much you risked."

For Ian, not for this woman. "I had my reasons."

"No matter. You kept the stone out of the wrong hands." Her dark gaze, warm and reassuring, met Tasya's. "But I am forgetting my manners. Won't you sit down, both of you?"

Paulinho opted for a deep-cushioned love seat, upholstered in heavy rose silk. Tasya perched on the edge of what she suspected was a prized antique, a chair with a dark wood frame, elaborately carved, its padded seat covered in an intricate pattern of embroidered flowers.

Dona Elizabete pulled a tasseled cord. "I had the cook hold dinner."

"Why did you send your nephew to escort us?" Tasya asked.

Dona Elizabete smiled. "I apologize for alarming you. An excess of caution on my part, but there have been rumors. A local gemstone dealer, a friend of a friend, was approached by a foreign collector interested in tourmalines. Large uncut stones."

"He did not contact you directly?" Paulinho said.

"No, the——" Before she could elaborate, a middle-aged woman in a maid's uniform entered the room. "Please tell Senhora da Rocha that my guests have arrived, Martina." Dona Elizabete waited until the maid was gone before continuing. "The dealer saw no reason to mention my name. It's common knowledge that Milagre was stolen many years ago."

"But you knew——" Paulinho said.

"Knew what?" Tasya frowned. "Knew where the stone was?"

Dona Elizabete smiled. "No, but I knew Milagre would come home again. It was foretold."

Tasya glanced from Dona Elizabete to Paulinho, then back to Dona Elizabete. "I'm confused."

The old woman turned to Paulinho. "Does she know about Father Duarte?"

"No."

Tasya looked from one to the other. "Who is Father Duarte?"

Dona Elizabete smiled. "Was, not is. Father Duarte was a Catholic priest, younger brother of my great-great-great-great-great-great-great-grandfather. In 1728, the church sent him to Ouro Preto, a mining town in Brazil's interior. His mission was to convert the slaves working in the mines.

"Father Duarte was a good Catholic, but he was also . . . open-minded, shall we say? And of a curious bent. He learned as much about the slaves' religious beliefs as they learned of his." Dona Elizabete paused. "One of the men he tried to convert was an old *babalaô*, a priest of the Ifa cult." She shot Tasya a questioning look. "Have you heard of the Ifa cult?"

"Paulinho has an *opele*, an Ifa necklace he uses to predict the future."

"The *babalaô* Dona Elizabete speaks of was my ancestor," Paulinho said.

"When the Africans came to this country, they brought their beliefs with them," Dona Elizabete continued. "Candomblé, which flourishes in Bahia, is the purest form of the religion, closest to its African roots. Here in Rio, Macumba is the more common form. The Ifa cult, restricted to men, has virtually died out. Which is a great loss, because their divination tool, the *opele*, never lies." She paused again. "Indeed, a true *babalaô* is never wrong in his prognostications.

"In Yoruba, *babalaô* means 'father of the mystery.' One might say the *babalaôs* are the guardians of the greatest mystery of all."

Tasya shot Paulinho a questioning look.

"Time," he said.

"Because they can predict the future?"

Dona Elizabete nodded. "And because they understand time's true nature."

Tasya shook her head in confusion. "I still don't understand."

"Paulinho's ancestor, the *babalaô*, worked in a gemstone mine near Ouro Preto. One day, the man digging next to him let out a howl and dropped a rock, screaming that it had burned his fingers."

"He'd found Milagre," Tasya guessed. "It feels hot to me, too."

Dona Elizabete and Paulinho exchanged a look Tasya couldn't interpret. "The overseer checked the man for injuries, but there were none," Dona Elizabete said. "However, when the overseer ordered the slave to get back to work, the man refused to touch the rock again, saying it was cursed. Angry, the overseer picked up the rock himself to prove there was nothing wrong with it."

"And he burned his hands," Tasya said.

Paulinho frowned at her.

Dona Elizabete didn't seem to have minded her interruption, though. Smiling, she shook her head. "He felt nothing. Angry, suspecting the slave was trying to pull some sort of trick, he thrust the rock back into the man's hands." Dona Elizabete stared straight ahead, her gaze unfocused. "Here is where the story gets very strange, but the *babalaô* swore to Father Duarte that it was the truth."

Her gaze sharpened as she turned to Tasya. "The slave's eyes grew round. He screamed with pain and shouted something in Yoruba.

"The *babalaô* heard a faint humming. The hair on his body stood up. He couldn't breathe. He said it was as if the air rippled, as if perhaps the world itself rippled. A wave of dizziness knocked him off his feet."

"Earthquake?" Tasya said.

"If so, it was a very small tremor, restricted to the immediate vicinity. Men working twenty feet away heard nothing, saw nothing, felt nothing."

"How about the overseer?"

"He'd turned his back and walked away as soon as he handed the rock to the slave. Apparently he felt nothing, either. Though when he heard the slave scream, he rushed back. Only by then the man had disappeared."

"He ran away?"

"No, vanished."

"Like that," Paulinho said, snapping his fingers.

"But vanished how? Vanished where?"

"Back to Africa? Back through the decades? Who knows?"

The elderly majordomo shuffled into the room. "Dinner is served," he said.

Dona Elizabete stood. "Shall we?"

*   *   *

Dona Elizabete refused to say another word until they had eaten, but Tasya was so anxious to hear the rest of the *babalaô*'s story, she could only pick at her food.

After an endless interval, they returned to the sitting room. A maid set a heavy silver tray on the table next to Dona Elizabete's chair, then left the room. "*Cafezinho,*" Dona Elizabete said, pouring small cups of rich aromatic coffee. She handed one to Tasya.

"Best with sugar." Paulinho added a spoonful to his.

Tasya turned to Dona Elizabete. "You suggested the slave who vanished might have gone to Africa, but how did he get out of the mine, much less out of the country?"

"According to what the *babalaô* told Father Duarte, one minute the man was holding the stone, and the next the stone lay on the ground and the man was gone. He vanished right in front of fifteen other men." Dona Elizabete paused. "Perhaps you would care to see a painting of the scene? Yes?"

"Father Duarte was an amateur artist," Paulinho explained. "He captured the *babalaô*'s story in oils."

Tasya followed Dona Elizabete to the far end of the room. A small, undistinguished painting overpowered by an ornate gilt frame hung next to a mahogany secretary. Paulinho was right. Father Duarte had, indeed, been an amateur. The people he'd depicted, including a tall man she supposed must represent the *babalaô*, were little more than stick figures. The tall man held something red in his left hand. Milagre, Tasya assumed, though it could just as easily have been an apple. The man's right arm was outstretched as if he were giving an oration. Or a blessing.

"Father Duarte's work is rather primitive," Dona Elizabete said, "of little artistic value, but my family has always treasured the painting for sentimental reasons." She ushered them back to their seats.

"Where was I? Oh, yes. The overseer suspected a trick. He ordered the slaves to pick up the rock and bring it to him, but none of them dared. They'd just seen one of themselves disappear. They were more frightened of the stone than of the overseer's whip.

"Finally, the overseer picked it up himself, tossed it into a basket, and ordered the slaves back to work."

"What about the slave who disappeared?"

"They searched but never found him. That night, back in the slave quarters, the *babalaô* asked the spirits for an explanation of the man's disappearance. He suspected it had something to do with the stone and the words the man had spoken before he disappeared. In their own cryptic way, the spirits confirmed it. The same two *odums* appeared every time he threw the *opele,* one referring to 'time,' the other to 'two.'"

Tasya frowned. "I don't see the connection."

"'Two' referred to the stone itself, a crystal cluster—"

"Wait," Tasya interrupted. "A crystal cluster? Then it wasn't Milagre?"

"Milagre formed half of the cluster. A second, nearly identical tourmaline was embedded in the same matrix."

"*Two* tourmalines?" Tasya said.

"Milagre and Gêmeo. *Gêmeo* means 'twin,'" Paulinho explained in English.

Dona Elizabete sipped her *cafezinho.* "Just before the slave disappeared, he begged to return to his childhood. The more the *babalaô* pondered the second *odum,* time, the more he wondered if the stones had sent the man back to his youth, back to Africa."

"An interesting speculation," Tasya said. "But where's the proof?"

"The man wished himself back in Africa, and poof!" Paulinho said. "He was gone."

"Not just because he wished it," Dona Elizabete said. "Because he wished it while he held the tourmaline cluster, Milagre and its twin stone, Gêmeo."

Tasya chewed at her lip. A legend wasn't proof. "What happened to Gêmeo? How did the twins become separated?"

"The separation occurred later," Dona Elizabete said. "The *babalaô* entrusted the twins to my ancestor, Father Duarte, and it was he who cut them apart as a safety precaution, fearing the crystals might fall into unscrupulous hands. Separating the stones lessened the danger. Individually, the stones manifested healing properties but did not send people hurtling off into the far reaches of time and space."

"I don't want to be rude," Tasya said, "But 'far reaches of time and space' sounds like science fiction."

"What is your theory, then?" Paulinho said. "What do you think happened to the man who vanished?"

"I don't know. Maybe he ducked behind a rock or slipped away when no one was looking."

"The *babalaô,* too, was skeptical at first." Dona Elizabete traced the floral design on her cup with the manicured tip of one nail. "He didn't trust the evidence of his own eyes. When the overseer was looking in the other direction, he picked up the stone himself."

"But nothing happened. He felt nothing," Paulinho said. "No heat. No electricity. No hint of supernatural power."

"Yet a man was missing, and his *opele* suggested the stone was responsible. He experimented," Dona Elizabete said. "He asked other miners to touch the stone, hoping to find someone who would react as the first man had."

"I thought the slaves were afraid to touch it."

"They were frightened, yes." Dona Elizabete nodded in emphasis. "But they accorded Paulinho's ancestor great respect because he was a *babalaô*."

"Did he find another who was sensitive to the stone?"

"Three others," Dona Elizabete said.

"And did they—"

"Vanish? One of them did, yes." Dona Elizabete's gaze probed Tasya's. "You do not believe me?"

"I'm sensitive to the stone. So was . . ." She fought for composure. "So was Ian. But neither of us disappeared into the twilight zone."

"Milagre is too weak by itself. It takes both twins to generate enough power."

Tasya's heart skipped a beat. "You're saying if I had both stones, all I would have to do is say, 'I wish I were in Africa in 1720,' and zap! I'd be in Africa in 1720?" Tasya felt a trickle of excitement. "You're saying with the twin tourmalines, a person could travel through time?"

"Not everyone," Dona Elizabete said. "Just a chosen few."

Tasya's mind spun in dizzying circles. "I don't believe this." Though she wanted to. Dear God, how she wanted to.

Dona Elizabete touched her hand. "Some people think of time as a river, but it is a place, each second a different destination. Life is the river that flows through it. Does that make sense?"

"No." Tasya pulled her hand away. None of this made sense. Yet it made no sense that the stone felt hot to her and cool to others, either. If it truly were possible to move through time . . . If she could go back in time . . .

"Think of it this way," Dona Elizabete said. "The power of the tourmalines is like the power of the swimmer's muscles as they propel him against the current."

"You're saying with Milagre's help I could swim upstream into the past?"

"Not with Milagre alone, no, but if you had both stones, yes, perhaps you could."

Tasya's heart raced. If she could go back to the time before Alex Farrell double-crossed Ian, before Ian ended up crippled and imprisoned, she could change everything. Fix everything. She pinned Dona Elizabete with a sharp look. "Where is Gêmeo?"

The older woman met her look with a steady appraisal. She said nothing.

Paulinho answered for her. "The twin has been lost for almost two hundred and fifty years."

The first things Tasya saw when she walked into her hotel room were the sleeping pills and brandy waiting for her on the nightstand. A great temptation, but . . . not tonight. Not if there was the slightest chance the crazy story about the tourmalines was true. If she could locate the second stone, if she could convince Paulinho and Dona Elizabete to let her try time travel, if she could find her way to Tahiti in the early 1970s, if she could stop Ian from accompanying Alex to Rio in the first place, then everything would be different. Ian wouldn't languish in prison for thirty years, bitter and crippled, and most importantly, he wouldn't die in the cottage at La Magia.

She stared at her reflection in the mirror above the dresser. A hectic flush stained her cheekbones. Black circles shadowed her eyes. Her mouth trembled.

It's a legend. No more real than her mother's tales of the witch Baba Yaga.

But what if it wasn't? What if it was true? She could save Ian from prison.

Saving Ian from prison isn't the only reason you want to do this.

All right, yes, she had an ulterior motive. She wanted to save Ian for herself.

But the Ian of 1972 isn't in love with you. He doesn't even know you. What makes you think he'll listen to you?

She would make him listen—whatever it took.

How? By seducing him? What happens to your grand plan if he's already in love with someone else?

She knew Ian hadn't been celibate prior to his paralysis. But his joking references to "French lessons" hadn't struck her as the reminiscences of a man who'd lost the love of his life.

Say you get him to listen. What will you tell him? The truth?

That you've come from the future to save him from his former apprentice?

Tasya gazed in despair at the woman in the mirror. God, what could she tell him? What would he believe?

Nothing. Not the truth, at any rate.

15

THE INSTANT THE BENTLEY pulled under the porte cochere, Paulinho walked out to meet it. He bent down to window level to introduce himself to the driver, only to find Vania behind the wheel once again. He mimed, *Roll down the window*, which she did with obvious reluctance. Cool air poured out. The Bentley might be over thirty years old, but its air conditioner still worked at top efficiency.

She frowned at him. "Where's Senhorita Flynn? Dona Elizabete told me to collect both of you."

"She overslept. She will be down shortly. Do you mind if I wait inside the car? It is warm out here."

"Suit yourself."

Judging by her expression, Paulinho suspected "Shoot yourself" was closer to her real sentiments. No surprise there. The little pain in the neck had grown up to be a big pain in the neck. He let himself in on the passenger's side. "I gather you got drafted for chauffeur duty again. Is the driver's ankle still troubling him?"

"You mean my idiot cousin Artur, who thinks he's the next Pelé?" She snorted. "His ankle is swollen as big as a melon. He's hobbling around on crutches. It will be days before he can put any weight on his foot."

"I am sorry to hear that."

Vania mumbled something he didn't catch.

"What was that?"

"I said, not as sorry as I am. I had planned to go to the beach this weekend with a friend."

He shot her a sharp look. "A friend? Not your husband?"

She stared straight ahead, avoiding his gaze. "My husband died three years ago," she said in a flat, emotionless voice. "A massive coronary. He was thirty-five."

Paulinho did not know what to say. "I am sorry" seemed inadequate, but it was the only phrase he could think of.

"I'd rather not talk about it," she said.

Which was fine with Paulinho, since he was not sure what sentiments were appropriate anyway. "Did you love him?" did not seem proper. Nor did asking if the friend she had planned to meet was a man or a woman. No way to work that casually into the conversation—especially now, since there *was* no conversation.

Vania cleared her throat. "How long have you and Senhorita Flynn been friends?"

Friends meaning friends? Or friends meaning lovers? Was that what this was about? Little Vania did not approve? "A few months," he said.

"Is your lover always this rude? Does she make a habit of keeping you waiting?"

Paulinho stared at her in surprise. This was not the Vania he remembered. Razor-tongued, yes. She had often cut him off at the knees, but cattiness was not her style. "Tasya recently suffered a great personal loss. She has not been sleeping well. And for the record, she is not my lover. She is my friend."

Vania took a moment to digest this. "I see," she said.

He raised an eyebrow. "Do you, Mosca?" *Mosca.* Portuguese for fly. An insulting childhood nickname chosen on purpose to stir her up.

"Mosca?" Her eyes narrowed dangerously. She smacked his arm. "No one has called me that for years."

"See how you have missed me, my annoying little insect?"

Her beautiful face went still for a moment. Then her eyes filled with tears. She blinked them back. "Yes," she said, her voice a little wobbly, "I did miss you, Paulinho."

He realized his mouth was hanging open and shut it. Vania Marcia Freire da Rocha, the pest who, as a child, had spent great time and energy torturing him, had missed him? He forced a laugh. "Missed having someone to pick on," he said.

"No." She latched onto his forearms and leaned closer, so close he could smell the spicy scent of her perfume, see the greenish flecks around her pupils, hear the soft sound of her indrawn breath. "I pestered you so you'd notice me, but you never did. Even after I started dating, you still treated me like a child. You never saw me as a woman."

"I—"

"No," she said. "Let me finish before I lose my nerve." Her grip tightened. "I'd been in love with you since I was two years old, but you were so blind, all you saw was little Mosca."

"I am sorry."

"So am I. When you married, you broke my heart."

As Angela broke mine.

"Don't do it again," she said. "Don't make me fall in love with you."

"I will not. I promise," he said and kissed her. Initially he did it to silence her and maybe because he felt a little sorry for her, but as the seconds ticked by on the sweetest, sexiest kiss he had ever experienced, he forgot his original motivations.

Someone pecked on the window behind him. He managed to ignore the irritating sound until Tasya shouted his name. He gave a guilty start and turned to find her grinning at him. "I knew it," she said.

Tasya, Paulinho, and Dona Elizabete were relaxing in the sitting room after lunch, making desultory conversation, when Tasya dropped her bombshell. "I want to travel back to 1972."

Paulinho goggled at her, but Dona Elizabete gave no sign she'd even heard what Tasya had said. She gazed off into space. Impossible to tell what she was thinking behind that polite mask.

Silence gripped the room, the only sound the buzzing of a fly that had blundered into the folds of the heavy rose damask draperies. Paulinho cleared his throat, then opened his mouth as if he were about to say something. He repeated the process twice before closing his mouth without uttering a word.

Dona Elizabete shook her head. "The danger is too great."

"Besides," Paulinho said, finding his voice at last, "it is impossible without Gêmeo."

"Then we must find Gêmeo," she said, ignoring their objections. "Under what circumstances did it disappear?"

"It didn't disappear," Dona Elizabete told her. "Father Duarte hid it."

"But you must have some idea where!" She gripped the arms of her chair so the others wouldn't notice that her hands were trembling. *This is why I was meant to come to Brazil.* She knew it as surely as she knew her own name.

"I am afraid not," Dona Elizabete said. "According to legend, Father Duarte left a hint to Gêmeo's whereabouts in his diary, but the family has never been able to confirm that part of the story. The diary was not found among his possessions after his death." She shrugged. "Perhaps he hid it. Or perhaps it never existed."

Paulinho grunted as if Dona Elizabete had just punched him in the gut.

She stared at him, eyebrows raised. "Paulinho?"

"It existed," he said. "It exists. I have it. The diary. My family has guarded its secrets for generations."

Dona Elizabete raised her eyebrows. "And yet you said nothing?"

"Until now, there was no reason," he said. "You know the legend as well as I do."

"The traveler," she said. "Tasya?"

He nodded.

Dizzy with hope, sick with apprehension, Tasya

searched Paulinho's face, then Dona Elizabete's. "Do you mean what I think you mean?"

Dona Elizabete shot her a troubled look. "The *babalaô* predicted the stones would be reunited by a traveler, a woman determined to save the man she loved."

Excitement stole her breath. "Me?" she whispered.

"Paulinho thinks so. I am not convinced." Dona Elizabete pressed her lips together in a tight line. "And even if it is so, the dangers are too great. It is said that power corrupts. With power of this magnitude, I fear the risk of corruption would increase dramatically. Think of it. A time traveler could manipulate the stock exchange, upset the balance of power, profit from prior knowledge of natural disasters."

"Or save lives, right wrongs, correct mistakes," Tasya argued. Save Ian's life, keep him out of prison, prevent him from coming out of retirement to help Alex Farrell steal Milagre.

Dona Elizabete sighed. "Every action, even the noblest, has repercussions, many of which cannot be predicted."

"That's as true of the actions we take in the present as it would be for actions we might take in the past."

"Tasya has a point," Paulinho said. "If we were to consider every possible result of a given action, we would completely immobilize ourselves for fear of causing unsuspected harm."

Dona Elizabete silenced them with a gesture. "I am not convinced."

Tasya met her gaze. *Then I will convince you.*

*　　*　　*

"I will convince her. I must," Tasya told Paulinho the next morning as they followed the elderly manservant around to the terrace behind the Sodré mansion.

"Dona Elizabete is a very stubborn woman," he said.

"So am I," Tasya said.

Paulinho grinned an acknowledgment. "It will take much to change her mind, but I will help if I can."

Tasya squeezed his hand. "Thank you."

The manservant announced them, and Dona Elizabete greeted them cordially. "Have a seat. Would you like to join me in a cup of coffee? Yes? Ronaldo, please ask Senhora da Rocha to fix a tray."

The manservant nodded and left.

Tasya sat on one of the wicker garden chairs.

"I brought Father Duarte's diary," Paulinho said.

"Yes?" Dona Elizabete sounded quite composed, but the glint in her eyes betrayed her excitement.

Paulinho set a carved ivory box on the umbrella-shaded table, removed its contents, then released the mechanism that held the false bottom in place. He drew a slim leather-bound volume from the hidden recess.

Dona Elizabete's hands trembled as she took the diary from him. "I can't believe I'm actually holding it," she said, her voice choked with emotion. She caressed the worn leather. "So old. So fragile."

Tasya leaned across the table to get a closer look. It was much less elaborate than she'd expected, the cover cracked, the gilt lettering faded with time.

"Open to the last page," Paulinho said. "That is where he left his hint."

Careful not to crack the spine or damage the yellowed

paper, Dona Elizabete opened to the page that held the clue to Gêmeo's whereabouts. She studied it for a long time, reading and rereading.

Tasya willed herself to relax, leaning back in her chair to follow the flight of an iridescent blue butterfly. It fluttered to and fro, seemingly at random, first landing on a hibiscus flower the size of a saucer, then perching on the edge of the sundial, as if trying to decipher the words carved into the stone. *Tempus fugit.* Time flies.

Dona Elizabete shook her head. "I was convinced Father Duarte's diary held the key, but I was wrong. He writes in riddles. 'Therefore must the traveler look to the *babalaô* to show the way,'" she quoted. "But how can the *babalaô* show us anything? He's been dead for two and a half centuries."

"It makes no sense to me, either," Paulinho said. "But then, I am not the traveler."

Dona Elizabete frowned. "What are you suggesting?"

"According to the legend, the traveler will reunite the stones. Therefore, it is hardly surprising that the clue means nothing to us. But if, as I believe, Tasya is the traveler, then Father Duarte's words should lead her to Gêmeo."

Tasya's stomach muscles tightened. This was Paulinho's idea of help? Placing her in an impossible position? If she failed . . .

Dona Elizabete frowned. "This is not a game, Paulinho. You know the dangers as well as I."

"Read the clue again," he said. "Listen carefully this time, Tasya."

She started to protest that she was no good at guessing

games, then faltered to a stop as a memory surfaced. She jumped to her feet so abruptly that her chair flipped backward.

"What?" Paulinho asked.

"I—I think I know how to find Gêmeo."

The other two stared at her as if she'd lost her mind.

As perhaps she had, but . . . "This way." She strode into the house, too focused on her goal to pay attention to whether or not Paulinho and Dona Elizabete followed her. She dashed upstairs to the sitting room where Dona Elizabete had entertained them their first night in Rio and stopped in front of Father Duarte's painting.

She studied the *babalaô*. He wasn't giving a speech or extending a blessing, as she'd originally thought. His outstretched arm pointed the way.

"*Meu Deus!*" Paulinho said behind her.

Tasya turned to face him. "Father Duarte hid the stone in the frame."

Paulinho grinned. "I think you are right, *moça*." He angled to face Dona Elizabete, who stood at his side, her expression wavering between troubled and hopeful. "What do you say? Shall we see if Tasya is right?"

Dona Elizabete hesitated, obviously torn. "Destroy a cherished family heirloom just to test a theory? I'm not sure that's the wisest course of action."

"Touch the frame," Paulinho told Tasya. "Milagre burned her fingers," he told Dona Elizabete. "If Gêmeo lies hidden within the frame, she should feel the heat."

"Yes," Tasya said. "I hadn't thought of that, but Paulinho's right. If the tourmaline is there, I'll know." She imagined a line extending from the end of the *babalaô*'s outstretched fingers, then stretched up on tiptoes to place her hand on the spot where the imaginary line intersected the frame.

She'd expected warmth, but the intensity of the heat took her by surprise. With a strangled cry, she snatched her hand away.

"It burned her," Paulinho said. "What more proof do we need?" He dug a Swiss army knife from his pocket. "You permit?" he said to Dona Elizabete.

She stared wide-eyed from Tasya to Paulinho, then inclined her head in the faintest of nods.

Paulinho chipped at the plaster frame, soon revealing a cloth-wrapped package tied with twine. With a slash of the knife, he cut through the wrappings.

He lifted the stone and it caught the light from the window. A deep ruby red, it seemed to burn with an inner fire.

Dona Elizabete gasped; then her eyes narrowed, and she pinned Tasya with a sharp look. "How did you know?"

"I—I'm not sure."

"I told you," Paulinho said. "She is the traveler." He placed the tourmaline in Dona Elizabete's hands. "It is as the legend predicted. Tasya deserves a chance."

"The danger is too great."

"If she is willing to risk it . . ."

"No." Dona Elizabete shook her head. "I refuse to be pushed into making a hasty decision I may later regret. I need time to consider the matter." She focused her troubled gaze on Tasya. "As do you."

"But—" Paulinho started.

"No," she said. "Not another word." She swept from the room, taking Gêmeo with her.

"Paulinho?" After the emotional ups and downs of the last half hour, Tasya felt as if she were on the verge of a complete meltdown.

He patted her shoulder. "Do not abandon hope yet, *moça*. Already Dona Elizabete is half convinced. Give her time."

After lunch Paulinho seated himself at the table in Dona Elizabete's garden. He tried to concentrate on his *opele*, despite the distraction of Mosca sitting across from him. How was he supposed to make a proper divination under such circumstances? If he did not know better, he would swear she was interfering on purpose. "Shouldn't you be shepherding a flock of tourists through the Museu Nacional?"

"I have the afternoon off." Vania leaned forward on her elbows to study the pattern formed by the *opele*, and the deep scoop neck of her dress displayed rather more of her charms than the designer had intended. Paulinho caught a glimpse of white lace bra and generous *café com leite* curves.

"*Nossa Senhora*," he murmured under his breath, half in exasperation, half in prayer.

Vania smiled at him, a smile that sent all his blood rushing south. "Making any progress?"

He stared at her blankly. At least he hoped it was blankly, praying none of the lustful thoughts stuffing his head showed in his expression. "Not yet."

She sighed, and her curves rose and fell.

Unbearable temptation. He closed his eyes, but it didn't help. He could still smell her—the spicy scent of her perfume, the minty sweetness of her breath. *Meu Deus,* if something as ordinary as toothpaste could spark all these inappropriate thoughts, he was in serious trouble.

"Paulinho, are you all right?" The delicate touch of her fingers along his cheekbone shoved him right over the edge. No longer merely distracted, he was now in the throes of full-fledged lust. His eyes popped open, and he saw his own tortured face reflected in the depths of her beautiful eyes.

"No, Mosca, I am not all right. I am very much not all right. You are driving me crazy."

She leaned closer, cupping his face in her hands. "Crazy enough to kiss me?"

"Crazier than that," he said.

She moistened her lips with the tip of her tongue. "How crazy, Paulinho?"

He swallowed, but his voice still came out raspy. "Crazy enough to be jealous of the clothes that caress your body."

Again she brushed his cheek with her fingertips. "I do admire a man with a poet's soul."

"Crazy enough to throw you over my shoulder and haul you off to the nearest cave."

"A man of action is even better."

"Crazy enough to make mad, passionate love to you for three weeks straight."

She moaned softly. "A man with stamina is best of all."

Smiling, Paulinho gathered her hands in his. "After Angela betrayed me, I swore a vow of celibacy. But I think the time has come to risk my heart again. And you, Mosca? Are you ready to live dangerously?"

Vania kissed him full on the lips. A sweet, soft, sensuous kiss that promised delicious dangers ahead. Soft shoulders. And curves. Lots of curves.

Despite the fact Tasya wasn't a hundred percent convinced that time travel existed outside the pages of science fiction, she sat in a corner of Dona Elizabete's library, compiling lists of time-traveling pros and cons. Topping the con list was, *Aside from Father Duarte's claims, we have no proof this works.*

On the other hand, what did she have to lose by trying? If she disappeared in a puff of smoke, what would it matter? And conversely, if it worked, she could change Ian's life, fix it so he didn't spend thirty years in a wheelchair in prison.

Or was that, fix it so he fell in love with her and put her life back on track?

Okay, her determination to save Ian was not entirely selfless. She'd been cheated of her happy ending the first time around. A second chance was only fair.

Since when is life fair?

Since never, but . . .

Besides, he won't remember anything that's happened between the two of you because—surprise, surprise—it won't have happened yet. What makes you think even if you do manage to track him down that he'll fall in love with you again? What if he decides you're not his type? What if he's already in love with someone else? What will you do then?

She didn't know what she'd do then, but she wanted the opportunity to find out. If she didn't try to save Ian, she'd never forgive herself.

On the pro side, she wrote: *I can make him happy. I can make myself happy.*

"Tasya?" Dona Elizabete poked her head into the room. "You'll never guess what I just saw."

Tasya smiled at the older woman's excitement. "What?"

"Paulinho and Vania kissing."

"Really?"

Dona Elizabete gave a giddy laugh. "I was never so surprised in my life. Is it not romantic?"

Romantic? Yes. Surprising? No. Tasya had known from that first blistering moment of eye contact in the hotel lobby that the two were meant for each other.

Suddenly, a degree of wariness and speculation tempered Dona Elizabete's enthusiasm. "But perhaps you felt something more than friendship for Paulinho? You expected—"

Tasya shook her head. "I love Paulinho, but only as a friend." She stared out the window, thinking of Ian. Not Ian in his grave, but Ian as he had been in real life and in her oh-so-vivid dreams. She smiled, remembering. Definitely a sexual component to that relationship.

"You are pleased, then?" Dona Elizabete said.

"About Paulinho and Vania? Certainly." She paused. "Dona Elizabete, I have something to ask you."

"Yes?"

"Do you believe Father Duarte's claim? Do you think it's possible to travel through time?"

"Yes, but it is not a journey to undertake lightly." Her

eyes radiated compassion. "You're thinking about Ian MacPherson."

"Yes—if only he had never agreed to help steal Milagre, things would have been different. He wouldn't have wasted half his life in prison. He wouldn't have lost the use of his legs."

"Nor would he have met you."

"I want to go back, Dona Elizabete. I want to interrupt the chain of events that destroyed his life. If there's the slightest chance I can rescue him, then I owe it to him to try."

"You realize the man in the past is not the same man you knew?"

"Yes."

"You loved him, didn't you?"

"Very much."

"How would you feel meeting him again as a stranger?"

Tasya clenched her hands together in her lap. "I know it won't be easy, but I want to try. The stones belong to you, however, so the choice is yours."

Dona Elizabete shook her head, a faint smile playing about the corners of her mouth.

"Don't say no. Please."

"Child, you misunderstand. I am guardian of the stones, but I don't own them. No one does. The stones choose who travels."

"What do you mean?"

A worried expression came over Dona Elizabete's face. "Not everyone is suited for time travel. Father Duarte believed only a few people have the right physiology."

"Only those who feel the heat," Tasya guessed.

Dona Elizabete gripped Tasya's hands. "The stones can't generate heat. Tourmalines aren't alive."

"But I felt it. More than once."

"What you felt was the heat produced by your own body."

"Then why doesn't everyone feel it?"

"Because there are variations in body chemistry. Yours is atypical. The heat your body generates creates a pyro-electric charge in the tourmaline, a charge that I suspect promotes healing and enables time travel.

"Father Duarte believed there was a continuum of sensitivity, but there's no way to judge where on the continuum a person falls. With healing, it makes little difference, but with time traveling, it makes all the difference."

"You mean some people are successful and some people aren't. That's all right. I don't mind failing, but I'll never forgive myself if I don't try."

Dona Elizabete sighed. "If only it were so simple." She squeezed Tasya's hands. "Some people are successful," she said. "And some people die."

"I don't care. I have to try. Without Ian, I might as well be dead."

"According to the legend," Dona Elizabete said, "the *babalaô* predicted that a traveler would appear to reunite Milagre and Gêmeo, then use the stones to journey to the past." Dona Elizabete shot her a worried look. "But not even the *babalaô* could tell whether or not the traveler would succeed."

Tasya lay in bed in her hotel room on Copacabana Beach, unable to sleep. Some time after midnight, she'd made up her mind. She was going to try time travel.

If her gamble paid off, there was a good chance she could save Ian years of pain and frustration. If not, she'd die. Electrocuted, according to Father Duarte's eyewitness account of a failed attempt.

Shivering, she pulled the covers up to her chin.

Electrocution. A more painful way to die than the barbiturate overdose she'd planned. She tried not to think about it.

Unfortunately she could think of little else. She had read Father Duarte's diary from cover to cover. In it, he'd described the tragedy in elaborate detail. Blackened fingers cooked onto the crystals. Smoke rising from the victim's head moments before his hair caught fire. The body jerked by involuntary spasms so violent they'd dislocated vertebrae.

Focus on something else.

Okay, given she survived the trip up the river of life, would she recognize the uncrippled, uncareworn, unembittered thirty-year-old version of Ian MacPherson? *What did you look like back then, Ian? What about you was different? And more important, what about you was the same?*

Even Paulinho had pointed out that there were no guarantees. The younger version of Ian did not know her. He might not come to feel the same way about her that the older version had. How would she feel, Paulinho had demanded, if she made this sacrifice and Ian rejected her?

How would she feel? Devastated, certainly. And worse, betrayed. But she refused to let such worries dissuade her. Her mind was made up.

*　　　*　　　*

Tasya spent the next few weeks preparing for her journey. Her most challenging task was obtaining an out-of-date American passport. If the forger wondered why she wanted a passport that listed her birth date as August 28, 1951, he asked no questions, any qualms he might have felt soothed by a thick stack of crisp new reais.

Clothes were no problem. Current retro styles would work, and long, straight hair had been as fashionable then as now. To transform herself into an authentic child of the seventies, all she really had to do was use a pale lip gloss and switch to liquid eyeliner. "Forget the false eyelashes, though," she told Paulinho after sitting through an old James Bond movie—historical research—in which the heroine had worn stiff black fringes on her eyelids.

The day of her scheduled departure dawned clear and sunny. Vania took the day off work so she could be there to lend moral support. "Don't worry about anachronisms," she told Tasya. "Since no one there knows what the future looks like, they aren't apt to be suspicious if you accidentally mention Tiger Woods or DVD players."

Tasya traced the words etched into Dona Elizabete's sundial. *Tempus fugit*.

Vania squeezed her arm. "It will be all right."

"I wish I were certain of that," Paulinho said. "I wish you luck, *moça*."

An awkward silence fell.

They had gathered in the shade of the palms on the tiled terrace behind the Sodré mansion—Tasya, Vania, and Paulinho. Dona Elizabete was inside, retrieving the tourmalines.

"It's a beautiful day," Vania said, obviously uncomfortable with the silence.

A beautiful day to die.

No, she wouldn't think that way. Tasya shifted her weight from foot to foot. *Think about Ian. Think about all the pain you can spare him.*

Paulinho touched her shoulder, and his troubled gaze snared hers. "Are you sure about this, *moça?*"

She nodded, afraid she'd cry if she tried to speak.

He gathered her in his arms and folded her close. "I will miss you."

And I you. She hugged him tight.

Vania tapped her shoulder. "My turn," she said, holding out her arms.

Paulinho released her, and she and Vania embraced. "You are so brave," Vania whispered, "but if it were Paulinho in danger, I would do the same—whatever the cost."

Tasya held her at arm's length, smiling despite the whirlpool of emotions threatening to drag her under. She swallowed hard. "Thank you."

Dona Elizabete emerged from the house, carrying a stone in each hand. A shaft of sunlight penetrated the palm fronds to bounce off Milagre in a dazzle of refracted and reflected rays. Dona Elizabete took a step forward and the light hit Gêmeo, too. For a split second, the glare blinded Tasya.

Then Dona Elizabete moved into the shade, and the miniature fireballs changed back into tourmalines. "It is time," she said.

*   *   *

It began with the pain. Tasya had experienced Milagre's power firsthand. She thought she knew what to expect, but she was wrong. Not even Richard, damn his soul, had prepared her for this. Fiery bursts of agony ricocheted up her arms and down her legs. They rocketed through her torso, exploded in her brain. "Tahiti," she said. "May 1972. Tahiti, May 1972."

Her lungs burned. Her nerve endings screamed. Every hair on her body stood up. Oh, God, was this the part where she burst into flames? "Tahiti, May 1972. Tahiti, May 1972."

The humming drowned her out, growing in volume and intensity until it reached thunderous proportions, as loud as a jet engine, as loud as an avalanche, as loud as the end of the world. And she vibrated to its frequency.

Something was happening to her. Something more than the heat scorching her body, more than the fearsome cacophony assaulting her ears. Something inside.

She felt as if her internal glue had come unstuck, as if she were no longer a sum of parts but the parts themselves, individual atoms quivering on the verge of dissolution. Maybe no one traveled through time. Maybe those who didn't burst into flames, disintegrated, shattering into millions of invisible splinters.

"Tahiti, May 1972. Tahiti, May 1972."

The roar and the pain crescendoed in tandem. A brilliant blue light engulfed her for an instant. Then the sound and heat were gone, as if they'd never been. The garden rippled once, then stabilized. Solidified.

She flexed her hands. The stones had vanished, but she was still there. Still alive. Still in Brazil. She'd gazed long into the abyss, and the abyss had spit in her eye, eliminating the last hope, destroying the last dream. Disappointment leached the color from her world. She closed her eyes, weary and brokenhearted, too spent for bitterness, too sad for tears.

"Meu Deus!" Dona Elizabete said from behind her.

She'd forgotten the others. If only they'd forgotten her. She was too tired to deal with a post mortem of her failure; all she wanted was time alone.

"Meu Deus," Dona Elizabete said, more softly this time.

Steeling herself, Tasya turned. Or tried to. She stumbled into a gardenia bush she hadn't remembered being there.

"Bem-vinda ao Brasil. Bem-vinda, viajante. Welcome to Brazil. Welcome, traveler."

Tasya met Dona Elizabete's gaze, and shock waves shuddered through her. She recognized Dona Elizabete's eyes, Dona Elizabete's voice, but this was not the Dona Elizabete she knew. This was the dark-haired woman of her long-ago dream.

"What year is this?" Tasya said.

PART THREE

Revision

In a minute there is time
For decisions and revisions which a minute
will reverse.

—T. S. ELIOT,
"THE LOVE SONG OF J. ALFRED PRUFROCK"

16

IAN DREAMED OF BEAUTIFUL bare-breasted women with hibiscus flowers tucked behind their ears. They danced the tamure to the beat of an unseen drum, their shredded-bark skirts swishing in a hypnotic rhythm, revealing glimpses of silky, sun-kissed thighs. An excellent dream, aside from that damned annoying thumping. If he were awake, he'd punt the bloody drum to hell and gone.

He woke with a start, realizing the racket wasn't drums at all but someone pounding on his bedroom door. "Sod off!" He buried his head under the pillow.

The pounding continued—on the door and in his head as well, a throbbing testimony to the foolishness of mixing beer and rum.

"Get up, MacPherson, you lazy bastard. It's half past one. You've slept the morning through." The voice belonged to his neighbor Peter Wheatley, expatriate Englishman, sometime novelist, and bloody great pain in the arse.

"Go away!" Ian said, his vehemence muffled somewhat by the pillow.

Instead the door opened, and Wheatley clomped in, his size tens pounding the floorboards, each step striking a virtual sledgehammer blow to Ian's tender head. "I say, MacPherson, I didn't realize you slept in the buff." With his deep baritone and plummy upper-crust accent, Wheatley sounded the way Ian supposed God would sound if he'd attended Eton and Cambridge. *I say, Noah, old boy, hang on for bit longer. The precipitation will taper off presently.*

"Get out."

"Out? You just invited me in."

"No, I didn't."

"Really? Perhaps if you'd enunciate more clearly—"

Ian tossed the pillow aside, glaring at his neighbor. "Bugger off," he said, bloody enunciating his brains out. "I've got a filthy headache, and I'm in no mood for company."

Wheatley raised his aristocratic eyebrows and stared down the length of his aristocratic nose. "I do apologize for disturbing you, but I assumed you'd be interested to know Fortier rented the beach house."

"What?" Ian sat bolt upright, shoving the mosquito netting aside.

Wheatley handed him his dressing gown. "Fortier rented the beach house," he repeated.

"Bloody hell." The beach house in question was a ramshackle building with peeling paint, a rusty corrugated iron roof, and a sagging verandah. For months Ian had been trying to convince Michel Fortier, the fat Frenchman who'd sold him ten acres of jungle and the Fortier family plantation house, to sell him the cottage as well. Ian wanted to tear down the old eyesore, not only because it was ugly but because it spoiled his view of the lagoon. "This is a trick. Mark my words. That sneaky French bastard's trying to run up the price."

Wheatley gnawed on his lower lip. "Yes, I dare say, but you haven't heard the best part, the identity of our new neighbor."

With his luck a fertile young couple with half a dozen screaming brats all under six. Or an eccentric octogenarian with a penchant for playing the trumpet at odd hours.

"Her name's Tasya Flynn. She has an American passport, but according to rumor, she's a Russian spy."

"Oh, for pity's sake, Peter, what would a Russian spy be doing in a shack on the beach ten miles from Papeete? The place doesn't even have a telephone."

"Two words, MacPherson." Wheatley tapped his nose, giving Ian a knowing look. "Shortwave radio."

After Wheatley's rumormongering, Ian had been expecting his new neighbor to look like the Soviet agent in *From Russia with Love*, sleek and sophisticated. What he hadn't expected was the ponytailed gamine in shorts and a T-shirt who awakened him at six the next morning, nailing patches on her roof.

At first he thought it was Wheatley come round to share more gossip, but when repeated exhortations to bugger off had no effect, he realized the racket was coming from outside.

He pulled on a shirt and shorts, shoved his feet in canvas deck shoes, and grabbed his sunglasses. "Six o'clock in the morning. Six o'clock in the bleeding morning," he grumbled under his breath as he stomped down to the beach, irritably kicking pebbles out of his way and nearly treading on a lizard sunning itself in the middle of the path.

She had her backside to him, and a comely backside it was, despite the ill-fitting clothes. That absurd ponytail—more *Gidget Goes Hawaiian* than *From Russia with Love*—flopped up and down with each blow of the hammer.

"You don't look like a KGB agent," he said.

She gave a squeak, and the hammer flew out of her hand, flipping backward onto the sand to land a mere six inches from his right foot. "You missed," he said.

She glared down at him from her perch on the roof ridge. "I'll try harder next time."

"You *are* Miss Flynn?"

"*Ms.* Flynn."

Great. One of those. "It's six in the morning," he said, working so hard to keep any trace of either self-pity or indignation out of his voice that he ended up sounding as bland as a BBC announcer.

"Yes," she agreed, her voice as expressionless as his, though he thought he caught a sparkle of mischief in her eyes.

"It's hard to sleep with all that hammering going on."

"Try sleeping with rain pouring through the roof."

The non sequitur caught him off guard, derailing his complaint. "I beg your pardon."

She waved her hand in a dismissive gesture. "No need, I'm sure. The weather is hardly your fault."

"The weather?" Though the sun hung low in the east at this early hour, the temperature was a comfortable seventy degrees Fahrenheit, not a cloud in the sky. He frowned, more confused than ever. Perhaps he was still asleep. Perhaps this was a dream like the one about the *tamure* dancers.

"It rained last night, a tropical deluge."

"I didn't notice."

"You would have if your roof leaked like a sieve the way mine does."

"You're doing your own repairs? Shouldn't that be your landlord's responsibility?"

"I don't think responsibility is in my landlord's vocabulary. I rode my bicycle two miles to the nearest telephone box to call and let him know about the waterfall in my bedroom. And do you know what that fat pig said?"

Ian smiled at the mental image of Fortier as a pig. The man had the snout for it. No question about that. "No, what did that fat pig say?"

She stared at him suspiciously. "He's not a friend of yours, is he?"

"Hardly."

"That's okay, then. I didn't want to badmouth him if he was your friend, but since he's not"—her voice grew increasingly indignant—"I don't mind telling you he was not the least bit helpful. When I complained about the leak, he told me to shift my bed over to the dry side of the room and go back to sleep."

"But you didn't."

"Well, what good would it have done? The mattress was already soaked."

"And now you're taking matters into your own hands."

"Exactly." A frown wrinkled her brow. "Or trying to. There's more to this roof-patching business than meets the eye. I keep cutting my fingers on the edges of the metal, and I'm afraid every nail I hammer in is creating a new leak."

"A distinct possibility," he said. "Have you had breakfast?"

"Breakfast?" As if she were unfamiliar with the word.

"You KGB operatives do eat, don't you?"

She laughed, a low, sultry sound that jump-started his heart and provoked a new line of speculation. "I'm not a spy."

"And I'm not a former priest, excommunicated for seducing every nun in a Parisian convent. But that's the story on the coconut radio. Tahiti's version of the grapevine," he added in response to her puzzled look.

She laughed. "Hold on. I'm coming down." Apparently she had a ladder leaned up against the other side of the building, because she disappeared over the edge of the roof, reappearing around the northwest corner of the cottage moments later.

She was taller than he'd thought, five-seven at a guess, slender with long legs and an athlete's well-defined muscles. She had a classic oval face, lovely black-lashed gray eyes, and blond-streaked hair.

She set her hammer on the railing of the wraparound verandah, then met his gaze, her eyes sparkling, her lips curved in a teasing smile. "So, if the gossips are wrong and you're not a defrocked priest, what are you?"

"Ian MacPherson, retired cat burglar, at your service." He sketched a mocking bow.

"What a coincidence," she said. "So am I. A retired cat burglar, I mean."

"Cruise liner in port." Ian nodded toward the pier. The balcony of the café where he'd brought Tasya for breakfast overlooked Papeete's crescent-shaped waterfront. A fascinating view, but not to her mind as fascinating as Ian's chiseled cheekbones. "Which means," he said, "the shops will be packed with tourists today."

"An excellent reason to avoid them."

He raised an eyebrow. "What woman avoids shopping?"

"A woman who hates crowds?" She grinned. "I grew up on an Idaho dairy farm. What do you expect?"

"You're not Russian, then?"

"No. My mother was, but I'm an American. How about you?"

"Scot by birth, American by choice." He smiled, and her heartbeat kicked up a notch. He wasn't exactly the Ian she remembered. This younger version had an angular, square-jawed face, unlined aside from the creases bracketing his mouth and the faint crow's feet at the outer corners of his eyes. His hair was dark, his skin tanned to a gleaming bronze by the tropical sun. But some things were achingly familiar—that voice, that smile, those wicked eyebrows.

Dear God, I'm falling in love all over again.

Her heart skipped a beat. She had her second chance, and this time no one was going to spoil it.

She tore her gaze away from his. Sunlight sparkled on the water beyond the quay, where yachts, schooners, and pearling luggers were dwarfed by the enormous ocean liner Ian had pointed out. Smaller craft, motorized outriggers and speedboats, buzzed around the harbor, their noise echoed and amplified a thousandfold by the boisterous wheeled traffic jamming Boulevard Pomare. She glanced back at Ian and found him studying her.

"You've had a rough time of it, haven't you?" he said.

"What gave you that idea?" Was she so transparent?

"Your eyes. Even when you smile, the sadness lingers."

She stared at the remains of her omelet. "I lost someone I loved. When he died, I wanted to die, too." She met his gaze. "Have you ever loved anyone that much?"

He shook his head, an odd expression on his face, part envy, part something else. "No. Never found the right woman." The corners of his mouth twitched in the sardonic smile she remembered so well. "Though I've put in a good bit of practice on the wrong ones." He yawned, then shot a sheepish grin her direction. "Sorry. It's not the company. Blame a full stomach and a short night."

"I'm feeling a bit groggy myself."

The corners of his mouth twitched again. "Next time you're rained out, feel free to share my bed. What are neighbors for if not to help in time of need?"

The smile might seem lazy, the comment merely casual flirtation, but his dark eyes told another story.

"Aren't you afraid you might let something slip? Isn't that how spies get their best information? From pillow talk?"

He raised an eyebrow. "But you're not a spy. You're a retired cat burglar."

"That was a joke. Actually, I'm writing a travel book on the islands of the South Pacific."

"In that case, I'll have to introduce you to my friend Wheatley. He's the modern Somerset Maugham—or so he claims. Lives in a bungalow on the hill north and west of your cottage. You may not have noticed his house hidden in that tangle of acacias and tamarinds, but I'll wager old Peter's noticed every move you've made. Likely has his telescope trained on your bedroom window. Likes to study human nature, Wheatley does. Especially the female of the species."

She laughed. "He sounds . . . interesting. Tell me, are all your friends perverts?"

"Absolutely. I find ordinary people a dead bore."

As they left the outskirts of Papeete town behind, Ian put his foot down on the accelerator. Growling in satisfaction, the Jaguar convertible chewed up the miles. His new neighbor gave a shout of delighted laughter, then jumped to her feet, arms extended, her ridiculous ponytail flagging in the breeze. "I'm the king of the world!" she yelled.

"Your reign won't last long," he said, "if I hit a bump and toss you out on your head."

She shot him a look of sheer joy. "At least I'll die happy."

He loved her wild abandon but was, at the same time, half terrified she'd lose her footing. "Fasten your seat belt, or I swear I'll make you walk the rest of the way home."

"Old fuddy-duddy," she muttered in muted rebellion, though she did sit back down and fasten her seat belt as ordered.

"I suppose I do seem old to someone your age. Exactly how old are you, Tasya? I'm not going to be arrested for contributing to the delinquency of a minor, am I?"

She leaned over and patted his thigh. "Going on twenty-two," she said. "You're safe."

Safe, he thought, was a relative term, considering the heat of her hand on his leg. He wondered if she had any notion how close he was to pulling over to the side of the road and dragging her off into the bushes.

"So you're twenty-one to my almost thirty. That's quite an age gap."

She smiled the sort of smile that made him want to kiss her breathless. "I prefer older men," she said. And smiled again.

"Who's that?" Tasya asked, pointing to the blond man in jeans and a gaudy flowered shirt lounging on the wide verandah of Ian's plantation house.

Ian scowled. "Wheatley, damn his hide."

"Your friend, the novelist?"

"My friend, the gooseberry."

She glanced sideways at him, looking for an explanation, but he just shook his head. "Never mind."

Ian parked on the crushed shell driveway, then dashed around the car to open her door, an old-fashioned display of gallantry she found both flattering and amusing, particularly since she was still wearing the same ratty old shorts and T-shirt she'd donned to patch the roof.

And her hair. Oh, my God, her hair! Not only raked back into a ponytail but windblown now as well after driving ten miles with the top down. She could feel stray wisps tickling her cheeks and the back of her neck. Great. How was she supposed to attract Ian when she looked like a grubby teenager?

Apparently Wheatley-the-peeping-Tom didn't find her dishabille off-putting, though. He sprang from his chair and clattered down the broad wooden steps to greet them, his hungry gaze taking in every detail of her appearance, particularly those details from the neck down. "Ms. Flynn, I presume." He crushed her hand in an enthusiastic greeting. "Enchanted, I'm sure."

"Tasya," Ian said, "this is Peter Wheatley, novelist."

"Sometime novelist," Wheatley corrected him. He smiled at Tasya, revealing an endearing gap between his front teeth. "And this is not the time. Today I'm devoting myself entirely to social pursuits."

"He's quite charming for a pervert," she said to Ian, who gave a snort of laughter.

Wheatley glared at him. "You told her I was a pervert?"

"It was a joke."

"I'm not laughing, MacPherson."

"All right, I apologize," Ian said. "The truth is, I wanted to be certain she'd fall for me, not you. You always steal the best-looking women."

"I can't help it. My accent drives women wild."

"Ian has an accent."

Wheatley sniffed. "Scottish vowels larded over with American colloquialisms? Hardly an advantage." He shot Ian a smug look. "I, on the other hand, sound like James Mason. Everyone says so. I dare say I look rather like him, too. Younger, of course, and fairer. A bit more muscular perhaps."

"Don't forget taller," Ian said, almost straight-faced. "Make yourself comfortable, you two. I'll see if I can scare up some drinks." He disappeared into the house, stranding her with the Englishman.

Wheatley escorted her onto the verandah, one hand under her elbow. "What's your unbiased opinion, Ms. Flynn? Would you say I favor James Mason?"

Tasya perched on one of the white wicker chairs. Wheatley took a seat across from her on the verandah railing. She stared at the pattern of giant purple gardenias on his shirt, not sure how to respond since she had no idea who James Mason was. Someone with an English accent, presumably. An actor maybe? Obviously attractive, if he looked anything like Peter Wheatley, who could pass for a Ralph Lauren model any day of the week, Hawaiian shirt or no Hawaiian shirt. "Definitely polo.com."

She didn't realize she'd spoken out loud until Wheatley said, "Are you a polo aficionado? I had to sell my ponies when I moved out here. Saddest day of my life." He pressed a hand to his heart. "Emotionally wrenching."

Ian bumped the screen door open with his shoulder, and Wheatley's pained expression disappeared as if by magic. "Why, bless you, MacPherson, I'm dying of thirst."

Ian set a wooden tray on the small rattan table next to Tasya. "Fresh squeezed orange juice." He handed her a glass.

"What? No vodka?" Wheatley said.

Ian gave him the raised eyebrow look. "At nine in the morning?" He passed a glass to Wheatley.

The Englishman took a sip, grimacing comically. "A screwdriver's not the same without vodka. You've Russian blood in your veins, Ms. Flynn. Tell him you vote for vodka, too."

"Too early for me," she said.

Ian shook his head. "The tropics are turning you into a sot, Wheatley."

"Not true." The Englishman grinned. "I was a hopeless sot long before I set foot on Tahiti. Ask anyone."

Ian laughed. "What brings you here so bright and early?"

The Englishman pulled a paper from his pocket. "In the excitement of meeting Ms. Flynn, I nearly forgot. A man from the telegraph office tried to deliver this to you, but as you weren't home, he left it at my place."

"Who'd be sending me a telegram?"

"Some chap named Farrell in Los Angeles."

Tasya's heart skipped a beat. A message from Alex Farrell? So soon? No longer thirsty, she set her glass on the table.

"You read my telegram?" Ian said.

"One would have to be blind not to."

Shooting an exasperated look at Wheatley, Ian took the telegram and sat down on one end of the settee to read it for himself.

She'd thought she'd have more time. It was only June. Ian wasn't supposed to go to Rio with Alex until the end of August. She'd counted on those two months free of Alex's influence to . . . what? Get her hooks in Ian? Make him fall in love with her? Make him listen?

God, she was an idiot. Worse, despite the danger she'd risked to get this far, despite all her careful planning, all her best efforts, history was about to repeat itself.

"What did he mean, MacPherson, by 'APPRENTICE FLIES SOLO IN RIO. STOP. WISH ME LUCK. STOP'? Made no sense to me whatsoever."

"Friend of mine just landed a new job, wanted to share the good news, that's all." Ian stuffed the telegram in his pocket and took a long swallow of his juice.

A surge of relief left Tasya dizzy. For one dreadful moment, it had seemed she'd lost the battle before it started. Not so. Alex hadn't sent that telegram to solicit Ian's help. He'd sent it to brag. Typical, really. The sort of gesture she might have expected from an egomaniac like Alex Farrell.

Have faith, she told herself. The future wasn't written in stone. She could save Ian. And she would.

"Something wrong with your juice?" Ian said.

"No." Tasya forced a smile.

He studied her face. "Have we met before? You seem so familiar."

"Good Lord, MacPherson," Wheatley drawled, "that's the worst pickup line I ever heard."

"It's not a line. I'm serious. Have you ever been to Monte Carlo, Tasya?"

"She's a spy, old man. Even if your paths have crossed, you can't expect her to admit it and blow her cover."

She grinned at Wheatley's foolishness. "I'm not a spy. I told you before. I'm writing a travel book on the islands of the South Pacific."

"Nonsense," Ian said. "You lack the requisite pedantic pomposity of the true writer."

"I say!" Wheatley raised his chin, clearly affronted. "I'll have you know *I'm* a writer."

"Quite." Ian's smile drifted dangerously close to a smirk.

Tasya wondered what would happen to that smug expression if she told him the truth: *I'm here from the twenty-first century to save you. Without my intervention, you're going to spend thirty years condemned to a wheelchair, rotting in a Brazilian prison.* He'd have her number then, wouldn't he? Number one loony-tuner.

"So, we've established you're not a writer." Ian paused for her response. When she said nothing, he continued. "And I doubt you're a Soviet agent, either, despite the rumors."

Again he paused. Again she said nothing.

"And as for a retired jewel thief? You're much too young to be a retired anything. So what are you, Tasya?"

"I have it," Wheatley said. "She's an actress. I daresay you saw her in a film."

"Perhaps," Ian said. "That would explain why you seem so familiar, like someone I used to know."

"In another life?" She couldn't stop herself from making the suggestion.

"I know I've heard that voice before. How about you, Wheatley? Do you recognize her voice?"

Wheatley tossed off the last of his juice. "Can't say that I do. Perhaps your ear is better than mine."

Ian smiled at her. "I do have a good ear."

"Two good ears," she said. "To go along with your excellent eyes, your first-rate nose, and your absolutely gorgeous mouth."

"You forgot his eyebrows," Wheatley said. "The man has terribly clever eyebrows."

"And terribly clever eyebrows," she added.

Ian's smile faded. He stared at her, not saying a thing—or maybe he did say something, but his words were drowned out by the whizzing and popping of the electricity suddenly sparking between them.

Wheatley gave a little cough, half polite, half embarrassed. Probably the first time he ever saw two people mentally undressing each other at nine-thirty in the morning. "I think I'll be going now."

"Yes, do," Ian said.

17

IAN WAS SO FOCUSED ON TASYA, he scarcely noticed Wheatley leaving. She fascinated him, though he wasn't sure why. She was lovely—even with her face innocent of makeup—but Tahiti was famous for its beautiful women. Wasn't that one reason he'd retired here? Yet no other beautiful woman had affected him the way Tasya Flynn did. He wanted her. He'd known her less than three hours, but he wanted her with the desperate, aching desire of a man who hadn't been with a woman in decades. Images flashed through his brain: Tasya in a blood-red evening gown, Tasya in a white singlet and pink boxers. Not quite memories. More like memories of memories. Or memories of dreams.

Color flushed her cheeks.

Had he telegraphed his intentions? Frightened her off? She stood. "I probably ought to be leaving, too."

"Don't go," he said quickly. "I know we just met, but I feel we have a connection." Oh, hell. Wheatley was right. He sounded like some two-bit island gigolo. He wouldn't blame her if she bolted.

Instead she joined him on the settee. "I feel it, too. That connection."

She felt it, too? This confusing sense of familiarity coupled with fierce sexual attraction?

She trailed her fingertips along his cheek, a touch so electric it short-circuited his brain. "I like your hair dark," she said. "Not quite black, but almost."

"Same color I was born with." Moronic comment, but the best he could manage under the circumstances.

"And your voice. I love your voice. If I close my eyes"—she suited action to words—"it's like . . ." Her sentence trailed off, and her eyes fluttered open. The pupils were huge, nearly obscuring the silvery irises.

"Like what?"

"Nothing." She leaned forward. Her breasts brushed his chest, and his heart tried to slam its way past his ribs. "Maybe," she said, "if you kiss me, it'll jog our memories."

Jog. Memories. Kiss. Yes. No problem. Kissing was only one step up from a handshake. He could handle a little kissing without reverting to a troglodyte. Absolutely. As long as he kept his wayward hands to himself.

His mouth found hers. She tasted of oranges and sunlight. Oranges and sunlight and sweet, sweet seduction.

One hand? his libido begged. *I promise, swear to God, no breast fondling or errant forays below the waist. I just want to cup the back of her head.*

So you can force your tongue down her throat, Reason argued. *I'm onto your tricks.*

Tasya parted her lips.

Reason tried to whisper a warning, but Libido drowned him out.

Groaning in pleasure, Ian drank her in like a man dying of thirst. He wrapped one hand around the back of her head, working his fingers under the elastic that bound her ponytail. It gave with a snap that stung his fingers, a small price to pay for the pleasure of seeing all that soft pale hair cascading around her shoulders.

His other hand found her right breast and cupped its warmth, his thumb tracing slow erotic circles around a nipple that was already tightly pebbled.

With a tremulous sigh, she broke off the kiss.

He thought for a second he'd botched it. Then he got a good look at her face. No panic there. No hint that he had gone too far, too fast. On the contrary, she looked like a woman who was right where she wanted to be. With her eyes half closed, a faint smile on her face, Tasya pressed two fingers to his mouth. "Just the same," she said.

He nibbled at the fingers, then captured her hand in his, kissing her knuckles one by one, pressing a kiss to the inside of her wrist. "Same as what?"

"Same . . . as I imagined."

"What? Not better?"

She laughed. "Since when have you needed your ego stroked? You're the most self-confident person I know."

"And you are the most enigmatic." He touched her face, knowing the texture of her skin, the play of muscles beneath it, as well as he knew his own name. She was the perfect oxymoron, the familiar stranger.

Or was he deluding himself? Seeing something that wasn't there? Projecting qualities he wanted to find?

Suddenly she scrambled to her feet. Confused, he wasn't

sure whether to apologize or remonstrate. "Are you going, then?"

One corner of her mouth curved up in a half smile. "That wasn't the plan, no."

Then what? he started to say, the words shriveling in his throat as she stripped off her T-shirt. She shot him an impish grin, then kicked off her sandals and stepped out of her shorts.

Tasya in baggy clothes and a ponytail had posed a temptation. Tasya in pink lace underwear, her long hair loose and disheveled, personified sin.

She climbed onto his lap, unbuttoned his shirt, and proceeded to drive him mad, flicking his nipples with the tip of her tongue, then blowing puffs of warm breath across the damp and sensitive skin. He gritted his teeth and gripped the settee, hanging on for dear life. "Do you like that, Ian? How does this feel?" she asked after each fresh torment, each new pleasure.

But when she shifted her attention to the button at his waistband, he grabbed her hands. "No," he said, his voice as rough as the coral reef enclosing the lagoon.

"Why?"

Because I'm scared silly I'm going to come in my trousers like an oversexed teenager. One touch of those dexterous fingers. That's all it would take.

When he didn't answer immediately, color stained her cheeks, and fear or something very like it flickered in her eyes for a moment before she lowered her lashes like a veil.

He leaned forward and kissed her on the end of the nose.

Her eyelashes fluttered. Her mouth trembled. "You're not irritated? I'm not being too pushy?"

"No, you're doing everything right. Too right. Embarrassing as it is to admit, where you're concerned I seem to have a hair trigger." He gave her a sheepish smile. "I need a minute to . . . regain control."

"Oh." She appeared to think about this for a moment, then, "Oh!" she said and scrambled to her feet.

Ian stood, too. "This probably isn't the best location anyway. My bed's more comfortable." More private, too.

She smiled sweetly. "I expect comfort is a concern for a man of your advanced years."

Advanced years? Ian grabbed for her, but she slipped past him into the house, hooking the screen door shut behind her.

"Hey!" he yelled, banging on the door frame. "Open up!" He grabbed the handle and gave a tremendous jerk. The wood splintered, the eyebolt went skittering across the floor, the door swung open, and he was inside.

Tasya popped her head through the dining room archway, saw him hunkered in the entry, shrieked, and fled.

She was quick and agile, but he knew the house. When she ran up the main staircase, he took the back stairs two at a time and cornered her at the end of the upstairs hall just outside his bedroom. He backed her against the wall. Both of them were breathing hard. And laughing.

Using his hips to pin her to the paneling, Ian gathered her wrists in one hand and shoved them over her head. Then he tilted her face to his and kissed her, a kiss that started fierce and punishing—I'll show *you* advanced years—but quickly evolved into something warm and sweet and curiously tender.

Her body seemed to melt into his. Hot and fluid. Wildly erotic. All that beautiful golden skin pressed tightly to his body, the soft warmth of her breasts, the firm heat of her thighs. The scent of her, a blend of tropical fragrances—gardenia, citrus, a hint of vanilla—tormented him. He wanted her. Needed her.

Yet enmeshed with the fierce sensual urges she aroused were other equally powerful if unfamiliar feelings: protectiveness, possessiveness, tenderness.

He relaxed his grip on her wrists, and her arms slid free. She draped them around his neck and pulled him closer, her fingers stroking the muscles of his neck and shoulders and tangling themselves in his hair. "Please." She whispered the word against his mouth.

This is crazy, Reason said. *You don't know this woman.*

But he did know her. Knew her and . . .

You want her. She's willing. What's the problem? That was Libido weighing in with his assessment.

But there was more to it. He . . .

"Please." Tasya squirmed against him in a way that delighted his libido.

To hell with it. His mouth found hers again, and he lost himself in the heat. She felt soft and warm and achingly familiar. Ian slid his hands across her skin, somehow knowing the smooth curve of her hip, the fragile angle of her crooked right collarbone.

Richard. The name slithered through his mind. Dark. Poisonous. Evil.

Tasya shuddered, as if she'd caught an echo of his thoughts. "What is it?"

"Nothing," he said, reassuring her with his mouth and hands. But why Richard? he wondered. He'd known several Richards in his life, none of them evil. Odd. Very odd.

Then Tasya melted against him again, and he quit thinking. He maneuvered her into the bedroom, kicking the door shut behind them in case his cleaning lady decided to fit him into her schedule this morning. Vaitiara knew a closed door meant he didn't want to be disturbed. At least not by Vaitiara.

Tasya Flynn, on the other hand, could disturb him all she wanted.

She smiled then, a knowing Mona Lisa smile that set his heart hammering. Maintaining eye contact, she released the front clasp of her bra, slipped it off, and tossed it on the floor.

Her breasts were the same warm honey color as the rest of her, fuller than he'd expected, with pale pink nipples. Thank God Wheatley's telescope couldn't see past the jacaranda trees to peep in this window.

He watched her watching him as he stripped, pleased to see her silver eyes widen, glistening like mirrors. She crossed to him and caught his face between her hands, gazing at him for a heartbeat, fire burning in her eyes. "Oh, Ian," she said, and then she was kissing him again, her sweet warmth invading his senses, seducing his body, and branding his soul.

How could he feel this way about someone he'd known so short a time? It was wild and impossible and utterly insane. But also inexplicably right.

The backs of his legs bumped the edge of the bed. Had she steered him in that direction, or had his body acted on its own initiative? No matter. He lay back on the rumpled sheets, pulling her down next to him, and almost lost it for the second time when his erection brushed the bare skin of her thigh. *Bloody hell, what was his problem?*

Tasya wrapped herself around him, all warm, sweet seduction and hot, desperate urgency. He could feel her hands on his shoulders, his back, his buttocks. Her breasts nudged his chest. Her legs twined around his. And she moved, arching against him, rubbing, touching, tantalizing.

Dear God, he couldn't hang on much longer. He worked an arm free and flailed through the drawer of the bedside table, scrabbling for a condom. *Don't let me be out. Don't let me be out. Please, God, don't let me be out.* Flashlight, pen, notebook, tissues, a jar of red hots. *Oh, bloody hell, he was out. He was . . . No, wait.* His fingers closed on the familiar outlines of a foil-wrapped packet, and he nearly sobbed in relief.

"What?" Tasya caught his lower lip between her teeth.

"Protection." Extricating himself from the tangle of limbs and bedclothes, he covered himself, then turned back to see Tasya'd *un*covered herself.

The pink lace panties dangled from one finger. She grinned, tossed them past a swag of mosquito netting, and reached for him.

He grabbed her hands and pinned them to the bed. He wanted to come inside her, with her.

Smiling up at him, she spread her thighs, and he entered her in one slow, smooth thrust. Her eyes widened, and she exhaled softly. "Ian." Just that. Just his name.

He meant to go slowly, to make it last, but Tasya was too impatient, too aroused. With breathy sighs and eager moans, she moved against him, beneath him, around him. Insanity. Sweet, sweet insanity.

She came quickly in a noisy climax, her shuddering spasms precipitating his own release. If release was the right word. It felt more like an explosion, a ten-megaton blast.

Gradually he regained a modicum of brain function, realized he was still lying on top of her, and rolled their entwined bodies so she was on top. Then he wrapped his arms around her and held her close. Long after the last of the pleasure jolts had ebbed away, he cradled her, breathing in the flowery scent of her hair and the headier scent of sex. Tasya. So warm and sweet. So passionate, so fierce.

"Ian?" One hand splayed out on his chest next to her cheek. The other gripped his biceps. Both tightened.

"What?"

She lifted her head and smiled down at him. "That was everything I'd hoped for." She brushed his chin with the tips of her fingers. "Beard stubble and all."

He touched his face. He'd tumbled out of bed so early, angry at being awakened by her hammering, he hadn't thought to shave.

Her smile widened, as if she found his chagrin amusing. She pressed her lips to his. "Don't worry. I think you're perfect," she said. "Well worth w——"

Worth what? he wondered. He'd never know. Before

she could complete her thought, a racket erupted downstairs. Someone banging on the door.

"That damned Wheatley," he muttered. "Maybe if we're quiet, he'll go away."

"I don't think so. He knows you're here."

"And you, too. Not to mention being perfectly well aware of what we're doing. If the man had an ounce of proper feeling, he'd butt out."

Another torrent of knocking assailed their ears. "Monsieur MacPherson! Monsieur MacPherson! Are you there?"

"Oh, no," he whispered. "It's worse than I thought."

"Monsieur MacPherson. *C'est moi*. Michel Fortier."

"I'm in bed. Come back later," he yelled, hoping Fortier would take the hint.

"Fortier," Tasya said. "That fat pig of a Frenchman. I wonder what he wants."

"Perhaps he's come to fix your roof."

Shooting him a dubious look, she rolled off the bed and began gathering up her underwear just as the Frenchman opened the door and walked in.

Tasya screamed, but Fortier, focused on the view, did not appear to hear her.

Ian ripped the top sheet loose and tossed it to Tasya, then turned on Fortier with a scowl. "What the bloody hell are you doing in my bedroom?"

Fortier, obviously offended, put a hand to his heart. "But you told me to come. I hear this with my own ears."

"What I said was, 'Come back later.'"

"Oh, well, then. My mistake." He shrugged. "I came to tell you about your new neighbor, but I see you have already met Mademoiselle Flynn."

Smirk, and you're going to lose your front teeth, you overfed French bastard. "Obviously," Ian said.

Fortier took a hasty step backward.

Damned good job of intimidation, Ian congratulated himself. Particularly for someone wearing nothing but beard stubble and a condom.

"And were you aware that the mademoiselle is a well-known Soviet agent, rumored to have seduced two United States senators and one nuclear physicist?"

Ian stripped off the condom, tossed it in the wastebasket, cleaned himself on his T-shirt, tossed that in the wastebasket, too, then pulled on a pair of shorts. Frowning, he turned to the Frenchman. "She told me *one* United States senator and *two* nuclear physicists, a husband-and-wife team."

Fortier's eyes bulged. "*Mon dieu,* is this true?"

"No, of course not. He's joking," Tasya said. She'd managed to wrap the sheet around herself, toga-style. "Defrocked priests are good at that."

Ian feared Fortier's eyes were about to pop right out of his head. "You were a priest? I thought you told me you'd been involved in the jewelry trade."

"Oh, good one." Tasya winked at him. "I'd love to stay and swap lies for what's left of the morning, gentlemen, but I have a waterlogged mattress to dry out and a roof that needs patching." She turned to Fortier. "Dare I hope that's why you're here?"

"Actually—" Fortier started, but she cut him off.

"If you'll excuse me—" She gathered her bra and panties into a bundle and swept from the room, the white percale sheet still clutched to her bosom.

Fortier watched her go. Ian really couldn't blame him. It was a very thin sheet.

When he heard the screen door bang shut behind her, Ian turned once again to the Frenchman. "About that leaky roof—"

Tasya lay in the hammock on the verandah of her cottage, trying to work up enough energy to go for a swim. Not that it would be much hassle. She was already in her bikini, and the lagoon was only fifty feet away. Still, swimming would require effort, and she was too comfortable to exert herself.

Besides, the hammock was the perfect spot for thinking, and she had a lot to process. She closed her eyes, her thoughts focusing on the time she'd spent with Ian. From their initial confrontation over her early morning roof repairs to that wonderful, fabulous, oh-so-very-much-worth-waiting-for sex, each moment had been magic.

All except maybe the moment when Wheatley had produced the telegram from Alex Farrell. She'd been terrified Alex had decided to alter the schedule on the Rio caper. Thank God, it had been a false alarm. To cheat fate, she needed to earn Ian's trust well before Alex tried to convince him to help steal Milagre. If Alex were to show up prematurely . . .

She shuddered. She couldn't let history repeat itself. She *wouldn't*.

Don't even think about failing.

Good advice, because sometimes what looked like failure wasn't. In the first moments after she'd rematerialized in Dona Elizabete's garden, she'd thought she'd failed. But her only failure was in not understanding what the tour-malines could and couldn't do. They *could* move people through time; they *couldn't* move people through space. Father Duarte'd got that part wrong. She smiled, remembering Dona Elizabete's excitement when she'd realized time travel was more than a theory, more than a legend.

So the lesson was, never give up. And be damned to Alex Farrell. They'd defeated him once. They could do it again. Only how was she to convince Ian of the danger?

She surveyed her surroundings. Evil had never seemed so remote. The sky was blue, and the day was warm, with just enough breeze off the ocean to keep it from feeling sultry. Waves broke against the reef in a peaceful sere-nade, and the scent of flowers filled the air. Leggy, over-grown hibiscus bushes clustered along the east side of the cottage, while fragrant frangipani grew wild on the hill-side above. With one bare foot, she pushed against the porch upright to set the hammock rocking.

How strange to see Ian looking so young. Strange, but not as hard to get used to as she'd feared. His eyes were the same. And his voice, though the burr was more pro-nounced now than it had been in the future. His smile, on the other hand, was exactly as she remembered it. So were his broad shoulders and strong, competent hands. Be-neath the unlined skin, the clean-shaven jaw, and the glossy dark hair, he was the same man she'd fallen in love with. Same man, different century.

"Yoo-hoo! Ahoy the cottage!"

Tasya sat up so abruptly she nearly got pitched out of the hammock. Steadying herself, she peered across the water. Nothing. The lagoon was empty.

"There you are!" Peter Wheatley popped around the corner like a jack-in-the-box.

"And there *you* are. I couldn't figure out where your voice was coming from. The 'ahoy' confused me. I half expected to see a ship full of pirates anchored in the lagoon."

He laughed. "Permission to come aboard?"

She extended a hand in welcome. "Permission granted."

Pocketing his sunglasses, he clambered up the rickety steps and propped himself against the railing. It groaned a protest but appeared in no imminent danger of collapse. "I see you got your roof fixed. The shiny new patches nearly knocked my eyes out as I came down the hill."

"Ian shamed Monsieur Fortier into taking care of it. He sent two nice young Tahitian men out to do the work. They didn't speak a word of English but seemed to understand my pitiful traveler's-phrase-book French. I had no idea what they were saying, though."

"Just as well, I imagine. Quite liberal in their speech, the Tahitians. Quite liberal altogether. They invented free love, you know, long before the hippies got into it."

"Moral issues aside, they were very helpful. After fixing my roof, they dragged my soggy mattress outside to dry in the sun."

"Pity your stay got off to such a poor start."

"A little rain is hardly a disaster." God knew she'd endured worse.

"That's the attitude. Life out here has its minor inconveniences—occasional power outages, rampant VD, rats, those nasty rockfish in the lagoon—but all in all, Tahiti lives up to its reputation."

"Rockfish?"

"Wretched creatures. About a foot long with poisonous spines along their backs. They lurk in shallow water, blending with the rocks and coral. One unwary step and . . ." He shook his head. "I stepped on one of the bloody things my first week out here and was laid up for a month in absolute agony. There is an antidote, but in my case it was administered too late to do much good." He shrugged. "I learned my lesson. Avoid lagoons."

"But if I can't swim in the lagoon—"

"You can. People do. But you have to be careful. Personally, I never cared much for salt water anyway. Burns my eyes. I generally swim at the pool below the waterfall." He tilted his head to indicate the direction. "It's on Ian's property, but he doesn't mind if other people use it."

Tasya stretched, then relaxed against the pillows. "I'm feeling too lazy to go swimming anyway. What brings you out in the heat of the afternoon?"

Wheatley, who'd been staring at her legs in apparent fascination, gave a start and dragged his gaze back up to her face. "It's Tuesday," he said.

"Last time I checked the calendar, yes."

His face flushed a little beneath his tan. "Tuesdays, Thursdays, and Saturdays, Ian and I typically drop in at Quinn's. Thought you might like to join us. Enjoy a bit of local color."

"Quinn's?"

"It's a bar on the waterfront. A dive, really. Everyone hangs out there. Sailors, prostitutes, tourists, locals. If you haven't been to Quinn's, you haven't seen the real Tahiti."

"Sounds . . . interesting." She grinned. "I'd love to go."

"Go where?"

A tiny frisson of pleasure rippled through her at the sound of Ian's voice. She tipped her head back to look behind her. Peter Wheatley had approached from the west, Ian from the east. She smiled at him upside down. "Come join the party."

He hopped over the railing onto the verandah. "Go where?" He glanced at Wheatley, his expression menacing.

"Peter invited me to join you two tonight at Quinn's."

"Actually"—Ian stood next to her, so close she could smell the clean soap-and-shaving-cream scent of him—"I have other plans." Judging by his expression, plans that included her and a box of condoms. Despite the trade winds wafting across the verandah, oxygen suddenly seemed in short supply.

"Well, I suppose Peter and I can manage by ourselves."

The Englishman grinned, obviously delighted by her response.

Ian, not quite so delighted, raised an eyebrow. "No need. I'm flexible. Quinn's it is. Eight-thirty all right?"

Wheatley looked like a toddler who'd just watched both scoops of his double-decker ice-cream cone plop off onto the sidewalk. "Eight-thirty's fine."

"We'll meet you there," Ian told him. "The Jaguar's a two-seater. Otherwise we could all go together."

"If we took my car—"

"Get serious. You can't expect Tasya to ride in that disaster. Dust an inch thick on the dash. Sand ground into the floor mats—"

"I could dust. I could vacuum."

"You could, but you never do. Bird droppings plastered all over the bonnet, dead insects obscuring the windscreen—"

"I could polish. I could scrub."

Ian flashed a grin at her. "Notice how he always says 'could,' not 'will'?" He turned to his friend. "Wouldn't help anyway. Not when you insist on parking under the acacias. Besides, there's the annoying rattle of all those empty beer bottles in the boot."

"I've been meaning to get rid of them."

"We'll meet you there," Ian said again.

"What do people wear to Quinn's?" Tasya asked.

"What's wrong with what you have on?" Wheatley said.

Ian shot him an exasperated look. "It's a pretty casual place. Perhaps not bikini casual, but aside from that . . . You'll likely see everything from socialites in designer sportswear to local girls in pareus."

"Pareus?"

"Like Dorothy Lamour wore in that old *Road* movie," Wheatley said. "A flowered sarong thingy."

"How about a miniskirt?"

"Works for me." Wheatley's enthusiasm made her laugh.

"Me, too," Ian said.

Her laughter evaporated under the fierce heat of his gaze.

"Whatever you do, wear something cool," Wheatley said. "It's going to be a warm night."

"Hot," Ian said. "A very hot night."

18

THE CUSTOMERS AT Quinn's Tahitian Hut seemed even more boisterous than usual. Ian fought his way to the circular bar, dragging Tasya in his wake. "Two beers." He eyed the gyrating crowd packing the dance floor.

Maybe the band, a group from Samoa who relied more on a driving drumbeat and twanging electric guitars than talent, was generating the extra rowdiness. Or perhaps the heightened activity was due to the number of thrill-seeking cruise ship passengers and inebriated French sailors crowding the place. Or maybe nothing had changed but his perspective. Maybe it only seemed different tonight because he was seeing it through Tasya's eyes.

The bartender slapped the beers down on the bar, and Ian paid for them. "What do you think of the place so far?" he asked Tasya.

She grinned. "Interesting." She raised her arms above her head and did a little shimmy. "What's that dance they're doing?"

"The *tamure*, the Tahitian version of the hula."

Setting her hands on her hips, Tasya did a few experimental hip twitches. "Looks like fun."

"Think so?" Ian considered dancing a spectator sport. He never ventured onto the dance floor himself—not unless he'd exceeded his three-drink limit.

"Oh, look," Tasya said. "There's Peter."

Wheatley was waving at them from across the room, where he sat talking to a middle-aged man in a double-breasted navy blazer and yachtsman's cap. Ian waved back, then, juggling their beers in one hand and towing Tasya with the other, launched himself into the crowd. Several minutes later he arrived at Wheatley's table with most of the beer and all of Tasya intact.

"Greetings and salutations." Wheatley's expansiveness suggested he'd been imbibing freely. "Sir Rupert, my friends Ian MacPherson and Tasya Flynn. Ian and Tasya, Sir Rupert Rutledge, an old family friend. Sir Rupert is cruising the Society Islands in his schooner *Orpheus*."

Sir Rupert nodded a greeting. "Quite festive tonight, eh?"

Tasya shot a dubious look at the churning crowd. "Someone pinched my rear end."

"Likely one of the Italian seamen off the cruise liner," Wheatley said. "That entire race has a fanny fetish."

"As opposed to the Americans, with their absurd obsession with breasts," Sir Rupert said.

"I'm not American," Wheatley said, "but I appreciate a lovely pair of breasts as much as the next bloke. And legs. Nothing like a good set of legs."

"I'm a leg man myself," Sir Rupert said with an arch

glance at Tasya, whose legs were very much in evidence beneath the hem of her miniskirt.

Ian, sensing Tasya was not happy with the discussion, gave her hand a squeeze. She leaned closer to whisper in his ear. "Not exactly PC, are they?"

Ian wasn't sure what she meant but was afraid to ask for fear of causing a fuss, so he just squeezed her hand again.

"Oh, there you are!" Sir Rupert greeted two women in pearls and little black cocktail dresses. One woman was tall, with short sable hair and eyes so impossibly blue they had to be contact-lens-enhanced. The other was a petite strawberry blonde with a typically English peaches-and-cream complexion, her beauty marred only by a petulant mouth. A mouth Ian knew only too well—he'd had a brief affair with its owner, Olivia Kimbrough-Yeats.

The yachtsman launched into introductions, but Olivia cut him off. "Pamela and I have known Peter for ages, haven't we, Pammy? And Ian, where was it we met? The Costa del Sol?"

"Monte Carlo," he said.

She patted his arm. "Yes, at the casino. Rather thrilling circumstances, as I recall. Heavy James Bond overtones."

"Really?" Tasya said. "I thought I was the only one suspected of being a spy."

Seeing no way around it, Ian introduced the two women.

"What did you mean when you said you were suspected of being a spy?" Olivia asked Tasya.

"Local gossip," Wheatley said. "Not a word of truth in it, of course. I mean, if the girl were KGB, she wouldn't hang around a political backwater like Papeete, would she? She'd be in London, worming her way into the confidence of fat politicians."

Olivia pursed her lips. "I don't know. I should think a clever operative could learn things even here. I mean, given the right social contacts. After all, Pammy's father's an MP, and Rupert's son Freddy is working with the Defense Ministry on some terribly hush-hush project."

"Quick, before I forget, someone loan me a pen so I can scribble notes on a napkin. What was it you said again?" Tasya asked. "Pammy's father's an MP, and Sir Rupert's son Freddy's working on a top-secret project?"

"Not funny," Ian said. "That's how rumors get started."

"Drag me out on the dance floor," she said. "That'll keep me out of trouble."

Wheatley laughed. "You don't want to dance with MacPherson. The man's got two left feet." He stood, only a trifle unsteadily. "Unlike me, England's answer to Fred Astaire. Shall we?" He offered Tasya his arm.

"Ian?" she said.

"Go on. He's harmless as long as you keep him at arm's length. But if they start playing a slow dance, run."

Laughing, she stepped behind Wheatley and placed her hands on his shoulders. "Lead the way, Fred. I'm right behind you." She winked at Ian. "See? Arm's length, as per instructions."

The two disappeared into the throng of dancers.

Pamela Whoever took Wheatley's vacated seat. Olivia sat next to Sir Rupert. Catching Ian's hand, she pulled him down beside her. "We need to talk," she said. Four of the most terrifying words in the English language.

"How about another round of drinks?" he suggested.

Olivia directed some eyebrow-wriggling-cum-telepathy toward her friend. Ian couldn't decipher the message, but apparently Pammy was on the right wavelength, because she popped to her feet, saying, "Sir Rupert and I will go get them, won't we, sweetie?"

Sir Rupert's face had a glazed expression. Either he was as confused by the eyebrow signals as Ian, or being called "sweetie" by a young lovely like Pammy had temporarily addled his brains.

"Back in a jiff." Pammy led Sir Rupert toward the bar.

Ian searched the crowded dance floor to see where Tasya and Wheatley had got to. He spotted them on the far side of the room, Wheatley jerking and twitching like a marionette in the hands of a demented puppeteer, Tasya drawing a crowd of appreciative onlookers as she performed a very creditable version of the tamure.

Olivia raked his forearm with her pearl pink nails, not hard enough to break the skin, just hard enough to get his attention. "You broke my heart, you bastard."

"You broke my foot. I guess that makes us even."

She pushed out her lip in an exaggerated pout, accompanied by a flirtatious sweep of false eyelashes. "But it was all your fault. If you hadn't gone waterskiing without telling me—"

"You deliberately stomped my bare foot with your high heel."

"You deserved it."

If she'd been a man, he'd have told her to sod off. Instead, he took a deep breath and counted silently to ten.

"We were good together, Ian. We can be good together

again. I'm here for a week. Think of it, darling, seven days of wild, uninhibited sex." She leaned closer, resting her left breast on his arm, the same arm she'd just scratched.

"It didn't work out. Let's leave it at that." He glanced back toward Tasya and Wheatley. Tasya had kicked off her platform sandals and was up on the bar, twitching her hips faster and faster to the beat of the drums while Wheatley and a crowd of enthusiastic fans cheered her on.

Lady Olivia followed his gaze. "So that's the way the wind blows, is it?" She laughed. "I thought you had better taste. Good God, Ian, she's a nobody." Olivia gave a delicate, ladylike shudder. "I've never seen such a blatant public display, but then, perhaps she's drumming up business. I wonder who she'll wangle more money out of—you or poor besotted Peter?"

Ian wanted to tell her to shut her mouth. Hell, he wanted to shut her mouth *for* her. But no matter how much the vile-tongued bitch deserved it, he couldn't. Instead he left the table without a word and elbowed his way across the room.

Tasya's eyes lit up when she saw him. She yelled something he couldn't hear over the noise of the band.

He shook his head, giving her a palms-up, and she motioned for him to join her on the bar.

Laughing, he shook his head again, then extended his arms.

Without hesitation she leaped off the bar. He caught her, and the crowd roared their approval. Wheatley gave them an A-OK sign.

Ian pulled Tasya close, so close he could feel her heart thumping as wildly as the drums. "Let's go," he mouthed.

"Wait!" someone shouted. He turned to see Wheatley worming his way toward them. Wheatley handed Tasya her sandals and slapped Ian on the back. "Best man wins and all that," he said in Ian's ear. "Lucky bastard."

"Who are you, Tasya? Who are you really?" Ian asked as they drove home through the darkness.

"You know who I am." She forced a laugh. "Tasya Flynn, super spy—slash—travel writer."

"You're not a spy, and I'm pretty sure you're not a writer, either. There's no typewriter in your cottage."

She shot him a questioning look.

"While you were in the bathroom putting the finishing touches on your makeup, I had a look around."

She clenched her hands together in her lap, trying to think of something to tell him. Not the truth. At least not the whole truth. He'd never believe it. Yet how could she expect him to trust her if she didn't tell him who and what she really was? An impossible conundrum. "What do you want to know?"

"Start at the beginning. Did you have a happy childhood?"

"Happy enough until my parents died. A car wreck. I was fifteen. Afterward I went to live with relatives."

"Judging by your voice, that wasn't a success."

"No." She paused. "The court eventually placed me in foster care. A year later, I ended up on the streets."

He pulled onto the shoulder of the road next to a coconut plantation, switched off the ignition, then angled toward her in the moonlight. "I didn't mean to make you dredge up bad memories."

She took a deep breath. Little did he know how very bad some of those memories were.

He traced the line of her crooked collarbone. "Richard."

A shudder worked its way down her spine. "What?" she whispered.

"He hurt you, didn't he? He hurt you terribly."

"How could you possibly know about—"

Ian frowned. "I'm not sure."

Tasya studied the regimented rows of palm trees. Their fronds rustled secrets in the night breeze. Maybe if she listened closely enough, they would explain how Ian could know what Richard had done. Would do. Depravity in the future tense.

"Seems quite impossible, doesn't it?" He took her hands in his. "I never believed in fortune-telling or mind reading or any of that ESP rubbish, but where you're concerned, I seem to have rather finely tuned intuition." His thumbs slid across the backs of her hands. Back and forth. Back and forth. "Perhaps it's because we're fundamentally alike, both battling the demons of our checkered pasts." He brought her hands to his mouth and kissed them. "I really am a retired cat burglar, you know. It's not a joke or a rumor started on the coconut radio. I stole for a living — mostly jewelry—from people who could well afford the loss, people like Sir Rupert and his friends."

"But why—"

"It's a long story."

"My favorite kind."

"All right." He gave her hands a final squeeze before releasing them. "My father lost everything in the war—his wife, his parents, even Clach Dubh, the home that had been in his family for two centuries—everything but me and his unshakable optimism. 'Count your blessings, boy, not your pennies,' he always said."

"I like him already." Tasya smiled.

"I went off to school in Edinburgh, and he settled in as estate agent for the English family who'd bought Clach Dubh. All went well until the new owners found themselves in financial straits. They faked the theft of some jewelry in order to collect the insurance. Only the local constable didn't buy the story of a break-in, so the new owners planted a few inferior pieces in my father's room to throw suspicion on him."

"That's terrible!"

"It gets worse. My father's shock at being hauled in for questioning triggered a fatal heart attack."

"I'm so sorry." Sorry for the father. Sorry for the son. She touched his arm and felt the tension in his muscles.

"At his funeral one of the Clach Dubh housemaids told me she'd seen the mistress wearing some of the jewelry that had been reported stolen. Wasn't hard after that to figure out what they'd done." He paused, gazing out at the ocean. "So I stole the 'stolen' jewels, bought my father the finest headstone in all Scotland, and booked myself on the next flight to America."

"Poetic justice," Tasya said.

"I doubt the authorities would agree, particularly since that caper was only the beginning. Burglary's addictive, Tasya. Pulling a high-stakes heist is a full-out adrenaline rush." A rueful smile tilted the corners of his mouth. "I was a thief. It was wrong, and I knew it. There are no excuses for what I did. Reasons, yes, but no excuses."

Tasya smiled. "So you're not perfect."

"Hardly."

She tilted her head, studying his face in the moonlight. "Close enough," she said.

He stared at her a moment, then restarted the engine and drove back onto the road. "Tell me about him."

"Richard?"

"No, the man you loved, the man who died."

His request took her by surprise. She gazed out the windshield, staring at the lights of an oncoming car, playing for time. How much could she share without making him suspicious? "When we first met, you introduced yourself as a retired cat burglar? Do you remember what I said?"

"'What a coincidence. So am I.'" He shot her a sideways glance. "Are you?"

"Not retired. Novice is more like it. I've been involved in two capers, and one really doesn't count because I gave back the ring I stole."

"Gave it back?" he said, as if that were a worse crime than stealing it in the first place.

"The ring wasn't my objective. The purpose of the heist was to prove I could pull it off. The theft was a sort of final exam arranged by my mentor."

"And your mentor—"

"Was the man I loved, the man who died." Not *who's dead* but *who died*. A subtle difference.

"What happened? Did the caper go wrong?"

"No, his death had nothing to do with the job." She drew a long shaky breath. "Richard tracked me down. I'd run away, but he caught up with me. My mentor died trying to protect me."

"And Richard?"

"He died, too." A silence stretched between them.

"Odd, isn't it," Ian said at length, "how his name popped into my head? One of several strange experiences I've had lately."

"For example?"

"You. I . . . a couple of times I've . . ."

"What?"

"It's hard to explain without sounding daft." He frowned. "Remember I told you that you seemed familiar?"

"Yes."

"It's bizarre, really. I relax for a moment, and stray images float to the surface of my brain."

"Images of me? You fantasize about me?"

"No. I mean yes, but this is different. The images aren't fantasies or daydreams. They're more like . . . memories." He shifted in his seat. "How strange is that?"

Despite the warmth of the tropical night, she shivered. How strange was that? Pretty damned strange.

Ian helped Tasya drag her mattress back inside. "You can't sleep on that," he said. "It's still damp."

She smiled, and for a second all he could think about was how much he wanted to kiss her. "So I'll sleep in the hammock."

"Impossible. The insects will eat you alive."

Still smiling, she took a step closer and rested her palms on his chest. Studying the buttons of his sports shirt, she said, "Whatever shall I do?"

He wrapped his arms around her, pulling her closer

yet. "I expect Wheatley would let you camp out in his spare room."

He felt her laughter more than heard it. "I should go stay with Peter just to spite you." She slid her hands up his chest and wrapped them around his neck. Standing on tiptoe, she kissed the end of his chin, the only part of his face within reach. "Bend down here so I can kiss you properly."

"I'll bend," he said, "but only if you promise to kiss me *im*properly."

She leaned away from him. "What do you consider improper?"

Frowning, he tipped his head to the side. "Pretty much anything French," he said. "French films. French love songs. French underwear. French perfume." He raised his eyebrows and grinned. "French letters. French kissing."

"How about French poodles?" she suggested with such an innocent expression it made him laugh. "Or French fries?"

He grabbed her hand and pulled her toward the door. "Come home with me. We can practice our French on one another."

She kissed the tip of one finger, then pressed it to his lips. "*Veux-tu coucher avec moi?*" she whispered.

"*Mais oui,*" he said.

Ian's bedroom looked different without sunlight peeping through the slats of the shutters—more formal, less welcoming. The wide plank flooring gleamed like the deck of a ship in the lamplight. Stark white walls contrasted with dark wood furniture, heavy antique pieces, probably original to the house. No paintings on the walls. No collectibles aside from the books that filled the shelves along one wall. Not even curtains to soften the angles of the big windows, just heavy wooden shutters, open now to let in the breeze.

Riding with the top down had mussed Ian's hair. It fell in a tumble across his brow. Without thinking, she brushed the stray locks back off his forehead.

His mouth curved in a smile. He captured her hand, brought it to his lips, and kissed her palm. "Feel what you do to me." He pressed her hand to his chest. His heart hammered fast and strong beneath her fingertips.

She placed his hand over her heart. "You have the same effect on me."

Unlike Peter Wheatley, Ian never would have made it as a Ralph Lauren model. His face was too severe, too overtly sensual. Yet below his devilish winged black brows, he had the most beautiful eyes Tasya had ever seen, deep-set, heavily fringed by thick black lashes. His irises were a rich dark brown and provided the only hint of softness in a harshly handsome face.

She stared, mesmerized, unable to blink or look away, and the world narrowed to this room, this time, this man with his hand on her breast and desire flickering in his eyes, promising danger and excitement.

"What do you want?" he said.

I loved you as you were, and I love you as you are. I wanted you then, and I want you now.

He leaned forward until his lips were all but touching hers. "Tell me what you want, Tasya."

"You. I want you."

*   *   *

Ian woke a little after nine to find himself curled around Tasya, one hand cupping a breast. When was the last time he'd spent the entire night with a woman? When had he felt such urgency, such desire to possess any woman, that he'd made love to her more than once in a single night?

Yet his feelings for Tasya were not solely about sex. She elicited other, more confusing emotions, too. Protectiveness. A desire for friendship. He'd never had a female friend, a woman he enjoyed as much out of bed as in. Until now.

And why is that, MacPherson?

Because Tasya was different. Special. He admired her spirit as much as her beautiful face, cherished her zest for life as much as her oh-so-perfect body. But—and this was the tricky part—even though she'd tapped this hitherto unsuspected well of tenderness, he wasn't sure he trusted her.

Somewhere around three in the morning, they'd descended on the kitchen. Between them, they'd devoured two papayas, six rashers of bacon, half a dozen eggs, and four thick slices of wheat toast slathered with butter and guava jelly. She'd made some offhand comment about his mattress being far superior to hers—even before its soaking, and he'd asked why she'd rented a dump like that in the first place.

"If I hadn't rented the cottage, I wouldn't have met you," she'd said, taking an enormous bite of toast.

He'd reached across the table with a napkin to wipe a smear of jelly from her top lip. "Tahiti's an island. Everyone meets sooner or later."

"Yes," she'd said, her smile making his blood boil. "But sooner's better than later."

"Except when it comes to sex," he'd said, and proceeded to prove his point.

But now, as he lay in bed, her body soft and warm in his arms, he couldn't help wondering why she'd rented Fortier's ramshackle cottage when there were so many other, better rentals in town. Nicer places for less money.

Because she wanted to meet you.

But why? Because she wanted him? Or because she wanted something from him? Something more than mind-blowing sex? Something more than protection or friendship? She'd admitted she was a novice jewel thief. Could she be looking for a new mentor?

He ran a hand over one silken shoulder, and she sighed in her sleep, snuggling closer. The scent of warm female and gardenias enveloped him, triggering another of those weird flashes of faux memory. The feel of her hands on his back, slick with soap, scrubbing in slow, sensuous circles.

He squeezed his eyes shut, trying to capture more of the scene, but it faded as quickly as a dream.

I am losing it. Sexual overload has fried my brain.

He felt himself drifting, edging closer to sleep. Later, he promised himself. Later today, tomorrow at the latest, he'd contact that private investigator in San Francisco he'd used in the past. See what he could dig up on Tasya. Because—Ian yawned—God forbid he fall for someone he didn't trust.

19

T ASYA SAT ACROSS THE TABLE from Ian at Quinn's. As June had given way to July, her feelings for this younger version of Ian had grown deeper and stronger. Like her old familiar Ian, this one was a list-maker, a plotter, his apparent goal in life to be prepared for any eventuality. Yet much as he tried to rein it in, he also had a reckless streak, and she took great pleasure in leading him astray, forcing him to relinquish control. To have fun. Try as she might, though, she still couldn't get him on the dance floor.

"Have you decided yet what you want for your birthday, Tasya?"

"A dance with you."

Ian rolled his eyes. "Try again."

"Okay, how about flowers? I love those gardenias called tiare Tahiti. Hint, hint."

"I was thinking more along the lines of jewelry."

"Don't rob anyone on my account."

"Brat," he said.

"Oh, my. Check out the woman who just walked in

with Peter." She nodded toward the entrance, where Peter Wheatley stood talking to a striking brunette. "I think I'm jealous. Did you ever see such a gorgeous female?"

Ian studied Peter's companion. "Not bad." He turned to Tasya with a look that upped her heart rate by a good twenty beats a minute. "Though personally I prefer suspected Russian spies."

"She doesn't look Russian, does she? What nationality would you guess? French?"

"No. Not Spanish, either. Italian, perhaps?" Ian said.

"How about Greek?"

"I doubt it. She does look a bit like Sophia Loren, though. Yes, definitely Italian."

She shot him a challenging look. "Okay, you say Italian and I say Greek. If you're so confident, how about a friendly wager?"

He raised an eyebrow. "What did you have in mind?"

"If I'm right, you have to dance with me. And if you're right, I have to accompany you and Peter on that fishing trip you've been pestering me about, even though I know I'll be seasick the entire time."

"What happens if we're both wrong?"

"Then the bet's off."

"Deal," he said, and they shook on it.

Ian caught Peter's eye and waved him over. "Ah. Look at that bag. Proof positive. I know Gucci when I see Gucci. Perhaps you should stock up on Dramamine."

"I doubt you're a bad enough dancer to make me seasick."

"Fancy seeing you here on a Friday night," Peter said.

"I thought you limited yourself to Tuesdays, Thursdays, and Saturdays, MacPherson."

"Tasya tells me I'm a slave to routine and need to get out of my rut." He turned to Peter's date. "I don't believe we've met. I'm Ian MacPherson, and this is Tasya Flynn."

"Sorry," Peter said. "Ian, Tasya, may I present Alexis Papandreou. Her family's stopping off in Papeete for a few days."

Ian raised his eyebrows. "That family wouldn't, by any chance, include Stavros Papandreou, the shipping magnate?"

"I believe so, yes," Peter said.

"I am please to meet you." Alexis smiled, revealing a row of straight white teeth.

"She doesn't speak much English," Peter said. "And the most I can manage in Greek is, 'Ouzo, please,' but we've been muddling along in French." He turned to the girl. "*Voulez-vous danser?*"

She smiled again. "*Oui.*"

"See you later." Peter led Alexis toward the dance floor.

Tasya nudged Ian. "You lose. *Veux-tu danser?*"

"Not on your nelly. You knew who she was all along, didn't you, you little wretch?"

Tasya laughed. "I might have seen her picture somewhere." The society pages of last month's *Vogue,* for instance.

"Then the bet's off."

"Unfair. There was nothing in the rules precluding the application of prior knowledge."

"A technicality." He drank the last of his Hinano and set

the bottle down with a clink. "Would you like another beer?"

"What I'd like is to dance with you."

"Not tonight."

"Okay, how about this? Dance with me now, and I'll let you have your way with me later."

A wicked grin spread across his face. "You'll let me have my way with you later anyway."

Tasya watched Ian sleep.

They'd spent the morning swimming below the waterfall, then picnicked under the acacia trees that edged the clearing. Lunch over, Ian lay sprawled on a beach towel in the shade. Thick black lashes fanned out on his cheeks, lending his face a youthful vulnerability.

She smoothed the hair back off his forehead. *I love you, Ian MacPherson.*

He smiled in his sleep as if he'd heard her thoughts.

Could he hear her thoughts? See her memories? Was that the explanation for the dream images he'd told her about? Or was he tapping into his own future? Had her voyage through time somehow scrambled past, present, and future?

She frowned into the clear green depths of the pool below the waterfall as if she might find the answers to her questions lurking below the water's surface.

"What's wrong?"

She glanced at Ian and found him gazing up at her, the concern in his voice reflected in his eyes.

She smiled, a smile she knew must look more wistful than happy. "This place . . ." She spread her arms to encompass the water cascading down the mountain in a graceful white cataract, the lush tropical vegetation edging the clearing, the mirrored surface of the pool reflecting the blue perfection of the cloudless sky. "This place is paradise, but"—she frowned—"every paradise has its serpent. I keep wondering when ours will show up." Time was running out. She could almost feel Alex Farrell breathing down her neck.

Ian captured her hand and pulled her down on top of him. "Don't worry. If a reptile invades our Eden, I'll have my housekeeper roast him for dinner. They say snake tastes a bit like chicken."

Not this particular snake. Gall and wormwood was more like it. Bitter as treachery, caustic as betrayal.

"I love you, Ian. You make me happy." She scrambled to her feet.

He raised an eyebrow. "And you make me horny."

She grinned. "I noticed."

He stretched, then leaned back on his elbows. "So what are you going to do about it?"

"Nothing." She glanced at the waterfall, actually a series of small waterfalls cascading down the mountain. Peter Wheatley had told her some of the locals liked to prove their courage by jumping from pool to pool. Quite a thrill, that would be, since the pools ranged from thirty to fifty feet apart.

Ian lifted both eyebrows. "What do you mean, 'nothing'?"

"Your overactive hormones are hardly my problem." She laughed at the look on his face.

He jumped to his feet.

She let out a squeal, then spun around, scrambling up the cliff as quickly as she could. She'd thought her head start and gymnastics training gave her an unbeatable edge, but Ian had a good seven-inch height advantage, and he moved surprisingly fast.

He caught up with her as she reached the first pool, but she dodged into the water and out of reach, maintaining a precarious balance on the slippery rocks at the lip of the waterfall.

"Tasya, don't fool around," he said, all the laughter draining from his voice. "Be careful."

But her adrenaline level was too high. She couldn't back off. She didn't want to back off. She launched herself into space, aiming for the deepest, darkest part of the pool below.

Ian died a thousand deaths in the seconds it took Tasya to reach the water, submerge, and bob back to the surface. But he wouldn't have jumped—swear to God he wouldn't have—if she hadn't looked back up at him with such a gloating expression. *All-y, all-y in free.*

He hit the water with a tremendous splash, then plunged down, down, so far down he was half afraid he'd crush his legs on the bottom. Luckily, the pool was deeper than it looked. He clawed his way back to the top, sucking air in huge gasps when he finally broke the surface.

Tasya was waiting for him, laughing. "Nice try, but I win."

He grabbed her arm. "Are you mad?"

"Mad about you." She kissed him and they both went under.

He dragged her back to the surface. "I'm serious," he

said. "You could have been hurt. Aren't you afraid of anything?"

She blinked at him. Water beaded her eyelashes. "Yes, of course. I'm afraid of lots of things. Sharks, snakes, lightning, Baba Yagas . . ." She swam to the edge of the pool and clambered out onto the sand.

Ian followed. "Baba Yagas?"

"Characters from Russian folklore, bony hags with crooked noses." She squeezed the excess water from her hair, then stretched out in the sun, leaning back on her elbows.

Ian sat beside her. "What else frightens you?"

She lowered her lashes. "The dark. Most of all, I'm afraid of the dark. I can't sleep without a light."

Simple words softly spoken, but they resonated with significance. Not an ordinary childhood fear, then. Something deeper. More complicated.

Ian took Tasya's hand in his, sliding his thumb back and forth across her palm. "And here I thought you left the light on because you liked to watch me sleep."

"I do." A hint of the old mischief sparkled in her eyes. "It's my second most favorite guilty pleasure."

"The first being sex in the afternoon."

"The first being chocolate for breakfast."

"Well, that puts me in my place, doesn't it?" He dropped her hand. "Have you decided yet what you'd like for your birthday?"

She smiled at him, a smile that brought his blood to a full rolling boil. "What are my choices?"

"A car? A mink coat? Diamonds?" An engagement ring?

"The car's out," she said. "I can't drive. As for a mink

coat?" She shuddered. "Aside from its being impractical in the tropics, I find the thought of draping myself in dead animal skins totally disgusting."

"You wear leather shoes," he pointed out.

She made a moue of distaste. "I hadn't thought of that."

"So it's diamonds then."

"What's wrong with flowers?"

"Flowers die. Diamonds are forever."

"I thought they were a girl's best friend."

"You already have a best friend," he said. "Me."

His heart skipped a beat at the look on her face. *Marry me.* It was all he could do to bite back the words. But he'd devoted too much time and effort planning the perfect marriage proposal to jump the gun. He'd bloody well wait for her birthday if it killed him.

August 1972
Tahiti

As Alex's plane circled, ready to begin the final descent to the airport built across Faa'a Lagoon, his spirits hit a new depressing low. In striking contrast, all around him the other passengers chattered with excitement at finally reaching Tahiti, the glowing pearl of the South Pacific. But then, they had come to enjoy the sybaritic excesses of this tropical paradise. He was there to eat crow.

The heist had taken him two weeks to plan, a month to arrange, and ten minutes to blow. How the hell was he supposed to have known the Sodré woman owned an attack cat? Attack *dogs*, yes. He'd vetted the place to be sure the heiress didn't have any Dobermans or pit bulls run-

ning tame in the mansion in Rio's Laranjeiras section. But
hell, he hadn't worried about the cat. Cats didn't bark at
intruders. Cats didn't rouse their owners in the middle of
the night to announce that a stranger had just picked the
lock on the back door. Cats didn't give a shit.

Correction. Most cats didn't give a shit. It wasn't his
fault the Sodré feline was a freak. Who on earth would
have wasted an instant's worry over a pet Siamese?

Ian MacPherson, that's who. Cat never pulled a job
without exploring every variable, considering every
angle, preparing for every contingency. Even a goddamned pampered Siamese.

The last thing Alex wanted to do was admit his mistake, especially after sending that cocky telegram the day
he'd sealed the deal with Gentry. Not that Cat would ever
say, "I told you so." Not out loud. But he'd be thinking it.
Gloating because Alex's fuckup proved what Ian had
known all along: Alex was too careless to make it as a cat
burglar.

He didn't want to admit his mistake, much less ask for
help, but he was out of options. All but a few hundred
bucks of the money Gentry had given him for expenses
was down the tubes. What remained would barely cover a
cut-rate fare back to L.A. No way could he scrounge
enough cash to buy the tools he'd need to break into the
mansion now that Elizabete Ribeiro Sodré had hired a
night watchman and installed a new security system.

Cat was his only hope.

"Are you expecting someone?" Tasya sat up.

"No." Ian was surprised he'd been able to manage even

that brief syllable. Tasya's abrupt change of position had shoved him deeper inside her, and the resulting physical sensations redefined the word *great* as it applied to sex.

"I think a car just drove in."

"I didn't hear anything." Aside from the thunder of his heart, the roar in his ears, and the rasp of his ragged breathing. "God, Tasya, have pity. You're killing me."

"Really?" Smiling down at him, she gave an experimental wriggle. "How's that?"

He groaned. Forget words. Too little blood left in his brain.

"And this?" She lifted herself until only the very tip of him remained inside her. Then she slid down, fast and hard, pushing him even deeper.

"Have you no mercy, woman?"

Evidently not. Laughing, she repeated the trick over and over until he was sure he was going to die, because nobody had sex like this and lived to tell the tale. He shuddered on the verge of climax, waiting for her.

"Tasya, damn it." He knew she could see it in his eyes, but still she laughed. Laughed and plunged down yet again.

He reached up to drag that impudent mouth down to his, thinking she'd be laughing out of the other side of her face once he got through with her. Only on the way his fingertips brushed her breast.

That did it. Her eyes went round. She gasped, then shuddered, her muscles squeezing as she came around him. Her orgasm triggered his—a heart-stopping, breathtaking, muscle-clenching mega-climax.

"What is that noise?"

It took him a few seconds to realize she wasn't talking about the thumping in his head. This thumping was farther away, the sound of someone's fist knocking on the front door. The locked front door. After Michel Fortier's unwelcome intrusion back in June, he'd taken to locking up whenever he and Tasya were alone in the house. He didn't like interruptions.

"Someone's at the door," she said, rolling off him and fumbling for her underwear.

He swore under his breath. He'd planned to spend the rest of the evening with Tasya enjoying a leisurely dinner, followed by some more not-so-leisurely sex.

He pulled on a pair of shorts, ran a hand back over his head to smooth his rumpled hair, then padded barefoot down the staircase to see who was at the door.

He crossed the wide entry, gathering up the clothes they'd discarded on their way to the bedroom. He stuffed the wadded clothing in the front closet, then peeked out the peephole in the front door.

"Alex Farrell!" he exclaimed, pulling the door wide. "What are you doing in Tahiti? The last I heard, you were headed for Rio to pull off the caper of the century."

Alex, who looked like he hadn't slept in days, gave a rueful half smile. "Complications, Cat."

"Aren't there always?" Ian said. "Come on in and tell me about it."

Clad in a pair of Ian's boxers and a T-shirt she'd found in his chest of drawers, Tasya tiptoed down the hall, pausing to listen at the top of the steps. Whoever'd knocked at the front door was now in Ian's study. She could hear two male voices, Ian's rich baritone with its faint Scottish burr and another less readily identifiable one. Not Wheatley's or Fortier's. Their accents were distinctive. This voice belonged to an American and sounded vaguely familiar.

The truth sucker-punched her. She grabbed the banister to keep from falling. Dear God, not vaguely familiar. Frighteningly familiar. The voice belonged to Alex Farrell. The man who'd ruined Ian's life. The man who'd double-crossed him, crippled him, and sent him to prison.

Only this was 1972, and Alex Farrell hadn't done any of those things. Yet.

But he would. If she didn't stop him, he would. Her heart pounded. Her hands shook. She wasn't ready for this.

"Oh, mademoiselle!" Vaitiara, the housekeeper, said behind her, sounding as surprised as Tasya to discover someone else up here on the second floor. "Almost you give me a heart attack." The plump, middle-aged maid patted her ample bosom, covered today in several acres of red-and-white-flowered fabric.

"Sorry," Tasya said. "I didn't know you were here."

"I am always here on Tuesday," Vaitiara said with dignity. "Is Monsieur Ian's friend staying for dinner?"

Friend. Anger gripped Tasya by the throat. "I have no idea."

Vaitiara raised her eyebrows. "You do not like this man?"

"I haven't met him."

Vaitiara didn't say anything, but Tasya could tell she wasn't buying it.

"I haven't met him, but I've heard of him. He's a liar and

a cheat. I'm terrified he's going to get Ian in trouble."

Vaitiara smiled and patted her arm. "Not to worry. Monsieur Ian is a big boy, *non*? He can look after himself."

"Ian doesn't know what Farrell has planned."

Vaitiara shrugged. "Then you must tell him."

Tell him the truth? He'd never believe it. Worse, he'd think she'd lost her mind. "If only it were that simple."

"The truth is always simple. It's the lies that get complicated." A slight frown creased Vaitiara's brow. "I brought *fafa* cooked with chicken and mango pudding, both left over from my grandmother's ninetieth birthday *tamaaraa* last night. Plenty for two, but for three? I don't know."

"Not a problem," Tasya said. "If the friend stays, I won't."

Tasya left Vaitiara in the upstairs hall, aware that the woman was staring holes in her back as she headed for the study. The door was open, but she knocked anyway before poking her head inside. "Ian? Am I disturbing something?"

Both men turned, Ian with a smile, Alex with an almost comical look of surprise. This younger Alex—no more than a year or two her senior—was even handsomer than the older version, despite shoulder-length hair and a gaudy medal hung from a chain around his neck. If she hadn't known what a danger he posed, she'd have found his appearance laughable. Seventies rock star chic. Tight white bell-bottoms and a white silk shirt, half unbuttoned to show off his chest hair.

"Come in," Ian said. "I have someone I'd like you to meet."

After Ian made the introductions, Tasya asked, "Are we

still on for dinner? Or would you rather spend time with your friend?"

"Why don't we all dine together?"

Alex frowned, then apparently realizing what he was doing, smoothed his expression. "Actually, I have some business to discuss with you, Cat."

"Cat?" Tasya raised her eyebrows.

"A nickname," Ian said, "a relic from my days as a cat burglar."

Now it was Alex's turn to raise his eyebrows. "She knows?"

"She's in the business herself," Ian said.

"Really?" Alex sounded stiff. "Your new apprentice?"

Ian laughed. "I'm retired. No more capers. No more apprentices."

"I'm more in the nature of a distraction," Tasya said.

"Or an obsession."

Alex's arrival had thrown her into a panic, making it hard to concentrate on anything but the fear gnawing at her insides. But when Ian took her hand, her gaze met his, and the expression on his face turned her bones to jelly. She sank down abruptly on the nearest chair.

Farrell looked from Ian to her, then back to Ian. "I see."

"I hope so," Ian said. "Tasya's off limits."

Alex's smile edged into smirk territory. "Understood."

Cocky little twerp. Tasya got a viselike grip on the arms of her chair, battling the urge to smack the smug look off his face.

The men sat down, Ian behind his desk and Alex in a chair. "What's this business you're so anxious to discuss?" Ian asked.

Alex glanced sideways at her, then at Ian. "You trust her?"

Ian smiled. "As much as one can trust a rumored Russian spy." He laughed at Alex's expression. "I'm joking. You can talk in front of Tasya. She would never betray a confidence."

Alex still looked uncertain.

"Is this about the big score in Rio?" she asked, and both men stared at her. She lifted her shoulders in a shrug. "I was here when the telegram arrived."

"I never told you who sent it," Ian said.

"Peter did, remember? Besides, I can add two and two." She pointed at Alex. "He said he wanted to discuss business, and robbery is your business."

"*Was* my business," Ian said. "I'm retired."

Tasya didn't like the way he kept repeating that, almost as if he were trying to convince himself. She stood. "Mr. Farrell is obviously uncomfortable speaking in front of me, so—"

"You don't have to leave," Ian said.

She didn't have to stay, either, since she already knew what Alex planned to discuss. "I have things to do." She headed for the door.

"This shouldn't take long," Ian said. "What do you say we all have dinner in Papeete, then drop by Quinn's afterward?"

"Vaitiara's feelings would be hurt if you ate in town. She has a special dinner planned. And besides, the Jaguar's a two-seater. I'll meet you at Quinn's. Peter will give me a ride." She breezed out before he could muster any more arguments.

Of course, her casual attitude was as much a pretense as Alex's friendliness, but provoking a confrontation at this point seemed like a recipe for failure. Leaving Ian with Alex was a calculated risk, but with any luck, Ian would be so preoccupied about her thighs being within reach of Wheatley-the-leg-man in the front seat of Wheatley's Ford that he'd be immune to Alex's blandishments. Last time he'd been bored, spoiling to get back in the game. This time he wouldn't be so easily lured to Rio.

Unless she was fooling herself. Unless in the grand scheme of things, her actions were immaterial. Unless everything in life was preordained and she was doomed to failure, no matter how hard she struggled against fate. A black mood enveloped her as she trudged down the path to the cottage.

20

TASYA AND PETER didn't make it to Quinn's until after nine. Ian and Alex were waiting just inside. "Where have you been?" Ian spoke in a civilized tone, but his nostrils were flaring, never a good sign.

Peter, no fool, moved behind her, out of the line of fire.

"My fault," she said. "I talked Peter into a little side trip." She turned in a slow circle to show off the blue-and-white-flowered pareu she'd bought. "I'm going native tonight." She'd even tucked a deep red hibiscus behind her right ear.

Alex, still in his white rock star outfit, gave her an appraising look that immediately put her hackles up.

"Very nice," Ian said, moving closer to kiss her cheek.

"Nice wasn't what I had in mind," she whispered in his ear.

"I stand corrected. There's one small problem, though." He plucked the flower from her hair and tucked it behind her left ear. "Worn on the right, it's means you're available. On the left, it means you're taken."

"Am I taken?" She met his gaze, her heartbeat quickening in anticipation.

"You are." He wrapped an arm around her waist to prove it.

"I'll scout out a table." Peter headed off into the crowd.

"Did you gentlemen finish your business?"

"No," Alex said.

"Yes," Ian said at the same time.

She looked from one to the other. "Which is it?"

"Yes," Ian said.

Smiling, Alex shrugged. "I'm still trying to convince him."

"Convince him of what?"

A silent communication seemed to pass between the two men. "Let's not talk business," Ian said. "We're here to have fun."

"Okay." She grabbed his hand. "In that case, let's dance."

"*We* indicates more than one person, but if *we* go dance," Ian said, "*you*'re the only one who's going to be having fun."

Tasya sang lyrics from a Cyndi Lauper song that hadn't been written yet, emphasizing the "fuh-un."

Ian shook his head. "She's always doing this," he told Alex.

"And you love it." She draped herself across his chest. "Come on, Ian. One dance won't kill you."

"You're the one who'd be in danger. My feet are lethal weapons."

"Your friend found us a table," Alex said. "Over in the corner."

Wheatley waved at them.

Tasya waved back. "Fuh-un," she repeated. Ian raised his eyebrows. "Dance with me. Just once. Please."

"Dance with Wheatley. Or Alex. I have to buy us a round of drinks." He headed for the bar.

"Slippery as an oiled eel," she said.

"How long have you and Ian known each other?" Alex asked as they wove their way through the crowd.

"Not nearly long enough."

"You do realize he's not husband material? Hell, the man's an adrenaline junkie. Once the thrill is gone, he is, too."

"I appreciate the warning."

He smiled, the same charming smile he'd probably been using to manipulate people since the day he was born.

She stumbled over someone's foot, and Alex steadied her, his hand on her arm. "I'd hate to see you get hurt." Translation: Back off, bitch. Stay out of my way, or you'll regret it.

She moved, dislodging his hand. "I'm tougher than I look."

Ian stared at the collection of empty beer bottles littering the table, only half listening to Alex, who was taking advantage of their being alone to pester him about the Rio job. "I'm retired," he said for probably the dozenth time.

Alex paid no more attention than he had the first eleven times, so Ian tuned him out, his gaze drawn to the dance floor, where Tasya and Wheatley were slow-dancing to "Sloop John B," an old Beach Boys song popular with the yachting crowd. He scowled. Why was Tasya so bloody obsessed with dancing?

"Okay." Alex set his beer bottle on the table. "No more bullshit. Here's the thing. I can't do this alone. I tried, and I screwed up. I need your help, Cat. I'm desperate."

Ian sighed, more exasperated than irritated. "You failed. It happens. Write it off to experience and move on."

"I can't."

"Why not? And don't try to feed me that pig swill about the poor dying girl whose father's convinced Milagre can cure her."

"What does it matter why Gentry wants the stone? He wants it, and he's willing to pay big bucks for it. A million big bucks." He scowled at the tabletop. "I need the money, Cat."

Neither of them said anything for a moment. Ian took a pull on his beer, then set it on the table with a decisive clink. "You've been gambling again."

Alex didn't answer, but judging by the ruddy color flushing the younger man's cheeks, Ian had guessed right.

"How much?"

"A couple thousand."

Ian raised his eyebrows.

"Okay, fifteen thousand. And I don't have it."

"Didn't Gentry give you money for expenses?"

"Yes, but it's gone."

"You gambled it away, you mean."

"Damn it, who crowned you king of morality?"

Ian didn't answer, concentrating instead on the enticing curve of Tasya's backside moving beneath the thin cotton pareu.

"Oh, I get it now. It's the girl. You think you're in love with her, don't you? You think *she's* in love with you." Alex laughed. "You poor deluded son of a bitch." His laughter faded, and a look of concern took its place. "Have you ever looked into her eyes? She may be young, but she's been around. I hate to say this, but I doubt it's the size of your equipment that thrills her as much as the size of your bank account."

"Shut your mouth." Ian enunciated each word clearly.

Alex blinked, but he didn't flinch. "Cat, I'm your friend. We've known each other a long time."

"Six years."

"How long have you known Tasya? More importantly, what do you know *about* Tasya?"

"Enough." He never had got around to asking that PI firm to do a background check. Too busy screwing Tasya's brains out. But damn it, he trusted her. More, he loved her. He leaned toward Alex. "I'll let you in on a secret. Tasya has a birthday coming up on Monday, her twenty-second. I plan to propose then."

"Holy shit." Alex blinked. "I had no idea." He raised his beer in a toast. "Congratulations."

"Thanks."

"Cat MacPherson married. It boggles the mind." He grinned. "But Monday's almost a week away. You could fly to Rio with me, pull the job, and still make it back here in plenty of time to pop the question."

"Sorry. Not interested."

Alex leaned closer. "I know you're living every man's fantasy here in paradise, but tell the truth. Don't you miss the thrill of pulling off a high-stakes caper? Remember our last job together in Istanbul, the Osman emeralds? What was that? Six months ago?"

"Nine," Ian said. The owner of the emeralds, a reclusive billionaire with his own private army of security guards, had given them a run for their money.

"Escaping by helicopter while the bullets whizzed past—now *that* was a full-out adrenaline rush." Alex grinned. "Don't you miss the excitement, Cat?"

"Occasionally," he admitted.

"So how about it?" Alex asked. "Help me out this one last time. You know you want to."

Yes, he did, but . . . "I'm retired," he said, feeling like a broken record.

Alex closed his eyes for a second. When he opened them again, all the charm, all the cajolery, all the false bonhomie, were gone. He looked pale and sick and terrified. For a second, Ian caught a glimpse of the frightened teenager he'd first seen cowering behind a row of trash cans in an alley off the Vegas strip. "Please, Cat. I'm begging you. I'm in really deep shit. I need to pull this heist before the guy I owe pulls my plug. Bottom line, it's my life at stake here." His sincerity struck a chord.

In the old days, they'd watched each other's backs. It had been Alex who'd stalled the baroness that time in Zurich, Alex who'd blocked the exit of a Chicago parking garage long enough for Ian to escape, Alex who'd provided Ian's alibi in Morocco. And yes, he'd saved Alex's bacon a time or two. If they were keeping score, Alex probably owed him, but still, where was the harm in helping an old friend? Wasn't as if he didn't have the time to spare. As Alex had pointed out, it *was* almost a week until Tasya's birthday.

"All right, I'll do it."

"What?" Alex looked so dumbfounded, Ian couldn't help but smile.

"I'll do it. This one last caper."

"Yes! I knew I could count on you."

"But I have one condition."

"Anything. You name it."

"Tasya comes to Rio with me."

"You're joking." Alex stared in disbelief.

"Tasya's in, or I'm out. That's my condition."

Alex opened his mouth as if he intended to argue the point, then shut it again and forced a smile. "Deal." The two men shook on it.

"Deal?" Wheatley said. He and Tasya had come up on the table unnoticed. "What kind of deal."

"Business." Ian turned to Tasya with a smile. "How would you like to visit Rio?"

August 1972
Rio de Janeiro, Brazil

Tasya gazed out her hotel window at the traffic on the Avenida Atlântica. Ironically, she, Ian, and Alex were staying at the same beachfront hotel where she and Paulinho had stayed—would stay? She frowned, her mind too mired in worry to sort through tenses.

It wasn't supposed to have happened this way. She'd meant to keep Ian in Tahiti, far from danger. But she'd failed. Ian was in Rio. Ian had agreed to help Alex. The two were working on their plan now. And if they put it in motion, if she couldn't figure out some way to thwart them, the whole chain of events was going to repeat itself. The theft. The double-cross. The fall. The murder. The prison sentence.

How was she to stop it? Time was running out.

A stray memory surfaced. Dona Elizabete's garden. Sunlight highlighting the inscription carved into the stone sundial. *Tempus fugit*. Time flies.

Great. Here she was in desperate need of inspiration, and what did her brain produce? A reminder that time was the enemy, and the enemy was getting away. "Time flies," she said aloud.

"Especially when you're having fun."

Tasya started. She'd been so preoccupied, she hadn't heard Ian enter the room.

He turned her to face him. "*Are* you having fun?"

She forced a smile. "Not yet. I'm still jet-lagged."

He pulled her close in a quick hug. "Take a nap, then. Alex and I have to go out for a while."

She nodded. "How long will you be? Should I order room service? Or will we go out for dinner?"

"We shouldn't be more than two or three hours."

"I have a bad feeling about this. I wish—"

"Shh." He pressed a finger to her mouth. "I'm very good at what I do. Trust me."

"I do," she said. "I do trust you."

"But not Alex? Is that it?"

"I know he's your friend, but I don't like him."

"You don't know him."

"I don't want to know him."

"Two days, and we're out of here. Two days. You can stand Alex for that long, can't you?"

"I—"

"Tell you what. I'm free tomorrow afternoon. Why don't we do something, just the two of us? Tour the city, walk on the beach, whatever you want."

"All I want is to go home."

"We'll be home for your birthday. Cross my heart." He smiled. "But as long as we're here, we might as well enjoy ourselves. How about a trip up Corcovado? The view's incredible, especially at sunset. I'll make arrangements on my way out."

"Ian—"

"I'm not ignoring you, Tasya. I know we need to talk." He brushed the hair from her cheek, his fingers lingering for a moment. "I don't have time right now, but we'll hash it out later." He kissed her. "I promise."

He left as suddenly as he'd appeared, leaving her alone. Alone with her fear. Alone with the growing certainty that she was up against forces beyond her understanding or control.

She sprawled across the bed, paralyzed by indecision. What to do? What to do?

Ian and Alex had rented a nondescript Volkswagen van— beige, no distinguishing marks—then spent two hours filling it with the equipment they'd need to break in through the skylight of the Sodré mansion. Ian's rudimentary Portuguese, learned by necessity five years ago when he'd pulled several jobs in the São Paolo area, had facilitated their shopping expedition. They'd finished sooner than expected, for which Ian was thankful. He didn't like leaving Tasya alone. Stupid, maybe. Overprotective, probably. But he couldn't help how he felt.

And how do you feel? he asked himself. Like a lovesick

teenager, that's how he felt. Not to mention guilty as hell for hiring a private investigator to research her past. If Alex hadn't planted the seed . . . Ah well, when Harper called with the report, he'd say forget it. He didn't care what secrets lay hidden in her past. The Tasya he knew was the only one who interested him—the Tasya he trusted, the Tasya he loved.

The inscription on Dona Elizabete's sundial nagged at Tasya. *Tempus fugit. Tempus fugit.* Like an annoying jingle—once heard, impossible to forget—the words repeated themselves in her brain. *Tempus fugit. Tempus fugit.*

She grabbed her head, as if she could stop the endless iteration by applying pressure with her fingertips. *Tempus fugit. Tempus fugit.* Damn it, she knew *tempus fugit.* She knew she had to act, and soon. What she didn't know was what action to take. *Tempus fugit. Tempus fugit.*

Unless . . . What if that irritating fragment of memory was more than a reminder that time was slipping away? What if it was a prompt, a clue, a destination? Of course. If she hadn't been mired in despair, she'd have realized what her subconscious had known all along. She must seek out Dona Elizabete's help.

Forty-five minutes later Tasya stood in front of the heavy gate in the wall that surrounded the Sodré mansion. No buzzer. Apparently it hadn't been installed yet. She lifted her fist and pounded on the carved wooden panels.

"They are not expecting you?" the taxi driver called.

"No." She should have called first. Why hadn't she thought to call first?

"Do you need help?"

"No," she said. "I can handle it. Please wait, though. I shouldn't be long." She banged again.

"Who are you?"

Tasya stared at the gate. It hadn't opened—not even a crack. So where had the voice come from?

"Up here."

She tilted her head and spotted him, a skinny little boy in shorts and tennis shoes perched atop one of the pineapple finials that crowned the gateposts. She didn't know him at first. The Afro threw her. Then she recognized his smile—even without the gold tooth. "Paulinho," she said. "Go tell Dona Elizabete that Tasya Flynn is here to see her on a very important matter."

Paulinho's smile faded. He regarded her with suspicion. "How do you know my name? I do not know you."

"Dona Elizabete has spoken of you." She tried not to look like the kind of stranger parents warned their children against. "Please tell her Tasya is here and needs to speak with her."

"Dona Elizabete is resting. My father would be very angry if I disturbed her afternoon nap."

"It's urgent, Paulinho. If you don't want to bother Dona Elizabete, then summon your father or Vania's mother instead."

He frowned at her. "You know Mosca?"

"Please go fetch someone to let me in. It's very important."

He didn't answer, just slid off the back of the finial and dropped out of sight. Seconds later, she heard the bolts being drawn. The gate swung open, and Paulinho waved her in.

"Wait for me," she called to the taxi driver.

He nodded, already tuning his radio to a samba station.

Tasya followed Paulinho into the courtyard. He bolted the gate behind them, stretching on tiptoes to reach.

She tried to work out how old he was. "You must be about seven, right?"

"Seven and a half," he said. "And tall for my age. Everyone says so. You are lucky I was here. If it had been Mosca, you would still be waiting outside. She is too small to reach the bolts." He held a hand out at waist level. "Three years old. Just a baby. She is napping, too, I think."

She followed the little boy around to the back garden, where Dona Elizabete drowsed on a chaise longue in the dappled shade of palms and one huge monkeypod tree. She opened her eyes when she heard them coming. "Tasya," she said. "You've returned. I'd almost convinced myself you were a dream."

Tasya clenched her hands together. "More like a nightmare. Remember the story I told you? That I'd come back to right a terrible wrong?"

Dona Elizabete held a finger to her lips and nodded toward Paulinho, who was still within earshot, playing at the base of the sundial. "Go ask Senhora da Rocha to fix a tea tray," she said to him, waiting until he was out of sight before she spoke again. "You were not able to persuade your Ian to remain in Tahiti."

"No."

"Did you not warn him of his fate?"

"How could I? He wouldn't have believed me."

"I did."

"Yes," Tasya said, "but you saw me materialize."

"Three months ago. Right here in the garden," she agreed. "You crushed my poor gardenia bush."

"And you'd heard the legend, so you already knew about the stones' power."

"Yes." Dona Elizabete nodded. "I see your problem, my dear, and yet what else but the truth can save him?"

"We finished faster than I expected," Alex said. "You want to drive past the mansion and scout out a good spot to leave the van?"

All Ian wanted to do was get back to the hotel and grab a shower, a bite to eat, and Tasya—not necessarily in that order. "Where did you park last time?"

"Two blocks away, and that's the point. I damned near got caught before. I don't want to take any chances this time."

"How long will it take?"

Alex glanced at his watch. "Call it twenty minutes each way and another fifteen or so to find a good out-of-the-way spot to leave the van."

Tasya had looked exhausted. It would probably be a kindness to let her sleep a little longer; chances were, they wouldn't be getting much sleep tonight. He smiled in anticipation. "All right. Let's do it then."

The drive took less time than Alex had predicted. They got lucky finding a place to park, too. On a side street half a block from the mansion, they located the perfect spot.

"So." Alex tapped the steering wheel as if it were a bongo drum. "This evening we test the rigging in the empty warehouse we rented, do a run-through, and get our timing down. Then if all goes well, tomorrow night we lift the stone."

Ian nodded. "With you in the rigging and me up top."

Alex's face lit up. "Me in the rigging? Holy shit!"

"It's your score. I'm just along as backup."

"But you're ten times better than I am, Cat. Hell, you're the best damned second-story man in the business."

"Except I'm not in the business any longer. I'm retired." He smiled at the younger man's enthusiasm. "It's your big score. Why should I have all the fun?"

"Hot damn." Alex beat on the steering wheel with renewed energy. "I appreciate this." He pulled into the street, paused at the intersection, then turned left. "Oh, shit," he said. "Is that who I think it is?"

Ian's heart stopped beating for a slow three count. Tasya? His breath caught in his chest. He watched in stunned disbelief as she waved to someone out of sight, shut the heavy wooden gate, and turned toward the taxi parked at the curb.

Alex went red in the face. "What the hell was your girlfriend doing in the Sodré mansion?"

"There must be a reasonable explanation," Ian heard himself say, knowing even as he said it that he was grabbing at straws. She'd betrayed him. This woman he loved more than life itself had lied to him, used him, made a fool of him.

"Reasonable explanation? Like what? She's casing the joint from the inside? Christ, how did she even know where to come? You didn't let any names slip, did you?"

"No, of course not." How *had* she known which mansion they planned to hit? This couldn't be some colossal coincidence, could it? "Pull in behind the taxi."

"And let her know we're onto her?"

"Just do it."

Cursing under his breath, Alex pulled to the curb.

"Keep the motor running," Ian said and bailed out.

Tasya's face lit up when she saw him. Was she that accomplished an actress? "Ian? What are you doing here?"

"Just what I was about to ask you."

"I . . ." Her smile faded. "Oh, God, Ian, don't look at me like that. It's not what you think."

"No?"

"I was trying to—"

"What? Double-cross me?"

Her face paled. She stared at him in silence.

"Nothing to say for yourself?" He paused. "Well, no matter. You'll have plenty of time to explain on the ride back to Copacabana."

"W-with you?" she said. "What about my taxi?"

"I'll take care of it." He strode over to the waiting taxi and shoved a handful of bills at the driver. The man grinned his thanks and drove off, singing along to the radio.

Dreading what lay ahead, Ian turned.

The empty sidewalk mocked him. In the brief time it had taken him to pay off the taxi driver, Tasya had disappeared.

"Tasya?" A confusing mixture of fear and anger roiled his gut. "Tasya, where are you?"

"Over here." Alex waved him toward the van.

As Ian drew closer, he spotted her body, sprawled limp

and motionless across the front seat. Despite the warmth of the afternoon sun, gooseflesh rose along his arms. "My God, Alex, what have you done?"

"Chloroformed her." Alex shrugged. "Had no choice. The second you turned your back, she tried to make a run for it."

"And you saved the day," Ian said, his voice heavy with sarcasm. "Lucky you had the chloroform handy."

"Luck had nothing to do with it," Alex said. "'Be prepared for every eventuality.' Isn't that what you drilled into my head all those years?"

Ian didn't want to listen to his own words thrown back in his face. He shouldered Alex aside, climbed in on the passenger's side, and gathered Tasya into his arms. "You shouldn't have drugged her. Chloroform's dangerous." The proper dose rendered a person unconscious. Too much, and the victim never woke up.

Tasya's head lolled back against his arm. Ian pressed his fingers to her throat and felt her pulse beating fast and strong, a good sign. He breathed a little easier.

Alex stomped around to the driver's side and boosted himself in. "Damn it, I'm not going to apologize for doing what had to be done." He jerked the van in gear. "Why was your girlfriend inside the Sodré mansion? Answer me that."

"If you hadn't knocked her out, she could answer for herself."

A muscle twitched in Alex's cheek. "She's been lying to you all along. She betrayed you. Betrayed us. Don't you get it?"

Ian didn't know what to think. His gut told him Tasya

loved him as much as he loved her. His gut told him she would never betray him. His gut told him there must be some reasonable explanation for her being in the Sodré mansion.

But common sense argued that Tasya had trained as a cat burglar. Common sense argued that she was working for someone else, someone like Porfirio DeLeon or Gotthard Vanderpool. Common sense argued that perhaps Alex wasn't the only thief Gentry had contacted.

Slowing once they were safely out of the Laranjeiras district, Alex glanced sideways at Ian. "What if she's not working for the competition? You thought about that? What if she's an Interpol agent? Be quite a boost to her career to nab legendary cat burglar Ian MacPherson, wouldn't it?"

"That's sheer speculation."

"Speculation, my ass. Face it, Cat, whatever her game, she was planning to screw you."

21

"I SAY WE KILL HER and dump the body in Guanabara Bay."

"No need for draconian measures."

"The hell there's not. She's seen our faces. She knows our names. If we don't get rid of her, we're going to find ourselves doing hard time. You ever seen the inside of a Brazilian prison, Cat? I hear the cockroaches are as big as your thumb."

"I don't care if they're as big as house cats. Get this through your thick skull. Tasya is off limits. You lift one finger against her, and you're a dead man."

The arguing woke Tasya. She'd been fighting the return to consciousness, afraid of what she might see if she opened her eyes. But the angry voices in the other room penetrated the fog. Despite a throbbing headache, she forced her eyelids open.

She'd been right to be afraid. She was back in the hotel in Copacabana, lying on the bed in the room she and Ian were sharing. But what made her blood run cold was discovering her wrists and ankles lashed to the bedposts. Richard's favorite trick.

"Ian?" she called, ashamed of the tremor in her voice.

"Sounds like your girlfriend's awake," she heard Alex say. "You want to ask the questions? Or shall I?"

He and Ian entered from the sitting room. Alex looked like he was enjoying himself. Ian's face was expressionless.

She glared at Alex. "Why am I tied up?"

"You're asking the wrong man." Ian's voice was so cold she hardly recognized it. "I restrained you."

Ian had done this to her? *Ian?* "But why?"

"Because I don't trust you."

A kick in the teeth couldn't have hurt as much. She blinked back tears.

Alex sneered. "Bawling's not going to work, bitch."

"Keep a civil tongue in your head." Ian shot him a fierce look, then turned that same look on her. "He's right. All I want from you is the truth."

What else but the truth can save him? Dona Elizabete's words seemed to echo in her ears.

But he wouldn't believe the truth. It sounded too bizarre.

"This is a goddamned waste of time," Alex said.

"Shut up." Ian flicked a glance at Alex, then shifted his gaze back to her, his eyes as dull as mud. "Just tell me the truth, Tasya. That's all I ask. If you're here to steal the tourmaline, fine. I'm a thief. You're a thief. No hard feelings. Tell me who you're working for, and you're free to go."

"I didn't come to Rio to steal Milagre."

Alex smacked the door frame. "Oh, for Christ's sake, she knows the damn rock by name. If she's not working for DeLeon or Vanderpool, she's got to be Interpol."

"I'm not Interpol, and I'm not working for anyone."

"Damn it, Tasya. I can forgive anything but a lie." Ian's gaze snared hers again, and this time he didn't hide his feelings. His eyes pleaded with her. *Tell me the truth. Prove you love me. Convince me this isn't a scam.*

In an intuitive flash, she saw how badly she'd hurt him. Behind his calm facade, Ian was angry and confused, half convinced she'd betrayed him, but even worse, afraid he'd betrayed himself by opening his heart.

The only way to put things right was to tell him all of it, but oh, dear God, what if he didn't believe her?

His face hardened. "The truth, Tasya."

She chose her words with care. "My uncle, the foster homes, Richard, my mentor. All true, but not all the truth. I told you the what but not the when."

"You're talking in riddles."

"A delaying tactic to give her time to come up with a plausible story," Alex said.

Tasya tuned him out, concentrating on Ian. "I know how crazy this is going to sound—"

"Here it comes."

"Let her talk," Ian said.

She took a deep breath. "The truth is, I'm from the future. Your future."

Silence reigned for a heartbeat. Then Alex laughed scornfully. "From the *future?* Damned if I'm going to waste my time listening to this shit." He slammed out, and once more silence claimed the room.

She drew a shaky breath. "I traveled back in time to save you. That's the truth. I swear."

Ian's mouth tightened. "You wouldn't know the truth if you heard it directly from God Himself. I checked up on you, Tasya. Called a private investigator I know, asked him to research your background. He got back to me this afternoon, and guess what. You don't have a background. There are no records for anyone named Tasya Flynn. Even your passport's a fake."

"Of course he found no records. I'm from the future. I won't be born for another eleven years."

Ian's nostrils flared. "My investigator did, however, discover something rather interesting. Apparently two months ago you deposited $20,000 in a Rio de Janeiro bank and have been drawing on it ever since. Coincidentally, a week before you made your deposit, someone withdrew $20,000 from my numbered Swiss account. I don't know how you managed it, but that was quite a trick. I salute you."

"Ian, don't you see? That proves it. How could I have gained access to your account if you hadn't authorized it? If you hadn't given me the number yourself?"

"But I didn't authorize it. I didn't give you my number."

"Not yet."

"Not ever."

She forced herself to meet his gaze. "I told you the truth, and you don't believe me. I don't blame you. I wouldn't believe me, either. So go ahead. Despise me if you want. Judge me a liar and a thief. Believe I was only interested in your money. It's all irrelevant. The only thing that matters is this: You cannot go through with the plan to steal Milagre. If you do, you're going to spend the next thirty years confined to a wheelchair, rotting in a Brazilian prison."

"That's what you were doing this afternoon? Warning the Sodré woman? Arranging a police ambush?"

"No!"

"You did speak with Elizabete Ribeiro Sodré, though."

"Yes."

"And it wasn't the first time, either, was it? My investigator says you stayed with her the last time you were in Rio. In fact, you flew directly to Tahiti from Brazil."

The silence was deafening. She took another deep breath, but it didn't help. Her mind whirled. "Ian—"

"You rented Fortier's cottage because you thought it would be easier to get acquainted with me if you were living nearby."

"I—"

"And I fell for it."

"Ian, it wasn't like that. I wanted to get to know you, yes. I knew that you'd only agreed to help Alex originally because you were bored with life in paradise. And I thought—"

"If I were infatuated with you, Rio wouldn't tempt me. Too bad it didn't work out. You prostituted yourself for nothing."

Tasya's temper flared. "You're twisting everything. I slept with you because I loved you. I loved you old, and I love you young. Even if you go through with this, even if you end up crippled and imprisoned again for thirty years, I will still love you. I will always love you."

"Oh, brava." Alex Farrell leaned against the doorjamb,

applauding. "You are good. Isn't she good, Cat? You deserve an Oscar for that performance."

She glared at him. "You think you've won, but you'll never win. In the short run, you may walk off with the million-dollar prize, but ultimately your greed is going to catch up with you."

He laughed. "Spoken like a true oracle."

"He's going to double-cross you, Ian. He's going to release the rigging when you're in the Sodré mansion and send you plummeting four stories."

"Give it a rest," Alex said. "Ian isn't even going to be in the harness. I am."

She looked to Ian for confirmation. He nodded grimly.

"Then something will come up to prevent his following through. I know what's going to happen, Ian. I came back to prevent it. What can I say to make you believe me?"

"Who are you, Tasya?" Ian demanded.

"You know who I am."

"Who are you working for?"

"I'm not working for anyone."

"You told me you'd trained as a cat burglar. With whom?"

"You," she said. "I trained with you."

"Damn it, Tasya!" Ian hit the bedpost with his fist, and she felt the vibration in her bones.

"You can't remember because for you it hasn't happened yet. It won't happen for thirty years. You didn't recruit me until after your release from prison."

"Recruit you for what?"

"To help you get even with Alex for double-crossing you. We set up a squeeze play with Eddie Casale, a Vegas gambler, on one side and Kenji Takimoto, a Japanese crime boss, on the other. Casale was after the money Alex owed him. Takimoto wanted Milagre. He'd learned about its healing properties, perhaps even about its connection to time travel." She sobbed in frustration. The more she told him, the crazier it sounded. "Please," she said. "Just open your mind. The stones helped me make the leap, but that doesn't mean time travel's some arcane magical process. I'm sure there's a scientific basis for the phenomenon, even if I can't explain it."

Ian stared at her, his face expressionless. She could feel the battle slipping away from her. Her mind raced, searching for something, any shred of evidence, that might convince him. "How is time travel any stranger, any more impossible, than your knowing Richard's name? There's no logical explanation for that, but I believe you."

"You could have—"

"Don't try to rationalize it. Before I breathed a word about Richard, you knew his name and recognized his true nature. He kept me tied to the bed for hours at a time. Did you know that? Tied to the bed just like this. He liked me helpless. He liked me to beg. Please, Richard, don't hurt me. Please, Richard, don't make me do that. Please, Richard. Please, Richard. Please, Richard!" Her voice spiraled out of control.

"Tasya—"

"Let me finish!" Tears leaked down her cheeks, but she ignored them. "When I escaped from him, I swore I would never beg again, but I am begging you, Ian. Please don't go after the tourmaline. If you do, I won't be able to alter the sequence. I won't be able to save you. Please, Ian. Please."

He stared at her, his eyes as black as midnight.

"This is pointless," Alex said. "Come on, Cat. We can deal with her later." He headed for the door.

"Ian, please!"

He didn't say a word, just shut the door as he left.

"Ian!" she screamed. "Please!"

But he didn't answer.

Dread wrapped itself around her heart. Later, Alex had said. Meaning after he had the stone, after Ian was in police custody. That's when Alex would deal with her, *deal with* being a euphemism for murder.

And once she was dead, who would prevent Ian from shooting himself? Who would help him get his revenge? Who would bring Milagre back to Brazil?

Nobody.

Her trip through time hadn't set things right. It had only made them worse.

Alex had watched Cat going through the motions during their practice session in the empty warehouse. He still had the moves and the reflexes, but his focus was elsewhere. On Tasya.

Frowning, Alex dismantled the rigging and packed it into the van. How the hell had she figured out what he had planned? Nobody was that good a guesser.

And he wasn't buying the time-travel shit, either. No, she must have connections Ian's investigator hadn't discovered. People who knew just how badly he needed Gentry's payoff. People who knew just how much he owed Eddie Casale.

Ian was starting to waver. Alex could read the signs. He

might not believe the girl's story, but he was beginning to have doubts about the job.

He stood near the back end of the van, coiling a hundred-foot length of nylon rope. "Alex?" He paused in mid-coil, the loose end dangling from his hands like a dead snake. "Maybe we should call it off. We don't know what Tasya told the Sodré woman. What if we break in there tomorrow night, and the cops are waiting for us? I don't know about you, but I have no interest in an extended stay in a Brazilian prison."

Alex chewed on his thumbnail, thinking it through. "You're right. The only way to be safe is to alter our timetable. Tonight. We'll go in tonight."

MacPherson's Rule Number Forty-nine: Never give up. If you run through every option on your list, brainstorm a new list.

Tasya wondered if Ian's advice applied to her current situation. He, after all, was the one who'd limited her options.

She'd screamed herself hoarse and jerked on the ropes anchoring her wrists and ankles to the bedposts until she felt as if she were dislocating her joints, but she was no closer to effecting an escape than she had been an hour ago.

She didn't know where Ian and Alex had gone. She didn't know when they'd be back. All she knew was, she had to escape before they returned, or she might not get another chance.

A muffled noise set her heart racing. Was that someone at the door to the suite? She held her breath, listening intently, but she couldn't be sure. Ian had closed the bedroom door before he left—probably to ensure her cries for help went unheard.

Most likely she was imagining things. And even if she weren't, her voice was gone and had been for a good fifteen minutes. At best, her poor abused vocal cords might produce a scratchy croak.

Never give up.

"Help," she cried. Only it didn't sound like a cry. It didn't sound like *help*. It sounded like rusty hinges.

Her effort was rewarded by a sharp, "Who is there?" in Portuguese.

"Please," she said, resulting in more rusty hinge creaking.

The bedroom door inched open. A man she'd never seen before stuck his head in the narrow opening.

"Help me," she said in Portuguese.

"Senhorita Flynn?"

She nodded.

As his face split in a broad smile, relief flooded her.

Then he shoved the door open wide, and she saw the knife in his hand.

Alex had insisted they stop for a late dinner at the Gaucha, a churrascaria known for its beef. Already riding a wave of euphoria, he'd chosen the biggest steak on the menu. He'd tried to order a bottle of wine, too, but Ian had managed to talk him out of that particular foolishness.

Ian didn't order anything but a bottle of mineral water. He never ate before a job. A full stomach imparted a sense of well-being, blunting his reflexes. Besides, worrying about Tasya had destroyed his appetite.

"Before we head for the Sodré mansion, let's stop by the hotel. I want to make sure Tasya's all right. She's been tied up for hours."

Alex laughed. "I don't believe you. The woman lies to you, steals from you, and does her best to screw you out of half a million dollars, and you're worried about her? Give me a break. What do you think? She's going to die of thirst? Damn it, the room's air-conditioned. The worst that's going to happen is, she'll piss the bed."

"Half an hour, that's all it'll take. I forgot to leave a light on."

"So?"

"She's afraid of the dark."

Alex laughed again. "A cat burglar who's afraid of the dark. Now I've heard everything."

"Not quite everything. Either we go check on Tasya, or you pull the job on your own."

Alex looked as if he suspected Ian had lost his mind. "You're going to let her go, aren't you?"

"Once you're clear. No matter what lies she's told, no matter what she's done, I love her. I won't see her hurt." He watched as the unspoken threat registered.

"Okay, it's your funeral." Alex shrugged. "But as for checking on her, sorry. No can do. The Sodré woman's night watchman takes his dinner break from midnight to one. Figure half an hour to forty minutes for us to finish up here and drive to the mansion. Then figure another half hour to get everything set up on the roof. That'll put us right at twelve-thirty, leaving thirty minutes to get in and get out before the watchman resumes his rounds. If we detour back to Copacabana first, we'll never make it back within the window of opportunity. And if we wait until tomorrow night . . ."

"Point taken," Ian said, resigned but not happy about it.

"I'm sorry, Cat, honest to God." Alex reached out as if to pat his arm, managing somehow to tip over the bottle of mineral water and knock Ian's glass onto the floor. "Shit."

Ian grabbed the bottle, and Alex ducked beneath the table to retrieve the glass.

A waiter came running. He mopped up the mess, apologizing as profusely as if it had been his fault.

"Son of a bitch!" Alex tossed a handful of glass shards, the remains of Ian's water goblet, onto the damp tablecloth. A spattering of red drops stained the snowy linen.

"*Meu Deus*," the waiter cried. "O senhor is hurt."

Alex held out his right hand. A cut ran diagonally across his palm, oozing blood. Ian couldn't tell at a glance how deep it was.

"Come with me," the waiter said. "We fix. First aid."

"Get your hand seen to," Ian said.

Alex rolled his eyes. "It's nothing—just a scratch."

"Come. Come." The waiter tugged at his sleeve.

"Humor the man," Ian said.

With an exasperated shrug, Alex wrapped his hand in a napkin and followed the waiter back to the kitchen.

Ian stared at the mess on the table. Though Alex had his faults, clumsiness had never been one of them. *Then something will come up to prevent his following through.* He didn't believe Tasya's time-travel story, but maybe she knew something about Alex that he didn't.

A busboy had the table reset by the time Alex appeared, a bandage wrapped around his hand, a self-satisfied smirk on his face. "Dinner's on the house. The manager insisted." He took a seat. "Guess I'll have that dessert after all."

"We don't have time," Ian said.

Alex glanced at his watch and frowned. "Damn, and the night was going so well."

So well? He'd just sliced open his hand. Ian studied Alex's face.

Alex glanced at his bandaged hand, then shot Ian a grin. "That was irony, Cat. Once again, Farrell fucks up." He frowned. "Let's go."

"Sure you don't want me to drive?" Ian asked when Alex slotted himself in behind the wheel.

"I can manage." But by the time they arrived at the Sodré mansion, blood had soaked through his bandage.

"You can't do precision work with that hand."

"Damn it, Cat. I'm not as incompetent as you seem to think."

"I never said—"

"Shit, you don't have to say it. I can see it in your eyes. I'll never be a burglar of your caliber. I know that. But I'm not a complete screwup, either."

Ian shook his head. "This has nothing to do with ability. You're injured."

Alex shot him a mutinous look. "It's not that bad. I . . ." He stared at the crimson splotches staining his bandage. Rebellion slowly faded to resignation. "Okay," he said. "You win."

Tasya's words haunted him. *Then something will come up to prevent his following through.*

Yes, but switching places had been Ian's idea.

Only Alex hadn't put up much of a fight, had he?

*   *   *

Alex secured the rigging to the roof anchors, then threw his whole weight against it to make sure the ropes would hold. They'd cut away one section of the enormous stained glass skylight, balancing the heavy oval they'd removed against an ornamental cupola ten feet away.

Ian slipped into the harness, did his own test of the rigging, checked his tool belt one last time, then the light strapped to his head. When he was satisfied, he gave Alex a thumbs-up and let himself down the ropes, not in the free-fall swoop popularized by Hollywood, but in slow, careful increments.

So far everything had gone like clockwork. If Alex's luck held, by this time tomorrow, he would be on his way back to L.A. to collect his million bucks. Emphasis on the *his*.

How the hell had Tasya known he intended to cut Ian out of his share? That had been a spooky moment, hearing her denounce him as a double-crosser, hearing her reveal the details of his plan. His *secret* plan. No way he bought that time-travel shit. But damned if he could see how she'd copped to the truth.

Not that it mattered. Once he had Milagre tucked safely in his backpack, once he'd disposed of Ian, he'd take care of Tasya, too, shut her up for good this time.

Ian's gut gave a warning twinge the instant he lowered himself through the skylight. Something was seriously off-kilter. The question was, what? Had Tasya told the truth? Did Alex plan to double-cross him? Had he faked the injury to guarantee Ian ended up in the harness? Who should he trust?

He paused for a moment, and the silence enveloped him—absolute, uncanny. Most old buildings expressed themselves in creaks and groans and sighs. This one was mute, its still air heavy with the scent of dying flowers and a hint of something else. Something raw.

He drew a deep breath. Flowers. No mistaking their sickly funereal scent. No mistaking the other scent, either. Blood. Alex had said the Sodré woman was an expert on Macumba rituals. Rituals that included animal sacrifice?

His gut gave another twinge. Ignoring it, he resumed his descent.

Halfway down, his headlamp flickered and died. Inky darkness, thick with secrets, swallowed him whole. His heart lurched. He'd checked the equipment. Double-checked it.

"Cat?" Ian glanced up to see Alex's head and shoulders silhouetted against an oval of star-smeared sky. "You all right?"

"I'm fine. It's this wretched headlamp." He'd barely uttered the words before the light blinked on again.

"Seems to be working now," Alex said. "What do you think? Short circuit?"

"Perhaps." His mind embraced the logic of Alex's conclusion, but his gut wasn't convinced. Once again, he resumed his descent.

Moments later he spotted the display case, and the twinge in his gut blossomed into a full-blown ache. No tourmaline. The empty case gaped open, its glass dome shattered.

Ian swiveled in a semicircle so the light strapped to his forehead illuminated the high-ceilinged room. Roughly fifty feet square and almost as high, the vaulted space seemed even larger. Aside from the display case, the room held only seven statues—crude, garishly painted plaster figures representing the *orixás* or spirits of Macumba. Six huddled in a rough semicircle around the pedestal that supported the display case. The seventh, a fierce warrior with eyes as black and shiny as polished onyx, lay tipped on its back amid a scatter of beads and flower petals.

Danger. He could smell it in the musty air, taste it as a metallic sourness at the back of his throat. The silence pressed on him, a tangible weight that made it hard to breathe, harder yet to think.

He caught a flicker of movement from the corner of his eye and whipped around.

Nothing. No one. Except those damned statues.

A buxom female leered at him, her red-lipped plaster smile both sly and sensual. As he watched, a single petal detached itself from the cluster bunched at her cleavage and drifted slowly to the floor. The petal landed near the outstretched hand of an eighth figure he hadn't noticed until now. Half hidden by the female, it sprawled face-down in a dark puddle.

The truth knocked the wind out of him.

"Hurry." Alex's whisper pierced the silence. "The guard's due back in five minutes."

Ian stared in horror at the sprawled figure. Unlike the colorful *orixás* with their elaborate outfits, this figure wore functional beige. A uniform.

"Cat? Did you hear me?"

Ian cleared his throat. "I heard. Don't worry. The guard's not going to bother us or anyone else. He's lying on the floor in a pool of blood."

"Shit, what did you do?"

"Nothing," Ian said. "I found him that way."

"And the tourmaline?"

"Gone. Someone beat us to it."

Gone. The word reverberated in Alex's head. *Gone.* No Milagre. No million dollars. Once again, he was fucked. And no question who'd stuck it to him. *Tasya.*

He'd misjudged her. Underestimated her. The little bitch hadn't been trying to warn Elizabete Ribeiro Sodré earlier. And she wasn't with Interpol. She'd been casing the joint for herself . . . or whoever she was working for.

The night was dark and very quiet, no traffic at all on the street below, the only sounds the breeze rustling through the treetops, the whirr of insects in the shrubbery, and the furious thumping of his heart.

"Haul me up," Ian said.

Alex hesitated. No real point in following through with his original plan, now that there was no money involved.

"Alex?"

Besides, the girl would know where the stone was, and Ian had a better chance of getting her to talk than he did.

"Alex? Is there a problem?"

"Rope's twisted," he said. "Got it." He pulled with a steady pressure until Ian's head and shoulders emerged from the opening.

"Let's go," Ian said. "I have a bad feeling about this."

*   *   *

Ian drove back. Traffic was almost nonexistent until he got close to Copacabana, where the *boîtes* and strip clubs were just hitting their stride.

Alex drummed the dash, heedless of his injured hand. "You sure the guard was dead?"

"I didn't take his pulse, but he wasn't moving. Looked like he'd lost a lot of blood."

"Shit." Alex's drumming assumed a faster tempo. "He must have blundered in at the wrong moment. You say the case was shattered?"

Ian nodded. "Glass everywhere. One of the statues had been knocked over, too. Sloppy work. Amateurs."

Alex smacked the dash one last time. "So who did it? I'd assumed the girl was working for Vanderpool, but a messy job like that isn't his style."

Ian pulled up in front of the hotel. "We don't know Tasya was involved. There are other possibilities. Perhaps Gentry got tired of waiting for you and hired someone local."

Alex didn't say anything else until they got off the elevator on their floor, but he grabbed Ian's arm as he was fitting the key to the lock. "Quit kidding yourself, Cat. Tasya has to be in on it. Nothing else makes sense."

"I disagree. How could she be involved in anything that happened in Laranjeiras when she's been tied up here the whole time?" Shrugging off Alex's hand, he opened the door to the suite and flicked on the lights.

He froze just inside the door. The back of his neck prickled. Hair raised along his forearms. He glanced at Alex, whose eyes were opened so wide, the whites showed all around his irises.

Alex's nostrils flared. "What's that stench?"

Sweet, metallic . . . and familiar. An image of the murdered security guard flashed through Ian's mind. "Blood," he said.

"Where's it coming from?"

Ian scanned the sitting room. As far as he could remember, it looked exactly as it had when they'd left. Drapes open. Blinds shut. A two-day-old copy of the *New York Times,* folded to the half-finished crossword, lay on the floor next to the sofa where he'd dropped it. On the coffee table the orange peels left over from Alex's breakfast still formed the same untidy little pyramid next to his empty coffee cup. Nothing moved. Nothing out of place. Nothing to explain the smell.

"Didn't you close the door to your bedroom?" Alex said.

Ian's heart stopped, then shifted into overdrive. "I did."

"Then why is it open now?"

22

IAN APPROACHED THE BEDROOM with caution. The nearer he drew, the stronger the stench. He paused on the threshold, and Alex crowded close, peering over his shoulder. The sitting room light scarcely penetrated the shadowed room. "Back off," he said, but Alex ignored him.

Ian groped for the light switch. Found it. Flipped it.

"Oh, fucking sh—" Alex gagged in mid-expletive, clapped a hand to his mouth, and ran for the bathroom.

Ian registered the retching noises only peripherally, too focused on the slaughterhouse images in front of him to spare attention for anything else. Blood was everywhere—the walls, the floor, the bed. Especially the bed. The towels he'd used to pad Tasya's wrists and ankles were soaked with gore. The ropes that had bound her dangled from the bedposts like limp and bloody entrails.

For a shocked moment all he could do was stare in horror. Then he roused himself. Avoiding the sticky puddles on the floor, he combed the room. Though he wouldn't have been surprised to have stumbled across a few severed body parts, all he found was blood. And more blood. Too much. No one survived a loss of this magnitude. Tasya was dead.

The toilet flushed. Water ran in the sink. He heard splashing and spitting, interspersed with a litany of muttered profanity.

Guilt and regret pierced his heart. If only they'd checked on her earlier, the way he'd wanted, they might have prevented this bloodbath. If only Alex, damn his soul, hadn't wasted all that time in the restaurant. If only . . .

An unthinkable possibility—grotesque, revolting— blindsided him. What if Alex had kept him away from the hotel on purpose? What if Alex had arranged this? What if Tasya had been right about him all along?

Ian stared at the evidence of his former apprentice's treachery.

"Let's get the hell out of here," Alex said from the doorway.

Ian swiveled to face him.

"What?" Alex said, as if something in Ian's expression made him nervous.

"You bastard."

"What?" Alex still had a befuddled look on his face when Ian grabbed him by the throat and shoved him against the door frame.

"You're responsible for this."

He clawed at Ian's hands. "What are you talking about? I've been with you all night."

Ian kneed him in the groin. "You could"—releasing his

grip on Alex's throat, he grabbed his shoulder and punched him in the mouth—"have hired"—another punch, this one to the stomach—"someone"—hard uppercut to the jaw—"to do the dirty work for you." His fists were bloody now. Almost as bloody as Alex's face. Almost as bloody as the bed where he'd left Tasya trussed up, defenseless.

Ian loosened his hold on Alex's shoulder, and Alex sagged to his knees, gasping for air. "How could I have hired anyone to do this? Damn it, Cat, I don't even speak the language."

Ian stared at the bloody sheets, the dangling restraints. "It had to be you. You're the only one who knew Tasya was here."

Alex slumped to the floor with a groan, nursing his groin and his broken nose. "Someone else must be involved. Someone you don't know about. I had nothing to do with this. Swear to God."

Was he telling the truth? Ian surveyed the room. So much blood.

"Cat?"

Ian ignored him. Tasya was dead. Alex denied responsibility. Maybe he was telling the truth. Ian didn't know. But he did know he couldn't deny his own responsibility. She'd begged him to listen, not once but over and over again. Instead, he'd left her alone in the dark, bound and helpless, reliving all her worst nightmares. He hadn't killed her, but by his actions, he'd facilitated her murder.

Alex's whimpering drew his attention. His former apprentice lay curled in a fetal position on the floor. "Get out."

"But—"

"I said, get out. Out of my sight. Out of the hotel. Out of the country."

"What about the stone? Without the money from the stone—"

"I don't give a damn about the stone. Or about you, either." He grabbed Alex's shirt front and dragged him to his feet. "Go, and don't come back. The next time I see you, I'll finish what I started." He paused. "You can lay odds on that."

Getting through to L.A. from the airport pay phone had taken Alex almost an hour. The call used up most of his change and all of his patience. He finally reached Gentry, but before he could say a word, the other man informed him the deal was off. He was no longer interested in acquiring Milagre.

"You hired someone else to steal it, didn't you, you slippery son of a bitch?"

Gentry hung up on him.

Alex slammed down the receiver and returned to his gate. He slouched in a seat and tried to think. Christ, what a fucked-up mess. No stone. No million dollars. No way to pay off Casale.

But hey, things could be worse. At least, thank God, that blood-drenched hotel suite hadn't been reserved in *his* name with *his* credit card. And if and when the police got involved, it wasn't *his* girlfriend that had gone missing. Hurt his mouth to smile, but damned if he could help it. Serve Cat right if he ended up doing time for the little bitch's murder.

*   *   *

Who had killed Tasya? Ian slumped in a chair in the sitting room of his hotel suite and tried to work out the answer. Alex? Someone working for Alex? If Tasya had been telling the truth, her revelations might well have spurred him to eliminate her.

On the other hand, if, as Alex had maintained, she'd been working for a rival gang all along, her partners in crime might have jettisoned her once she'd served her purpose. Which didn't explain the gruesome charnel house scene in the bedroom. If they'd wanted to be rid of her, why not simply put a bullet through her brain or toss her out the window?

Unless rage rather than expediency had prompted the murder. Only why rage? What could she have done to trigger such violence?

Perhaps, he thought, it wasn't what she'd done, but what she hadn't done. What if, at the end, she *hadn't* cooperated? What if she'd tried instead to protect him?

His mind flashed again on the memory of the night watchman facedown in a pool of blood. A violent death, yes, but nothing to compare with the butchery that had taken place in the hotel.

He stared at the bedroom door, closed now, though it couldn't shut out the grisly images imprinted forever on his brain. The blood told a savage tale. Someone had tortured her, done unspeakable things to her. God knew the pain she'd suffered. God knew, too, who was to blame. It didn't matter who'd done the actual killing. Ultimately, Tasya's death was his fault.

He must have dozed for a while. He woke shortly after

dawn, still slumped in the chair, his neck stiff, his heart sore. What now? She was dead, and he might as well be. If he'd had a gun, he'd have used it. A bullet through his head, an end to his pain.

A sudden memory pierced his grief—Tasya's eyes, wild with fear, silvery with unshed tears, and her voice, choked with emotion as she tried to convince him her bizarre tale was true. Something . . . She'd said something about the power of the stones helping her make the leap through time.

He'd dismissed her words as nonsense at the time, just as he'd dismissed her claim that Alex meant to double-cross him. Yet Alex's actions—the uncharacteristic clumsiness, that moment of hesitation before pulling Ian up to the roof—suggested she'd been right about the intended double-cross. If she'd told the truth about Alex, perhaps she'd told the truth about her trip through time as well.

Stones, she'd said. Stones as in gemstones? Gemstones like Milagre? If Tasya's claim were true, it would explain why the Sodré woman had refused to sell the tourmaline and why a Hollywood mogul had offered Alex a million dollars to steal it.

If Tasya had been telling the truth all along, if she had, in fact, traveled back in time to save him, then perhaps he could do the same.

A dizzy excitement gripped him. He needn't go far, a few days at most. Even a few hours would be enough to alter the events leading to her death. He could redeem himself. He could put things right. Only—he groaned aloud—someone had stolen Milagre last night. For all he knew, it was on its way to California by now. Or Timbuktu.

Dear God, he had to find that stone.

He grabbed the telephone and called down to the desk for a newspaper and a pot of coffee. The break-in at the Sodré mansion, the theft of the tourmaline, and the murder of the security guard should be front-page news. Considering how sloppy the thieves had been, the police probably had several leads, perhaps had even made an arrest already.

Or perhaps not.

Three cups of strong black coffee later, his nerves were buzzing, but he was none the wiser as to Milagre's whereabouts. The newspaper made no mention of the crime. Elizabete Ribeiro Sodré couldn't have kept the police out of it. A man had been killed. But the press was another story. Apparently in Rio wealth and position afforded one privacy.

He needed information. But contacting the Sodré woman posed a significant risk. If, as he had every reason to suspect, she knew of his involvement in the plan to steal Milagre, she could have him thrown in prison. But she was his only lead to the stone, and without the stone, Tasya was lost to him forever.

No contest.

He called the switchboard, but there was no listing for Elizabete Ribeiro Sodré.

The only option left was to show up on her doorstep. Risky, but what choice did he have? Ian hung a Do Not Disturb sign on the door, hoping to delay discovery of the bloodbath in the bedroom. Then he took a taxi to Laranjeiras.

A police car hugged the curb in front of the Sodré mansion. The taxi driver pulled in behind it, and Ian passed him a wad of cruzeiros. "Wait. I won't be long." Unless, of course, the authorities arrested him, in which case the driver might be waiting a good long time—say five to seven, with time off for good behavior, longer if they pinned the guard's murder on him, too.

For a split second he considered climbing back into the cab and heading straight for the airport. Back to Tahiti. But without Tasya, paradise might as well be hell.

He bullied his way past the yardman, a maid, and the majordomo to find Elizabete Ribeiro Sodré ensconced in a sitting room on the second floor, speaking with a young man in a police uniform. She glanced up, raising her brows at the interruption.

"I am sorry, Dona Elizabete," the majordomo hurried to explain. "I told this person you were otherwise engaged, but he shoved his way in." At least, Ian thought that's what the man said. He spoke in a rush, and Ian's command of Portuguese was a little shaky.

"I need to save Tasya," he said in English.

Dona Elizabete looked him up and down. "*Não falo inglês, mas meu sobrinho . . .*"

The young policeman stood. He was a big man, taller than Ian by an inch or so and thirty pounds heavier. "I am the nephew of Dona Elizabete, and I speak the English."

"My name is Ian MacPherson. I'm a friend of Tasya Flynn, the young woman who visited this house yesterday. Tasya is"—admitting knowledge of a crime to a policeman probably wouldn't be wise—"missing," he said. The truth, after all. "I need your aunt's help to find her."

"Missing?" The nephew gave Ian a long, measuring

look, then translated what Ian had said into rapid-fire Portuguese.

Dona Elizabete considered his request for a moment. Then she rattled off a response that ended with a shrug. Ian couldn't tell if it was a "tough luck" shrug, a "take this scoundrel away" shrug, or an "I don't know what he's talking about" shrug.

"My aunt asks what you think she can to do for you."

"She owns a tourmaline known as Milagre. I believe the stone can provide the help I need."

The nephew translated, listened to his aunt's reply, then turned back to Ian, a strange look on his face. "My aunt asks what you are knowing of Milagre."

"It's rumored the stone can heal the sick—"

"You are ill?" the nephew interrupted.

He probably looked ill, if not deranged. "No, just worried." He hesitated. How to broach the topic of time travel without sounding completely mad? "Tasya told me Milagre has another unusual attribute, that with its help a person can change the past."

The nephew shot him a narrow-eyed look before translating for his aunt. Her gaze flicked over Ian, and for a moment, he could have sworn he saw a hint of compassion in her eyes. Then she spoke at length to her nephew.

"My aunt has asked me to share a family legend."

Ian fought to keep his impatience in check. Tasya was dead, and this woman wanted him to listen to fairy tales?

"Long ago near Ouro Preto, a slave working in the gemstone mines discovered two large tourmalines embedded in the same matrix. It soon became apparent that these were no ordinary stones. After two men disappeared and several others died horribly, Father Duarte, the priest who ministered to the slaves, separated the stones, believing that by doing so, he was lessening the danger. He kept one stone but hid the second. Hearing of this, a seer of some renown, a *babalaô* of the Ifa cult, predicted that one day the stones would be reunited to aid a traveler."

"Meaning?"

"Who knows? These predictions are always very vague, *não*?" The nephew shrugged. "But my aunt believes Ms. Flynn was the traveler the *babalaô* foretold. My aunt claims she witnessed the miracle with her own eyes."

"Miracle?"

"One moment her garden was empty, the next the traveler appeared out of thin air." The nephew obviously had his doubts about this part of the story, but it convinced Ian.

Tasya had told him the truth. She really had come from the future. He addressed Dona Elizabete directly in Portuguese. "I made a terrible mistake, and I must put it right. Please tell me. Do you know what happened to Milagre?"

She studied his face for a long moment, then inclined her head. "The thieves were thwarted. The stone is safe."

Oh, God. He still had a chance. "Then help me," he said. "Help me go back. Help me find her." Save her.

She shook her head. "You cannot travel."

"Tasya did."

"The process requires both stones. I have only one."

"Then tell me where to find the second stone."

Again he glimpsed compassion in her eyes. "I am sorry. I do not know its location. No one does."

"But—"

"Have faith," she said. "Life always comes full circle."

Ian frowned, thinking he'd misunderstood. "Translate, please," he said to the nephew.

"My aunt says life always is coming full circle."

"But what does that mean?" Ian asked him.

The nephew shrugged. "We live. We die." He stood. "I will show you to the door."

Ian asked the taxi driver to drop him in front of the big wooden doors of Gloria Church. From there he wandered the city, zigzagging aimlessly like a ship without a rudder. Tasya was dead. He knew that, but twice his foolish heart quickened as he caught sight of women he mistook for her. Each time he realized his mistake, his sense of loss deepened.

As the shadows lengthened, he found himself standing once again in front of his Copacabana hotel. Had the housekeeping staff discovered the blood-soaked bedroom? Had they called in the police? The rational part of his brain recognized the risk of loitering here, but grief overrode caution.

Sometime during the long day he'd realized what Dona Elizabete meant. *Life always comes full circle.* Tasya was dead, but there was still one way to reunite with her. He stared at the hotel, estimating its height. Fifteen stories perhaps? High enough? Probably. But probably wasn't good enough.

He turned to leave and noticed a uniformed driver standing next to a limousine. The man held a placard that said MACPHERSON in big block capitals. Who could have sent a car for him? Dona Elizabete? Had she perhaps learned something about the second stone's whereabouts? His heart sped up.

Then he remembered, and his brief flare of hope fizzled and died. He'd ordered the car himself. Was it only yesterday? He'd intended to take Tasya up Corcovado Mountain to the overlook below the Christ the Redeemer statue, a little side jaunt planned to distract her from their real purpose for visiting Rio.

The driver must have noticed him staring. "Mr. MacPherson?" he said, sounding dubious and more than a little nervous.

Ian was about to turn away when he recognized the driver as fate's messenger. "Yes, I ordered a car yesterday."

The driver frowned. "My instructions were to collect a party of two and—"

"Yes, yes, and drive them to the top of Corcovado. I know. I'm the one who made the arrangements. Unfortunately, there's been a change in plan. My companion is unable to make the trip."

"Perhaps I should check with my—"

"No need." Ian waved a stack of cruzeiros at the man. "Shall we go?"

The driver nodded and tucked the bills in his pocket. "I believe you will find everything as you requested it, sir. Champagne on ice. Caviar. Pâté de foie gras."

"Yes, thank you."

The driver opened the door. Ian climbed inside and was immediately assailed by one of those disturbing faux memories, this one of Tasya in a form-fitting beaded black evening gown and his own voice saying, "But why hide the ring in an hors d'oeuvre?"

Dear God, he couldn't bear it. All that sweet youth and beauty gone forever. A fierce, eviscerating pain ripped at his insides. Guilt, regret, and sorrow ate like acid at his soul. With shaking hands he poured himself champagne.

The limousine began the long ascent, and he raised his glass in a silent toast. *To Tasya. To love lost.*

The sun had disappeared behind the mountains, but the bank of clouds hanging low over the hills behind Niteroi reflected its dying fire in a dazzle of pinks and purples. One by one the lights of the city flickered to life in the gathering gloom.

At last the driver pulled into the parking lot. Ian swallowed the last of his champagne and climbed out. "You needn't wait," he told the driver.

"Are you sure? It's almost closing time, and the last tram is always crowded. You may not get a seat. It's up to you, of course, but it's a long hike down the mountain."

Ian gave him a bleak smile. "I don't plan to walk down."

The lights illuminating the statue blinked on as if by magic when he was halfway up the endless stairs leading to the overlook on top. All around him people paused, oohing and aahing, but he kept going. Like a salmon struggling upstream, he wove his way through the mob headed for the parking lot.

Ian arrived at the top to find the overlook emptying rapidly. He claimed a spot at the far end of the platform and rested his elbows on the railing. The wide sweep of Rio de Janeiro spread out beneath him: the glittering lights of the city, the familiar outline of Sugar Loaf, and, scattered across the bay, dark islands afloat on the mist-shrouded water.

He glanced around casually. Still too many people. He'd wait a while longer for the last of the diehards—he smiled in grim amusement—to leave.

The sky grew darker. One by one the tourists drifted away until only a handful remained, none of whom seemed to be paying any attention to him. He risked a quick peek over the railing. Not quite the sheer drop he'd hoped for, but steep enough.

I can't live with her blood on my hands. The words thundered in his head. For a second he thought perhaps he'd said them aloud. He looked up quickly to see if anyone was staring at him, and it was then he spotted her.

She stood by herself, gazing out at the lights of the city. Tasya. His heart raced.

MacPherson, you fool. Tasya was dead. He knew it. Why was he torturing himself? Hadn't he been through this twice already?

Yes, but this time it was no trick, no mistake. This time it really was Tasya. He was certain of it. Almost certain. *Tasya?*

She turned.

Oh, God. Her gaze met his, and time stopped for a moment, isolating them. Ian drank in the details of her appearance, from the shadows under her eyes to the flower tucked behind her ear.

"Ian?" Her voice trembled.

He thought for a moment his facial muscles had atrophied, but with an effort he managed a wobbly smile. "Tasya." Aloud this time.

She launched herself at him, and he caught her, hugging her close. He wanted to tell her how sorry he was for doubting her, how terrified he'd been that he'd lost her forever, how much, how very, very much he loved her, but he couldn't speak. Emotion welled up, rendering him mute.

He finally set her on her feet and let his eyes say all the things his mouth couldn't manage.

She lifted her hands to frame his face. The look on hers took his breath away. "You came." Then her eyes filled with tears, and he pulled her tight against his chest. She'd been as lost and frightened as he.

He rested his chin on the top of her head and caught the faint scent of gardenias. "I'm sorry," he whispered into her hair.

She pulled away, smiling up at him so sweetly, he thought for one panicked second he was going to break down in tears. "I'm sorry, too. I should have told you the truth right from the start, but I was afraid you wouldn't believe me."

He wouldn't have. He wasn't sure he did now. All he knew was, he loved her.

"When it got so late, I was afraid you weren't coming."

"Late?"

"My note said sunset."

"What note?"

"I left a note at the front desk, explaining everything."

"I never got it. I thought you were dead."

"Dead? Oh, no! But if you didn't get my note, what are you—" She searched his face. "Oh, my God," she whispered. "You came up here to kill yourself, didn't you?

That's how we met the first time. You were about to put a bullet in your brain when I crawled through your dog door."

"Life always comes full circle."

"What?"

"Something Dona Elizabete said. I thought she meant . . ."

She stiffened. "You went to Dona Elizabete? Are you crazy? She could have had you thrown in prison."

"I was desperate. I thought you were dead," he said again. "All that blood."

"Stage dressing meant to fool Alex. Januário's idea. His brother's a butcher."

"And who is Januário?"

"Dona Elizabete's night-watchman–slash–chauffeur. When she realized you'd seen me leaving the mansion, she knew I was in trouble. She sent Januário to free me. He faked my death, the theft of the stone, and his own murder. We figured with Milagre gone, Alex would have no reason to double-cross you or kill Januário. You wouldn't spend thirty years in prison, and Christina Gentry wouldn't end up married to Alex. Dona Elizabete even invited her to Rio so Milagre can cure her cancer."

If Dona Elizabete had known Tasya was alive, why hadn't she told him? But then he'd never actually said he thought Tasya was dead. The word he'd used was "missing."

"Of course, Alex and Richard and Takimoto are still running around free," Tasya said, "and they're bound to cause more trouble, but I guess I can't fix—"

He pressed his fingers to her mouth. "Shh."

She kissed his fingertips. "I love you," she said. "You don't have to believe any of the rest of it as long as you believe that."

"I do." He took her hand in his, using his thumb to trace his initials in her palm. "I love you, too."

She closed her eyes. Tears squeezed through her lashes and rolled down her cheeks.

Oh, God, he'd made her cry. His chest tightened. "Tasya?" He forced her name past the obstruction in his throat. "Dance with me?"

Her lashes fluttered open. She smiled uncertainly. "Dance? Here?"

"Here," he said.

She searched his face. "Have you been drinking?"

"One glass of champagne." He laughed. "Have you been reading Cicero?"

She stared at him as if he'd lost his mind.

"'*Neminem saltare sobrius, nisi forte insanit,*'" he quoted. "Latin for 'No sober man dances, unless he happens to be mad.' I'm not drunk, but I am mad . . . madly in love. Dance with me?"

"But all those times I tried to get you out on the dance floor, you turned me down."

"Forgive me."

She kissed her fingertips and pressed them to his lips. "Consider yourself forgiven."

Ian felt the prickle of tears behind his lids and blinked to stave them off. "So." He cleared his throat. "Tasya." No use. His voice still sounded raspy. He took a deep breath. Last try. "Dance with me?" *Marry me? Grow old with me?* He opened his arms. . . .

And she walked into his heart. Full circle.

Not sure what to read next?

Visit Pocket Books online at
www.SimonSays.com

Reading suggestions for
you and your reading group

New release news

Author appearances

Online chats with your favorite writers

Special offers

And much, much more!

POCKET BOOKS
A Division of Simon & Schuster
A VIACOM COMPANY

POCKET STAR BOOKS
A Division of Simon & Schuster
A VIACOM COMPANY

10421

LOVE IS IN THE AIR WITH THESE UNFORGETTABLE ROMANCES FROM POCKET BOOKS

ROXANNE ST. CLAIRE FRENCH TWIST

In the land of romance, love is everywhere...but so is danger.

DORIEN KELLY HOT NIGHTS IN BALLYMUIR

A passionate Irishman might be the answer to an American woman's dreams.

LORRAINE HEATH SMOOTH TALKIN' STRANGER

Was it one night of uncontrollable chemistry or the beginnings of the love of a lifetime?

JANET CHAPMAN THE SEDUCTIVE IMPOSTOR

He makes her want to risk everything—but can she trust him?

CAROL GRACE AN ACCIDENTAL GREEK WEDDING

Sparks are flying—only it's not between the bride and groom!

JULIE KENNER THE SPY WHO LOVES ME

He's Double-Oh-No. But she's about to change that...

SUSAN SIZEMORE I THIRST FOR YOU

A beautiful mortal becomes embraced by darkness and passion when a vampire desires her for all time.

www.simonsayslove.com • Wherever books are sold.

10413